**BLACKBONE PRISON CAMP—AS THE REICH'S
DARK DREAM SLOWLY DIED, A NIGHTMARE
WAS BEING BORN . . .**

MAJOR DAVID GILMAN—One tragic mistake had
cost him his first command. Another would cost him his
men—and his mind.

CAPTAIN ROGER WAYNE HOPKINS—A petty sa-
dist, he carved out an empire of graft and degradation
that he thought nothing but peace could destroy.

MAJOR WALTER STEUBEN—Even in prison camp,
his first duty was to ensure the safety of his men. But who
was he protecting them from? The Americans? A mad-
man within his own ranks? Or an enemy beyond rank,
nationality, reason, or nature?

LEUTNANT ROLF KIRST—The lone survivor of a
sunken Nazi U-boat, was his quiet obedience the mark of
a model prisoner . . . or the mask of an archetypal terror?

LORING HOLLOWAY—A beautiful young woman, she
would be thrust into the center of the battle to chain the
evil she had so innocently unleashed.

**AMERICANS AND GERMANS, GUARDS AND
PRISONERS, THEY WERE ALL HELD
HOSTAGE IN . . .**

BLACKBONE

Other Books by
George E. Simpson and Neal R. Burger

GHOSTBOAT
THIN AIR
FAIR WARNING
SEVERED TIES

= BLACKBONE =

George E. Simpson &
Neal R. Burger

A DELL BOOK

Published by
Dell Publishing Co., Inc.
1 Dag Hammarskjold Plaza
New York, New York 10017

Dell ® TM 681510, Dell Publishing Co., Inc.

ISBN: 0-440-10707-5

Printed in the United States of America
First printing—June 1985

Prologue

December 1944.

Leutnant Rolf Kirst plowed into the Atlantic with a stunning force that knocked the breath from his body.

He would have drowned then and there but for the buoyancy of his life preserver. It brought him to the surface, blinking salt-stung eyes, gulping air into tortured lungs. Horrified, he watched U-221, her conning tower and afterdeck a ruin of twisted steel, roll over and slip beneath the waves.

Kirst paddled furiously to escape the suction trying to drag him down with the boat. His mind raced to reconstruct the sequence of events that had catapulted him into the sea.

They had torpedoed the straggling Liberty Ship, then surfaced to finish her off with the deck gun. As gunnery officer, Kirst had been topside as his crew manned the 88-millimeter and pumped shell after shell into the stricken freighter, setting her ablaze from one end to the other.

How then had he ended up in the water?

Something roared over Kirst's head. An American patrol bomber flashed by, its blue-white underside illuminated by the glow from the burning freighter. Kirst shook his head, trying to recall details. Position—at least four hundred miles off the eastern coast of the United

States. Situation—bobbing in the Atlantic Ocean, imminently about to freeze or drown, whichever came first. He recalled his training, remembered the warnings—the icy waters could kill him in minutes.

He saw the crate break loose from a welter of smaller pieces of wood. It slid down a swell, riding high in the water.

Kirst lunged for it. Numbed fingers locked around hemp wrapping lines. He heaved himself out of the ocean and sprawled over rough planking, spreading his arms for balance, afraid that any abrupt weight shift would overturn the crate.

After a few minutes, Kirst realized that the crate was no lightweight empty box but contained some sort of cargo acting as ballast—watertight as well, or it would have sunk before now. If he could get it open, he might be able to crawl inside, out of the terrible cold.

Holding the wrapping lines in his left hand, he snaked his right down to his waist, found his sheath knife still attached to his belt, fumbled with the snap, then freed the blade.

He began sawing through the rope, realizing that once it was cut, he would have no handhold, but even more aware that if he didn't get inside, he might as well give up now, let go, and slide beneath—

The blade was sharp. In a moment, the hemp fell away. The crate rocked suddenly and Kirst nearly fell off. Jamming his knife into the wood and using it as a handhold, he drew his legs up and reversed position. Pulling the knife out again, he cut the line on the other side of the crate, then flattened himself once again. His fingers groped for nails: there were none. What held the crate together? He peered at the wood beneath his cheek. Between the planks he discovered a line of caulking.

Cursing whoever had sealed the crate, Kirst inserted the tip of his blade between two planks, sliced through the caulking, then gently levered the wood. One plank edged loose. He sliced up more of the caulking, turned the blade, and levered again, widening the space. He shifted the knife and slipped his right hand through the opening. He pushed the wood. The plank slid out of the frame and into the water. The opening was still too small to climb through. He went to work on the next plank.

A series of explosions across the water buffeted him. The crate heaved and tipped crazily. His knife dropped through the opening. Kirst locked his fingers around the edge of the second plank to avoid being thrown back into the ocean.

Chunks of white-hot metal whizzed through the air and splashed around him. The Atlantic was taking the Liberty Ship down.

She sank with a final grace. Tortured metal groaned as it constricted in the frigid water. Rapidly diminishing bubbles spat out debris that shot into the air, then fell back into the sea. The remains became a moving carpet of charred wood and bits of cork. Kirst was in a sea of garbage.

When things settled, Kirst moved gingerly, retrieving his knife from inside the crate. He raised his body and wedged the blade into the seam between the second and third plank. Exerting the last of his strength and muttering a long-forgotten prayer, Kirst twisted the knife handle.

Slowly the wood yielded. A gap opened. Triumphantly, he slid the blade down and worked the plank loose. Then again he jammed the knife into the lid and used it as a handhold. He forced his arm into the gap and pushed. The second plank popped out and fell into the water.

9

Kirst rolled through the opening.

He landed on packing material—burlap and lumpy wadding. At least it was dry. The crate was picked up on the swells and tossed about, and Kirst was rocked around inside. His fingers explored the walls and he discovered that the crate was lined with sticky caulking. The smell was terrible, but to Kirst it surpassed the finest perfume. It meant life, safety, survival.

First he had to warm his chilled body. With cold air whistling through the open top, Kirst tunneled deeper and wrapped himself in a burlap cocoon, ignoring hard lumps beneath his exhausted body. Burlap scratched his face but, lulled by the rocking motion as the crate was pushed through long Atlantic swells, Kirst drifted into a deep sleep.

He awoke with a start. Several seconds later, he remembered where he was. He fought panic and tried to take stock. He was alive, but for how long? He shifted and discovered that his whole body ached from stiffness. And he was cold, bitterly cold. Through the opening, stars shimmered in the night sky. He tried to focus on the distant points of light, but the crate kept rocking and the stars danced like manic fireflies. Something painful dug into his thigh. He felt beneath his legs and found a small wooden box.

He pulled it up and realized he was lying on a stack of such boxes. Though his fingers were still sticky from handling the caulking, he managed to work the box open. With a muted clatter, a smooth flat object with rounded edges dropped onto the burlap.

By the sound alone, Kirst knew it was nothing edible. He brought it up to his mouth anyway and tasted it, bit into it. He spat grit. It was rock.

10

Before he could grasp another box, the crate was hit by a wave. Seawater showered through the opening, and Kirst swallowed enough to burn his throat. He coughed and tried to hack it up, but the bitter taste remained in his mouth. He began to realize that without fresh water or food, his strange little craft would become his coffin.

He raised his hips and dug deeper, hoping desperately to find something edible. He pulled up six packages. Five were duplicates of the first, containing the same sort of flat, worn stone tablets. With mounting frustration, Kirst pitched each of them overboard.

The sixth was different. The box was square. He could feel a wooden frame under heavy paper sealed with wax. He tore at the paper and tried to pry the wood loose, but all parts of the box had been carefully glued shut. Someone had taken extra trouble with this one. Kirst shook it and heard from inside the reassuring gurgle of liquid.

Hope swelled in his brain. His stomach dictated every move he made thereafter. He sat up and stuck his head out of the crate. He grabbed the knife he had left embedded in the wood.

Shaking with anticipation and hunger, Kirst pried the glue apart and struggled to separate the lid from the box. The glue was old and dry and he heard it crack, then the box popped apart in his hands.

Something heavy fell into his lap. It caught the starlight from above and gleamed brightly. Kirst stared at it. It was some sort of flask or bottle, made of metal, with a smooth surface, warm to the touch. He held it up to the stars to see it better. It was five-sided, with a broad base tapering up to a narrow neck. The stopper was sealed to the neck with wire. Both the stopper and the flask, he realized, were made of pure silver. Kirst shook it. Again it gurgled.

Kirst laughed happily. Wine. Probably a very rare vintage. If he was to die out here, at least he would go in style.

Using the knife, he worked the wire loose and unwound it. He turned the stopper and was surprised to find that it came out easily. He dropped it in his lap and brought the open flask up to his nose, hoping to smell the pungent aroma of a *grand cru* burgundy, but nothing so wonderful teased his senses. There was no bouquet at all.

With a softly muttered "Heil," he brought the flask to his lips and drank greedily.

A warmth that Kirst hadn't felt in hours shot through his body. The liquid had a sour taste, not winelike at all, almost medicinal and very oily. It infused him with a sense of well-being. He arched his head back and swallowed the last of it.

Gagging on the bitter residue at the bottom, he leaned over the side of his makeshift boat and spat it into the sea.

As it struck the ocean, it sizzled and burst into flame.

Kirst watched it, amazed, briefly wondering whether he had poisoned himself.

Thoughts trailed away as the warmth moved inside him and helped him relax. A moment later, without knowing why, Kirst threw the empty flask as far away as he could. He watched it bob a moment, then saw it fill with water and sink from sight.

Part One

Chapter 1

Ishtar was the Babylonian goddess of love, worshiped by the largest cult of followers in ancient Mesopotamia. Loring Holloway turned the tiny carved image over and over in her hands, feeling the rough stone and delicate indentations beneath the pendulous breasts.

As much a goddess of war as of love, to the Phoenicians she was Astarte, to the Semites, Ashtoreth, and to the Sumerians, Inanna. But to the Babylonians she was chiefly an excuse for orgies of wild abandon and ritual prostitution.

To Loring Holloway she was exhibit number G814 in the new Mesopotamian display. She would have a place of honor in a glass case, lit from two sides and fixed upright on a pedestal covered in red satin, *if* Loring could get red satin somewhere during these wartime shortages, and *if* there was enough in the *if* budget to purchase it on the black market should that become necessary. Otherwise, little Ishtar would be resting on colored construction paper.

Loring leaned back in her creaking swivel stool. The light was bad down in the basement of the Metropolitan Museum. They were saving on electricity, too. She looked over at the stack of opened crates that were her responsibility. So much work left to do for a display date seven months away—she doubted she would make it without assistance. There wasn't even a secretary to handle the cataloging: she had to do it all herself—unpack the artifacts, check the master inventory and the descriptions, be sure there were no new defects, measure with calipers, draw a rendering as faithfully as possible, and write the museum catalog description that would eventually go to the printer. Then she had to decide where and how everything would be displayed, and write it all down so that the museum custodians would make no mistakes.

She groaned and rolled her shoulders. Her back ached. She had asked for a straight-backed chair three weeks ago. She couldn't believe that *chairs* were hard to find in wartime.

She thought back on the career she had dropped for the duration. Field archaeology was far more rewarding than museum staff work. But where Loring wanted to be, where she felt she belonged, was too dangerous at this time. The Middle East, though not the focal point of the war, was nevertheless embroiled in it.

Loring heard the elevator creaking and clanking. The doors opened with a series of crashes. She stared down the long dark basement corridor, past stacks of crates that belonged to other displays. Footsteps clacked on ancient linoleum, and a figure was silhouetted coming up the corridor and into the light.

"Hiya, honey."

His face appeared under the first conical work light. He took off his hat and kept coming, shrugging out of his coat. It was Warren Clark.

"Hi," she said back. His coat was stained with wet spots. "Is it raining out?"

"Can't you hear it?"

"Oh, yes . . ." She listened and heard the distant pat-

16

ter. "I thought you were in Washington. You said you weren't coming down till Saturday."

"It's a little slow up at State. I took an Army B-25. Boy, those things are cold. No heat."

He tossed his coat and hat on the long workbench, careful not to disturb anything. He reached over and ran a finger over Ishtar's left breast.

"Nice," he said. "Babylonian, right?"

"You're improving." She watched him pull a silver cigarette case from his jacket pocket. He lit a Camel, inhaled deeply, blew the smoke out, then leaned over and kissed her on the lips. She let him have only a peck, then sat back and smiled at him.

He dropped into a chair and worked on his cigarette.

Loring cocked her head and studied his features. He wasn't a bad-looking lout, old Warren Clark, just so obviously a product of eastern prep schools, and so painfully obviously stuck on her. He had a big square face with a square jaw and a square smile. His hair was slicked down and combed to one side, then brushed back at the top. He used a fragrant cream on it every day that turned sour by midafternoon. But there were other things that bothered Loring about Warren Clark—like his self-conscious awareness of being a rarity on the home front, a civilian bachelor with connections.

Since his State Department job had kept him out of the Army, he could have had his pick of available women, but he was obsessed with Loring Holloway. On the frequent occasions when she asked why, he would explain, "You're a challenge."

He reminded her of two young Harvard snots she had dated back in her college days. Both had been bent on conquest; both had lost their battles to enter her bed. But

17

Warren was useful, and it was wartime, when every girl needed someone useful.

"What brings you out, Warren? You didn't come all the way up from Washington three days early just to see me."

"No?" He watched her through a haze of his own smoke. She was busying herself with the Ishtar, dusting it with a thin brush. "Actually, I'm down on business, but as soon as I found out, I came right over here."

"Found out what?"

"That ship you asked me to keep track of—the *Delaware Trader?*"

Loring looked up. "What about it?"

"Six days overdue. Presumed lost."

Loring put down her brush. Her eyes fixed on the Ishtar and for a moment she felt she was staring right through solid stone. Terrifying scenes danced before her eyes—memories of disaster—and the unmistakably giddy feeling of *déjà vu*—as if somehow she had known this would happen at the very moment she had finalized arrangements with London—

She glanced at Warren. "Are you sure?"

"I double-checked with Charlie Hemphill, port captain of New York."

She still didn't believe it, didn't want to believe it. "Presumed lost. That doesn't mean definitely, does it? I mean, it could have gone to another harbor. You just don't know for certain, do you?"

"I'm not suggesting you should assume the worst—just be prepared for it. It left London; it failed to arrive in New York; something happened."

"An accident?" She tried to keep the stricken look off her face, but Warren was frowning at her. He sensed that her concern was intensely personal.

18

"Forget that optimistic propaganda in the newspapers, okay? There are still German U-boats in the Atlantic."

Loring's eyes blazed. She clutched the Ishtar tightly, letting all her tension flow into that grip. White-knuckled, she set the piece down, then shoved herself away from the table. The stool rolled. She jumped up.

"What am I supposed to do? Sit still and wait for more news?"

"Well, I guess you'll have to. Then again, we may never find out and—and *presumed lost* would remain on the books."

Loring's backbone quivered. "You mean if they don't find the ship or any wreckage, I'll never know what happened?"

Warren folded his arms across his chest. "I think you ought to fill me in."

"I told you before—museum business. I've got a consignment of artifacts aboard that ship, sent from the British Museum."

"Hardly vital war materiel."

"But important to *me,* Warren!"

He shrugged. "I can't get an air and sea search going for a museum consignment."

"What *can* you do?"

He stared at her, starting to feel used again. She sensed it and backed down. She came over to him and stood by his chair. He was conscious of the curve of her hip beneath the heavy wool skirt. He wanted to reach out and touch—

"You're right, Warren. I ask too many favors. I'll handle this myself." She moved to the coatrack, slipped on her rain gear, and shoved her feet into galoshes.

"Uh—where are you going?"

She snatched up a note pad from her table and tossed it

to him. "This Charlie Hemphill you mentioned. Give me his address."

"The port captain? You want the port captain's address?"

"Phone number will do. Save me a trip in the rain."

"You're serious."

She stood in front of him and directed his gaze into her eyes so he could see just how serious. "I have to find out about that ship, Warren. It's no joke, it's no game, and it's more important than you can imagine. Now, one of us is going to contact Charlie Hemphill, and if he doesn't provide answers, I'll go right up the chain until I get what I need. If you can help, I would be more than grateful. It might mean a lot to our friendship."

Warren was motionless, not knowing what to make of that. Friendship, indeed. She touched his shoulder, and he looked at her hand, then her eyes. She was pleading. If Loring Holloway was capable of a plea, it was there on her face now. And as much as he wanted to say "No," he felt a garbled "Yes" rising in his throat.

When he was gone, after getting his obligatory peck on the cheek, Loring stripped off her raincoat and pulled off the galoshes, wondering what it was that had convinced Warren to do as she asked. Probably her hand on his shoulder—he always shuddered at her touch, and he would do anything for more.

Her parents liked Warren Clark, and to Loring that in itself was the kiss of death. Of course, he was careful to promote their approval, always half again as nice to her mother and father as he was to her. For every pair of nylon stockings he brought Loring, there were two for her mother. And then there was the set of tires he had wangled for her father. Even the rich knew shortages in this war.

To Loring's dad, Warren had become one of the family, already affectionately referred to as "sonny boy" and "our Warren." But it would go no farther if Loring had any say in it. She knew that soon Warren would have to be informed that courting her family did not mean he was winning *her* hand. Whenever she felt guilty over her hesitation about telling him this, she simply reminded herself that he had elected to pursue her, not vice versa.

But for right now, she would have to *use* him. He was her only link with a situation that she felt was about to get out of hand. She already knew, with that fine, intestinal-churning sense known as female intuition, that the *Delaware Trader* was a goner, and her shipment of artifacts that had survived twenty-five hundred years buried in the desert was most probably gone with it.

But she also knew that she would not be able to sleep or even rest until she knew for certain.

Commander Bernard Heller considered himself a lucky man. A doctor, he had been called up for active duty in 1942. With the exception of a six-month tour at Walter Reed Hospital in Washington, he had done his service at the Brooklyn Navy Yard, less than thirty minutes from his home on Eastern Parkway. Six nights out of seven, he slept in his own bed under his own roof.

He removed his stethoscope from Kirst's chest and made a notation on a medical chart. "You can put your shirt on now," he said in flawless German.

Kirst murmured, *"Danke,"* and reached for the garment.

Heller cocked his head at Kingsly, the intelligence officer. "Artie," he called, stepping around the shore patrolman standing in the doorway, "I'd like a word with you."

21

Kingsly joined him. "What's *your* verdict, Doc?"

Heller scanned the medical chart. "Same as the others. He's healthier than you and me put together. Medically speaking, his story doesn't make sense."

Kingsly sighed. "You too, huh? Look. His uniform, his ID disk, and his papers all check out. He's Rolf Kirst. What's the big puzzle?"

"Two days in an open crate out in the Atlantic, Artie. There's not a goddamned thing wrong with him. No dehydration, no exposure. It doesn't add up. I don't want to tell you how to do your job, but if I were you I'd recheck his story."

"Already have. I know it's nutty, but I believe him. Now sign him off, so I can get him the hell out of here."

"Forms'll be ready in an hour. Where's he being sent?"

"To the wide open spaces. He's going to see more of America than I have."

Kirst gave up trying to understand the conversation in the hallway. English was a mystery to him. He finished tying his shoes, then straightened up and returned the stolid gaze of the big American guarding him. He opened his mouth to speak and once again, with a familiar, frightening rush, his vocal cords were paralyzed and he choked on his words. His jaw clamped shut involuntarily and the panic in his eyes was instantly clouded over. The guard stared at him briefly, frowning, then relaxed.

On a drunken binge with fellow officers, Kirst had once boasted that he didn't know the meaning of fear. In the last several days he had grown to understand it better, never more so than when words formed in his throat only to be torn away by an invisible hand. Fear kept him pressed to the table as he thought of bounding to the door, bowling the guard over, and running away. He

22

tried to move his hand but it wouldn't budge. He wanted to stick fingers down his throat and vomit up the oppressive power inside him. Knowledge floated in and out, knowledge and awareness of something beyond himself, stronger than his own will, yet deeply, firmly embedded in his vitals, waiting and drawing on his energy—

Right now it was closing its invisible grip on his heart, squeezing, sending fear and panic welling up inside him and—

To the guard, Kirst was just a listless, helpless German perched on the examining table. So far he had offered no resistance. He had sat almost perfectly still as the doctor examined him, had responded almost automatically to the requests to raise a knee, breathe deeply, expose his throat. . . . *A pussy, this one,* thought the guard. *What weed patch did he spring from? German officer stock—shit.*

Kirst silently promised the whatever-it-was inside him that he wouldn't bolt, wouldn't run or try to escape or do anything it didn't want done, if it would just leave him the hell alone for a few minutes. Almost magically, it responded to his thoughts and, with great relief, he felt the warmth stir in his stomach and the grip on his heart relax. He felt his eyes directed to the guard and, without understanding why, he gave the man a stare that bore right through him and into his brain and caused him to step forward—

Kirst's eyes closed. He could still see the guard floating on his inner lids. There was an aura about him, a pulsing unnameable color that felt to him like the visual embodiment of strength. He wanted to—no, the warmth inside him wanted to—The image on his inner lids shimmered and shook, then exploded into shards—

Blackness floated in its place, and Kirst knew it was

seeing through eyes not his own, that while his lids were clamped shut, it was viewing the world with malevolent delight—

Panic rose up inside him again. Just as quickly, the blackness engulfed him and drove his feelings down into his stomach until they were no more than a tiny rock-hard knot of tension waiting to spring free once more.

Kirst's eyes opened again. The blackness was gone. The warmth shrank inside him and he was permitted to get up. He stood shakily under the guard's curious gaze. He tried to remember when all this had started. Certainly not when he was aboard U-221. It must have been later, when he was in the water or—

He saw himself heaving his body out of the sea and flopping down atop that crate. He saw his hands struggling with the knife and the boards, opening it, getting inside—

The rest faded into nothingness.

He forced himself to think, but that only brought the warmth rolling up through his torso and into his head, filling it with a blackness that blotted out his growing anxiety. Finally, the only thing he could recall with any clarity was the gray hull of the rescue ship.

His mind drifted. The blackness subsided.

Captain Roger Wayne Hopkins left the noon mess in a foul mood. He checked his watch and tested the air. The temperature had dropped since this morning. Above the camp, the sky was bleak and overcast. The slopes of Blackbone Mountain glistened with winter dampness. Patches of snow still clung to the rocks. There hadn't been a storm in ten days but, according to Armed Forces Weather, one was due any minute. And Hopkins' moods had a habit of fluctuating with the barometer.

Hopkins zipped up his fur-lined jacket and slogged back to headquarters, glancing through the fence to see what the Germans were up to. A little volleyball, a little schmoozing, a lot of walking around and staring at each other. Same as always. They never did anything unusual. Smoke curled from the stack in the rec hut, and he could see Germans hanging around the front porch. He glanced up at the nearest perimeter guard post. The man in the tower had one leg up on the railing and a hand on his machine gun. Ready but relaxed.

A rabbit cut across Hopkins' path and paused to stare at the Germans. Hopkins laughed, then made as if to grab it. The rabbit took off. Maybe it didn't like the Germans, but it had no use for Hopkins either. Hopkins walked on, scratching flakes off the back of his head and making a mental note to get on the quartermaster's ass about some decent shampoo. Maybe he could heist it from the Germans' Red Cross packages. They were always getting useful crap like that. The larcenous possibility pleased him. He chuckled to himself, then thought about his leave. He had a couple of weeks coming—a chance to get the hell out of this backwoods Antarctica and go someplace warm and sunny, with hot and cold running women. Oh, Christ, women. He hadn't seen a real tit in months. Just those magazines that Private Carlton kept getting from his uncle in Jersey. Oh, for those two goddamned weeks and a chance to catch up on his sex life. He closed his eyes and stood rock-still for a moment, and there in the bitter cold, with an icy breeze tickling his nose and lips, he thought of the most beautiful woman he had ever laid eyes on and what it would be like to have his hands on her right now, this minute. . . .

A rush of cold air cut through his thoughts. He sighed and moved along. Fat chance about leave. Not with the new commandant reporting in today. Hopkins wondered about him. Would he be like the last C.O.—easygoing, disinterested, quiet, keep-to-himself Major Mancroft?

What a cushy deal that had been! Hopkins smiled, remembering Mancroft closeted with his books, his black-market liquor, and his classical music, venturing out once a day to inspect the camp, but leaving Hopkins to run things. Would the new C.O. be the same?

The scuttlebutt sounded good. Major Gilman. New York boy, prep schools, Dartmouth. Volunteered for service before the war, went through OCS, got his command just as the war got under way. Hopkins had peeked at his dossier, but he didn't have the latest information. Rumor had it that Gilman screwed up in France and lost a whole battalion. Rumor aside, the end result was clear: Gilman was relieved of command, busted a grade, and shipped back stateside. The assignment to Blackbone was clearly a punishment. Gilman would probably spend his entire tour hiding his head, doing as little as possible.

Fine with Hopkins, but he did find it curious that the camp C.O.s were always losers. Take the last one—Mancroft. Fucked up some things for a general, got himself blown out of a cushy desk job, ended up here a burnt-out case with Hopkins holding everything together. Hopkins shook his head—you really had to be a colossal screw-up to get the top job here.

But what if Major Gilman came boiling in and tried to toss his weight around? Hopkins sniffed and smiled. The climate and the independence of the MPs would put him in his place. Hopkins could just go on being Hopkins, the man in charge.

He entered headquarters, called the clerks to attention, and ran a brisk inspection. The jeep bringing Gilman from his train was due in thirty minutes.

Blackbone Military Detention Facility was little more than a compound of barracks-type huts, surrounded by a chain link fence topped with barbed wire. There were guard posts at intervals around the perimeter—tiny open huts atop wood scaffolding. The support huts, housing the American MPs, were no different from the prisoners' accommodations. The MPs were assigned to guard more than two hundred German prisoners of war, all of them commissioned officers captured in Europe and shipped to the States for internment. There were other camps around the country, many of them more comfortable than Blackbone. Noncommissioned officers were sent to work camps in sunny California, where they spent the rest of the war picking oranges. Most of the field-grade troublemakers ended up at Blackbone, where there was little to do but think.

The camp was backed up against a hill that contained a played-out silver mine. Behind it loomed Blackbone Mountain. Rugged, sparsely forested, steep and gloomy, it was the most lifeless hunk of real estate in the Little Belt Range, stuck away in a corner of Meagher County, Montana. It was isolated fifty miles from the nearest town, which was the railroad stop at White Sulphur Springs. There was nowhere to go on a weekend pass, so none were handed out. In winter, the MPs couldn't even go hunting: the animals were smart enough not to hang around. Everybody—Americans as well as Germans—wanted out. So when it snowed—frequently—and it got wet and freezing cold, tempers would grow short. The Americans would look to the source of their misery, and the Germans would gird their loins for a dose of bad treatment.

Most of it was tolerated with mute approval by Hopkins. But he liked it even better when he started it himself. In his tour of duty at Blackbone, he had evolved into a master of subtle indignities, which he enjoyed inflicting on his prisoners with what he called "the velvet touch." He would go out of his way to make them uncomfortable while leading them to believe he was sympathetic. They wanted better rations—he got them canned beets and rhubarb, grits and black-eyed peas, porridge and lard, hardtack and matzos. They asked for meat—they got hog jowls, chitlins, and gizzards. They requested reading matter—they got Spanish-language newspapers, government form letters, and old laundry tickets. When they complained of rats and vermin, Hopkins sent them a large cooking pot.

His favorite trick was roll call. He would wait till it

was pouring rain or there was a blizzard going, then he would roust the Germans and, from the protection of a covered jeep, slowly and haltingly call the roll. His tongue would tie itself in knots over names like von Lechterhoeven and Schliechenvaldmer. If the Germans protested, he would immediately inflict something worse.

The Germans had resigned themselves to Hopkins. Nevertheless, their morale had hit bottom long before Major Mancroft was transferred. The news that a replacement was coming had little effect. They figured it would still be Hopkins on the throne.

Christmas was coming, and it would be Major Walter Steuben's second at Blackbone, an anniversary he was not looking forward to. He stepped out on the rec-hut porch and lit a cigarette, inhaled deeply, and scanned the camp. The volleyball game was breaking up. Some of the men were running in place to continue the exercise. There was some spirited joking, but that faded quickly, replaced by the usual gloom that settled in when nothing was happening.

Steuben thought about organizing another perimeter patrol: the men had responded to the last one enthusiastically. They had stripped to their underwear, lined up in two ranks, and marched around the camp, just inside the warning wire, singing *"Deutschland, Deutschland, über alles . . ."* and thumbing their noses at the MPs. The men needed something like that to unite them.

Steuben was the senior German officer and as such had appointed himself guardian of the general morale. But he hardly felt successful at it. He glanced back into the rec hut. There was a fast game of poker going on inside. His men had learned at least one vice from the Americans.

And they would gamble with anything on hand: pine cones, pebbles, even dried rabbit turds.

Steuben reached inside his open coat and scratched the rash at his groin. Everybody in the camp had something that the medics couldn't treat. Lice they could handle, but crotch rot, athlete's foot, acne, and anything related to a vitamin deficiency went practically untreated. At least they ate regularly, but oh, God, what they ate. Steuben winced, remembering last night's culinary masterpiece. Pork something something, with some horrid greens that could not have grown on any land Steuben had ever seen. His chefs, three German noncoms imported from another camp, were hard-pressed to deal with some of the odd groceries supplied by Hopkins. They always managed to serve something, but not everyone managed to eat it. In the quiet moments before falling asleep, just as his eyes were about to close, Steuben would be haunted by memories of restaurants and beer gardens and cafes, and wonderful meals and marvelous wines. . . . Then it would be hours before sleep caught him.

Something was happening on the other side of the fence. MPs were running out of the barracks and forming up near the headquarters hut. Steuben drew on the nub of his cigarette, then flicked it into a patch of snow. He crossed the yard and headed up the slope to the fence. Others joined him. Bruckner came up, leading his mutt on a rope leash.

"What do you suppose?" Bruckner said, his eyes moving furtively.

Hopkins came out of headquarters briskly, wearing a clean uniform, sparkling like a tin soldier. He called the ranks of MPs to attention and yelled at them for a few moments.

Several of the Germans looked at Steuben. "New commandant is coming," Steuben said. "Should be arriving any minute." Automatically, Steuben buttoned up his coat, then sent someone to fetch his cap.

Bruckner looked at his dog. It was sniffing the ground, lapping at a puddle of melted snow. Always drinking, that dog. Bruckner worried that it suffered from dehydration. It was a mongrel—no wonder. One could expect sickness in an impure animal. But he had grown attached to the little bastard. They were inseparable. Leutnant Hans Bruckner was thin and pinch-faced, and his dog was the opposite, broad and puglike. Bruckner kept a little stick in his pocket and, whenever MPs were in the camp, he would throw the stick. The dog would fetch it and come back with the stick wedged in a corner of its mouth like a cigar, and Bruckner would call out loudly, "Here, Churchill!" The MPs, if they had never heard it before, would stop in their tracks and look around and, when they realized the joke, they would laugh with Bruckner. But Bruckner had only pulled that gag once around Hopkins. Hopkins had threatened to kill the dog and make Bruckner eat it.

Everyone fell silent as a jeep appeared around the back bend and roared up the road.

Dortmunder returned with Steuben's cap, which he quickly put on. Then he clasped his hands behind his back and stepped in front of the growing crowd of prisoners. He stood stiffly, watching the jeep come to a stop near the line of MPs.

The officer who got out of the jeep looked to be in his early thirties, seasoned and muscular, with angular features that stood out sharply. As the jeep slewed around and shot toward headquarters, the officer stood alone for a moment, his stocky body taut as he surveyed the camp.

31

Steuben knew immediately this was no *dummkopf.* This one looked *kräftig.*

Major David Gilman's gaze skimmed past the MPs to take in the entire camp. The isolation, the cold, the soldiers lined up—all instantly reminded him of France and the Second Battalion. He wanted to call that jeep back, leap in and drive on, just go off into the mountains and lose himself. This was his first command since the battalion, and he had been dreading it all through the cross-country train ride. He wanted to be anywhere but facing a bunch of soldiers who would be looking to him for their welfare.

Then the captain was walking toward him, and it was too late to run.

"Captain Hopkins reporting, sir. Welcome to Blackbone."

Gilman returned the salute. "Major Gilman, Captain."

Hopkins grinned and stuck out his hand—the gesture was openly informal and seemed to say, Let's show the men that you and I are gonna be pals.

Gilman made no move to acknowledge the gesture until Hopkins' grin faded, then Gilman gripped his hand. Thereafter, Hopkins was in an uncertain mood.

Gilman rushed through the formalities of assuming command. Hopkins called the MPs to attention, and they ran a quick inspection.

Gilman came to the end of the first rank and realized he hadn't looked a single one of these soldiers in the eye. He had stared at their boots, their belt buckles and buttons, but not their faces. He did the second rank less quickly, forcing himself to display some humanity, some interest, though doing so only made him anxious.

32

This was not going to be easy. He kept seeing those faces in France. Second Battalion.

He returned to position himself in front of the men. Hopkins stood before him stiffly. Gilman looked past him, through the fence at the row of Germans lined up behind the warning wire. He stared at them and for a moment the MPs didn't exist: there was only David Gilman and a bunch of Germans, the enemy. . . . Some feeling he didn't understand welled up inside him. Gilman thought it might be hate, but it felt more like despair.

He caught Hopkins staring at him. The captain's face betrayed nothing, but what had he seen in Gilman's eyes? Fear? Terror? Weakness? Gilman didn't give him a chance to think about it.

"I'd like to tour the camp, Captain."

"Wouldn't you rather get settled first, sir?"

"I'm settled just dandy. Let's go have a look at those Germans."

They went through the gate—Gilman, Hopkins, and four MPs. It was closed, chained, and padlocked after them. They went down the slope and were met by Steuben and Bruckner.

Ignoring Bruckner, Hopkins introduced Steuben. "Major Gilman, this is the senior Nazi officer at Blackbone, Major Walter Steuben."

"German officer, Captain Hopkins," Steuben said, matching the precise inflection of hostility that Hopkins had directed at him. "As I have reminded you many times, the Nazis are a political party of which I am not a member. I am an officer of the Wehrmacht. I realize it's difficult for you, but please make that distinction."

Steuben spoke excellent English with only the trace of an accent. Gilman figured him for about forty. He was heavyset, with wolfish features and an impressive air of authority. Bruckner, on the other hand, wore a phony smile. Behind it lurked pure terror. He kept glancing at Hopkins and tightening his grip on the dog's leash.

Steuben saluted Gilman. "Blackbone is not your typical American resort, Herr Major, but should you desire company, I am happy to offer my quarters as a refuge from the daily bore. You play poker, Major?"

Gilman returned the salute. "Sure do. But you know the rules—no fraternizing."

"Wie schade!"

"Yes, it is a pity."

"You speak German, Major?"

"Just enough to tell a prisoner what to do." Gilman grinned. Steuben's smile froze.

He recovered quickly and bowed with that curious European chickenlike nod. "I am happy to report that in my time in your country, I have acquired what the Americans call a sense of humor. I shall be most happy to take it home with me when the festivities are over."

Hopkins spat and glared at Steuben. "Don't be fooled by his jokes, Major. Steuben here is the leader of the pack. What he says, goes. If the Germans make trouble, you can be sure he's behind it."

Steuben bowed again. "I am sure Major Gilman knows a troublemaker when he sees one, Captain."

Hopkins took a step toward Steuben, his features going taut with anger. "I don't think the major needs to hear any more from you."

Steuben faced him without expression. There was nothing more Hopkins could say or do, so he whirled sharply and glared at Bruckner.

"You still got that damned dog?"

Bruckner shrank slightly and looked at Gilman with a

34

bent smile that seemed forced under his natural pinched scowl.

"Leutnant, I'd like you to speak freely," Gilman said. "How is it here? Are you comfortable?"

Bruckner stared at him. "*Ja,*" he said hesitantly.

"And your dog? How does he get along?"

"He eats scraps, Major," Steuben cut in. "He's really no bother."

Hopkins strolled around Gilman and approached the dog. Bruckner eyed him warily. "Don't worry, Leutnant," said Hopkins. "I'm not going to kick the sonofabitch. I don't kick dogs."

Gilman felt the tension even more than the chill in the air. He had learned one thing without anybody telling him to his face: the Germans hated Hopkins. And they feared him.

Gilman knelt down. Slowly he raised a hand. Cautiously, the dog approached and sniffed it. That led to some petting and stroking, then the dog was licking his hand and Gilman was scratching its ears, and Bruckner knelt down with him and together they petted the dog.

"His name is Churchill," Bruckner said, almost apologetically.

Gilman snorted a laugh. Then, out of the corner of his eye, he caught the Germans along the slope watching him and nodding to each other. Yes, sir, best move he could have made. Pet the dog, make some friends.

The barracks huts looked a lot worse close up—warped walls and rot, and great flaps of tar paper hanging over the edges of the roofs. The huts had been constructed on stilts with about eighteen inches of crawl space beneath. There were a few windows and a door at each end. None of the doors were seated right. And at

35

some of them, there were no steps, just a sharp drop—bad for sleepwalkers.

Inside, the huts were sectioned off into rooms on either side and an aisle down the center. The walls were thin plywood sheets. There were double bunks, and the Germans slept eight to a room. No frills. Some rooms had windows, others did not. The shower hut was a communal facility with a urinal trough, a few unenclosed pots, a long sink, and mirror for shaving and washing clothes. Most of the hut was taken up by a large shower stall with a concrete floor and drainage. The floor sloped sharply toward the drain, and Gilman noted a thick soapy scum around the sides. Overhead were shower pipes with unnozzled spouts.

"Hot water?" he asked Hopkins.

Hopkins took him outside and showed him the jury-rigged water heater, fed by a coal-burning stove. It was stone cold, and there was no coal in the bin.

"How often do you shower?" Gilman asked Steuben.

"Whenever we can heat the water," Steuben replied.

"How often is that?"

"Now and then."

"Major, would you care to register a complaint?"

Steuben studied him carefully, unsure how to answer that. He still hadn't figured out whose side Gilman would be on. "Not at this time," he said.

Gilman glanced at Hopkins, who shrugged. "Want to see your quarters, Major?" he asked.

"I'm not through here." Gilman motioned to Steuben and they went back into the shower hut. Gilman asked about towels, soap, toilet paper, supplies in general.

Steuben thought for a while, then said, "We have been short of these things in the past. Very short. But then, magically, they appear." He threw a look at Hopkins.

36

Hopkins snorted. "Sir, I think you should be directing those questions to me," he said.

"Okay." Gilman turned and looked him square in the eye. Hopkins motioned toward the mess hut and they all trooped after him.

Half the hut was a mess hall, crowded with tables and benches. There was a coal-burning stove in one corner. Behind another plywood partition was the kitchen, small and cramped. And beyond that, a locked pantry. Hopkins opened it and turned on the light. Inside, he displayed stacks of food—canned meats, soups, and vegetables by the gallon; sacks of flour, rice, and salt; crates of oranges and fresh vegetables. It was more than well-stocked—it was stuffed with food that Steuben hadn't seen in months. And he said so.

Hopkins smiled. "Oh, come on, Major. You know damn well there's a war on. There're always shortages. We got lucky this week. Big shipment came in."

"And when did you bring it into the camp?" Steuben asked. "In the dead of night? When we were all sleeping?"

"Sure. Made for a lot less fuss."

"Why wasn't I informed?"

"Don't you like surprises?"

Hopkins was enjoying his little joke.

"What about coal for the stoves?" asked Gilman. "Blankets?"

Hopkins took them out to a padlocked shed behind the mess hut. Opening it, he displayed two huge bins filled with coal. "Blankets came in yesterday," he added. "Still out in our supply shack. Haven't sorted them yet. But we'll have them distributed today."

He stood back and rocked on his heels, happy.

Steuben turned to Gilman, flushed with anger. "Major,

this is all for show. These items have been requisitioned for months, but we have always been given the same excuse—there's a war on. We are forced to live with shortages." He pointed to the full coal bins. "*This* is *not* normal!"

Gilman quietly asked, "Now do you want to make a formal complaint?"

Steuben shook his head. "Your concern is enough."

Gilman nodded. By now, he had Steuben pegged. Career soldier, army man down to his toes, responsible, unselfish, and proud. Bruckner reminded him of an eagle-eyed accountant and seemed out of place as a soldier. Tight-lipped, brooding, and suspicious, he clung to his dog's leash and carefully kept the animal away from Hopkins.

Hopkins was only one thing, with or without the uniform—a bully.

Gilman turned on his heel and walked away from the huts, heading for the warning wire, then beginning a hike around the perimeter. The others followed. The Germans hung back a little, but Hopkins caught up.

Hopkins said nothing for a long time, and Gilman had the feeling he was being gauged. "We do the best we can," Hopkins finally said. "But after all, sir, they are Germans."

"How goddamned observant of you, Hopkins."

"Sir—"

"Now listen to me and listen carefully. When we finish this little tour, I'm going over to the supply shack to check out inventories for the last six months. You want to tell me right now what I'm going to find, or should I tell you?"

Hopkins was silent.

"Okay. You've been skimping on everything. Coal,

blankets, food, soap—everything. Maybe you think it's clever to treat these men like shit. After all, they're your prisoners and they're Germans. They're not human, so you short their supplies. You starve them a little, and that reminds them who's boss. I don't believe you're siphoning the stuff off for profit, Hopkins. I don't think you're clever enough for that. But you've become an expert torturer. Maybe you don't think it's wrong. Maybe you think it's creative punishment and you ought to get a medal for what you're doing. Well, I'll tell you what you're going to get. You're going to get those goddamned blankets out *now* and, if you're still short, you take them off the MPs' bunks and *you* explain to them why. But I want every prisoner in this camp to have two new blankets by 1500 hours. And let them into those coal bins. And give Steuben a set of keys to the shed and the pantry. Now . . . what the fuck is this?"

Gilman stopped at the back perimeter, where the fence climbed the sharp slope of the Blackbone foothills, enclosing a caved-in area within the camp.

Hopkins was slow to answer: his ears still burned from Gilman's attack. Gilman snapped at him, "I asked you a question, Captain!" as Steuben and Bruckner joined them, followed by the MPs.

Hopkins stared at the cave-in. "It's an abandoned mine shaft," he explained. "Used to be a silver mine in Blackbone Mountain. When the Corps of Engineers laid out the camp, they sealed the shaft with explosives, then ran the fence around it."

"Why didn't they put the fence on this side of the shaft?"

"It . . . it was supposed to be sort of a symbol." Hopkins glanced up from his shoes.

"Of what?"

39

"Freedom. So near yet so far." Hopkins couldn't resist a little smile at the joke.

Gilman stared at him. "We're supposed to be holding these people, Captain—not tormenting them."

Hopkins quivered with anger. "Sir, I have to question the wisdom of leniency. After all, sir, they are the enemy. Anything we can do to make them miserable, to demoralize them, is a contribution to the war effort!"

With Steuben and Bruckner listening to every word, Gilman went nose to nose with Hopkins. "Treating them properly, Captain, is not leniency. It's good sense, maybe even vital. If we break the rules, what indignities do you imagine the Germans might feel free to inflict on Americans in their camps? These men are under our care, not our thumb. Now, get this camp up to standard and be quick about it. And move that fence so that caved-in mine shaft is outside the wire."

"Yes, sir." Hopkins' lip quivered bitterly. "But . . . we're out of fencing."

"Order some."

Gilman sent Hopkins back with the MPs, then hiked back toward the huts with Steuben. Bruckner remained a few paces behind, stopping once to let his dog take a leak.

"Blackbone isn't going to turn into a resort, Major," said Gilman, "but I don't think it should be an unpleasant place to sit out the war."

"Most appreciated, Major Gilman. *Du bist ein ehrenhafter Mann.*"

"Honorable?"

"*Ja.*" Steuben smiled. Gilman made no response. As they drew closer to the huts, he grew edgy seeing the crowd of faces studying him from the hut doors, from outside the huts, from beneath trees, Germans with curious eyes, hopeful eyes some of them, others hateful. . . .

"Ironisch, Herr Major," said Steuben. "We are both sitting out the war, and we both have the same job—looking after the welfare of these men."

Gilman stopped abruptly and stared straight ahead as if lost. Then he parted from Steuben without a word and marched stiffly past the Germans and up to the gate.

Steuben stared after him curiously.

Chapter 3 ═══════════════════════

Hopkins slammed the door as he walked into headquarters. The company clerk, Corporal Chilton, looked up from his typing briefly, then continued, out of the corner of his eye watching Hopkins go to the window. Hopkins lit a cigarette and stared out at the camp, his brow furrowed with anger. He rolled the cigarette around his fingers like a magician rolls a coin, over the knuckles and under the tips then back and up into his mouth for a long draw. He was thinking.

Chilton stopped typing and lit a cigarette for himself. Finally, their eyes met. "So, what's he like, sir?" said Chilton.

"He's like shit," said Hopkins.

"What's his beef?"

"That's what you're going to find out."

"Sir?"

"I want you to plug into the pipeline and get whatever dope is available on Major Gilman. I want to know exactly how he screwed up in France. I want names, dates, and places. I want to know if he crossed anybody, or fucked a general's wife." Hopkins rolled the butt through his fingers again. Then he flicked it across the room, and it landed squarely in Chilton's ashtray.

"I want something on him," Hopkins growled. "I don't care how you get it."

"Tall order, Captain."

"Is it worth a week in Frisco?"

"Are we talking leave, sir?"

"Could be."

"I'll get right on it, Captain."

Steuben's room served as the unofficial headquarters for the camp's senior officers. There was a pinup next to the door, a magazine photo of some buxom Bavarian blonde with an extremely prominent behind. Some claimed it was Steuben's wife, others his mistress. But everyone to a man who entered the room paused to pay homage, even if it was no more than an affectionate pat or a sideways glance. It served its purpose well, loosening tensions and promoting a lusty camaraderie.

But there were serious faces filing into Steuben's room after Gilman's walking tour. Within ten minutes after Steuben returned, the room was filled with fellow officers wanting to know what the new *amerikanischer Kommandant* was like.

"By the book," said Steuben. "Tough, direct, but fair. I think we'll see some improvement."

Leutnant Hoffman sneered. "How soft is he?"

"Not soft at all. He is as likely to come down on *us* as he did Hopkins."

"You think he'll transfer Hopkins out?"

"No, but he'll get him under control."

"I doubt that." Bruckner was sitting on the window-sill, stroking Churchill's ears. "Major Gilman may start off behaving like a saint, but he's not immune to temptation. He has a campful of enemy officers at his mercy. Was Hopkins such a bastard when he came here? No, it

43

took time for the disease to fester. It will be the same with Gilman—"

"That'll be enough, Bruckner," said Steuben.

But it wasn't enough for Bruckner. His eyes flashed and he tightened his grip on Churchill's leash. "They are plotting things, Hopkins and his pawns. And Gilman is part of it. He's going to be nice to us, give us food and blankets and extra coal, and make us think he's on our side. And then when he's got us where he wants us—"

"We're already where he wants us!" Steuben snapped. "We're prisoners! What more can they do to us?" He paused to control his anger then worked toward patience. "Hans, you have more theories and fears than I have hairs on my head. Accept one thing at face value, will you please? Nobody is plotting evil against us. We've been here too long and we've survived. Nobody has died in this camp! Nobody! Even Hopkins, with all his little tortures, has killed no one. We know the limits of what they will do. Hopkins is the worst, but he's unique. I am prepared to believe that Gilman is more representative of the way this government wants to treat us. And until we get evidence to the contrary, I believe we should be model prisoners. Offer no resistance, cause no trouble. Give them no reason to take reprisals. And that is how we will determine the true intentions of Major Gilman. I believe that, just as strongly as I believe that if we *do* step out of line, Gilman will act."

There were frowns and grumblings from the small core of true Nazis among the senior officers. While they didn't subscribe to Bruckner's wild statements, neither did they trust the Americans—any Americans. To them, Hopkins was more typical of the American character. Hopkins met all their expectations.

"Major Steuben." Mueller piped up from the rear,

coldly contemptuous. Mueller was the senior Luftwaffe officer and resident escape artist—or so he fancied himself.

"What is it, Mueller?"

"Same as always, Major. When will I get a hearing before the escape committee?"

"Let's give Major Gilman a little time to settle in before we start taking advantage."

"I don't understand that, Major. Are we supposed to hang up our balls until we find out if Gilman has any of his own? I've got serious plans that require discussion, and I'm willing to abide by the rules—no independent efforts. But there are other men involved, and *we want a hearing.*"

Hoffman stood behind him, nodding.

"So noted."

Mueller's eyes went icy with hatred. He was a disciplined officer, but his patience was sorely tried by Steuben's unbending reluctance to permit escape attempts. If Mueller didn't get his hearing soon, he might go without approval, and Steuben knew it.

"The escape committee will meet within the next forty-eight hours," Steuben said, "to discuss the general issue of escape. No plans will be heard at that time. But we will let you know our thinking."

Mueller's contempt only deepened. "What more could I ask for?" he said, then turned and walked out.

"At least we know one thing about Gilman," said Gebhard, the lone U-boat officer imprisoned at Blackbone. "He likes dogs."

Everybody glanced at Churchill and smiled. Churchill recognized the attention and let out a happy bark. Bruckner snorted. "Making love to the dog was for our benefit.

If Hopkins killed it, do you think Gilman would punish him?"

"It's your own fault," said Hoffman. "You had to go and name him Churchill."

"Right," said Gebhard. "Maybe if we call him Goering and kick him now and then—"

A few of the officers laughed. The Nazis in the corner glared at Gebhard.

Steuben dismissed the meeting and cleared the room. He stopped Bruckner at the door. "Hans," he said, "I don't understand where you get some of your ideas. Do you really believe the Americans are trying to find a way to kill us?"

"This is war, Major," Bruckner said with a bitter smile. "Some things you wouldn't dream of could already be reality."

Psychotic? Or just paranoid? Steuben wondered if he shouldn't turn Bruckner over to an American psychiatrist. There was no one on the prisoners' medical staff qualified to judge. But Bruckner was paranoid about American doctors, too, convinced that they were conducting horrifying experiments on war prisoners.

A few months ago, when he had run a fever and suffered chills, Bruckner had not even admitted he was sick, he was so afraid of being turned over to the Americans for treatment.

"In their hands, I would just disappear like a bug down a frog's throat," he had told Steuben in his delirium. "You would never see me again. I would end up cut into pieces. They would attach wires to what remains and run currents of electricity through me, and I would go on and off like a lamp." He had ranted and raved, and Steuben had ended up nursing him alone, not even permitting the German medics near him.

46

Since then, Bruckner had been more careful about his hygiene, his sleeping and eating habits. . . . And he had devoted himself to that dog, convinced that caring for another living being put him in good grace with God, and therefore he was protected.

"You are convinced we are losing this war," Bruckner told Steuben. "I don't blame you for that. In fact, I may believe it myself. But you are content to stay where you are, in the comforting bosom of America, the international tit. Your only concern is survival and, beyond that, repatriation. Some of these two hundred-odd men don't share that view. Mueller, for instance. You keep putting him off, expecting him to come around to your point of view and realize that escape is hopeless. But some of our men do not believe it is over. And they have grown rather unhappy with you."

Steuben was surprised to hear all this from Bruckner. "You mean they're finally paying attention to your portents of doom?" he said.

"No." Bruckner smiled. "I believe what I believe. They have their own ideas. And I . . ." He frowned, then gazed into space. "I live with what I know."

He shook Churchill's leash and made kissing sounds. The dog followed him down the corridor and out the door.

Steuben stepped back into his room and shut the door. Bruckner was right. His only interest was survival and, beyond that, going home. If there was a home to go back to. And it wasn't just for himself that he hoped. It was for all two hundred of the men in his care.

Steuben unbuttoned his tunic and lay down on his bunk. He closed his eyes and wished everyone away. Bruckner, Mueller, Hopkins, even Gilman. Send them all

47

to another planet. The only thing he wanted right now was a glass of schnapps and the warm flesh of his wife.

Lust faded quickly as he thought of his family back in Germany, trapped like helpless mice, directly in the path of the advancing Russian Army. And here he sat in the comforting bosom of America—safe.

Chapter 4

"Hi."

Loring held the door open. Warren Clark was leaning against the jamb—clothes rumpled, tie askew, damp stains on his shirt, drunk, and regarding her with a look of complete disgust. His head bobbed, and it seemed as if any second it might roll off his shoulders.

"It's past midnight, Warren. What do you want?"

"Me? What do I want?" He laughed then spoke again, trying to control a slur. "My pumpkin has become a coach, my footman has become a dog, and oops, my glass slippers have become *huaraches.*" He laughed again and sagged against the jamb. His coat rode up, pulling his shirttail out on one side.

"You're a mess. Go home and sleep it off."

Warren's face darkened. His foot lashed out, kicking the door wide. He tumbled into the room. "May I come in?"

Loring thought quickly. She decided it would be better to let him pass out in her apartment. In the morning, he would be his usual contrite, cooperative self, easier to get rid of. She shut the door. He fell onto the sofa, stretched out in a long heap, and stared at her.

"I've hit a dead end," he said. "I can't help you anymore. What do you think of that?"

Loring leaned against the door. "What sort of dead end?"

"You know. *Delaware Trader.*"

"What have you found out?"

"Wouldn't you like to know?"

"Yes, I would. Do I have to pull your teeth to find out?"

"Maybe—you might have to pull *something.*"

"Look, Warren, if you've got some gripe with me, can we settle it later? If you have any information about that ship, I would appreciate hearing it right now. It's vital!"

Warren lay motionless a moment then erupted. "Of course it's vital! Everything is vital to you except us! Well, shit! I'm tired of playing the lapdog! Warren, will you do this? Warren, will you check into that? Warren, would you use your connections? Warren, I don't want to tell you this, but I really think you're nothing more than the perfect doormat! And that's what I think of you!" He waved a demonstrative hand. "Isn't it?"

"No, and I'm sorry you feel that way."

"You're sorry for nothing. The only purpose I serve in your life is to run your goddamned errands and squire you around. You're using me!"

She stayed at the door. "Warren, you want too much."

"Too much? All I want is a sign that you care!"

She watched him a long moment then said quietly, "I've never encouraged you."

He sank deeper into the sofa. The anger flowed out of him, replaced by defeat. "That's right," he said. "That's right. You never have. Oh, God, you're a cold one. You knew this would happen, that you could just frost me and frost me and sooner or later I would complain, and then you could wriggle right out of it by saying, Sorry, Warren, old asshole, I never fucking encouraged you! And, by God, you never did. You certainly never did."

Loring moved away from the door. "I'll make some coffee."

"No!" Warren rolled over. His legs hit the floor and with effort he pulled himself up. He reeled from dizziness and dropped back again. "Okay. Go ahead. Make it. It's the least you can do for me."

Loring went to the kitchen, resisting an impulse to pick up a rolling pin and beat some sense into him. She put water up to boil then touched her cheeks. They were burning. Why should she be embarrassed, or feel guilty? She was only telling him the truth. She had never encouraged him. Simple as that. And he knew it, too, or he wouldn't be so angry. The sleeping dog wakes. But he knew something, or he would never have had the courage to come here, even drunk, and pull this nonsense. She went back into the living room, flashing a smile. He was still on the sofa, watching her balefully.

She could blame her mother for this. She had wanted to get rid of Warren after the first date, but Mother had begged her not to be hasty. Mother, the professional club woman and would-be marriage broker. She had successfully found husbands for seven young ladies from the better New Haven families, but she had failed miserably with her own daughter, who had rebelled from the time she could spell the word. Bryn Mawr and Radcliffe hadn't been good enough for Loring, even though her father—a Wall Street securities specialist whose portfolio remained fat no matter what the political climate—could afford to send his daughter to the top school in the world. Instead, she had picked plain old Columbia University in New York City. And not to study home economics, either. Entirely on her own and with no encouragement at

51

home, Loring had managed to turn herself into a professional archaeologist. And it utterly burned her parents' collective egos that she chose to soil her hands with field work. They would rather see her stashed away in a Park Avenue town house with good old Warren Clark, leading a life they could understand and at least partially control.

More than ever, Loring was convinced she could never let that happen. Besides, Warren did nothing for her sexually. Oh, he wanted it all right. The poor fool was beside himself with unresolved sexual tension. But he awakened nothing inside Loring, not even the remotest stir.

Especially not like this, when his courage—what there was of it—came from a bottle.

The kettle whistled. She returned to the kitchen, made the coffee strong and black, and brought him a large cup. She helped him sit up and got him to drink some of it.

When he was beginning to think more of his throbbing head than his rage at her, she sat down on the floor in front of him and waited.

For a long time, he wouldn't look at her. Then his eyes slid to her face, and some of the fight went out of him.

"What did Charlie Hemphill say?" she asked.

Warren ran a hand through his hair. "He wanted to know why I wanted to know, so I made up some bullshit about State Department business, hush-hush, connection with the museum, and then I mentioned your shipment. He had the cargo manifest as cabled from Liverpool, and we found it on there with no trouble. One crate shipped from the British Museum, care of Loring Holloway, Metropolitan Museum, New York. There's some kind of a lid on information regarding sinkings but—"

"Sinking?"

"Yeah . . . latest word is that the *Delaware Trader*

was torpedoed by a German U-boat seven days ago. She went down with all hands."

Loring's eyes shot to the floor.

"And cargo," Warren added.

She hardened. "All of it?"

"Well, now, that's the interesting part. There was a survivor—"

Loring looked up sharply.

"—from the U-boat. A German officer. Nice catch for the Navy. Seems that after they torpedoed the *Delaware Trader,* this U-boat surfaced to finish her off with their deck gun. Very dumb. They got nailed by one of our antisub patrol bombers. The survivor was their gunnery officer, one Herr Leutnant Rolf Kirst, rescued at sea by the destroyer escort USS *Sharpe."*

"When did they pick him up?"

"Oh, couple days later. He was found floating around in the Atlantic inside—guess what?—a crate."

L   ng stared at Warren. A weight descended in her stomach. "Where is it?"

"You're so sure it's yours, aren't you?"

Oh, Christ, Warren, she thought. *You don't know how sure I am, how I know, I know! But I have to know for certain and can't you please stop playing this little game and get on with it . . . ?*

"It's a goddamned miracle, is what it is."

"What do you mean?"

"That he's alive at all. I went to see Commander Lehman, captain of the *Sharpe,* over at the Brooklyn Naval Yard. He said nobody survives that amount of time in the Atlantic this time of year. Kirst should have died of exposure within minutes, but somehow he found that crate and crawled inside—"

"Was it my crate?"

Warren glared at her. He wanted to tell it his way. "Yes, damnit. Stickered and tagged, stenciled all over it— 'Property of Metropolitan Museum, New York City, U.S.A.' "

Loring's heart jumped. "You say he was found inside it? What about the—the shipment—the artifacts . . . ?"

"The only thing in the crate was Kirst."

"Well, what did he do with . . . ?"

"Nobody knows. He wouldn't talk. Lehman questioned him through an interpreter. He didn't even respond to German. Not a peep. But the crate was empty—"

"Did you . . . ?"

"I asked, yes. Lehman figured Kirst must have thrown everything out in order to make room for himself." Warren gave her a hard look. "He was trying to save his life. I doubt if he looked at your stuff and put his hand over his heart and said, Oh, my God, the museum needs this, I'd better jump out."

"I want to meet him."

"Not possible. He's been shipped to a POW camp."

"Where?"

Warren smiled thinly. "Ah, that's where Sherlock really had his work cut out for him. I had to hop my ass over to Naval Intelligence and see someone named Zalman Ball. I invoked the museum, the city of New York, the State Department, Anglo-American friendship, and he just kept saying, Sorry, the disposition of prisoners in this country is classified, and so is the location of POW camps. And since I couldn't exactly be too open with him about what was in the goddamned crate that was even remotely interesting to State—"

"The shipment contained archaeological artifacts from

a dig in Iraq. Call him up and tell him, and find out where they sent Kirst."

Warren stared at her with a little crooked, drunken smile. He sipped more coffee. "At last a morsel, a tidbit, a tiny scrap of a hint. What sort of artifacts?"

"Pottery, tablets, some things over two thousand years old—a major find, Warren." She didn't dare tell him more.

Warren sipped loudly. "A sad loss for the world of archaeology, I am sure."

"More than that."

"What more?"

"The significance would be . . . meaningless to you. It wouldn't make sense."

"It already doesn't."

Loring shifted uncomfortably.

"Look, Lor. The stuff in the crate is gone. It went to the bottom of the ocean so Kirst could get into the crate and save his ass. So make a report to the museum director and call it quits. You can't change what's happened, and you're certainly not the first person in this war to lose some shipping."

Loring jumped up. "I've got to know what happened!"

"Loring, for God's sake, the museum is wall-to-wall artifacts! What's another more or less?"

"It's not enough for somebody to tell me it went to the bottom of the sea. *I have to know for sure!"*

"You're obsessed with this."

Her eyes blazed. "Yes!"

Warren sat back grimly. "Oh, Christ, I'm a fool. I am just a goddamned pipeline for you. And I've been clinging to hope for months. Hope when there is none. I realized it today, when I was on the line to Washington trying to squeeze information out of some chicken general.

. . . You don't trust me—not with your life, your love, or your body. You don't even trust me with those god-damned errands you send me on. I'm pulling strings for you, but you keep me in the dark over *why!*"

He spread both hands on the sofa and heaved himself to his feet. "What's so goddamned important about the *Delaware Trader* and that shipment and you getting to that German officer? Why do you have to *know?*"

"Warren, I can't discuss it. Thanks for what you've—"

"Don't patronize me!"

"I can't tell you."

"Why not?"

"You wouldn't believe it."

"No?" He was shouting now. "Well, if *I* wouldn't, then *what about the people in Montana?*"

His face twisted with emotion, then all at once he was falling backward. He landed on the sofa and slid from there to the floor. He sat looking at her stupidly, then broke into a satisfied smirk. She knelt beside him.

"What people in Montana?"

Warren gingerly placed his coffee cup a few feet away on the floor. It was empty. He reached into his coat pocket and produced some papers, which he waved entic-ingly at Loring.

"Kirst," he said. "Herr Leutnant Kirst has been shipped to a POW camp at Blackbone Mountain, Mon-tana."

Relief flooded through Loring, along with the unpleas-ant certainty that if she took those papers from Warren, she would never see him again. She suddenly felt very guilty.

"These are for you." He placed the papers in her hand as if he were entrusting her with the Japanese invasion plans. "Travel instructions and a letter of introduction

56

State Department. I've already wired the com-
He's expecting you."

the papers. "Look, Warren—"

make a speech."

"I wish you'd understand. I have to follow through on this. . . ." He was already dragging himself to his feet. She stayed on the floor. "I promise—when I get back, we'll straighten out our lives, and it won't be the way it's been—"

"It sure won't, lady." He was moving toward the door.

Loring rose and made a move to follow, but something held her back. Warren reached the door and opened it. He turned and gave her a bitter smile. "I've turned away some interesting possibilities since I've known you. I'm not going to do that anymore. I'm going to find some-body who wants me."

He straightened his coat and tie and walked out. "Thanks for the coffee," he said as he shut the door.

Loring stared after him, feeling nothing but the touch of the papers in her hand.

She turned away and looked for somewhere to sit, and at last the tears started to come. Determined not to give in to this, she swore at herself, but the tears still came, because deep inside she knew that despite never having given Warren Clark any real encouragement, she hadn't been completely honest with him either. She should have told him way back at the beginning, when she suspected that his ultimate purpose was to win himself a wife who would cook for him, poop out his babies, and rise up the Washington social ladder on his arm. An ornament, not a woman. His very presence had always carried the hint that her career was an illusion, that reality lay within what Warren Clark had to offer, and not within the world she had built for herself. The trouble with that was, the was no room for the real Loring in Warren's world.

Look forward, she told herself, clutching the papers tightly. Look forward to what? What she had been dreading ever since Warren told her the ship was overdue? It went further back than that. Back to Iraq, to the tablets and the silver flask and the legends and the rock splitting and water gushing and all the nightmares she hadn't been able to deal with throughout the long dark hours of the war.

Fleeing Iraq, returning to London, burying the artifacts in the bowels of the museum with instructions that they not be touched, researching their origins, learning, learning. . . . It all flooded back into her mind. She hurried to the kitchen and poured coffee for herself, then thought, no, that would keep her awake the rest of the night, but yes, perhaps it would keep her from dreaming, because she knew what tonight's dream would be—the faces, the swirling bodies and groping arms, the cries. . . .

Shakily, she sipped the coffee and opened the papers on her kitchen counter, studying Warren's neatly worded letter "To Whom It May Concern:" . . . The letter faded from her vision and she saw a frightened young woman after her first year in the field, huddled in the library at the British Museum, poring over Arabic texts and maps and illustrations, growing more and more terrified by the hour. Sleepless nights, long days with her nose in those books, learning, learning. . . . Taking courage only from the thought that the flask was safely stored in the bottom of the museum, that no one else would ever touch it or even know it was there or what it was. Hoping as she left England and returned to America that it would remain untouched forever, until she died, and the

58

terrible responsibility fell to someone else. . . . What folly! How stupid to think that she could escape it!

And finally bringing it to America, having it packed in a watertight crate with all the other Iraqi artifacts, believing the propaganda as Warren had said, that the U-boats were finished in the Atlantic. But no, they were far from finished. They had one last little job to do, and they had done it well.

Kirst. She had to get to him, speak to him, learn what he had done with the flask. And that could merely be the beginning.

Chapter 5

Mahmud Yazir carefully measured milk into his tea and stirred it delicately. He tossed the used bag into his wastebasket, then raised the cup and sipped. He edged the old leather chair back so he could squeeze in behind his desk, between the sagging bookshelves and the stacks of borrowed library volumes. Through his closed office door, he heard the laughter of students passing in the corridor. Ignoring them, Yazir tried to relax with his tea. But it was difficult. Loring's call last night had been anxious, her tone urgent. Yazir was not looking forward to this meeting. Stress was bad for his heart.

He looked up at the faded wall maps opposite his desk, maps of the present-day Middle East and of the ancient Babylonian Empire, the latter covered with thumbtacked notations written in an Arabic scrawl. Beneath the maps were more stacks of books and yellowed periodicals. Yazir thought fleetingly of reorganizing the clutter, then he gazed out the window and saw Loring Holloway hurrying up the walkway to the first-floor entrance.

Yazir recalled the last time she had been to see him, shortly after her return from England. She had breezed in, nervous and excited, wanting to tell him all about her field work in Iraq, but at the last minute, after raising his interest to unbearable heights, she had abruptly decided not to tell him anything. One minute she was in the room with him, the next minute she was gone.

Yazir sighed. Perhaps now he was going to get the story, but why would it be urgent so many years later? It was 1940 when Loring was attached to the British Museum expedition. For months she had worked a dig in the desert lands near the Euphrates River. Before that, she had been one of Yazir's top students here at Columbia University. She had gone through History of Ancient Civilization with him, then continued through his upper-division Middle Eastern Folklore program, then she had taken her master's degree in archaeology. Yazir had sponsored her for the British expedition, and before leaving, Loring had showered him with gratitude. But upon returning, except for the one brief, exasperating meeting, she had avoided him.

He had provided references for her job with the Metropolitan, but she had not requested them. Yazir bore no grudge: he had many former students who didn't like to be reminded that before they became experts they had been pupils.

But now Loring was back, and Yazir's sharp sixth sense told him he was about to be drawn into something unpleasant. He stood up and drained the last of his tea.

She looked better than he remembered, although the Middle Eastern tan was gone and she was back to that New York City museum pallor. But she seemed flushed with excitement, or was it agitation?

Yazir guided her to a chair and offered to make tea. She accepted graciously and thanked him for agreeing to see her. Yazir got the hot plate going again and smiled at her. "So, student, how can I help you?"

She managed a smile. "I hope you still have that great open mind that I recall from the old days."

61

"I hope so, too."

"When I came home from Iraq, I wanted to tell you about this. You were the only one I could trust, but, as I was about to tell it, it suddenly seemed so far away and unbelievable. So . . . I ran out. I'm sorry."

"Apology accepted, but if you do it again I shall be very upset."

There was no reply. He glanced back. She was working her hands together and frowning. He brought her the tea and waited. When she looked up, he saw fear in her eyes. He knew what was coming—one of those farfetched, mystical experiences that every archaeologist dreams of having, and many concoct because their imaginations demand it.

"There were three of us at the dig," she began. "Aside from the workers, there was Selim Bayar—an Armenian linguistics expert, and Ismet Moulin—a hieroglyphics man from Syria."

Yazir sat down. "I know Moulin. Good fellow. Experienced."

Loring relaxed. "We were on our own. Working apart from the rest of the expedition, we dug through the ruins of a building and found a cache of artifacts, many of them smashed by the weight of accruing sand. But some of them had identifying marks which Moulin was able to decipher. We determined that they had all been the property of a Babylonian sorcerer named Korbazrah."

"Sorcerer?"

"Necromancer, magician, whatever you want to call him. He lived in Ur-Tawaq, a small city in constant friction with Babylon during the reign of Nebuchadnezzar. For most of his life he produced crafted silver and made a living from a small shop in the city, but in his last years he became a secret ally to the king and was probably responsible for a panic that brought the city to its knees and permitted Nebuchadnezzar to destroy it. The ruins we uncovered were evidently Korbazrah's work chamber. Moulin deciphered a stack of clay tablets that turned out to be a cabala, a set of occult rituals."

Yazir showed mild interest, but inwardly his stomach was beginning to protest.

"I found a box made entirely of handworked silver, covered with satyrs and devils and winged lions—Babylonian imagery crossed with the occult. Inside the box were several clay tablets and a silver flask, which was stoppered and sealed and . . . warm to the touch. It contained some sort of liquid, but we never opened it to find out precisely what." Her voice caught, and there was a fleeting look of regret in her eyes. "Moulin took the tablets away to translate. A few nights later, he sat down with us around the fire and told us what he had deciphered. The tablets described how Korbazrah had trapped a demon in that silver flask—"

"A demon?" Yazir's eyebrows went up.

Loring nodded. "And that anyone opening it would be releasing a plague of evil."

She sat quietly a moment. Yazir stared at his wall maps but said nothing. Finally, he nodded for her to continue.

"The Iraqis, who were around the fire with us, were terribly frightened. They demanded that we put everything back where we had found it, rebury the site, and leave. Moulin and Bayar did their best to calm the men down, but they were insistent. They threatened Bayar, until finally he went down into the excavation to prove there was nothing harmful. He made a lot of noise— shouting at imaginary demons, warning them to leave or risk being destroyed by a man without fear. Quite a performance."

"Did it work?"

"On the Iraqis, boasting is very effective. They relaxed and went to sleep. Moulin and I stayed up drinking. Nervous. We started kidding around. Moulin read some of his translations from the hieroglyphics. He gave me one of Korbazrah's spells—a chant that was supposed to bring water."

She stopped a moment and sipped her tea, lost in reflection. "I thought it would be interesting to see what would happen, so I climbed up on a rock and began chanting. It was—it was a joke." She hesitated. "But then I fell into the rhythm of it and there was a moment when . . . when I knew I was doing it right. . . . The sound became a singsong effect I copied from the Iraqis. . . . All of a sudden I knew how that chant should sound . . . and then . . . then there was the water."

"Water?" Yazir's brow darkened.

"A boulder over the excavation disintegrated—and water erupted out of it. It came rushing down—"

She stopped with her hands in the air and sorted through a torrent of thoughts.

"It completely flooded the excavation, overran the dig, washed down into our camp, and then"—her eyes went wide and her voice quavered—"I just couldn't get down there fast enough. I was shouting—Moulin and I were both shouting to warn them, but they didn't hear us over the roar of the water—" She choked. "They never had a chance—"

"The workers . . ."

Loring nodded, her eyes filling with tears. Her hand covered her mouth. "They were all caught sleeping. All of them—drowned."

She was very still for a moment. Yazir stared at her but she couldn't meet his gaze. "I see," he said. "You recited a chant, a rock broke, water flooded the excavation and drowned the Iraqis—leading you to the inescapable conclusion that *you* were somehow responsible."

Loring looked at him miserably. Yazir packed a pipe with a foul-smelling Turkish tobacco and lit it. He spoke around the stem. "What did you do about this *accident?*"

"Nothing," she said.

"Did you report it?"

"They were washed away without a trace—down a gully into a canyon filled with erosion holes. We searched when the water stopped flowing. We tramped down miles of that gully and never found anything."

"Then what did you do?"

"Packed up the artifacts . . . the silver flask and the clay tablets . . . whatever was left up on the ridge. We returned to the expedition and told them that our workers had run off and the excavation had been destroyed in a flood."

"Ah." Yazir puffed hard on his pipe.

"What was I going to tell them? What could I possibly have said to the Iraqi authorities? They would have reacted exactly as you—"

"Never mind my reaction. What did you do next?"

"Returned to England, deposited everything in a basement vault at the British Museum, left orders that nothing was to be disturbed. Moulin swore never to speak of it again. I don't think he returned to Iraq. He disappeared, and took all the translations with him. I lost track of Bayar, too. I stayed at the museum for a while and researched what we had found. . . . Eventually, I caught a boat home and took the job at the Metropolitan. The last few years I've been on staff, and occasionally I've done more research. I had been planning to go back after the war, to get the artifacts out of storage and work on them but never could get up the courage. Then recently I was informed that the British Museum was dispersing its collection to get it out of danger. I didn't want that material inspected, so I arranged to have it sent here. But the ship it was on, the *Delaware Trader,* was torpedoed and sunk a few days ago in the Atlantic by a German U-boat. I thought that was the end of it—the stuff went to the bottom of the sea and there was nothing more to worry about. Then it turned out that the U-boat was almost immediately bombed and sunk by one of our planes. A survivor saved himself by climbing onto the crate containing my artifacts, which he evidently dumped out to make room for himself. I hope."

She was silent a long time, then she got up and paced to the map. Her hand floated over the area labeled Babylon. "There is a book of collected tales about ancient Babylon called *The Light of Days*—"

"I know it."

"In it, Korbazrah is described as a tall, thin, ascetic silversmith who specialized in occult designs on shields, goblets, and urns. Sorcery was a profitable sideline. He hired himself out as a demon remover. He would go to the homes of people suffering from unknown maladies, and he would invariably diagnose demonic possession. He would then perform an elaborate ritual—burning incense, placing silver objects decorated with occult designs all around the room, speaking in strange tongues—it was a hell of a show. Then he would force the victim to ingest a substance to make him vomit up the demon. The bile was collected in a silver container which the family paid for in advance. Afterward, Korbazrah would seal the container and supposedly place it in a secret vault, where it would be kept for all eternity. He sold a lot of demon containers. More likely, he sold the same one many times

66

over. The victims would recover from whatever ailment they had—probably nothing more serious than a case of flu. But the whole performance was probably a great comfort to the Mesopotamians. In *The Light of Days* this is all passed down as part of the folklore. Korbazrah's giant catacomb with its endless shelves of silver urns—most likely never existed."

"I recall that story," said Yazir. "I've read other accounts."

"Imagine a quack like that suddenly finding himself face-to-face with a real demon."

"The one in the flask?" Yazir's pipe had gone out. He ignored it.

Loring smiled back at him. "That flask was not one of Korbazrah's customary demon containers. It was specially designed for a special demon. A djinn."

Yazir removed the pipe and fixed Loring with a reproachful stare. "Miss Holloway, a djinn is nothing more than a Middle Eastern gremlin. The goat won't eat, the crops won't grow, the sun is obscured—there must be a djinn around somewhere. Please—we're going now from water spells and exorcism to the sublimely ridiculous!"

Loring waited for him to finish, then said, "The demon in that flask is mentioned in *The Light of Days* and in two other books. The flask is described as being made of crafted silver, with a pentagonal base tapering up to a long rounded neck, a five-sided opening, and corresponding stopper."

Yazir frowned. Loring went to her chair, sat down, and opened her handbag. She gave him a sheet of paper listing book titles and page references. Yazir recognized several titles.

"These titles are all cross-referenced," said Loring, "and I've summarized them here." She produced a thick typescript, yellowed and dog-eared. Yazir flipped through it.

Loring continued, "This is no ordinary gremlin—no genie in a bottle—no wish-granting mythical being with long fingernails and pointy ears. This is a monster in every sense of the word. Of course, Korbazrah's mumbojumbo must have been useless. No incantations and vomiting into a silver container. Capturing it must have been a very difficult, dangerous job."

Yazir cleared his throat. "There is an expulsion ritual for djinn—"

"Invoking certain passages from the Koran? This djinn has been sealed away in the flask for twenty-five hundred years—that's longer than recorded Arab history. It predates the Koran. The ritual would have effect. If there is a spell for dealing with the djinn, it might be in the tablets, but there isn't enough time to start a manhunt for Moulin—"

"I think, my dear, you are getting ahead of yourself. How did Korbazrah capture the djinn?"

Loring stared at him; for the first time a flicker of doubt crossed her face. "I'm afraid those accounts are inconsistent. But I think it went something like this. . . . He managed to find the demon a host body to live in—an assistant over whom he had complete power. He was then able to coax the demon into doing his bidding. He struck a bargain with it. That's not hard to do. Traditionally, the forces of evil love a good bargain. Throughout the folklore, the djinn are described as mischievous creatures who thrive on beguiling humans. Korbazrah probably thought he had the upper hand and, for a while, perhaps he did.

"When Nebuchadnezzar laid siege to Ur-Tawaq, Korbazrah sold the king his conjuring services. I found enough evidence to suggest he was being paid by Nebuchadnezzar. In return for his money he got the demon to do what it did best, unleash a plague of psychological terror, reducing the citizens to a state of panic. Ultimately demoralized, many of them killed by strange inexplicable incidents, they surrendered to the Babylonians. Nebuchadnezzar had them all slaughtered.

"Korbazrah was then ordered to subdue his demon, which he did, believing he was about to come into his life's great reward. He fashioned a silver flask in the shape of a pentagon—the flask that I found. He lured the demon into it—how, I don't know—then slammed on the stopper and sealed it. After that, he probably hid it in his chamber, figuring he might need it again. Then he went to the king. And the king . . . the king had him executed. The body was burned, the work chamber sealed, and the location heavily salted to keep the demon from rising again."

"Salt," mumbled Yazir. "Salt and silver . . ."

"Yes," echoed Loring, relieved that Yazir's resistance was crumbling. "Salt and silver—two of the ancient deterrents against demons. When we excavated our dig, we found the ground heavily laced with salt. The water that burst from the rock was salty. That far inland, an underground spring should have produced fresh water—pure and sweet, not salty. And the flask, made of silver—and the shape of it—a pentagon . . ."

"Yes . . ."

"According to the folklore, these are all things used to combat demons."

"Yes, they are. According to . . . folklore."

Loring sat down. "You don't believe me."

Yazir relit his pipe. "Let's say that I do not find it unusual that a group of illiterate Iraqis assigned to an

69

archaeological expedition should permit themselves to be ruled by the ancient superstitions. I do however find it odd that an intelligent, well-educated American woman should become so stirred by these things. So influenced."

"You think that's what it is? Influence, mass hysteria?"

"Couldn't it have been? After all, the events at the dig prompted your search for all this other information, and when one has crossed the line from scientific objectivity into the realm of *willing to believe* . . . one can prove anything."

Loring checked her rising anger and tried to display the objectivity Yazir was hoping for. "I saw the rock burst open and the water rush out. It *was* salty."

"Yes, but that is an event added on top of others. First we must accept that Moulin translated the tablets accurately, and that what you were reciting really was a spell to bring water, and that the moon was not in confluence with Jupiter, and there was no coincidental earthquake and so on. Otherwise, you are relating an isolated, though admittedly unusual event."

Loring shook her head. "You're picking me apart."

Yazir threw up his hands and flashed a smile. "My dear, you have not come to me to have your story tested. You obviously believe it and will continue to do so until something happens to prove you wrong. What do you really think about this demon, this djinn?"

Loring thought carefully. "It could be the original genie in the bottle. I believe this story became part of the folklore that comes down to us in a watered-down form as the tale of Aladdin and his magic lamp. You know as well as I do that the djinn are as real to the Islamics as Satan is to the Christians."

"Some believe, some do not," said Yazir.

"Do you?"

Yazir laughed. "There are moments when I am as superstitious as the most ignorant Bedouin, but not often."

"Imagine what you would feel if all this had happened to you."

Yazir shifted uncomfortably. His stomach roiled again.

"The shape of that flask was not randomly chosen. It was crafted for its magical properties. The pentagon is the base form of the pentangle, a geometric design of great occult power. It is most often applied as a restraint against dark forces—"

"I seem to recall those words."

Loring grinned. "One of your lectures—ten years ago."

"How flattering."

"The chamber where we found the artifacts had five walls. A pentagon." Loring leaned forward. Her eyes shone with fevered certainty. "The entire city of Ur-Tawaq was laid out inside a pentagon—five walls of equal length, height, and thickness surrounding the inhabitants. It was a common architectural form in those days and was supposed to help ward off evil spirits."

Yazir's brow knitted. "Or keep them in," he said. "This man who was rescued from your crate . . . did he have the flask with him? No—right. As you said, he had nothing. And you are concerned about where it is, yes?"

"Very."

"You're afraid he may have opened it and set loose the demon, yes?"

"Yes."

"Or he might simply have dropped it into the sea."

"I have to find that out." She explained to him about Kirst being sent to Blackbone Detention Camp in Montana, about her plans to go there—

"I wouldn't advise that. If there really is a demon such

as you have described, then you are hardly equipped to deal with it."

"But people have to be warned—"

"By you?" Yazir laughed. "Please, between us I am the Middle Eastern folklore expert—though I must admit you have exceeded me in this area—but I would not risk my professional standing by publicly claiming that a twenty-five-hundred-year-old demon is loose in Montana. No one would believe me. And as for you . . . this German might be headed for a prison camp, but where would they send you?"

Tears formed in Loring's eyes. She pleaded with Yazir. "If it's loose and it's traveling with Kirst, God only knows what it can do. I need help."

"From me?"

"Yes. You do know the folklore better than I do. You know how to research the deterrents—ways to deal with this thing—weapons, spells, incantations—I don't care how wild! I need whatever you can come up with—and fast! Don't you see? *I brought that thing out of the ground.* Whatever happens now is on my conscience! I have to do something!"

She stopped and stared at Yazir desperately.

Yazir sighed. "Remember what they say in Islam. . . ." He laid a hand on her cheek. *"Kutibat.* It is written." His hand dropped away. "The fate of those who come in contact with the djinn is already history."

Chapter 6

One hour west of Aberdeen, South Dakota, Corporal Strann was getting impatient. He wanted to see the Missouri River. His daddy had always said it was a hell of a sight. "If you're ever traveling west on the Chicago, Milwaukee, St. Paul & Pacific," he had said, "don't be caught napping when she crosses the Missouri. The river's five miles wide at that point and the grandest sight you'll ever see. When she passes Mobridge, get out on the platform and soak it up."

It was night, though. Shouldn't matter much. Lots of moonlight.

Kirst was staring at him with the blankest eyes Strann had ever seen, even for a kraut. Ever since leaving New York, Kirst had been a zombie, hardly acknowledging when he was spoken to. Next to him, the other MP, Kalmus, was asleep, dead to the world. Strann growled to himself.

Fuck this detail. Thought you were a real smart sonofabitch, getting out of the infantry to become an MP. Well, look what it gets you. Three days' duty transporting a kraut across country to a prison camp in Montana, for Christ's sake. A kraut. You used to kill krauts.

Strann ran a hand over his grimy face and felt the harsh stubble. He sniffed his armpit. God, he reeked.

Can't even take a shower watching this lousy kraut. And Kalmus does nothing but sleep all the time. Hope he wakes before Mobridge.

Strann considered kicking Kalmus awake and blaming it on Kirst. Then maybe there would be some sparks. He glanced over to be sure Kirst was still handcuffed to the seat.

Christ, I wish he'd close his eyes or at least stop looking at me.

Strann cupped his balls. "Hey, kraut, want to see something cute?"

Kirst's head rolled with the motion of the train.

The clickety rhythm must have him in a trance. Some guys are like that. Bet the bastard stares at me all the way to White Sulphur Springs.

Strann unzipped his fly and hauled out his penis. He winked at Kirst. "Hey, kraut? Ever seen Yankee cock before? Hey, I've fucked a lot of kraut girls with this, and the kraut guys with my gun. You know the difference? One is for shooting—the other's for fun."

No reaction.

Strann's smile faded. He put his penis away. "Know how many Germans I've killed? Nine. That's right, kraut. North Africa, with Patton. Right there in the goddamned desert, I killed nine of you fuckers. And what have you been doing? Sneaking around the Atlantic in a fucking U-boat. They're gonna love you at Blackbone, kraut. They're MPs like me. They're gonna cut your goddamned balls off and put 'em in your soup. Krautball soup! What do you think of that? Huh? Hey—you might at least blink!" Strann snapped his fingers under Kirst's eyes. "Lemme know you're alive!"

Something gleamed briefly in Kirst's eye.

Strann missed it. He thought he saw a flicker of interest, but then it went right back to that cold stare. Strann growled again, then he kicked Kalmus.

Fifteen minutes later, the porter came by to make up the berths. While Kalmus held the muzzle of his .45 to Kirst's chin, Strann unlocked the cuffs. Then he pushed the German down on the bunk, handcuffed him again, and threw a blanket over him.

Kirst never took his eyes off Strann. He never spoke either.

"I'll take the first watch," said Kalmus.

"Like shit you will," Strann replied. "Park your ass in that upper berth. I'm going out for a smoke."

"Okay, okay." Kalmus had learned not to argue with Strann. He hoisted himself into the upper berth and watched Strann walk up the aisle.

Strann opened the vestibule door and was struck by the cold wind, the racketing noise, and the back and forth motion of connecting cars. He released the door and it shot closed, leaving him in the open vestibule. He hauled out his Camels and cupped his hands to light one. When he looked up, the train was passing through Mobridge.

The Missouri River was less than four miles away.

Blackness stirred inside Rolf Kirst. It flowed through his organs, sluggishly searching for the arteries where the blood pumped in rhythmic jets. It flooded his chest cavity and seeped into his heart, where its molecules thrashed excitedly with every beat of the muscle. The blackness thinned and flowed like soup heating on a stove. For now, Kirst generated enough energy to sustain his unwanted guest and, as he lay immobilized on the bunk, his mind dulled by a soothing, shrouding narcotic, he was driven to laugh inwardly at the ludicrous bracelet chaining him to the bunk.

He wasn't going anywhere, not without his guest's permission. From the hospital bed in Brooklyn clear across this strange new country, Kirst's awareness had been stifled by the gloomy darkness inside him.

His whole body went limp as the thing fed on his circulatory system. The green metal of the upper berth casing swam before his eyes, turned liquid, and flowed into his brain, merging with the black, swallowed up in it until all was quiet and Kirst floated in limbo, and the blackness filled his body, gathering strength for its first foray into the world in centuries.

Kalmus sat with his legs dangling over the side, bored. Most of the other berths had been made up and their heavy green curtains were already drawn. There was a lady up the aisle in a long flannel nightgown, brushing out her hair in front of a portable mirror she had hooked to the upper bunk. She was at least forty-five, but Kalmus didn't care: he hadn't seen anything so sweet and domestic since leaving home and joining up. His mother used to stand like that, combing her hair. But Kalmus wasn't thinking of his mother. He was thinking it would be nice to trot down the aisle and pull up that flannel nightgown and let his hands roam over the woman's flesh. . . .

She finished brushing, then shook her head and let her hair fall naturally. Satisfied, she reached into the upper bunk for a whiskey flask and passed it to someone unseen in the lower berth. Then she bent over, rested her hands on her knees, and chatted quietly with whoever it was.

Kalmus's eyes were glued to her ass, the curve of it prominent beneath the flannel. The flask was returned. She took a long pull, then a man's hairy arms came out of the berth and pulled her in. She gave a sharp laugh, then the curtains were drawn.

Kalmus sat still, contemplating what old hairy arms was up to. . . . Gradually, he became aware of a gentle pressure on his leg and looked down to see what it was. Kirst's hand settled on his ankle and held it. Kalmus kicked it away and jumped off the bunk.

Kirst's hand groped involuntarily, his fingers clutched and unclutched. His eyes were closed, lips slightly parted. Kalmus felt an inner chill as he watched. The fingers twitched again, extended, then curled, and for one brief instant the hand was a quivering claw, then it relaxed and dropped, dangling outside the bunk.

Kalmus hesitantly picked it up and placed it on Kirst's chest. He wondered if the sonofabitch kraut had died on him. Only one way to tell. He leaned over and placed his ear to Kirst's chest. He listened. There was a heartbeat, slow but steady. He moved his cheek to within an inch of Kirst's open mouth. He felt hot breath on his skin. Hot like the man was on fire. Kalmus laid his palm on Kirst's forehead. Odd. It was cool. Hot breath, cool forehead.

Kalmus shrugged and decided to forget it. He pulled Kirst's curtains then climbed back into the upper. He swung his legs up and relaxed against the pillow. Okay, Strann, he thought. You want to go stand out in the cold, fine. Me for comfort.

The *nightform* spilled out of the lower berth and flowed across the floor, a thick black vaporous substance that hugged the shadows to remain unseen. It hovered just above the rattling floor, trying to make sense of its surroundings, disturbed by the sensations of speed and noise.

But it couldn't wait any longer. Avoiding the aisle lights, it undulated toward the vestibule door, its excitement mounting. What it hadn't tasted in eons lurked only a few feet away. It burbled with anticipation. Tendrils of oily blackness whipped above the rolling mass and snapped at the air. In all the time it had lain dormant, nothing had changed. Men were still quick to feel fear, and fear was emotional turmoil, and from that could be drawn power, power to live and to grow, and the greatest fear of all was fear in the certainty of death. When death stared man in the face, his emotions boiled at fever pitch, and from that could be drawn energy for growth, the energy of victims, supplying the strongest power of all. Because the host was constantly aware of the parasitic presence inside him, he was in a perpetual state of fear and panic, and that energy could be drawn upon to sustain the seething blackness harbored within the body. Whenever this feeding took place, the host would be plunged into paroxysms of fear that death was imminent. The fear and feeding would then build on each other. Eventually, death would come to the host, but long before that his energy would be depleted. So even now the nightform probed the air for a replacement. It would not be needed for some time yet: there was still good feeding in this host, but soon . . .

The nightform gathered itself against the cold steel of the vestibule door, angered at the obstruction. Good feeding was outside. It would not be held back. There. A narrow slot. Room to slip through.

Beneath the vestibule door, a black smudge flowed through and emerged unseen by the man outside. It rolled past his boots, buffeted by the wind but holding its ground. Even in its weakened, unfed state, it was stronger than any mere natural force.

It reared up a few inches and tasted the air—the man's thoughts, emotions. In a moment, it knew exactly what to do.

Strann stood at the platform railing, fighting the sway and the bumping tracks clacking beneath his feet. He stared out at the Missouri River, at the broad expanse of moonlight-spackled water, the twinkling lights of Mobridge dwindling in the distance. He watched for a long time, drawing on his second Camel and wondering why he was disappointed. What the hell had impressed his father so much? It was just a huge goddamned river, just flowing water. Nowhere near as thrilling as killing krauts.

He thought of the nine men he had killed in North Africa. Nine in two days. And the pride he had felt after the job was done and everybody was counting. No thrill in standing there waiting as they advanced across the desert, wondering if they were going to get him or he was going to get them. No fun in that at all. It was the killing itself, then the luxury of success that he liked.

Germans. With those coal-scuttle helmets and sand-colored uniforms, they mocked him in his dreams, inviting him to come back and fight again, because next time they would get him.

"Fucking krauts," Strann grumbled, trying to banish them from his thoughts. He knew that killing nine men in two days was pure luck. That's why he had become an MP. If he had to go through it again, those nine men might still be alive, and it might be *his* bones lying in the sand, bleaching under the sun. He could still see them— the Germans—slogging across the desert ahead of their tanks, coming closer, right up to his position, so close he could see the fear in their eyes. He looked up at the roof of the next car.

One of them was up there, big hands wrapped around

a rifle stock, holding it steady, aiming it directly at him. The rifle swayed slightly with the motion of the train.

Strann rocked from side to side, his eyes fixed on it, knowing it was a figment of his imagination. He almost laughed, but the sound choked off in his throat.

Something's wrong. This is no dream. There is someone up there—

He couldn't see a face, but there *was* a coal-scuttle helmet and one ferocious eye sighting down the barrel at him.

Then the rifle flashed fire and something ripped past Strann's cheek. Wood splintered behind him.

Strann turned in shock and stared at the jagged three inches of torn frame.

Impossible! A goddamned German soldier—on this train?

The next shot clanged off the steel platform and ricocheted away in the dark. Then all at once Strann was in motion, scrabbling for the .45 at his belt, digging it out and firing back.

The bullets flew in both directions as Strann scrambled backward, trying to find cover. But there was no cover—it was the perfect trap.

Kirst! Gotta be someone trying to rescue Kirst!

The rifle flashed again and again, so close, right in Strann's face it seemed. But why didn't the bullets hit? Or was he already dead, with the bullets going through him like hot blades through butter? He flinched with each shot and jumped around, watching the goddamned rifle follow and fire, follow and fire.

He twisted against the railing and leaned over the edge of the train and saw the water below. He thought of the door, of jumping back inside and hollering for help. But the German was firing round after round into the wood around the door, warning him away.

That's water down there, you fucking idiot. Come on, you can swim. Go for it.

He leaped up on the railing—and then the shots were banging into the steel at the edge of the car behind him, ricocheting wildly. It was now or never. He felt the sensation of jumping and, as he jumped, he saw his mistake. He saw the west bank coming up just underneath, and a long sloping wall appear under the bridge. He saw it come up fast and heard the shots still echoing, and then he felt himself hit the wall with all the force of a cannonball.

Somewhere between consciousness and the murky certainty of approaching death, Corporal Michael Strann slid helplessly down that rough wall and into the cold embrace of the Missouri River. Blackness closed over him, enveloped him, and seemed to suck the desperation and terror from his body. A scream finally tore from his mouth and, as it echoed around him, he thought he heard distantly the whistle of the train and the rattling wheels.

By the time Kalmus got his ass out of the upper berth, grabbed his weapon, and nudged his way past the other passengers stepping into the aisle, the shots had stopped and that awful sustained scream had died. He bulled his way past and got out to the platform. Wind lifted him back against the vestibule door, and he stumbled over a dark mass at his feet. The lights were out. He couldn't see a thing. He held his .45 ready and blinked to get accustomed to the gloom. The Missouri River was a half mile back and they were coming up on Moreau Jo, then suddenly they passed the first light and Kalmus glimpsed the thing at his feet.

It was Strann, sprawled shapelessly on the platform, his back against the wall, his jacket up around his chest as if he had slid down the wall. His eyes were stiff and glazed, and his gun was in his hand.

A steward appeared with a lantern. He stared bug-eyed at Kalmus kneeling by the body on the platform. Then Kalmus shouted at him to get a doctor. Kalmus snatched the lantern and shoved him away. The steward plunged through the vestibule door and tried to push through the crowd, but they flowed past him and, in the next second, there were ten people on the platform.

Kalmus took the .45 from Strann's hand and touched the barrel. It was still warm. He checked the chamber—empty. He ran a hand over Strann's face. The eyes moved. Strann was alive. Kalmus smelled something disagreeable and ran his hand under Strann's ass to be sure. Christ, the guy had a full load in his pants.

Passengers were mumbling around him. The woman in the flannel nightgown stood above Kalmus, asking if the other soldier was dead. Kalmus shook his head and stood up. The steward came back with a doctor, an elderly gentleman with a white goatee and a thick southern accent that flowed like syrup as he shooed the passengers off the platform.

"What happened?" he asked Kalmus. Kalmus shrugged. The doctor knelt down by Strann, took his face in his hands, and studied the eyes. "Shock," he declared, and rummaged in his bag for smelling salts.

Kalmus stood up and studied the platform. What had Strann been shooting at? Kalmus swept his gaze up to the top of the next car. He raised the lantern to see better and discovered that bullets had chewed up the roof. Kalmus frowned. He searched the platform on his side. If Strann had been shooting at someone up there, then shouldn't there be evidence of returned fire? There was nothing. His side of the vestibule was intact, untouched. Kalmus turned and stared at Strann, who was starting to come around, and starting to cry uncontrollably.

During all the ruckus, before the steward arrived with the lantern, the nightform had slipped down from the roof of the next car, rolled back under the vestibule door, and drifted along the shadows, past milling feet, until it had found the closed curtains of Rolf Kirst's berth. Frustrated because it lacked the power to complete its feeding, it licked at the air and tasted the confusion. It had come close. It had found the victim's weakness and preyed on it but had been so weakened over the dark ages of imprisonment that the final moment, the climactic release of terror, had slipped out of its grasp. And something else—these people were stronger. In its own epoch, man had known that demons lurked in the void and had been properly frightened and therefore easier to feed upon. It made his task that much more difficult—dealing with a race of men who had no universal concept of evil, no instinctive awareness of what to be terrified about. No matter. The nightform would teach them.

Without a sound, it was swallowed up in the darkness behind the curtain.

Part Two ═══════════

Chapter 7

Chilton stood at the door to the officers' rec room, waiting for Hopkins to finish his favorite joke. After the obligatory laughs, Chilton called to him softly.

Hopkins excused himself and went out, following Chilton up the road past headquarters.

"Got it through the grapevine, sir, just what we were looking for. Kinda skimpy, but I have a line on where to get the full story."

"Let's hear what you've got."

"Yes, sir. Well, it appears that while stationed in France, Lieutenant Colonel Gilman disobeyed a direct order and subsequently lost his entire battalion."

"Lost?"

"Wiped out, killed."

"Everybody?"

Chilton nodded vigorously. "Gilman was relieved of command, busted to major, and sent home."

"Jesus Christ." Hopkins whistled. "Jesus H. Christ! Why didn't they throw the book at him?"

"Don't know, sir."

"How did he end up here?"

"Well, sir, you have to look at where *here* is." Chilton grinned.

Hopkins glared at him. "Where here is happens to be where *we* are, Corporal."

"Yes, sir."

"And personally, I don't like the idea of associating with some prick who can't obey an order."

"You want me to keep on it, sir?"

"Yes! I want all of it! Every goddamned detail."

"Yes, sir. I'll keep going until I have every scrap of information available, and then and only then we can discuss that leave, sir."

"Leave?"

Chilton reminded him of their deal. "San Francisco—one week's leave."

"Well, Corp, you just keep that in mind."

"Yes, sir. We all need motivation."

"I'll motivate you with a boot in the ass if you breathe a word of this to anyone."

"Yes, sir. I am fully motivated, *sir!*"

Hopkins turned up late for the officers' meeting. He banged into Gilman's office and grabbed a chair. "Sorry, sir," he said to Gilman, fixing the clipboard on his lap and opening up his silver-plated pen.

"Help yourself to the coffee," Gilman said.

"Thank you, sir. I've had sufficient."

Gilman turned back to his agenda. As he went through it, assigning tasks, Hopkins doodled on his clipboard and waited for the inevitable pile of crap that would be coming his way. But Gilman handed even the shit jobs to Cosco and Blish.

Lieutenant Cosco was the adjutant—trim, well-built, and under twenty-five. His job was to shuffle paperwork, cut orders, requisition supplies, and expedite with clean efficiency. Nobody ever complained about Cosco's work, and Gilman was mindful of that.

Lieutenant Blish was head of the MP detachment. Though stocky and gruff, he was not known for his initiative. It was rumored he was a secret drinker, but it never seemed to affect his ability to carry out orders.

Major Borden, the medical officer, was a retread from World War One. He was fifty years old and resented having been called up out of private practice to serve his country once again. And he doubly resented being sentenced to Blackbone. But Borden had integrity; he was dependable, knowledgeable, and a crackerjack doctor. He spoke German and was the only reliable interpreter in the camp. Borden was pasty white, with an iron-gray crew cut that showed off his Clark Gable ears. He smoked too heavily and hacked when he laughed. His glasses had lenses as thick as Coke bottles.

Gilman tore off the next page of his agenda and handed it to Cosco. "Type this up and see that everyone gets a copy, then let's go to work on it. Basically, it's everything we've discussed about making up shortages, fixing leaks, moving that fence, passing the prisoners' mail through without holding it up six months for censorship—all that stuff. Hopkins, I want you to take the list around and personally make sure that every guard in this camp understands my policy. The prisoners are not our playthings. Anybody who can't live with that gets transferred out."

Hopkins nodded sullenly. "Yes, sir."

With business concluded, Gilman broke out drinks. They switched from coffee to scotch. Cosco declined; Blish made a show of sipping quietly. Borden wanted to talk about the '14–'18 War, how much tougher and nastier it was. Hopkins interrupted.

"That's old news. I'd like to hear what's happening now. Major, what's going on in France?"

Gilman was silent a moment then said, "If you're reading the papers, you know as much as I do. They're not hiding anything."

"Oh, I don't mean the political shit. I mean the inside poop. You were a line officer in Europe. How tough was it?"

"Some other time."

"Oh, come on, Major. We're stuck here on the back side of the moon. We don't know what the hell's going on. Fill us in."

Gilman remained silent.

"What's the matter, Major?"

"Lay off, Hopkins." Borden swirled his scotch at Hopkins.

"I wasn't addressing you, sir."

Borden's gaze zeroed in on the single line of ribbons on Hopkins' jacket. "Never been in combat, have you, Captain?"

Hopkins stiffened, then smiled. "That's why I'm asking the major. Maybe he can pass on some experience—tell us what real fighting is all about."

"If you really want to know, Captain," said Borden, "put in for a transfer. Go up on the line. Then you won't have to hear it from old farts like me. You'll get your experience firsthand."

Hopkins went red. "Are you calling me a coward?"

"No . . . just out of line. Some men don't share your zeal for war stories, old or new."

Hopkins returned Borden's stare.

You old bastard. I'll take care of you.

Gilman polished off his scotch and stood up. "This meeting is adjourned," he declared.

The others finished their drinks and filed out. Hopkins took his time. Gilman studied him, wondering if his questions were as innocent as he had taken the trouble to make them sound. Hopkins finally tossed Gilman a smile and left.

Gilman shut the door and leaned against it. His mouth was dry and his palms were damp. He rubbed them on his trousers.

France. Window Hill. Second Battalion.

Gilman's face screwed up. A wave of nausea sent him hurrying to the bathroom.

Chapter 8

Central Park was thickly carpeted in white after the first pre-winter snowfall. Loring Holloway huddled inside her thick camel's-hair coat and braved the icy wind to get to the West Side. Cabs were scarce in wartime and after the first snowfall all but extinct.

Yazir was lecturing at Fordham University at 10 A.M. She reached the lecture hall at 10:30 and stood next to the radiator in the lobby drying out for a half hour. Yazir came out trailing students at each elbow, fielding their questions, looking tired and preoccupied. He spotted Loring and made his excuses, then hurried to meet her.

"Let's go sit down," he said, pulling a woolen scarf up around his ears and jamming a tweed cap over his head. He led Loring across campus to the faculty lounge, where they sat and had tea.

"Once a week, I do an hour lecture at Fordham, subbing for a friend of mine. I tell you, the exertion of getting around town in these times, and in this weather— Any more word on your German officer?"

"No. But I'm leaving tomorrow."

"Still set on going." She nodded. He managed a smile and a frown all at once. Two slack-jawed, white-haired professors came by carrying trays and pausing to grunt at

Yazir. He acknowledged them, then returned his full attention to Loring.

"I hope you understand that when we met before I was obliged to be skeptical. It would have been unwise for both of us to get carried away."

Loring nodded.

"I have gone back into my research and talked with some colleagues—Islamic mullahs, holy men. As I indicated before, I had heard the story of Korbazrah but, like a lot of the folklore, thought it to be merely legend. You apparently discovered enough hard evidence to earn him a niche in the real world."

"You believe me then?"

Yazir pursed his lips. "I believe your evidence. Whether it all adds up to a living, breathing demon is what we are here to discuss. If you go chasing after it, you must be scientific. You can't just barge into a prisoner of war camp and tell the same story you told me. You'll be back on the train in no time flat. You must devise certain tests to prove to yourself and to anyone else that the demon really exists. Of course, this may be impossible; you may find nothing, in which case it would be best to assume that the flask was lost at sea. You will look a bit foolish but at least your conscience will be eased."

Loring wasn't so sure of that.

"The Arabic belief in the djinn is mostly superstitious, but superstitions usually have their roots in reality. Once on this earth perhaps there really were demons. Perhaps Korbazrah really did trap one, but he could have invented it, too. Realizing that Nebuchadnezzar would eventually succeed in capturing the city of Ur-Tawaq, and that he would be put to the sword along with everyone else, he might have convinced the king that he had captured a demon and could use it to disrupt the city, create a panic, and ultimately bring about a surrender. But, for the moment, let us say that you are correct and something supernatural was involved."

Loring eyed him coolly. "Go on."

"The mullahs that I spoke to, as I said, were aware of the story. One of them had in his possession a very old book in Latin which we spent much of last night translating. In it there is a section that describes the Babylonian sacking of Ur-Tawaq. The siege was accompanied by a general panic that came about because of a series of mysterious deaths. There was a man who killed his friend, believing the friend had slept with his wife. Another man was driven to hang himself. Another drowned in his own home when a nearby well flooded for no apparent reason. Others died by suffocation, by fire, beneath collapsing buildings. Another died of heart failure believing he was being pursued by imaginary beasts. . . . In many cases, they succumbed to their own worst fears, which magnified the fears of those who survived. Surrounded and cut off from the rest of the world by the Babylonian Army and terrorized from within, they were collectively isolated, virtually imprisoned in their five-walled city while something natural or unnatural preyed upon them."

"The djinn," said Loring.

"Perhaps. There is no mention of a demon in this Latin text. *The Light of Days,* which you have quoted to me, is pure folklore. The other texts on your list are of questionable authenticity but—"

"As you said, superstitions have their roots in reality."

"Yes."

"So?"

"So let us make the leap for the time being and accept that the terror in Ur-Tawaq *was* caused by a demon that preyed on the fears and weaknesses of its victims. All of these incidents occurred at night, leading us to conclude that the demon is inactive during the day, probably lying dormant inside the host—whoever or whatever that happens to be. By night, though, it goes out and does its work. You suggested that it was working for Korbazrah. I find that unlikely. A demon has no need for employment. It does what it wants, when it is convenient. I think it is more likely that Korbazrah supplied it with a host—his assistant—who then remained under the sorcerer's control. The demon used the assistant's body. Korbazrah merely exploited the situation."

Loring leaned back, awed. Yazir's hypothesis made sense. "But the silver flask . . ."

"Yes, well, silver is one of the things that can be used to combat a djinn. Silver, salt, the mystical symbol of the pentangle—there are a number of reported deterrents, but it's hard to know which if any have the desired effect —to banish the demon or capture it . . . or kill it."

"Are you saying that it's not known which of these things will do what?"

"I believe that you will have to apply certain tests—first to determine if the djinn is there, second, to discover how it can be affected. Certain of the djinn—the lesser demons especially, the relatively harmless ones—are known to hide inside inanimate objects such as trees, bushes, rocks. The larger, more fearsome, dangerous ones take up residence inside animals, and it is often impossible to determine if a beast is so possessed, unless you are present at the very moment when the djinn emerges to do its work. There is in the folklore an even more dangerous type of demon who will venture into a human being and become an unseen parasite, draining the host of energy and using him as a base from which to attack other victims. This would seem to be the nature of Korbazrah's demon. And it is, as you can imagine, the most dangerous of all.

"Just why it stayed within the walls of Ur-Tawaq is difficult to determine. Also, what might have happened had Korbazrah not sealed it away in that flask. . . ." Yazir shrugged. "It could have gone after the Babylonian Army, it could have devoured Babylon itself, and then gone out into the world and . . ." He gestured broadly and held his hand out for a moment to encompass the very room they were sitting in. His eyes bored into Loring's with deep significance.

She shuddered.

Into the world. The entire world, devoured by a monster that she had loosed after a twenty-five-hundred-year enforced hibernation.

"It's more than you want to believe, isn't it?" Yazir said.

"I think I see what you're getting at," she said. "If I believe the smallest part of this, then I have to believe the worst."

"Yes. If the djinn was ingested by Korbazrah's assistant and lived inside him during the day and came out only at night, then that is what you must look for with respect to this German submarine officer. It won't be enough to simply ask him what he did with the flask. Why should he tell the truth? Why would he if the very thing you are after has him under control?"

"Find out if it's there, then find out what works against it." She echoed his words.

"Yes. Now . . . the mullahs were concerned that someone with no religious training whatsoever would be going off to deal with a demon. But when I explained that even their vast knowledge and experience would be useless in handling a djinn of pre-Islamic antiquity, they came to this conclusion. A layman, such as yourself, might have a better chance than a holy man trying to do his duty. They are bound by their beliefs, by knowledge of the Koran. They would never in an emergency be able to separate themselves from their beliefs. Their tendency would be to rely on things that couldn't work, and the djinn would then prevail. It would prey on the uncertainty of faith, shake their belief in God, and destroy them through that. But if a layman goes in with a clear mind and nothing but a simple purpose, he might have a chance. An awareness of what you're confronting and a firm belief that it exists are in themselves great weapons."

Loring nodded. She was firm and aware and convinced of what she was after. But she was also frightened and realized that for the first time. How would she survive going up against a demon that preys on fear?

"It will try to confound you," Yazir continued, "to shake your belief in its existence, to foil any tests—because to do its work it must hide. No one must know it's there. It's hiding inside a mortal body that can be killed. Korbazrah did it, according to the stories. He slew his assistant, the host, and forced the demon to take refuge in the flask. If he did it, you might have to do it. But if you kill the host and fail to convince the people around you that there is a demon . . ."

She saw the picture without further elaboration. The steps were clear. Find Kirst, try to make him tell what he did with the flask, find out if the djinn is inside him and, if it is, convince the others, expose it, capture it, or kill it.

"The best advice I can give you about weapons is to search for a natural substance that will repel the djinn. There has to be something—that much is consistent in the folklore. The djinn are not invincible. Korbazrah

97

found a way. He put something in the flask that attracted the djinn. Try everything. Salt, for instance, was known to the ancients as a cleansing agent for wounds. Its healing properties might very well repel a djinn, even kill it. Silver, iron, light—it might be sensitive to light since it operates only in darkness. Use your imagination."

Yazir went on, detailing an endless list of elements that might be potential weapons against the djinn. Loring's mind grew heavy with the possibilities. She wanted Yazir to shut up, to leave this to her. It was her mission, her purpose, her conscience that had to be played out on this journey. She selfishly wanted to hug the coming battle to her soul as she had never embraced anything else in her life.

She thanked Yazir, interrupting him. He stared at her, worried.

"What time are you leaving tomorrow?" he asked. She told him and he promised to be there. "Tonight I will be seeing the mullahs once again and, if they have any further ideas, I think you should hear them before you go."

"Fine. But please be on time."

He watched her slip back into her coat. He watched the fever in her eyes and thought of the terrible waste— that a woman as attractive as Loring Holloway would even think of throwing herself into battle with a centuries-old demon instead of into the arms of a man. He closed his eyes for a moment and tried to recall her as a student sitting in his class. He remembered only their lengthy discussions in his office—her almost total preoccupation with the subject, her scruffiness and disinterest in her appearance, her dedication and single-mindedness.

Yes, perhaps she is the right person to do this.

He opened his eyes and saw her smile. "I have to go," she said. "I have to pack."

He stood up. "I hope that you find absolutely nothing."

She smiled, shook his hand, and hurried off, finding it strange that she hoped exactly the opposite.

Corporal Kalmus was still shaken when he reported to Gilman after delivering Kirst.

"What the hell was he shooting at?" Gilman asked.

"I don't know, sir. The engineer thought it might have been somebody bumming a ride or an escaped convict. Corporal Strann claims it was a German soldier, but we didn't find a trace of returned fire." Kalmus shrugged. Even he didn't believe it.

"Where is Strann now?"

"Shipped back from Bismarck, North Dakota, sir. Relieved of this detail."

"Was the prisoner involved?"

"Oh no, sir. He was handcuffed to his bunk when it happened. In fact he was dead asleep through the whole thing. Didn't even wake up when the shooting started. But then he was like that all the way from New York, sir. Real quiet, didn't talk, hardly looked at us. Kinda spooky."

Gilman went to the window and looked out at the camp. It was bleak and chilly outside. Dark clouds were gathering over Blackbone Mountain. Maybe snow tomorrow. The Germans had another volleyball game going. They were big on volleyball. Despite the chill, some were stripped down to long underwear and boots, a few were shirtless. . . .

Kalmus was still at parade rest when Gilman turned back. "Well, I don't see anything in this that relates to the prisoner," said Gilman. "Do you?"

"No, sir."

"Okay. Go down the hall and make your report to Lieutenant Blish, head of our MP detachment. Then go to the mess hut and take a meal in the kitchen. When you're done, report to the adjutant. He'll have you driven back to the station at White Sulphur Springs."

"Yes, sir."

"What you do with your story beyond that is between you and your commanding officer. But I wouldn't like it circulated in this camp. Get me?" Kalmus nodded. "Blish will forward your report. Now, where is the prisoner?"

Kirst was sitting in a tiny room with a single barred window, relaxed and staring into space. An MP stationed himself at the door, gripping the butt of his sidearm, but he didn't impress Kirst. Gilman half expected him to jump up, salute, and introduce himself, but Kirst stayed right where he was. Gilman pulled up a chair and sat opposite him. Kirst's eyes traveled around and fixed disinterestedly on the American officer.

"I'm Major Gilman."

Kirst gave the outstretched hand an empty look. Then he shuddered, life surged into his eyes, and he looked around in panic, as if just discovering where he was. Gilman watched, puzzled. Maybe Kalmus was right, thought Gilman, and Kirst had slept through the whole cross-country ride.

Kirst's hand tentatively gripped Gilman's. "Kirst," he said. "Leutnant Rolf Kirst."

"Sprechen Sie English?"

Kirst thought it over, then shook his head. *"Nein."*

"Too bad." Gilman studied him again. He looked like a little lost boy, frightened, wondering where his momma was and why she had left him. Gilman thought about getting Borden up here to interrogate him, but that was against regulations. All the necessary interrogating had been handled back East, otherwise Kirst wouldn't even be here yet. And, according to the reports, they had gotten nothing out of him. Gilman finally decided there was only one thing he could do—send him through the usual way, but keep an eye on him.

"Process him," Gilman told the MP, then walked out.

The flash going off made Kirst flinch. Immediately the warmth inside him became agitated and coursed rapidly through his body. An undulating pain followed in its wake, so intense he wanted to cry out but couldn't. Through the pain he was dimly aware that the photographer, a buttery-lipped sergeant named Loats, was unhappy with the results. He changed bulbs, fumbled with a new plate, and grumbled to the officer sitting nearby. Kirst tried to remember his name . . . Gordon . . . Warden . . . Borden! The doctor. Kirst had already been through delousing and a physical, and Borden had been pleasant to him, asking him in German about his family, but Kirst had been unable to answer because there was this thing inside that rose up and blocked his throat with rolling pain whenever—

"He wants you to hold still for another picture," Borden told him in German.

Kirst tried to move his facial muscles to express misery, but it didn't happen. Nothing got across. Borden seemed satisfied and nodded to Loats.

Kirst forced himself to face the camera. The churning inside got worse. As Loats prepared to get his shot, Kirst was hit with a wave of uncontrollable anxiety.

The flash went off again.

Kirst went rigid. The thing inside him went wild. He stared at Borden and tried to shout with his eyes because his voice wouldn't work, but Borden was busy conversing with Loats.

Kirst forced his eyes shut. Then all hell broke loose inside him. The black oily thing roared past his closed lids and seized complete control.

When he again became aware of the world around him, Kirst found himself walking behind two MPs. Behind him trailed Borden with an unpleasant-looking officer named Hopkins.

Hopkins threw him a dark look and snapped his fingers, indicating he should face front. Kirst turned and tried to take in more of what was happening. There was something under his arm. He looked down at it—an issue kit, a bundle of whatever he was going to need inside this camp. He looked at where he was going. The ground sloped down toward the fence and the gate just ahead. An MP was opening it to let them in. As his gaze went to the fence and took in the length and breadth of it, the thing inside him began to move again. It roiled in his stomach and he stopped short, willing the anxiety not to return.

But the officer named Hopkins shoved him through the gate and turned him over to a German leutnant waiting for him on the other side. The leutnant had a small dog with him.

Kirst stood inside the fence and stared at the dog. Its ears went back and it shrank away from him. He got a curious look from the leutnant who was holding the leash, then his attention was drawn to Borden and Hopkins arguing. Borden said something sharp to Hopkins, who glared once at Kirst, then turned on his heel and stalked out of the camp.

Borden then spoke to Kirst in German. "If you're not feeling well, Kirst, you go on the sick list, understand? The medical hut—the *Krankenhaus*—is right over there." He pointed to a barracks hut distinguished from the others by a Red Cross symbol on the door. "The doctor is German, and he'll take care of you. This is Leutnant Bruckner. I'm turning you over to him." Borden paused, studying Kirst uncertainly. Then he said "Good Luck" in English and walked out through the gate with the MPs.

The gate swung shut and was chained and locked after him. Bruckner soothed the dog cowering behind his leg, then eyed Kirst suspiciously. "Major Borden thinks there is something wrong with you, Kirst?"

Kirst wanted to tell him what it was, but the thing inside him made him shake his head no.

"Hopkins thinks you're faking. He can make your life miserable, make you wish you had died on your U-boat. So which is it, Kirst? Are you sick or faking? Do you want to see the doctor?"

Kirst felt the grip on his vocal cords relax slightly. But it was still there—a silent warning. "I'm all right," he said.

"Good. Better that way." He tried to pull the dog around, but it stayed behind his legs. "What is this effect you have on dogs?"

Kirst extended a hand to pet the dog. The blackness

knifed down his arm. He snatched his hand back and saw Bruckner staring at him.

"He won't bite," Bruckner said.

"Another time," Kirst replied.

Bruckner shrugged. As they walked down to the camp, he delivered his standard orientation lecture. Kirst hardly listened. He felt his head involuntarily whipped about as the thing used his eyes to examine the camp, locking his gaze on the fence that completely encircled the compound. It was angular at five points, where the large sentry towers were located. Kirst's gaze swept from one tower to the other. What he was seeing registered dully—the importance of it lost on Kirst himself. But the thing rose up through his innards in a hot angry flush that threatened to explode out the top of his head. Five angles, five long sections of fence adding up to five equal walls. The camp perimeter formed a nearly perfect pentagon. Kirst had no idea what it meant. He was conscious only of pain twisting his vitals. He tried to yell, to get Bruckner's attention, but the thing's grip tightened.

Blackness clouded Kirst's eyes. Something had thrown his guest into a violent rage, and Kirst wildly tried to figure what it was so he could fix it and appease the thing—

But it wasn't about to tell him. It would never tell him anything—just continue to use him.

Hopkins examined Kalmus' report on Kirst in Blish's office. He snorted to himself. Somebody must have been drunk, probably Corporal Strann. A German on the roof of a passenger car, on the Chicago, Milwaukee, St. Paul & Pacific, no less. Definitely drunk. But what was this shit about Kirst being asleep during the whole ride? More bullshit. Hopkins knew a malingerer when he saw one.

"Can I have that back?" said Blish. "Gotta shoot a copy over the wire. Headquarters wants to see it. That frigging MP might face a court-martial."

Hopkins doubted it. Nothing had happened. The prisoner hadn't escaped. Strann had merely shot up the roof of a passenger car. They wouldn't make a big deal out of that, just take the cost of repairs out of his pay. Hopkins went to the orderly room and stood by the coffee urn thinking.

Kirst probably wasn't responsible for what had happened, probably had nothing to do with it, yet there was something slightly creepy about him. Most new prisoners had a ballsy attitude—haughty, chip-on-the-shoulder, all-knowing, telegraphing with their eyes that *you've got my body, but you'll never get my soul.*

Hopkins smirked. He had their souls: they just didn't want to admit it. But Kirst had the damnedest eyes—as if he were looking right through you. Creepy. Hopkins sipped his coffee, made a face, and glared at the orderly.

"Sorry, sir." The orderly leaped up, grabbed the pot, and rushed off to get a fresh brew going.

Hopkins put the cup on the orderly's desk so he would remember to wash it out, then he strolled down the hall, thinking about Kirst and some neat stuff he might pull if the malingering sonofabitch went on sick call.

Steuben tromped into Hut 7 and poked his nose into several rooms before he found them. Gebhard was trying to read aloud a tattered American children's book, part of a meager donation from a library in Billings. Eckmann was curled on a bunk, as usual writing a letter. The dog, Churchill, was crouched by the door and gave Steuben a worried look as he stepped inside.

"Herr Major Steuben," said Bruckner, "this is Leutnant Rolf Kirst."

Steuben found Kirst's hand cold and rubbery; his face was pale, and he seemed at first glance a bit dull-witted. "I hope you don't mind," said Steuben. "We put you in with Gebhard here, our only other U-boat officer."

Gebhard chucked his book into a corner. "Enough of this Cinderella nonsense. I want to hear good news. I want to hear about all the British and American ships we're sinking, about the fat targets and the new torpedoes, and improvements aboard the boats, and who the captains are. I've been here almost two years without another submariner to talk with. Kirst, you and I are going to be inseparable." He laughed. "Can I get you some coffee?"

"No . . . thank you."

"Tea, perhaps?"

"Nothing."

"There's not much else to do here, just drink tea and coffee, walk, play volleyball, write letters, listen to lies. . . . It's not much of a war. Not like when I was at sea and we were sinking everything in sight. We were good then. We were strong, invincible. Is it still like that, Kirst?"

Kirst studied Gebhard measuredly then slowly shook his head.

Gebhard's smile faded. "What do you mean?"

Kirst struggled to gather his thoughts. His gaze seemed to lick at Gebhard as he spoke. "The time when you were at sea . . . that's now called the Happy Time. Yes, our submarines were invincible; we owned the Atlantic; we sank everything—British, Russians, Americans. Our wolf packs made fish stew of the convoys. A

107

U-boat always returned with confirmed kills. We had our share of victories. But it's not that way now."

Gebhard was very still. Steuben frowned.

"The service is not what it was," Kirst went on, his voice curiously flat. "Morale has hit bottom. When the boats return—the few that do—the men are half dead with exhaustion and failure. A kill is something you long for . . . like a woman. Something you need to reaffirm yourself. When you get it, your joy is boundless. The sheer pleasure . . . the power over life. . . . Smell the fear, then strike. . . ."

There was silence in the little room with the four double bunks and the single window. Bruckner fidgeted. Steuben leaned back and sucked air deeply. Eckmann had stopped writing.

Kirst's murky eyes were fixed on the floorboards.

Damn you! Why are you doing this? How are you doing it? This is not me! Not Rolf Kirst! I want you all to see and hear the real me, but there is this awful thing inside me that won't allow the real Rolf Kirst to speak! Please! Please don't listen to it! Look at me! All of you, please! Damn you, let me go—let me raise my eyes so they can look inside and see that it's not me saying these things.

He shuddered and managed to get his head up. There was a fleeting wildness behind those inky eyes that caused Steuben to stiffen. Then it was gone, and Kirst was shaking his head sadly at Gebhard and going on:

"Losses. Boats gone to the bottom with thousands of our men. They try to keep the reports from us but, when we return to the pens, all we hear is remember Captain So-and-So, he's gone. And all those gunnery officers like me—gone to the bottom—"

Gebhard leaped up, black with anger. "Lies!"

Kirst's gaze locked on him.

Oh, God, no! Kirst felt a wild shock of pain as the blackness absorbed the full impact of Gebhard's emotion.

Gebhard reached for Kirst. Bruckner pulled him back.

"That's enough!" Steuben motioned to Kirst. "You come with me."

Gebhard jerked free of Bruckner and fled from the room, cursing. The door banged as he stomped outside.

Steuben led Kirst down the hall to the rear door. They stood on the stoop together, watching the men milling in groups outside. Then Steuben smiled.

"In a prisoner of war camp, morale is everything, Kirst. More important here than on the battlefield or under the sea, because we are not in control of our own destiny. Morale and discretion. In future, Kirst, when you are questioned about the war—and you will be questioned about it frequently, because you are closer to it than any of the rest of us—when they ask you what's going on, answer carefully. Truthfully, but carefully. Some of our men are fanatically loyal National Socialists, others are not. Some believe the war is lost, some do not. Some believe we are disgraced because we are prisoners, some do not. Some like to imagine that we are winning on all fronts. Whether they are party followers or wishful thinkers, they don't want to hear that we are losing. Their lives, their peace of mind, their very sanity, depend on believing something, even a lie. Time enough to face the truth when we are all free and home once again. But here, in this place, we try not to deal with it. We try to focus on today. What can we do? We can't fight, but we can tell ourselves that one day we will get back into the war. Some of us prefer to dwell on thoughts of home, family, real living. But in short, Herr Leutnant, we are here to *think, not to act.* Therefore, it serves no purpose to provoke the emotions, either consciously or unconsciously."

Steuben laid a reassuring hand on Kirst's shoulder. "In this camp, every man has his dream, eh?"

Kirst nodded slowly at first, then more vigorously.

"Good. We understand each other." Steuben smiled. It faded quickly, replaced by a fatalistic frown. "Now, Kirst, since I am one who does not flinch at the truth . . . tell me . . . what's happening inside Germany?"

Steuben missed the fleeting excitement in Kirst's eyes. The dark force reached out across the few inches separating them and probed Steuben's thoughts. Then, in Kirst's voice, it quietly told Steuben what he did not want to hear. The truth about how bad it really was back home. About shortages, bombings, Allied forces in a multipronged assault across Europe, closing in on Germany from the west and the south, the Russians closing in from the east, the fear that the Russians would get in first and avenge themselves by slaughtering the German people . . .

Steuben went down the steps to escape Kirst's words. Kirst stopped talking and walked beside him awhile, but Steuben hardly noticed. He was lost in reflection, worried about his family, certain now that his worst fears were justified. He cursed himself for having asked. He should have resisted the temptation. He glanced at Kirst, who seemed fascinated by the small groups of men they were passing.

What is it about him? As if he delights in bearing bad news, yet without a trace of glee in his voice or on his face. He's like a machine—pull the lever and out comes the truth whether you want it or not. I should have listened to my own advice—

"Herr Major!"

Mueller hurried over, motioning to Steuben. Steuben introduced him to Kirst. Mueller shook hands but was completely preoccupied. "I want the committee to hear my proposal, Major. You promised."

"I promised we would discuss it and decide whether or not to hear it. We haven't gotten around to that. I'll let you know, Mueller."

"I don't feel like waiting, Major. And there are others who feel as I do."

"Tell them to be patient."

"You tell them. Invite them before the committee and tell them yourself."

"Mueller has been here almost as long as Gebhard," Steuben explained to Kirst, "and he is anxious to get out, by any means possible."

"Not like some I can think of," Mueller retorted. "You like it here, Steuben, because you're in charge—"

"We'll take it up at the meeting, Mueller."

Mueller glared at him then saluted, turned on his heel, and stalked off.

Steuben sighed. "The first thing you must accept, Kirst, is that you are here to stay." He turned and walked off quickly.

Kirst looked after him, immobilized by the soaring pain inside him, wanting to scream out and writhe on the ground, but the djinn held him steady, unmoving, unblinking. He was like a seething volcano beneath a solid granite mountain that no one in a thousand years would ever expect to erupt. The idea that he was trapped here in this camp with this ripping, tearing force inside him was enough to make him wish for death. The djinn had no intention of letting Steuben's words govern its actions. It would find a way out. Soon it would have the power.

It looked after Mueller, instantly attuned to the young Luftwaffe officer's emotions. So much anger and frustration—the djinn could taste it on the air. And Steuben—so much strength and resolve, but beneath it lurked fear of what the Russians were going to do to his family. And the others, these Germans, all with their outward portraits of strength and unity and purpose, all just as weak, all perfect to feed upon. . . .

Kirst had control of himself for a moment as the djinn's hunger reached out to sample what floated on the ether. But there was barely enough time for Kirst to catch his breath before the djinn's steel grip returned to flood his body and supplant his will. For a brief moment of awareness, Kirst figured out what it could do—tap into his memory, press the buttons of his conditioned responses, and *be him*. Back in the hut when Gebhard had asked about the war, his answers had not been his own; he wouldn't have been so cruel or blunt. But the knowledge was all his. Kirst resolved to find Gebhard and tell him the things he had said were lies. . . .

Soothing darkness enveloped that thought and obliterated it. In a moment, he found himself tramping back into Hut 7 to his new quarters. Gebhard was gone. So were Bruckner and his dog. Eckmann was alone in the room, on his bunk writing.

Eckmann paused to stare at the little photo of his bride tacked over his bunk. The picture was creased and smudged, but as always Frieda smiled back at him, her face radiant with happiness and the promise of love.

Eckmann recalled when it was taken. A week before the wedding in Hamburg, outside her father's home near the city center. Frieda had been especially happy that week, showered with gifts and attention, saying good-bye to old admirers, sneaking off with Eckmann several times a day to sate his lust and demonstrate her vast capacity for affection. It had seemed endless and she had seemed the most beautiful and desirable woman in the world, and Eckmann had clung to that belief tenaciously throughout his seventeen months as a prisoner.

Frieda had always been an independent spirit, free and rebellious, as strong-willed and big and blond as the German ideal could ask for. And as Eckmann sat and thought of her loveliness, her charm, her sexual abandon, and her loyalty, he smiled and swayed slightly on the bed, feeling a tingling between his legs.

His eyes snapped open and he saw Kirst standing at the foot of his bunk, looking at Frieda's picture. "My wife," Eckmann said protectively.

"Very pretty," Kirst said.

"Are you married?"

"No."

Eckmann didn't like him staring at Frieda. He leaned over to intercept the look. "Girl?" he asked.

"None that I . . . that I remember."

Eckmann laughed, shaking his head. "The frauleins suffer so much at our hands. Left behind and forgotten as we march off to defend the Fatherland. They sacrifice as much as we do, you know? We give our lives, but we ask them to give their youth and fidelity." He stared at the photo wistfully. "We were only married two days before I was ordered back. Two days, you see? I told my Frieda to be patient, that I would return on my next leave, and then we would make a baby."

He shook his head again and looked back at Kirst. "In France, my staff car overturned. General Saghorst and another officer were killed. I was captured. They questioned me for twenty days, then shipped me overseas and brought me here."

Eckmann paused and sighed. "I have letters from Frieda, wonderful letters. She is so full of love. It's important that someone at home still cares, isn't it?"

Kirst nodded slowly.

Sergeant Loats switched on the overhead bulb in his tiny darkroom and stirred the prints in the bath. Using wooden tongs, he picked up the first one and let the water drip off, then stared at it and swore again. He was right. In normal light, it looked even worse. It appeared to be a picture of Kirst, but it was indistinct, almost blurred, with no feature detail at all. The sonofabitch must have moved the instant the shutter snapped.

Loats chucked the print into the ashcan and reached for the second one. It was even worse. Kirst's face could be seen, but the whole image was partially obscured by an indistinct mottling, as if the plate had been double-exposed—once to shoot Kirst, and prior to that to photograph some kind of animal.

"I've checked around, sir, and I don't think anybody could have tampered with my plates."

Gilman studied the two prints and held the negatives up to the light. He frowned curiously at the images. "Anybody borrow your equipment lately, Sergeant?"

"No, sir."

"It looks like somebody went off to do a portrait of a wolf then left his film in your holders."

"Yes, sir, that's what it looks like."

"Well, there's only one solution. Bring him back for another sitting."

"Whatever you say, sir."

Chapter 10

The train was waiting on track five. Loring stood on the platform in a crush of humanity, her eyes darting back and forth. The p.a. announced boarding again. Loring glanced at her watch. Five minutes to departure—where was Yazir? Finally, as she turned and climbed the steps, there was an anxious call behind her:

"Miss Holloway . . . !"

She looked back. Yazir was hurrying through the crowd clutching a large package. A conductor helped him board Loring's car. He paused to lean against a partition and catch his breath. He waved the package at Loring.

"Present for you," he gasped.

He came up and followed her down the aisle to her seat. She had managed to get a lower berth in the middle of the car. Her baggage was already stored, and the passenger who would be occupying the upper hadn't arrived yet.

Yazir gave her the package and insisted she open it. "It's not a cake," he said. "If I am unable to deter you from going, then at least I can provide some modest protection."

Loring fingered the wrapping. "I was up all last night," she said. She looked at him sadly. "I haven't a hope in hell, you know. If there is no djinn, I'll be the biggest fool who ever lived. If there is—how can *I* fight it?"

Yazir nodded at the parcel. "Open it."

Loring untied the string. There were two tissue-wrapped objects inside the box. She tore the paper off the first, revealing a silver decanter the size of a wine bottle. Plugged into the two-inch neck at the top was a stopper, also made of silver.

"The mullahs have assured me that all the appropriate incantations have been read over it . . . for what that's worth. But look at it this way—if such a device was useful to a would-be sorcerer twenty-five hundred years ago, it might help you today. All you have to do is coax the djinn into it and seal it."

Loring stared at it. "All I have to do, eh?"

"Yes . . . well . . . perhaps you will discover something that attracts it. As I suggested before, a natural substance which you can place inside to lure it . . ."

"It's very nice. Very thoughtful of the mullahs." Yazir looked embarrassed. She touched his hand. "I'm sorry. I'm being a real brat."

Yazir sat down. "My dear, you are going up against a supernatural creature of unknown power and danger. Against such incredible beings, sometimes the best weapons are the most trivial." He gave her a reassuring smile. "Open the other one."

The second packet was much smaller and flatter. She tore off the tissue and held it up. Hanging from the end of a thin chain was a three-inch talisman in the shape of a pentagon, enclosing a five-pointed star. It too was made of silver.

"The only thing of my own that I could find in such a hurry," said Yazir. "It's been in my family for genera-

116

tions. I had the chain attached so you could wear it. Please—put it on."

She sat fingering it, unmoving.

"I showed it to the mullahs. They said it's very powerful."

"What else would they say?" Loring felt a stab of hopelessness. "Professor, I'm a scientist and you're a scholar. I'm chasing a demon—and you're offering me a magic charm."

"Now who's the skeptic?"

He took the talisman from her and slipped the chain over her head. He dropped the talisman down her blouse and she felt its cool weight against her skin. It was like one of those fat old brooches her grandmother used to wear. She had always hated the look of them. They reminded her of age and vanity.

"If nothing else," said Yazir, "this will offer some small comfort—for both of us. As long as you are within the djinn's sphere of influence, do not take it off."

Her brows knitted in a troubled frown as she grew worried that this task was too dangerous to attempt alone. She almost asked Yazir to come with her. He must have sensed that coming because he leaned over, kissed her forehead, and said, "For luck. And remember this—all djinn have one thing in common."

"What's that?"

"A quick and violent temper. Its one great weakness and its greatest danger."

He stood up then, and as the last boarding whistle sounded, he turned and was gone.

"The situation must be improving with Doenitz in charge of the Navy, eh, Kirst? There's a man who understands that the U-boat is our only hope of victory."

117

Gebhard finished stoking the fire and adjusting the water flow, then tromped into the shower hut with Kirst following. On Steuben's advice, Gebhard had put behind him Kirst's disagreeable remarks at their first meeting. If anything, Steuben had reasoned, Kirst needed a friend who would help him get accustomed to life in the camp. Gebhard was the only other submariner, so it fell to him. And Gebhard knew just what a submariner would appreciate most in this camp.

Kirst stood eyeing the shower—the broad concrete floor, the overhead network of pipes and spouts, across from it the troughlike sink with its wall-length mirror.

As they stripped and hung their clothing on pegs, Gebhard quizzed Kirst about his service. "I hear the snorkel cut our losses considerably."

"The snorkel . . . ?"

Gebhard found Kirst exasperating: his mind was constantly adrift, as if he weren't really paying attention. Or maybe . . . another thought occurred to Gebhard . . . maybe he didn't really know any of this. . . . Maybe he knew it but it wasn't second nature to him as it would be to a real submariner with extensive sea duty. . . .

"The snorkel . . ." Kirst appeared to think for a while, then began to speak. "Yes, for a time it boosted morale, but with the intake and exhaust heads always sticking up out of the water, the boats were easily detected by enemy airborne radar. When our commanding officers began calculating losses to air attack as opposed to other—"

"They've stopped using the snorkel?"

"Oh, it's still in use. On U-221, the snorkel heads were encased in a rubberized shield that had a waffle pattern to deflect radar. . . ."

Gebhard frowned. Kirst talked like a textbook. He

118

'turned on the water and waited for it to run hot, but it came out merely tepid. Gebhard grumbled and stepped under the spray with his soap, then quickly lathered up. Kirst stepped under the next spout.

"Tell me more," Gebhard said.

The djinn searched Kirst's brain for half-buried facts. Kirst could almost feel gates opening inside his head as the blackness gained access to his memory. The words emerged as smooth as glass.

"One thing about the snorkel that no one likes—it shortens deep diving capability. Submerged depth is limited to the length of the snorkel pipe—"

Gebhard grinned. "Might as well stick your cock up in the air and wave it around for all the good that does."

They continued discussing submarine technology until Gebhard tired of it. He passed the soap to Kirst, and he lathered up, too. Gebhard rolled his head back and let water run into his mouth and overflow his lips. He gargled and spat. The water got warmer and he sighed gratefully.

"Feel that?" he said. "Takes forever, but the heat comes. Usually when you're about through." He reached for the soap. "Nothing like this on the U-boats, eh, Kirst? The purest luxury on earth." He soaped up a second time. "So, Kirst, how did they get you? The plane bombed your boat and you went into the water? What's the rest of it? How were you rescued?"

Kirst rolled his head under the spray. He almost blacked out as the thing rushed up inside him and slammed the mental doors it had opened earlier. He stood there like a department-store mannequin, the spray running into his open eyes and mouth and down his body. When he returned to reality only seconds later, Gebhard was repeating his question.

119

Kirst searched for the answer but could find neither words nor thoughts. His mind kept hitting a black wall. His frustration mounted as Gebhard studied him oddly. He wanted to answer the question, wanted desperately to regain control of himself and scream out the truth, but he couldn't. Something must have shown on his face because Gebhard was looking at him oddly, but then he realized it was pure curiosity—Gebhard had asked him something, and Kirst hadn't answered.

I have to answer! he screamed at the black wall.

His arm rose. His hand gripped the valve and shut off the spray then stretched out toward Gebhard, motioning for the soap. Gebhard gave it to him. Kirst had no idea what he was doing or why. His legs propelled him out of the shower area and over to the long sink. The mirror was fogged, but he turned the tap and ran water and began to lather his face with soap.

A shave!

The thing inside had rooted around in his mind for the next obvious thing Kirst would do after a shower, and it had come up with a shave. Fascinated and detached, he watched his hand spread soap over his stubble. Then it reached for a razor attached to a wall hook by a length of chain. His fingers opened the blade and ran it across the strop beneath the mirror.

The razor was motionless in his hand as his eyes locked on the cloudy mirror.

Everything was still for a moment, then the blackness tingled mischievously inside him and he grew aware of an urge, a pressing desire to bring that razor up to his bared throat. He fought it but the urge was stronger. The tingle ran down his hand holding the razor. The blackness pulsed in his head, mocking him with insane, thunderous laughter. His fear mounted. The blackness reached out and devoured it hungrily. But that didn't sate it. It wanted more. Kirst trembled inside as his hand was forced to the mirror surface to wipe away a clear space so that he could see to shave. To shave, he screamed inside. His hand holding the razor was forced up.

Gebhard switched off his shower and reached for his towel. He was humming to himself.

Kirst's palm wiped the glass in broad strokes. His eyes were shut. The razor was at his throat. The blackness boiled inside him, hysterically happy, feeding off his terror.

His eyes flew open and he saw his reflection, and it must have been the one thing *it* hadn't counted on, because the horror that shot through Kirst at what he saw was not devoured. It too was shocked at this single moment of lost control. Because where Kirst's face should have been were a pair of deep feral eyes, monstrous snarling jaws, sallow mottled skin, and reptilian scales. It was like no animal Kirst had ever seen. It flung him backward, recoiling in anger, ripping through him in an uncontrollable rage. It whipped him around and, through his eyes, stared at Gebhard—poor surprised Gebhard, who stood confused with the towel to his body—and then it made Kirst snatch up his gear—his clothing and towel —and run away from the mirror, out the door, and down the steps, making him dash naked across the compound.

Gebhard missed seeing the image in the mirror. He saw only Kirst bolting from the hut and assumed that he ran because he couldn't explain to a submariner how he had survived two days and nights in the freezing Atlantic. Why? Gebhard asked himself. Because he had something to hide?

The djinn laughed inside Kirst, a soundless laugh that sent blackness rippling through Kirst's body. He stopped and flung himself against a tree and sobbed in front of the prisoners lounging outside the rec hut. They stared at him. He tried to get dressed but fumbled with his shorts, suddenly panicked about his nakedness.

The djinn bellowed dark laughter into his ears and rushed to his loins.

Kirst felt a warmth build in his crotch. He looked down and saw his penis thicken and lengthen until it stood out from his body in a stiff purple arch—massive, threatening, bigger than he had ever seen it in his life. He groaned and prayed that it wouldn't burst, and he cursed the dark tenant that filled it.

The men at the rec hut spotted his giant erection. They pointed and laughed.

The djinn let Kirst struggle with his shorts. He stumbled about, trying to get them up over his knees then over that massive aching bone. He fell against the tree and choked out a sob, despair wracking his throat—

And filling the djinn with pleasurable sustenance.

Gradually, the djinn withdrew, and Kirst's erection subsided. He dressed hurriedly, ignoring the men at the rec hut. When he looked up, weak and wanting nothing more than a bed to lie on and warm covers to pull over his body, he saw two MPs marching toward him. They were grinning.

Kirst sat in Loats' posing chair again, limp and disinterested as the sergeant adjusted his flash and loaded the Speed Graphic. Loats was chuckling with the two MPs. Kirst knew they were joking about his cock. He heard words like horse and stallion and knew exactly what they were saying. *Well, the hell with them.* He fought to keep himself calm, not wanting to alert the imp in his gut. He could feel it curled up there like a little black ball, sated from feeding off his terror. But he knew that it slept with one eye open and, if he so much as blurted a word about its existence, it would roar through his body like an enraged lion. He had no desire to test it.

"Okay, Herr Leutnant Horse-cock," Loats said, "let's see if you can look pretty this time."

The ball stirred in his stomach and started to spread. But the flash went off before the djinn could emerge from its slumbering torpor. The explosion of light so terrified the djinn that it slammed Kirst's body backward violently. He flew from the chair and skidded across the floor.

Loats and the two MPs stared at him in amazement.

Kirst was conscious of furious blackness boiling inside his head, obscuring his vision. Through a whipping dark cloud, he glimpsed the three Americans bending over him, conversing, worried. His eyelids fluttered and he felt himself losing consciousness and, as he slipped into limbo, he was aware of the imp's rage and helplessness, and the image of the fence around the compound loomed in his mind, the fence and a sensation of freedom and a vicious anger that he wouldn't stay awake because—

It forced his eyes open.

Because he had to stay awake. He was needed. The imp needed him to express his needs—its needs—it had to stay outside the fence—*why outside the fence?—awake —stay awake so you can tell them—tell them what?—tell them you need—you need a doctor!—their doctor!—the one with the—*

Kirst got an image of eyeglasses.

Borden, you want Borden? The American doctor? Why? Awake—stay awake—

But Kirst slipped into unconsciousness, for one brief second feeling true happiness at the imp's displeasure.

123

"What about the picture?" Gilman said. "Did you get it?"

Loats shook his head. "Didn't come out. The negative is a blur. When the flash went off, he flew right the hell out of that chair, sir. Banged his head on the floor, out like a light."

Gilman grunted and looked down at Kirst, lying unconscious on a cot in Borden's dispensary. Borden finished examining him and rose, puzzled.

"No sign of concussion. No bruise, bump, no blood. I don't see any reason why he should be unconscious."

"He's faking." Hopkins stepped forward, hands on his hips, glaring at Kirst.

"Thank you, Dr. Hopkins," said Gilman. "Send us a bill for the consultation."

"Well, sir, that's my opinion. Back in the third grade, I knew a guy used to faint—just pass right out—whenever it looked like he'd have to do something he didn't like. Eyes would roll back up in his head, knees would buckle —always managed to land on something soft, though."

"Your head," muttered Borden.

"I heard that."

Gilman stepped between them. "This isn't helping. Borden, what's your recommendation?"

Borden glanced at Kirst then at his watch. "Getting close to evening mess, Major. I say let him sleep it off. We'll check him when he wakes and, if nothing's wrong, send him back inside."

Hopkins was horrified. "You mean keep him here—in our hospital?"

"Spare us the moral outrage," said Gilman. "Sergeant Loats, can we live without a picture?"

Loats scratched his chin. "I don't know, sir. What if he escapes and we can't show anybody what he looks like?"

"That's why he's not staying here." Gilman looked down at Kirst. "If he's sucking us into a game, then he'd better find other players. Major Borden, have him sent back to camp and placed on sick call."

"Yes, sir."

"Hopkins, have you done anything about moving that fence yet?"

"Uh, no, sir—haven't received the materials from supply."

"Why don't you give them a nudge?"

Hopkins glared once more at Kirst then left. Borden followed Gilman to the door. "You're the commandant, sir, but medically speaking, I think we ought to keep this man under observation. He might have an aggravated condition that we don't know about."

Gilman nodded. "We've all got aggravated conditions, Borden—some medical, some psychological. If he knows what it is and it bothers him enough, he'll say something about it."

"That's a kind of cold-blooded way to look at it. Suppose he's got a tumor or a growth or something, and he's just not aware of it."

"He's not going to tell us the truth. He's not obliged to. He's a prisoner of war. The only way he can continue

125

fighting in this camp is to lie, disrupt and confound us, the enemy. If he's hurting, let him convince his own people first. Send him back."

"Yes, sir."

Borden opened the door. Gilman hunched his jacket tighter and marched out into the cold. Borden closed the door and paused to light a cigarette, reflecting on the exigencies of command. If he were in Gilman's shoes, would he behave the same way? Probably. The greater good. When you're dealing with the enemy, assume deceit until proved otherwise. Drawing deeply on the cigarette, Borden strolled back to the ward and stopped at the first bed.

Kirst was sitting up on the cot, watching him.

"So, Gebhard, what were you *pulling* in the shower, eh?" Snickers ran round the rec hut as Dortmunder fixed Gebhard with a prissy grin. "Now we learn the truth, eh? Secrets of submarine life."

Open guffaws.

Dortmunder was Luftwaffe, though how anyone so huge and brawny could ever have squeezed himself into the cockpit of a fighter was a subject of bored speculation among many of his comrades. He sat at a card table with his ever-present crony, Hoffman, another pilot—short and wiry. They were the camp needlers, and they kept their sanity by picking on everyone's Achilles heel.

Gebhard ignored them and stayed where he was, stretched out on one of the two ratty sofas. Hut 10 was the prisoners' day room, their recreation center, as large as a barracks hut but without the dividing partitions. It was a long single room supplied with card tables, busted-down chairs, a windup phonograph, and a stack of 78s that dated from the early 1930s. There were Spanish-language magazines, children's books, and even some tattered restaurant menus to read—all courtesy of Hopkins and his perverse sense of humor. Mostly it was a place for the prisoners to hang out, smoke, chat, play cards, and trade lies.

"I saw a cock that big once," said Hoffman, "on a bull in a French pasture. We cut it off and had it stuffed. I had it with me when I was shot down. An American officer took it. God knows what he did with it."

Dortmunder snorted. "What's Kirst going to do with his? There isn't an asshole in this camp big enough for *that.*"

Hoffman grinned. "Yes, there is. Hopkins."

Gebhard tuned them out, staring at the ceiling with his hands tucked behind his head, filled with anger—not so much at Dortmunder and Hoffman because their behavior was normal, but very much at Kirst. Running out of the shower hut exposing himself, he had set everyone to speculating: Had he and Gebhard been engaged in a little meat-flashing? Embarrassing to Kirst but more so to Gebhard. And why? Why run out there with his maypole waving? To deliberately cast Gebhard in a bad light?

Gebhard ruminated on that and saw a pattern emerging. Frightened by Gebhard's questioning his miraculous rescue at sea, Kirst flees to the compound, displays himself, and is conveniently picked up by the MPs and escorted out the gate. What for?

Cause and effect. Gebhard reached a simple conclusion: Kirst was not what he appeared to be.

Laughter trailed off around him and he looked at what everybody else was looking at: Kirst—standing motionless in the doorway with nothing to indicate life other than his eyes, which fixed on Gebhard liquidly—and sent a chill up his spine.

Borden sat at the staff table, picking at his evening meal. Blish tore into a steak, Cosco carefully arranged peas on the edge of his plate before tackling his meat, and Gilman ate efficiently. Hopkins was trying to convince Gilman of the merits of rousting prisoners at odd hours. Gilman listened but kept shaking his head.

Borden kept seeing Kirst sitting up on the cot in the dispensary, eyeing him like an amoeba under a microscope. There was something about the man that gave Borden the willies. He searched his mind, sure that he had seen that look before, in another war. . . .

"Major, I have been dealing with these krauts a long time," Hopkins insisted, "and I know all their tricks. Take this new guy, Kirst."

"What about him?"

"An actor. A performer, a phony-baloney. I'll give you hundred-to-one odds this is just the beginning with him. He's going to pull every gag in the book until we don't know what he'll try next, then all of a sudden—wham!"

"Wham?"

Hopkins made a burrowing gesture. "Right through the gate and out of sight. And what will we be able to say about him? Not one single consistent thing, that's what."

"What do you want me to do?"

"Nothing, sir. You don't have to do a thing. Just let me get him alone for a little bit and I'll find out what he's up to. Use a little muscle, that's all. Not much, just enough to make him squirm."

Gilman put down his fork and glared at Hopkins. "What were you in your previous life, Hopkins? The Grand Inquisitor?"

Hopkins shrugged.

"'I told you before—we're not going to torture those

men. If they start trouble, we'll stop it. But we're not going to provoke them. Do you understand?"

Hopkins grudgingly nodded. Gilman picked up his fork and resumed eating. Borden thought of Kirst, lying like a sack of potatoes up against one of the huts after a little of Hopkins' treatment . . . eyes open and staring, half dead.

And then he remembered where he had seen that look before. On the face of a German soldier whom he had just bayoneted, lying spread-eagled over the edge of a trench on the last day of the Great War. No hatred in his eyes, only a dull surprise.

On the cot this afternoon, Kirst had given him that dull surprised look, but only in the position of his features, slack-jawed and pained. The eyes. The eyes had flashed something else: cold, calculated something . . .

Something what?

Then Borden realized why he couldn't eat, and what he had seen in Kirst's eyes.

Cold, calculated *hunger.*

During the prisoners' evening mess, Kirst sat surrounded by Naval, Luftwaffe, and Army officers downing lentil soup and bread. In response to their questions, the djinn had him painting a picture of war-ravaged Germany vainly trying to stave off the inevitable. As they listened to him, they grew increasingly depressed, which delighted the djinn as it fed on their emotions. Kirst was conscious only of being a conduit—out went the words, in came the emotions, which in turn assaulted him and supplied the djinn with added sustenance.

He still knew it only as a blackness that now and then obscured his vision, that raised dark walls in his mind, that flooded throughout his system and could settle anywhere and everywhere—now as a tight, weighted ball in the pit of his stomach—now as a churning fire—now as a freezing numbness—now as an aching hunger. He called it the "imp" when he could barely tolerate it. At other times it had other names—foul, disgusting names that hardly came close to describing what he felt about it. But mostly he felt only helplessness, and a slow drain on his emotions that he knew in the end would leave him a desiccated husk. Now, while it was active, he had an overriding sense that it was no longer the tenant in his body, but that he was. Rolf Kirst was trapped inside a body no longer his own, and all he wanted now was to be out and gone. Leave it behind, leave it to the imp.

Kirst tried to eat his soup, but there was something in it the imp didn't like, so it would only let him munch on bread. In their mutual silence, he screamed at it that he had to have food, that if he didn't eat he would die. *Then what would happen to you?* he asked the imp. It never answered.

Gebhard now dominated the conversation and was bombarding Kirst with technical questions about the U-boats, trying to trip him up. The djinn fed on Gebhard's suspicions and mocked him by pouring answers through Kirst's lips as if by rote. Torpedo range variations, characteristics of the magnetic exploder, advantages of electric drive . . .

Kirst was fascinated by what came out of him, only vaguely recalling learning all of this, realizing it must have been buried somewhere in his mind and the imp had unlocked it.

Across the mess hall, he glimpsed Steuben watching him sternly. Kirst tried to warn the imp to shut up, but it was having too much fun. It kept him chattering like a magpie. On his right, von Lechterhoeven ladled himself a second helping of lentil soup, then picked up a salt cellar and began liberally shaking its contents into his bowl.

Kirst's flow of words instantly stopped. He froze in his seat as the imp retreated into the farthest corner of his body, away from this maniac with his salt shaker. This was all lost on Kirst, who was only conscious of two things: one, a thick dark ache in his foot where the imp had gone, and two, he was once again in control of himself.

In surprise, Kirst dropped his bread. It splashed into his soup. Von Lechterhoeven glanced at him. They all looked at him, Gebhard intently. Kirst felt a sudden, tremendous, wonderful exhilaration, as if an incredible weight had been lifted from his shoulders, as if the cloud that had muddled his thinking for days had suddenly vanished and left him with a clarity he had never experienced before, as if all at once he knew the secret of the universe, that life was grand and wonderful and the greatest gift of all—

He opened his mouth to proclaim his freedom in his own voice, but before he could form the words, the ache in his foot tore up the length of his leg and shot into his crotch. He turned pale. Blackness spread upward and robbed him of his great discovery, as the imp took him back. It lifted his arm and worked his hand and made him fish the bread out of his soup and drop it on a napkin. Then it made him look at the officers around him sheepishly. It made him apologize.

And he heard himself tell them, "Seizures. I get them now and then. Not very painful, but . . . momentary blackouts."

A few of the officers nodded. They had heard of such things.

"How did you get into submarines with *that?*" Gebhard asked coldly.

The imp locked gazes with Gebhard. "I only began to get them during this last patrol," it said through Kirst.

The men were getting up around them, taking their plates to the washtubs outside the kitchen. Kirst ignored them. The imp had him take another slice of bread and work on that while everyone else cleared out.

Gebhard was the last to leave.

Chapter 12

A thick, low-hanging fog obscured Blackbone Mountain and covered the roofs of the huts. Gebhard walked the fence perimeter with Steuben and voiced his suspicions of Kirst.

"Most of the time you can hardly get two words out of him but, when he does talk, he sounds like a walking textbook. He's soulless."

"That's not enough to condemn a man," said Steuben.

"Did you see him at dinner? Seizures indeed. Every time it gets a little hot, he pulls a stunt."

Steuben pursed his lips. "There's a story going around that you attacked him in the shower."

Gebhard laughed bitterly. "I asked him to explain how he survived at sea for two days, and he ran like he'd seen a ghost. A few minutes later, I heard he had sprouted a bone in front of twenty of our men. Are the two things connected? I think so, but not the way he led everyone to believe. He's trying to discredit me—make me out to be a pervert, when he's—"

"What?"

"Major, he was blown off a U-boat. He's supposed to have survived two days' exposure to freezing water and air temperatures before he was rescued. But that's just not possible!"

"No?"

"Not in the Atlantic. Not at this time of year. I'm a submariner! He knows damned well I wouldn't believe that story! That I'd question it and eventually voice my doubts to the others. So he undercut me. He plays the victim, and I'm the goat!"

"If he didn't survive that ordeal, then how do you account for the fact that he's here?"

"Because he was never *there!* He was never rescued at sea! He's a spy!"

"A spy?"

"Planted by the Americans."

Steuben lapsed into silence. Gebhard stared into space and continued walking, mentally writing the scenario of Kirst's recruitment by the Americans to go to Blackbone and play ferret among his countrymen.

"Suppose he is a spy," said Steuben. "Then what?"

"Then we should do something."

"What?"

Gebhard was no cold-blooded bully, no heartless Gestapo. He couldn't simply say, Kill him. Submariners did not view themselves as killers. Unlike the army types, they were never involved in hand-to-hand combat. Their action was almost entirely impersonal. Torpedoes did the killing; images in the lens of a periscope did the dying.

"You see," said Steuben, "I don't find him quite so sinister. He's strange, he's quiet, hasn't much spirit, keeps to himself, and has an unfortunate habit of babbling unpleasant truths. But a spy?" Steuben shrugged.

"You don't think he's capable of it?"

"I don't know. He bears watching. But look at it this way—perhaps he doesn't trust *you.* Maybe he thinks you're a spy trying to pump *him.* Maybe he doesn't trust any of us."

"You think I'm imagining things."

"So far, he's guilty of only one crime—being indiscreet."

"Hah!"

"I mean about discussing the war. He seems to seize every opportunity to depress us with his bleak view of the situation. I warned him not to, but it appears he has no control over the impulse."

"What are you going to do about *that,* Major?"

Steuben stopped near the westernmost perimeter tower. He could feel the sentry's eyes on his back and knew the man was resisting a terrible temptation to plonk a German major and go home a hero. Gebhard stood near his left shoulder, hands in his pockets, waiting for an answer.

"You're the one who wants to do something, Leutnant Gebhard. Make a suggestion."

"Move him out of my hut."

"No."

"At least out of my room."

"No. If you're concerned that he should be watched, then you watch him. And report everything to me."

Gebhard frowned angrily then reconsidered. "All right," he said finally. "I'll watch him."

"Good."

Gebhard saluted. Steuben returned it and watched the little submariner stroll off toward the huts. Steuben grunted to himself. Psychology worked every time. In this camp, all any man wanted was something to relieve the boredom. Give him a task, the slightest chore, and he was in seventh heaven. Give him something remotely smacking of importance and he would tackle it like the search for the Grail. Steuben smiled: he had just turned

135

Gebhard into the very thing he believed Kirst to be—a spy.

Cold seeped up through cracks in the floorboards in Hut 7, but the presence of eight sleeping bodies in one small room kept the cold at floor level. Kirst was sunk into a deep sleep and lay on his back, snoring.

The djinn stirred inside him, flowed into his brain, and sealed off all awareness, plunging him into a trancelike state that bordered on coma. Kirst was becoming easier to manage. The djinn had familiarized itself completely with his memory and his behavioral impulses. Soon Kirst could be made to function with more natural demeanor. Soon even Gebhard would lose his suspicions. But by then it might be too late. With as much energy as the djinn required to rebuild itself, Kirst would be drained long before he became truly controlled and of optimum use.

The djinn gathered itself now for the tremendous effort ahead. From all parts of Kirst's body, it summoned its substance and rose up in the throat to sample the air. . . .

A moment later, an oily black smoke seeped from Kirst's open mouth and cascaded to the cold floor. The nightform spread over the boards in a murky pool. When it was all out, lying there like a detached shadow, it began to move across the floor, to drift higher, to extend tendrils of soft, wispy blackness. . . .

Exploring Eckmann and the photograph of Eckmann's wife, Frieda . . . hesitating over Gebhard . . . a tendril touching Gebhard's face and creeping around his temples, looking for the emotions that lay close to the surface in sleep . . . moving over the other men in the same way, as if making their acquaintance . . .

136

The tendrils collected back on the floor. An undulating blob of black, the nightform seeped under the door. It flowed along the corridor, past closed doors at which it hesitated only briefly, searching for the energy it couldn't get from Kirst, energy needed for growth, energy derived from the terror and even death of other victims. From Kirst it gained sustenance—from others, growth and power.

It spilled out of the hut and down the steps and rolled across the compound, clinging to the ground like a swirling black fog. Swept by spotlights from the guard towers, it went undiscovered.

A burly American sergeant named Vinge tramped through the blackness and took it for nothing more than a shadow. As soon as Vinge had passed, the nightform settled around the base of a tree to wait and watch.

Vinge was on patrol, playing his flashlight under the huts to see if any Germans were trying to tunnel out, or if they were hiding to jump him later. He found nothing but looking reassured him.

As Vinge stooped to inspect beneath Hut 7, a distant wolf howl sent a shiver up his back. Vinge hated wild animals. In his dreams they lurked beneath the huts, hid behind trees, crouched in the branches. He saw them everywhere in his mind, but at Blackbone he had encountered nothing more ferocious than a bunny. He knew they were around, the vicious ones. And he knew that someday something awful would chew through the fence and get into the camp and be waiting for him. . . .

At Hut 9 he hunkered down and peered into the crawl space. His light picked out stones, dead leaves, foundation blocks, and weeds—

And a pair of eyes gleaming in the shadows.

Vinge froze. He held his light on the eyes but could see

nothing more in the blackness. He switched the light off and on.

The eyes were gone. Vinge edged back. He heard something thumping along the ground, coming toward him. He tried to turn and run, but it bounded out from beneath the hut and shot right past him. Vinge was bowled over by his own fear. He saw it bounding away . . . a snow-white jackrabbit. . . .

Vinge lay on the ground, his heart beating frantically. Then he cursed aloud. "Shit! Fuck! Piss! Goddamn all animals everywhere!"

He got to his feet and glanced about, then moved on. *Rabbit stew. Rabbit drumsticks.*

He would make short goddamned work of that rabbit if it crossed his path again.

The nightform flowed away from the tree and rolled quickly after the rabbit.

Stopping to devour a tempting bit of garbage outside the mess hut, the rabbit never noticed the shadow creeping up behind him. The nightform swirled under the rabbit's feet and in an instant had him completely enveloped in black and rooted helplessly to the ground. Dark tendrils probed his white fur, found his ears, and seeped into his head.

The rabbit was conscious of a ravenous burning inside his brain. He erupted in terror, disrupting the nightform's hold. He sprang straight up into the air and kicked his hind legs wildly, tearing at the wispy black stuff, which whipped off in several directions then regrouped.

The rabbit bounded free, zigzagged madly across the compound and took refuge beneath another hut. There it curled up and hid, quivering, its heart shuddering in ter-

ror as the nightform found it and enveloped it in blackness. It fought and shook and whipped around but
couldn't escape. The nightform rushed into its ears and
nose and mouth and filled its body with an icy presence
that fed on its rising panic, devoured its frantic emotions—

Until finally the rabbit convulsed and lay still.

The nightform left it and moved away from the hut.

It drifted uphill toward the fence, crossing the long
distance from the huts to the perimeter in less time than
it would take a man to walk it. It drifted right up to the
wire and extended tendrils to touch it—

And recoiled violently.

The entire nightform bucked and weaved in pain. It
sprang out in rage, then tucked back in on itself, undulating in spasms of movement. Finally, it rose up in a sheet
of black shadow and defiantly faced the fence as if a show
of power would be enough to rip the imprisoning walls
from the ground.

The sentry's spotlight played slowly across the chain
links and barbed wire. As it approached, the nightform
settled and spread out on the ground. Light stirred black
tendrils but passed too quickly to cause pain. The
nightform hovered briefly as the djinn extended its sen-
sory capacity and tried to determine a way to thwart the
fence. Rage would not provide a solution, only natural
cunning could help now. The djinn recalled the five walls
of Ur-Tawaq and the maddening hunger that had driven
it to do the sorcerer's bidding, on the promise that after
the feeding inside the city was depleted, the djinn would
be allowed out in the only way it could get out, inside a
host. And once out, the sorcerer had promised it could
feed on the armies of Nebuchadnezzar. . . . But the sorcerer had cheated him, had slit the throat of the host,

139

compelling the djinn to abandon the body and hide inside the flask. . . .

But now it was out. It had a new host and enough men to feed on. And though there were still the walls, the magic circle, the pentagon, keeping it confined, at least this time there was no sorcerer.

And the djinn had had eons in which to reflect on past mistakes.

Now it rolled away from the fence and searched the confusing jumble of emotions it had robbed from the rabbit, looking for something a rabbit might fear, another animal indigenous to this area. In seconds, it had the image.

The nightform found a dark corner under one of the huts, drew itself together, and, as it had done with Strann on the train, turned itself into a being of seemingly solid substance. Its blackness balled up into a thick mass and convulsed into form, sprouting black fur and sharp claws. The eyes opened. It padded away from the hut.

Seeing Hopkins enter the compound with a pair of huge MPs, Gilman slammed on the brakes and backed the jeep up to the gate. He had been about to start an inspection drive around the outside perimeter, but now his suspicions were alerted. He signaled the gate sentry and shifted again—the jeep's gears were grinding in protest—then he drove through.

Just past the gate, Gilman swerved to miss something in his path. He slowed and watched it slink off into darkness. A black wildcat.

Wondering where it had come from and resolving to check the fence for broken spots or holes, Gilman stabbed his foot back on the gas and went banging down the slope after Hopkins. He squealed to a stop and pulled the brake. Hopkins flicked a cigarette away and turned to meet him.

"What's up?" Gilman said.

"Thought it might be a good idea to question Kirst about that incident on the train, sir."

Gilman stared at the MPs. He knew the type—soulless enforcers. They would be big-city cops if they had the brains to go with the brawn. Just the sort Hopkins would rely on in a pinch.

"There's nothing to question," Gilman said. "He slept through the whole thing."

"Beg pardon, sir, but that may not be the truth, if you know what I mean." Hopkins winked.

"I know exactly what you mean. What are you planning? A little midnight third degree? You and the two dwarfs there?"

"Major—"

"Get out, Hopkins. If I want you in this compound at night, I'll order you in."

Hopkins' jaw dropped. Gilman threw the jeep back into gear, cursed the grinding protest, then wheeled it around and back up the hill. The sentry had the gate open before he got there. He charged through.

Hopkins swallowed his anger and tramped back up the hill. The MPs followed obediently, wearing tiny smiles that Hopkins never saw.

The lights were out all through the camp when Sergeant Vinge tramped up the steps into the prison shower hut. Humming to himself, he went to the back urinal and unzipped his fly. A great peace came over him as he relieved himself in a steady stream. He stared at the wall and thought of the cigarettes he had forgotten to bring.

Oh, well, he was coming off duty in twenty minutes. Plenty of time for a smoke before hitting the sack.

The cat strolled into the gloomy shower hut. It rubbed against the doorjamb and peered hard at the overhead pipes. One of the shower heads was leaking. Water dripped from the rusted spout and pooled on the concrete. A small river ran from the pool toward the single drain.

The cat's gaze shifted to the long sink and the mirror over it. It shrank back slightly and nosed the air. Its ears pricked up as it caught the hissing sound coming from the rear of the hut. It peered into the darkness and saw Vinge shaking himself, then hitching up his pants, starting to whistle. The cat's gaze fixed on Vinge then shifted to the mirror again. Its eyes hardened.

Vinge moved away from the urinal and, still whistling, went down the hut to the sink. He ran a little water and rinsed his hands, studying his reflection in the mirror. He spotted a pimple on his upper lip and frowned. Goddamned skin problem had never gone away. He stopped whistling and leaned closer to study it. He pinched it between two fingers and squeezed.

In that moment of silence, Vinge heard something breathing.

He held very still and ran his eyes across the mirror, which afforded him a view of the entire hut. Nothing moved. But he still heard breathing. There were dark spots, of course, corners back in the potty stalls where he couldn't see, but who could be . . . ?

Vinge lowered his hands and resumed whistling. Trying to appear casual, he backed from the mirror and turned and rolled his head on his shoulders, so it would look like he was exercising tired muscles, but he was really doing it to get a good glimpse into those shadows. Nothing moved.

Wup. Something by the door—

Vinge whipped around. Blackness obscured his view and, in the same instant, the mirror exploded behind him. Shattered fragments blew outward, some striking his back, most crashing to the concrete floor and littering it with shards and gleaming bits. Vinge let out an instinctive, frightened yell. Out of the corner of his eye, he glimpsed a figure standing at the door—a German prisoner. It turned and was gone. Vinge shouted after it.

Outside, in its place, the nightform drifted away from the hut. It re-formed as the black wildcat and ran a short distance away then turned to crouch in the open as Vinge came charging out of the shower hut, his right hand scrabbling for his sidearm, his left awkwardly bent, trying to pull the glass out of his back. He was screaming curses. The gun came out and he looked wildly for the German—

Then he saw the cat.

The cat rose and crept toward him, emitting a low, throaty growl. It bared its fangs and hissed loudly and its steady pace became a lope.

Vinge stumbled backward, no longer cursing, letting out a long sustained yell as he pumped shots into the night. When the gun was empty, he looked for the body—

And saw nothing.

Something cold rushed up around his ears, a chill breeze out of nowhere. It made him instantly light-headed. He spun around and beat at the air, but saw only blackness. A sob caught in his throat. He shut his eyes and wished for it to go away. In the midst of his terror,

143

he heard whistles and the hissing of arc lamps going on, the creak of the gate, running feet. . . .

Vinge opened his eyes and looked around. He was alone except for the MPs charging down the slope toward him.

Chapter 13

The Germans hurried from their huts, pulling on trousers and shoes and buttoning shirts. Swept by searchlights and responding to harsh cries of *"Schnell! Schnell!"* they formed up in the yard in front of the huts and stood for roll call, all 231 of them, surrounded by MPs with automatic weapons.

A short distance away, Vinge stooped over a box while Borden worked on his back, picking bits of glass out of his flesh with a pair of tweezers, soaking the minor wounds with alcohol. Vinge bore it stoically, his eyes glued vengefully to the Germans standing before him.

Hopkins paced back and forth a short distance away, rolling a cigarette through his fingers and drawing on it frequently, giving the Germans a baleful gaze while he plotted reprisals.

Steuben emerged from the shower hut behind Gilman. They came forward grimly. Cosco finished calling the roll and reported to Gilman, "All present and accounted for, sir."

"Thank you, Lieutenant."

Hopkins glared at Bruckner and gave Churchill a particularly hateful look. The dog sat on its haunches at the end of a leash that Bruckner held tightly in his fist—it panted at Hopkins and licked its lips.

"Major Steuben," said Gilman, "will you please explain the situation to your men?"

Steuben turned. With his men still at attention, he spoke to them in German, nodding in Vinge's direction. "Sergeant Vinge reports that in a routine inspection of the shower hut he was attacked by a concealed prisoner. This prisoner threw an unidentified weapon at him. It missed him but shattered the washbasin mirror. The attacker then fled. Vinge pursued but was unable to apprehend him."

The Germans muttered among themselves as Borden translated Steuben's words for Gilman. Satisfied, Gilman hunkered down with Vinge.

"Sergeant, are you sure it was a German?"

"Dead sure, sir."

"Could you recognize him?"

Vinge hesitated. "I only got a glimpse, sir, but . . . yeah, I think I could pick him out."

Kirst stood at attention in the third rank along with everyone else, watching Borden tape gauze to Vinge's back. Lulled by the blackness clouding his mind, he had no recollection of the evening's adventure. He remembered going to sleep at lights-out but nothing else until Gebhard forcibly wakened him to stumble outside with the others.

Vinge shrugged into a jacket provided by another MP then began trudging down the front rank of prisoners, gazing into faces. Gilman, Steuben, and Hopkins formed a little parade behind him.

As Vinge rounded the end of the first rank and started along the second, the imp opened a little window inside Kirst's mind and gave him a fuzzy replay of the night's events. Kirst stood stiffly staring into space, seeing not the men in front of him and the sweeping searchlights but the interior of the shower hut from a point of view almost at floor level. He saw the mirror, the darkness, the man at the back urinal—Vinge taking a piss. He saw Vinge come forward, stop at the mirror, examine his face in its reflection. Then Vinge froze, turned suddenly, fear in his eyes—

Fear rising inside Kirst, heart pounding, dreading what he would see, what the imp would make him feel—

The mirror exploded. Glass embedded in Vinge's back. His scream. His look directly at—

The little head movie ended. Vinge was at the end of the second rank now, and Kirst's nerves went on edge. He knew he hadn't been out of bed tonight. He knew he hadn't been back to the shower hut. The imp had gone. . . . But why did it want him to see what had happened? His leg quivered. He felt his knees threaten to buckle as anxiety overwhelmed him.

Vinge came down the third rank. Gebhard was four men ahead of Kirst and was turning to stare at him.

Go screw yourself, Gebhard—it wasn't me!

The blackness danced inside Kirst's head, devouring his anxiety, which mounted as Vinge drew closer.

Vinge knew the face he was looking for—no doubt in his mind. He glanced at each pair of stiff, staring eyes. He reached Gebhard and passed him by, and the man after him, and after that, and another and then—

He stopped in front of Kirst.

The imp buzzed. Blood pounded in Kirst's ears. Fire burned his brain.

Vinge was very still for just a moment, then his hands lashed out, grabbed Kirst, and lifted him off the ground. "Sonofabitch!" he screamed in Kirst's face.

Gilman and Hopkins restrained him.

Then Steuben was nose-to-nose with Kirst, staring intently and angrily at him. Kirst glanced around. The prisoners were turning to see who Vinge had nailed. Vinge shook Hopkins off, pointed a finger at Kirst, and announced, "That's him! That's the one I saw!"

"Did you do it, Kirst?" said Steuben.

"Do what, Major?" Kirst surprised himself: inside he was going insane with terror, and the imp was wildly feeding off it but still controlling his voice, making it come out calm, innocent.

"Did you attack the American sergeant?"

"No, sir."

"Were you in the shower hut tonight?"

"No, sir."

"Did you leave Hut Seven?"

"Only for roll call, Major."

Steuben looked around. "Is that right, Eckmann? Gebhard?" Gebhard looked away and refused to answer. Eckmann reported that Kirst had been the first one asleep in their room and, as far as he knew, hadn't left the hut. He was corroborated by Schliebert, another prisoner from the same room. Steuben relayed all this to Gilman.

Vinge reddened and took another step forward. Gilman grabbed him. "You only got a glimpse, Sergeant," he said. "Let's be sure. You want to look a little more?"

"No, I don't want to look! Sir, that's him! I'm positive."

Gilman hesitated, uncertain what to do. Hopkins moved up. "Let me handle this, sir," he said. "You don't know these people and their bullshit tricks, Major. He's not going to tell you he did it. You gotta make him *want* to tell. Let me just turn the screws a little bit, take him outside and teach him a little American history—"

148

Kirst felt the imp stop its excited movements briefly, reacting to Hopkins. It moved his head slightly, focused his eyes on Hopkins, boring into him.

"No," said Gilman. "He stays inside."

"Sir—" Hopkins protested.

"Put a detail together and get that glass cleaned up."

"Why not make the Germans do it?"

"Because they might use the pieces to slit American throats, Hopkins. And somehow I don't think they'd start with mine."

Hopkins glanced around, aware that he wasn't among friends. "They're prisoners," he snapped. "They have to be reminded who's boss."

"And who is?"

Hopkins backed down with a thin smile. "Can't understand you, Major—sympathizing with the krauts after the way they chewed you up in France . . ."

"Get moving, Captain."

Hopkins motioned several MPs to follow him to the shower hut.

Gilman turned back to Steuben. Indicating Kirst and Vinge, he said, "I'm not inclined to call either of these men a liar, but somebody broke that mirror. I don't think Vinge did it—he'd have to be a contortionist to end up with glass in his back, also devious and pathologically vengeful. On the other hand, it didn't look to me as if anyone threw *anything* at that mirror. It looks as if it exploded off the wall. How I haven't a clue. The fact remains that Kirst—"

He frowned, unsure how to finish the thought. *Kirst has been consistently weird since his arrival?* Gilman detected the same unease in Steuben. Both men glanced at Kirst and saw only a stony-faced officer standing at attention.

Then Gilman noticed that nearly everybody—all the prisoners—were looking at Kirst—if not looking at him, at least thinking about him, or so it seemed.

"Well . . . something has to be done," Gilman said. "So I'm withdrawing privileges for all prisoners until this matter is settled through further investigation. The shower hut is off limits." Gilman flashed Kirst a look. "For everybody. I'm sure you can explain why, Major."

Steuben nodded.

"You may dismiss your men."

Gilman hiked up the hill, listening to Steuben's voice ringing across the compound in German.

German. Hopkins had struck a nerve. Gilman wondered how he could escape the fact that these Germans entrusted to his care were soldiers of the same army that had butchered his command in France? Confusion. Guilt. If only he had used some tact. Couldn't he have simply agreed with the general then ignored his orders and risked the consequences? No, he had felt compelled to argue logic, when he should have played the game. He failed his men. And now here he was charged with the well-being of the enemy.

Why should you care if Hopkins wants to torture Germans? You know why. Because now they are your command.

Back in the barracks hut up in the MP compound, Vinge fended off questions from his buddies. He cashed in a poker debt with Chilton, settling for a half-bottle of bourbon, which he downed in twenty minutes. Then he stripped down and hit the sack, lying on his belly and closing his eyes to escape the curious looks of the men around him. He felt foolish, not so much about the glass in his back or even the kraut escaping punishment . . .

But that goddamned black wildcat. Where the hell had that come from? Scared shit out of him, and that made him mad.

Cosco squatted down by the bunk, lit a cigarette, and passed it to him. "Thanks," he said.

"Gilman sent me to find out if you want to go on the sick list."

"No," growled Vinge. "Thanks anyway, sir."

"You're on patrol tomorrow night, too. I can switch you with someone else, put you on the gate or something."

Vinge inhaled deeply and thought about the wildcat. He hadn't told anyone that part of the story, not Gilman, not the guys, not Borden. . . . Tomorrow night on patrol, he could steal some time and hunt for it. Probably came over the fence, down off Blackbone Mountain. If it liked what it saw, it would be back, and Vinge could be waiting. For once in his life, he wouldn't run from any damned four-legged beast. Okay, so it had claws and speed and cunning. . . . But Vinge had a .45 strapped to his waist. His lip curled in a smile.

"I'll take the patrol," he told Cosco.

Behind him, someone applauded.

In Hut 7 it was 0300 before the prisoners settled down and got back to sleep. There was a lot of grousing about Kirst and the order placing the showers off limits, but nobody really knew what to make of it. In Kirst's room, they were sullen and suspicious. They lay in their bunks glancing at each other, glancing at Kirst—he had gone right back to sleep.

Gebhard replayed events in his mind. Eckmann had reported correctly: Kirst had been the first to close his eyes after lights-out but, once they were all asleep, who would have known if Kirst had taken a midnight stroll? Didn't make sense, though—all the noise from the shower hut—the crash of glass breaking, which some of the men heard, followed by a volley of gunshots, then whistles, then the camp being rousted—all within a couple of minutes. No time for Kirst to be in the shower hut, throw something at the mirror, and get all the way back to Hut 7 and into his bunk before . . .

Gebhard frowned. It made no sense. Nothing about Kirst made any sense. He looked around at Eckmann, Schliebert, Mueller, all still awake, puzzled.

Gebhard shrugged deeper under the covers. At least now he wasn't alone. Now they were all wondering about Kirst.

The djinn flooded Kirst's body with a soothing darkness, sated from its night's activities and pleased because it had stumbled on what it most needed in the near future —a potential new host. A wealth of repressed fear and anxiety bubbling beneath the surface, this new body would offer much greater sustaining power for the djinn. Its unstable emotional fabric would give the djinn a stronger energy base from which it could launch out and feed on others. Kirst was growing weaker emotionally. Soon he would be just a shell, a walking husk, depleted of all fear, left to wander the camp like some demented soul who has lost his god.

The djinn chuckled soundlessly. Lost his god, most assuredly. When the true god of all men is fear.

Fear in the host was devoured to fan the spark of life. And the terror of victims like Sergeant Vinge and Corporal Strann was food for growth.

Much opportunity for growth in this camp, despite the unpassable walls. The djinn sucked in on itself and curled

152

up in Kirst's beating heart. Much opportunity . . . and only beginning to take shape. Fear on the rise. Anger, confusion, ultimately panic . . . as it was in Ur-Tawaq . . . and cities before that . . . it would be that way here . . . only this time it would be different . . . the djinn would get out . . . pass through the walls inside the host, then leave the host and find another more wide-ranging host. . . .

The one outside . . . the one with the so-well-concealed fears . . . concealed to all but the djinn . . . nothing escapes the djinn. . . .

Soundless laughter thundered in Kirst's brain. But he was no longer terrified by it. Fear was becoming a hard tune to play—the more he produced, the more the imp wanted. He was distantly conscious of having not much more to give.

Smoke and mist. The smell of death on the cold morning air. Scorched earth and jagged tree stumps. Bits of shrapnel covered with gleaming dew. Craters rimmed with mounds of dirt and exposed roots. Shattered weapons and human limbs. Crushed and pulpy corpses stiffened into grotesque statues of flesh and bone. Rivers of blood spilling off rocks, down the sloping meadow, seeping into the ground . . .

French soil. Foreign ground. American soldiers splayed about the hill like clumps of seaweed on a beach. Dozens more blown to bits and scattered over the ground . . .

Window Hill.

Gilman's boots squashing in the crimson mud, stopping to examine the men of his battalion, the men he had fought with, joked with, counseled in their fear and helped through the war . . .

Gilman moves on, drawn to the faces but afraid to look because, in the end, each face he looks into is his own. . . .

Toeing over a corpse, the head—severed between the jaws—rolls off and stops against a rock. Teeth bite into burnt earth. Shock-filled eyes stare back at Gilman. His own eyes, his own bulging blue eyes stare back at him asking why—*why?*

Gilman sat bolt upright on his cot, his head pounding, blood pumping furiously in his veins, sweat pouring off his brow. He blinked away salty wetness.

Where are the men? Where are the men?

He could feel the boots on his feet and the cold ground beneath them, then gradually the past began to fade and he saw where he was. . . .

The darkened room in the commandant's private quarters, Blackbone Military Detention Facility. His own tiny room with its single window overlooking the prison compound, the lone cot and heavy oak schoolteacher's desk, the wardrobe with the full-length mirror, the yellow-enameled dresser, the portraits of President Roosevelt and Ike, the dresser caddy with his tie clasps and collar stays . . .

Gilman shut his eyes and tried to hold on to the dream, trying to remember those other Gilmans staring back at him on the French battlefield at Window Hill.

The dream was nearly all he had brought back from France. Certainly he had left the better part of himself on that bloody, mist-shrouded hill.

Gilman fell against the blankets, rubbing his face in the wool. Then he rolled off the cot and stood up, his body clammy with sweat. The floor was cold. He sat down and lit a cigarette. He tried to shake the dream by thinking of something else and ended up trading one trauma for another.

Nona.

They were supposed to have married when the war ended. But when he returned from France, his spirit broken, she was there to meet him in New York at Grand Central Station. Standing on the platform as he came off the train, she told him it was foolish to wait any longer. Now that he was home, they should marry immediately.

She gave him an aching, sympathetic smile and told him she shared his pain. He had written to her about Window Hill, had poured it all out to her in his letters. And her solution was written in that smile: "I'm going to reward you for failing, for being weak and proving you are only human. I am going to marry you for it."

He refused. She played the wounded woman. He told her she was posturing. He said that he was no longer the man she had loved, that he would never be that man again. She couldn't believe he had changed so much: he still looked the same, just a bit tired and gaunt. He told her the war had scarred him forever, but the scars were inside, not worn on his chest where she could be proud of them.

She followed him out of the station, protesting that she wanted to be helpful and understanding. He rejected her help and told her that by destroying their romance, he was doing her a service. He didn't deserve happiness. He had sacrificed it on the battlefield.

Gilman tamped out his cigarette. He had written Nona off, as he had written off his burgeoning military career. Now, at Blackbone, he was just marking time, like the Germans in his keep. And when the war ended, and the Germans went home to their wives and children and girl-

155

friends and what remained of their country, what would he do? What was left for David Gilman?

He moved to the window and stared out at the camp. Lights swept the fence. Nothing moved. Maybe he should have tried with Nona but, when she got to him, he was in no mood to heal: he hadn't suffered enough. But now he knew that it never would have worked. She might have come to understand the problem, but she would never have stopped believing that she was the solution.

Gilman climbed back into his cot and wished for only one thing before his eyes closed and he returned to sleep —that he could do it all over again, but this time do it right—*his* way. From now on, he decided, he would listen to the little voice in his head and, when it conflicted with orders, heed it.

Chapter 14

Loring Holloway held her window seat in the club car through breakfast and beyond. She drank a fourth cup of coffee and sat staring out the window at the bleak, overcast cornfields of South Dakota. She had never been this far west and found the scenery fascinating. It was the only thing about this train ride that kept her from thinking of what lay ahead. She wasn't sleeping very well, her dreams filled with visions of Babylon, Ur-Tawaq, Korbazrah, and drowning Iraqi workers. . . .

Across from her, a grim fat lady in a black cotton dress tippled brandy and dabbed at the sweat on her chest with a silk handkerchief. She had good reason to drink, having barraged Loring with her story immediately upon sitting down: she had two sons in the war, her daughter had eloped with a Mexican, and her husband had recently died of emphysema. She was en route to California to live with her spinster sister, whom she hated, and was dreading it. Loring had offered sympathy but had tuned out when the woman declined breakfast and ordered her second brandy.

Loring fingered the silver talisman Yazir had given her. It was still on her chest, draped from the chain around her neck. Whenever she got to thinking about how to deal with the djinn, her hand automatically checked to see that it was still in place. She hardly knew why. Upon leaving Grand Central, she had immediately dug back through her notes and found that, among the talismen presumed effective against djinn, the pentagon shape was the least commonly mentioned. It seemed to be part of a later mythology, more effective against satanic demons than Middle Eastern ones. But then, as both she and Yazir had pointed out to each other, all these things had their roots. The demons themselves, the tricks and games, the folklore, the weapons—all had their ancient antecedents. Just because the pentagon shape was not considered an official djinn deterrent did not mean that it wouldn't work.

And so it must be with all the other things, Loring thought. Iron, steel, salt, silver—the list was endless. She would have to try everything and see what worked, what might elicit a response from Kirst. And if nothing happened? If Kirst had no reaction whatsoever? Could she risk believing without proof that the djinn was gone? Or might it have grown stronger and cleverer during all its years of enforced captivity?

A lump of anxiety rose in her throat. She glanced at her hand and discovered it was shaking. Not nerves—too much coffee. She got up and left the fat lady with a few words of encouragement, then she made her way back to her car.

Tomorrow, she told herself, tomorrow you'll be there. Tomorrow you'll know. And by then, if the djinn was operating at capacity, everyone at Blackbone would know something was up. They might—and this she found heartening—they might be ready to listen.

"Frisco's not really my kind of town," said Corporal Chilton. "What about L.A.? I've got girls down there. My mother lives there."

"L.A. then. What've you got?" Hopkins closed the door to his office. Chilton sat down, held up a sheet of neat typescript, and read it like a proclamation.

"The skinny on Major David Gilman, formerly Lieutenant Colonel David Gilman, commanding Second Battalion of the Third Division under Major General Benton Malkin, Seventh Army, under Lieutenant General Alexander M. Patch. On fifteen August 1944, Lieutenant Colonel Gilman's unit landed on the Mediterranean coast of France as part of the southern invasion force following D-day, assigned to keep the Germans in the south from linking up with units in the north and opposing the Normandy operation. They set up a line of communications along the Mediterranean ports, then swept north and in mid-September hooked up with the Allies near Dijon. They were involved in several skirmishes and distinguished themselves in a manner befitting—"

"Stop glamorizing," said Hopkins.

"Thought you'd want the flavor, sir."

"Never mind the flavor. Get to the meat."

"Yes, sir. Basically, it happened like this . . ." From here on Chilton stopped reading and used his report only as a referral. "Somewhere in mid- to northern France, Gilman was informed by General Malkin that a captured German officer had revealed the following piece of intelligence—a certain area designated Window Hill had recently been evacuated by the Germans. Malkin wanted Gilman to move his battalion up and take the hill. Gilman was reluctant to do it, pleading for time to soften up the area with artillery then send in a recon patrol. Malkin was impatient and ordered him to go in at once.

Gilman protested that they were relying on the word of a prisoner, and he didn't want to risk casualties without a chance to reconnoiter."

Hopkins sat back, seeing the confrontation in his mind's eye: pushy light colonel versus tough general. He had heard about Malkin—no one to trifle with. He fished out his cigarettes, offered one to Chilton. "Go on," he said.

"Malkin accused Gilman of disobeying a direct order and relieved him of command. The exec was placed in charge and ordered to take the men in. Malkin chewed Gilman out and threatened to court-martial him. Second Battalion took off for Window Hill."

Hopkins chuckled, enjoying this.

"Then the report came in. Gilman's unit had been suckered into a trap. The entire battalion was annihilated. No survivors."

"Wow," said Hopkins.

Chilton went on spinning his tale, oblivious to the weight of the events he was recounting. "Gilman became an embarrassment. General Malkin refused to admit he was at fault for not questioning the word of a prisoner more closely. He met privately with Gilman—notes were taken by the general's aide and later transcribed by a clerk—"

"I was wondering how you got all this," Hopkins snorted. "The network of brother clerks."

"Yes, sir." Chilton flashed a smile, then continued. "Anyway, the general told Gilman that he would deny ever having discussed softening up Window Hill, so there would be no point in Gilman relying on that to back up his own actions. It came down to this—no one would believe a light colonel over a two-star general. Then he said he would forget about the court-martial if Gilman would quietly allow himself to be transferred out of Europe." Chilton paused, grinning.

"What happened?"

"Gilman punched him out."

"He punched a general?"

"He fucking well did, sir. Flattened him."

Hopkins whistled.

"Malkin threw Gilman into detention for a week. But he must have realized he could never court-martial Gilman for the punch without the other crap coming out. So he busted him a grade, shipped him home, and had him transferred here."

Chilton pushed the report across to Hopkins with a flourish that ended in a burnt-hand gesture. Hopkins studied it a long moment, impressed by the crisp typing and even paragraphing. Chilton did great work.

Hopkins unceremoniously tore the report in half, then in half again. He crumpled the pieces and dropped them into his wastebasket. Chilton was stunned.

"Nice work, Corporal," said Hopkins. "Two weeks in L.A., earliest opportunity."

"Thank you, sir."

"On one condition?"

"Sir?"

"If that story gets back to you with some details a little out of joint, don't bother to correct them, get me?"

Chilton didn't quite get him, but he nodded anyway.

"After all," said Hopkins, "losing your command for refusing an order and punching a general in the bargain —that's bad news. Word gets around, former light colonel Gilman could lose whatever friends he's making here."

Chilton was puzzled. "Yes, sir, but . . . it was more the general's fault, don't you think?"

161

Hopkins eyed him coldly. "The way I hear the story, it sounds more like Gilman blew it. It's going to sound that way to you, too, when you come back from L.A."

Chilton stared at him. Finally, he got it.

Hopkins seemed uncommonly smug when he reported to Gilman after the morning roll call. Gilman ignored it and showed him a dispatch. "Got a job suited to your talents, Hopkins. Prepare accommodations for a visitor. Someone from the State Department is en route here to interview the prisoner Kirst. What are you grinning at?"

"Nothing much, sir," said Hopkins. "Just recalling that last night you wouldn't let me put the screws to him, now here comes the State Department."

"I doubt the two things are related, and I hope whoever they're sending is at least marginally more qualified than you."

Hopkins' grin froze.

"Let's just concentrate on the job at hand, okay? State wants to question a captured German submariner, that's all there is to it. So we'll go out of our way to cooperate with this"—he glanced at the cable—"Mr. Holloway."

There were a dozen men in Hut 10 when Gebhard entered. Everybody else was outside, involved in a mass soccer game. The Luftwaffe had challenged the Navy. Gebhard couldn't care less: he was interested neither in soccer nor interservice rivalry. At the moment he was disgusted, angry, and brooding. Spotting Kirst on a sofa, Gebhard walked past him, glared at him, then took a table less than five yards away.

Gebhard picked up a worn deck of cards and began shuffling. He looked around. The others were occupied in relaxing. There was a sullenness among them that Gebhard attributed to last night's events and Kirst's presence in the room. Nobody liked him now, Gebhard realized with satisfaction. Even his own wild suspicions no longer mattered: he had something else to hate Kirst for.

Directly or indirectly, in Gebhard's view, Kirst was responsible for the shower hut being closed. For that, Gebhard could never forgive him. Gebhard loved his showers.

Dortmunder and Hoffman finished a game of gin rummy and leaned back, studying Kirst. "How's your periscope, Kirst?" said Hoffman. Dortmunder spat a laugh. Kirst didn't move. Not getting a rise out of him, Hoffman looked around for someone else to needle.

Eckmann walked in, happier than usual, waving a letter from his wife.

Hoffman scooted up to the table, grabbed the cards, expertly shuffled and cut, winked at Dortmunder, then said, "Eckmann, what's that you've got there?"

Eckmann came over, proudly displaying the letter. "From Frieda," he said.

"Is that so?" said Hoffman, hardly surprised. Eckmann got them at the rate of one or two a month. His wife was a devoted pen pal. "Come and sit down, Eckmann."

Eckmann drew up a chair and held the letter in his outstretched hands. The envelope was slit. He had already read it. Probably ten times, Hoffman decided.

"Eckmann," he said, "you depend too much on those letters. You don't play soccer, you don't play cards, you don't joke—your whole life is wrapped up in Frieda."

Dortmunder snickered. He leaned toward Eckmann. "Come and sit on my lap, little Frieda!" He snatched Eckmann's letter and placed it on his thigh. Eckmann tried to grab it back, but Dortmunder scooted his chair aside.

"Easy, Eckmann," said Hoffman. "Dortmunder just wants to hold it. You know, he hasn't held anything softer than Bruckner's dog since he arrived here."

Eckmann hesitated, frowning. They were always playing games, these two. Ordinarily he could take it, but he hated it when they picked on his devotion to Frieda.

Dortmunder rubbed the letter across his crotch. "Ah, my gorgeous Frieda," he murmured. "Your breasts white as twin alps, your legs like alabaster columns, your cunt —" He slapped the letter up to his nose and sniffed.

Eckmann jumped up. Hoffman got between them. Dortmunder opened the letter and shoved his fingers into the envelope, stirring them about with a lascivious grin. Eckmann shook with anger at the way his property was being defiled.

Dortmunder drew something out of the envelope and held it pressed between his thumb and forefinger. It was a single curly hair. "God in heaven," he said. "She has sent him a hair from her pussy!"

"Damn you!" Eckmann lunged at Dortmunder. Hoffman slammed him backward. Eckmann collapsed into his chair.

Fascinated, Dortmunder waved the hair before his eyes. "Brunette. . . . Eckmann, I thought your Frieda was a blonde."

"Go disembowel yourself."

Dortmunder brought the hair to his nose, swayed in ecstasy, then sniffed loudly. He grimaced and dropped the hair with a cry of disgust.

"What's the matter?" said Hoffman.

Dortmunder wrinkled his nose. "Christ, that's not from her pussy at all. It's from her asshole."

Eckmann kicked his chair back then grabbed the table and overturned it. Cards scattered. He snatched his letter from Dortmunder's lap.

"I'm not finished," Dortmunder said.

"You—you—" Eckmann could hardly get the words out. "My wife is the most beautiful woman on earth! You would be lucky if she lowered herself to look at you—"

"I would be lucky if she lowered herself on this." Dortmunder gripped his crotch. "And that's probably what she's been doing since you've been gone. Face it, Eckmann—you had one day of marriage. Letters are easy to write. Keeping her legs closed is a bit harder."

"He's right," Hoffman agreed. "No woman would put that much on paper unless she had a lot to atone for. She does it to conceal her sins."

Shaken, Eckmann stuffed the letter into his pocket and backed away from them and turned—

To see Kirst staring at him.

He whirled and ran for the door, pursued by laughter.

Through it all, Gebhard had watched Kirst. As soon as Hoffman and Dortmunder started their game, Kirst's face had become a mask. Whatever his response to Eckmann's razzing—if he had a response—he was not letting it show. Now the empty look shifted to Gebhard.

And for just a flash, Gebhard thought he saw an indescribably hideous grin.

The soccer game was raucous and half-assed. Rules were ignored because everybody knew the game was merely a cover for committee meetings, which were always held during mass physical activity in order to foil the MPs. There was no way so many key people could meet at night or in the huts without attracting the sentries' attention.

The committees were everywhere. The food committee was meeting among a cheering section of Luftwaffe officers, discussing how to more equitably divide up the Red Cross parcels due the following week. The health committee was meeting outside the *Krankenhaus*, where the medic, Leutnant Cuno, had set up an emergency field hospital complete with two stretchers and a first-aid table. Behind him, two National Socialist army officers argued with the number two medic, Leutnant Heilbruner, about getting priority care in the event of a flu epidemic. Heilbruner stated flatly that, if that were enforced, he would withhold services.

The escape committee was on the warm-up bench and, like the players, stripped down to shorts, undershirts, and bare feet. The ground was icy cold, so most sat cross-legged or with legs tucked beneath them. There were Steuben, Bruckner and Churchill, and three others.

Steuben and Bruckner applauded as their side thwarted a near goal. In the ensuing brawl, two Navy men were flattened and had to be carried off amid much boisterous laughter.

Steuben nodded to Mueller that he could join them now. Mueller strolled over and squatted down in front of the escape committee. "All right, Mueller," said Steuben, "let's hear your plan."

Mueller nodded toward Blackbone Mountain. "The old mine cave-in near the fence."

"What about it?" said Steuben.

"Look at it."

They all looked. Not much of it was visible, just a depression in the ground surrounded by winter-dried bushes, behind it a bulge in the hill, and above that the fence line.

166

"Digging at night, I believe I can cut through that and get into the main shaft."

"With what?" said Bruckner.

"Tools made from ration tins, homemade shovels, and scoops concealed beneath one of the huts."

"You'd be seen easily."

"I can rig a simple lean-to around those bushes with sticks sunk into the ground, a blanket thrown over them, and a layer of dirt over that. Even in daylight, it will look exactly as it does now. And if it snows—even better."

"How long to do the digging?" Steuben asked.

"Not more than a few days."

Steuben eyed the cave-in skeptically. "Not enough time. As soon as supplies arrive, they're going to move that fence. In any case, I would think the entire shaft collapsed back when they blew up that entrance."

"If that were true," said Mueller, "you would see depressed ground all the way up to the fence and beyond. I'm convinced that no more than the first twenty feet could have sustained damage. We can get through that easily. The important thing is that this shaft goes up into the mountains and lets out on the other side of Blackbone. I've heard the MPs mention a river over there. The miners who used to work here had to have a river to transport ore, which means that this is the back door . . . and the main entrance is on the *river* side. They blew up this end to keep us from using the tunnel, but they wouldn't have bothered with the other side. It *should* still be open." Mueller beamed. "And as for moving the fence, we'll worry about that when those supplies arrive."

"They could have closed the other end," said Steuben. "It could have collapsed. You just don't know."

"Could it hurt to go in and find out?"

167

Steuben hesitated.

"Sir, I'm sure we can get through. We can find the river, wade upstream so we don't leave a trail, find a farmhouse, steal a vehicle and some food—Why are you laughing?"

Steuben forced himself to be serious. "Where will you go?"

"Canada."

"Ah, yes, Canada. One of the Fatherland's staunchest allies, Herr Mueller. Good thinking. Bold, daring—you're a determined adventurer, but unrealistic. You have no maps, no idea of terrain or distance, or whether there are any nearby farms, or whether they have vehicles or food, or whether the river flows north, south, west, or east. . . . This is winter. The big storms are about to hit us. You're in enemy country, planning to escape to another enemy country. Trading one bad situation for another. And all to no purpose. No, Leutnant Mueller, I cannot permit you to endanger your life and the lives of others."

The soccer game erupted in their laps. The ball arrived on a rebound off someone's knee. With it came a frantic pile of players. The escape committee scattered off the bench and re-formed at the goal line. Mueller was incensed. "It is the duty of officers to escape," he told Steuben.

"I know that, Mueller. But there is no point in being utterly foolish. If you wish to present the committee with a more viable plan, we are prepared to hear you. But forget this—it won't work." He turned to the others. "Do I speak for all of us?"

They nodded. Bruckner added, "I hope you realize, Major, that the very reasons you're giving Mueller apply

168

to *any* escape attempt." He looked around the valley and said, "Escape to where?"

Mueller wheeled and departed angrily. The committee broke up. Several of them joined the game as replacements. Bruckner took Churchill for a pee and a drink. Steuben reflected on what Bruckner had said—Of course there was nowhere to go, and the committee would go on rejecting ideas that risked lives. But they couldn't flatly turn down every single escape plan. Some attempts might be worthwhile—even if they failed, they would cause the Americans considerable trouble. Orders were the same for all prisoners everywhere—escape if you can—confuse and confound the enemy. But Mueller was a fanatic for personal reasons, and that made him dangerous.

Steuben saw Hopkins approaching, flanked by MPs and grinning at Steuben's underwear. He called out, "Too bad your men are working up such a glorious sweat. The shower hut is still off limits. I don't suppose Kirst has confessed yet, has he?"

"No."

"That's unfortunate, but I'm sure you wonderful people can endure your precious bodily stench for as long as it takes."

Steuben gave him a cold grin. "Would you care to join us for some soccer? We need a new ball."

One of the MPs snorted. Hopkins acknowledged the barb with a smile. "Use your scrotum. Around here it's not good for much else."

Steuben shrugged and went into the game. Hopkins brushed past Gebhard and walked along the edge of the foul line, a rough furrow in the ground. He watched the Germans chase the ball and threw smiles as he passed men on the sidelines.

Gebhard walked to the shower hut, stared at the padlocked door, and trembled with anger.

Dearest Frieda,
   Your letters are the soul of my life, the warmth of my winter nights. In my solitude, your words are my prayers. In my dreams, you come to me and whisper your love in my ear. I tiptoe to your bed, lie down with you, our bodies barely touching. My hand clasps yours. We gaze at each other, and we both know that nothing has changed. Our marriage is before us— only the wedding is over. Trust in me, my loving Frieda. I shall return.

A near beatific smile creased Eckmann's face as he looked to Schliebert for approval. Schliebert turned away, embarrassed. Eckmann turned to Kirst. "What do you think, Kirst? Shall I make it more poetic?"

Kirst looked up from his bunk and fixed Eckmann with a murky stare. But Eckmann was already back at work, scribbling quickly, whispering to himself as he wrote. Kirst sank back on his bunk, tired. He closed his eyes for a moment. They flew open as Mueller stormed in, banged his empty coffee mug on the table, and moved to the window. He looked out at the back end of the camp, at the cave-in and the fence, and he swore.

"The tunnel is out," he told Eckmann. "Steuben said no. The fool is perfectly content to sit out the rest of the war and force the rest of us to do the same. Someday he will pay for his timidity."

Mueller glanced at Kirst then shifted uneasily. "What are you looking at?" he said sharply. Kirst turned away.

Eckmann put down his pencil and looked out the window with Mueller, who then voiced what Eckmann was thinking. "I'm sorry, Eckmann—it will be a long time before you see your wife."

Mueller straightened, clasped Eckmann's shoulder, gave Kirst a foul look, then walked out. Eckmann sank back against the wall, his letter forgotten, his gaze settling on his wife's photograph.

"Frieda . . ." he said quietly.

Kirst was barely conscious, weakened by the djinn's increased appetite for his emotions, his eyes kept open by his curious tenant. At last, the churning that had been going on inside him all day began to subside, and he was flooded with a peaceful, relaxing warmth. He sensed a new feeling forming in his brain. A feeling of readiness.

Loring Holloway stood on the platform at the tiny station in Ringling, Montana, waiting for the connection to White Sulphur Springs. It was night. A rusted wall thermometer read forty-one degrees, and she was shivering despite her thick coat. Her baggage was on a bench by the station door. She could have chosen to wait inside, but it was no warmer in there: the local handyman responsible for supplying wood was home with a sniffle. No wood for the stove, no heat.

She moved under a conical light and fumbled to fix her makeup. Her hand shook with the cold. Her fingers were numb and, as she struggled to hold it steady, the compact slipped from her grasp and crashed to the platform.

"Damn!" She stooped to pick it up. As she lifted it, pieces of glass fell out. The mirror was broken. She sighed and swore again. What was she going to do with her face half made up? She couldn't board the train looking like a clown.

Remembering the silver talisman around her neck, Loring drew it out on the chain and held it up to catch the light. She stared into it and discovered something she hadn't seen before—an inscription within the pentangle. In Arabic, it translated as, *"In the name of Allah . . ."* That was all.

She frowned. What use was this against a demon who predated Islam? Yazir had meant well, but this little hunk of silver was probably useless as anything other than a substitute compact mirror.

She heard a far-off approaching horn and quickly finished her makeup. By the time the train arrived, she was standing on the edge of the platform with her bags. A conductor helped her aboard for the final leg of her journey. She took a lower berth in a nearly empty car and fell on the bed, pulled up the covers, and waited to drift off to sleep, cold and exhausted.

Silver. Silver talisman. Silver flask.

Korbazrah had trapped the djinn in a five-sided silver flask. Yazir's talisman had five sides and was silver. But the decanter he had given her was round. Her head began to spin with worry and, with a sinking, angry feeling, she realized this would be another near-sleepless night.

The train pulled out of Ringling, picked up speed, and was soon roaring toward White Sulphur Springs.

Chapter 15

Light swept across the crawl space beneath Hut 7 and stopped. Vinge got down on his knees and peered at the huddled white mass caught in the beam of his flashlight. It wasn't moving. And it wasn't black, so it obviously wasn't his wildcat friend. Vinge lowered his sidearm and shivered. The first breeze of the coming storm whipped under his coat and chilled his throbbing back. Borden had changed the dressing twice today, dousing the wounds with iodine. His flesh there was raw and sweating despite the cold. Cosco had asked him again if he wanted off night duty. Again he had refused, but as night had drawn closer, his nervous anticipation had risen. It was fear he was fighting, not anger. That basic fear of animals that had always haunted him. He was determined to get rid of it once and for all by bagging the cat.

But it wasn't a cat he had in his light. He got down on hands and knees and started to crawl forward, wriggling under the hut, the light bouncing off the floorboards as he moved, the light in one hand, gun in the other.

It was past midnight, and the Germans were asleep in Hut 7 as Kirst's lips parted and his cheeks drew back in a distended grin, and the nightform spilled from his mouth and pooled on the floor.

Blackness edged across the room, approaching the

bunk where Bauhopf slept below Eckmann. Curling around the corner post, the nightform drew itself under the bunks, then bled into the shadows beneath Schliebert's bed.

Vinge rose to avoid catching his crotch on a sharp rock embedded in the dirt. His back scraped along the floorboards and he froze at the pain. It shuddered deep into his flesh and he had to force himself to keep from crying out. Tears welled up in his eyes and blurred his vision. He swiveled the light and fixed the white furry mass in its beam. He pulled up his right leg and, keeping his body against the cold ground, continued toward his goal.

He stopped, hearing something above.

Eckmann stirred in his sleep, woke drowsily, and turned. He looked up at the ceiling and listened. Nothing. . . . Wait. . . . Something. A rustling sound, as of sheets moving together. A muffled grunting. Eckmann snorted to himself. Just Bauhopf jacking off. He rolled over and faced the wall, staring at Frieda's picture.

Vinge pulled himself across the last two yards and drew up even with the white animal. It was dead. He knew it before he got there. He could smell it. Holding the light steady, he reached out with the gun and prodded it. It was stiff, unmoving. He nosed the gun barrel beneath it and, with a quick jerk of his wrist, flipped it over.

It was a dead white rabbit. The ears were back, eyes wide, snout pulled back in a terrified grimace.

Vinge stared at it. What the hell had killed it? He prodded the body again, turning it around, looking for blood. There was none. No wounds of any kind, no teeth marks.

Frowning, caught up in the puzzle before him, he almost didn't hear the sounds coming from above. They were faint and indistinct.

Uhm . . . uh . . . oh . . . ah . . .

What the hell is that idiot doing? Eckmann rolled back again and peered over the edge of his bunk at Bauhopf below, whose face was concealed in shadow.

"Hey," Eckmann whispered. "Bauhopf."

There was no reply, then:

Oh . . . uh . . . ah . . .

And the brief, muffled chuckle of a woman.

It wasn't coming from Bauhopf's bed.

Vinge heard only the grunts, then the wind picked up and carried the sound away before it could reach his ears. He turned back to the rabbit. Pointless to haul it out of here, he decided. What would he do with it? Show it to Gilman? Hopkins? What for? They would only want to know how it got into the compound. They would institute a search for a break in the fence, and then he might have to tell them about the black cat, and he didn't want to do that. He wanted to find it himself, kill it. . . .

Vinge turned away and left the rabbit, crawling out as he had come in, pausing to listen once again as the wind shifted and he thought he heard a woman laugh.

Eckmann rolled upright and listened again. He scanned the darkened room and made out sleeping shapes in the beds. No one moved. Every bed was filled.

A woman? Must have been dreaming.

He dropped to his pillow and tried to get back to sleep.

Oh . . . ah . . . oh . . . ah . . .

The sound grew, became insistent. Then another voice —lower, throatier, but distinctly feminine.

Uhmmm . . . oooh . . . jaaa . . .

German! She was German. How did they get a German woman into this camp? Eckmann sat up, eyes narrowing suspiciously. A prank. One of his roommates was playing a joke. Again his eyes swept the room, this time stopping at the top bunk directly opposite his own, catching slight movement under the covers. Schliebert making love to himself, playing five against one, hand-to-cock combat, and fantasizing that he had a woman under there—

Oooh . . . jaaa . . . ungh!

The covers moved rapidly. They rose up and down with ferocious speed then slowed, collapsed . . . then came up again. Moaning and grunting overlapped and became indistinguishable—

Uh . . . oh . . . oooh . . . ungh . . . jaaa . . . uhmmm . . .

Two voices.

Eckmann stared and imagined Schliebert faking two people making love, as the covers jerked from side to side and up and down. Schliebert waving his arms beneath the covers, moaning and grunting in separate voices—why play such a stupid game?

Obviously it's for your benefit, he told himself. A prank for the sensitive Leutnant Eckmann. Seeing no one else awake or even stirring, despite the noise, Eckmann was sure of it. They were all in on it.

Oh . . . aaahhh . . . Frieda . . .

Eckmann's eyes widened. Schliebert's covers moved vigorously.

Frieda . . . oooohh . . . Frieda . . .

176

Eckmann swung his legs over the side and dropped to the floor.

Frieda . . . mein Liebchen . . . *ungh!*

A woman groaned in ecstasy. Schliebert faking, Eckmann was sure. No, not so sure. That voice! He remembered that groan from his wedding night. Common sense told him no, this is a joke, don't be taken in, but that voice!

He couldn't stand it any longer. He crossed to the other bunk in a bound. He jumped onto the lower bed and snatched Schliebert's covers off, expecting to find Schliebert performing some gross parody of the sex act—

Her eyes flashed at him madly, her tongue shot out and licked the air in a rapid quiver. She threw out her chest and laughed, and Eckmann flew back in shock. He lost his footing on the bed below, sprawled on the floor, and looked up. She was naked and sitting on Schliebert's hips, grinding herself over him, lost in sexual abandon. She was blond and beautiful. She was his own darling Frieda!

He sprang up in rage and yanked the covers off. They came tumbling down—the man, the woman, and the mattress—all crashed to the floor. He whirled and stared at Frieda sitting up in the center of the room, unhurt but naked, her breasts flushed with excitement, skin glistening with sweat. She leered at Eckmann. Her laughter filled the room, mocking him, burning into his heart.

Schliebert gazed up at Eckmann in surprise. Others in the room woke. Eckmann turned from his beautiful but grossly unfaithful Frieda and bellowed as he grabbed Schliebert's neck and wrung it, and banged his head repeatedly on the floor. Schliebert thrashed and choked and coughed for help, but Eckmann was too strong, superhumanly strong, growing even stronger as rage took over his entire body and made it a weapon of vengeance.

Her laughter rang in his ears. Schliebert felt his hands clutching something firm but squashy and squeezing and throwing it against the floor, and he saw it as his Frieda's thigh, his Frieda's beautiful, soft, unfaithful thigh, and he smashed harder and harder, as frustration exploded inside him.

Others tumbled out of bed and grabbed Eckmann. Ignoring their clawing hands, he continued bashing the life out of Schliebert, who struggled weakly then lapsed into unconsciousness. Blackness rose up Eckmann's back, beneath his undershirt, closing around his neck and drawing energy from his seething brain—life-giving, power-giving energy—energy the djinn needed to grow and make itself stronger—power from Eckmann, from Schliebert's terror, from the others' confusion—power that would enable the djinn to go out and get more power—

Power from death.

Power from terror.

Energy, sweet bubbling electricity of the mind, the human mind that the djinn knew so well. Fear for power. Fear and frustration, the human equation, the formula for power.

Bauhopf and Mueller struggled with Eckmann but couldn't break his grip on Schliebert's neck. Eckmann's sobs and groans filled the tiny room, and only the dead could have slept through it.

Kirst did.

And in the commotion, unseen by the men dragging Eckmann off Schliebert, the nightform oozed back toward Kirst and was swallowed up between his parted lips.

Eckmann cried out then, throwing his hands to his head and realizing in one blinding instant what he had just done. As they held him down, struggling and kicking, he looked around wildly.

"Frieda! He had Frieda! He was fucking her! He was fucking my Frieda!"

His eyes shot in all directions, searching for his Frieda's sweat-streaked body. She was gone. The door slammed open and Sergeant Vinge crashed into the room, brandishing his .45.

Gilman ran off without a coat. The duty officer who had rousted him now double-timed behind him. Gilman charged through the gate and was out of breath as he stumbled into Hut 7. Hopkins was waiting for him, calm and cool but giving off an aura of impending vengeance. Everybody from Eckmann's room was lined up in the corridor for interrogation, guarded by a squad of nervous MPs. Eckmann was at the far end of the hut, handcuffed under guard, sobbing uncontrollably.

Gilman glanced at the Germans. They were pale and frightened, eyeing him expectantly, worried. All except—

Kirst again.

He was slumped against the wall, hands stuffed deep in his pockets, lost in a world of his own, apart from the others. Gilman stared at him.

"In here, sir," Hopkins said in his ear. Gilman turned. Hopkins toed the door open with his foot.

Gilman edged past Vinge, who was just inside, and stared down at the body covered with a blanket. "Who is it?" he asked.

"The prisoner Schliebert, sir," said Hopkins, barely concealing an excited gloat.

Gilman swore under his breath. "Go wake Steuben."

"Don't you think I'd better interrogate the—"

"That's an order!"

179

Hopkins grabbed an MP and hustled out the door. Gilman lifted the blanket.

Schliebert's bulging eyes stared up at him. His tongue was a black knob nearly bitten off between clenched teeth. There was a pool of blood beneath his head. Gilman glanced at the wound. The skin was broken. He could see cracked bone.

"He *is* dead, Herr Major."

Gilman stiffened and looked around. A German officer was sitting on a bunk, hands clasped between his open knees. He had a shiny bald head with a wispy fringe from ear to ear around the back. "I am Leutnant Cuno," he said. "The medic. There was nothing I could do."

Gilman glanced at Vinge. The sergeant was as pale as the Germans in the corridor. As he looked down at Schliebert, something worked behind his eyes. Fear? Anger? Gilman wasn't sure, but he sensed something was going on among the MPs. It wasn't just Vinge. The men in the doorway were giving him grim, sidelong looks, as if they knew he wouldn't handle this right.

"What happened?" Gilman asked Vinge.

Vinge quickly explained about hearing the excitement, bursting in, discovering the others restraining Eckmann, who was raving, and finding Schliebert dead on the floor.

Gilman turned to the medic. "Cuno, I suggest you get back to the *Krankenhaus.*"

"Certainly, Herr Major." Cuno stood up and walked to the door. He paused. "What shall we do about Eckmann? He's sick, you know."

Gilman felt all eyes on him. "We'll see," he said.

Solitary was a small hut separated from the rest. There were eight cells lined up four and four opposite each other with a narrow corridor between them. The cells each had a single barred window, a cot, blankets, and a thick door with a tiny barred window in it. The only light was in the corridor so, under the sentry's wavering flash beam, Gilman had Eckmann placed in one of the cells with a round-the-clock guard. There were no other prisoners in solitary at that moment. Gilman was not inclined to use it for any but the most incorrigible offenders. But in Eckmann's case, it was a necessity for mutual protection. He didn't want the Germans taking matters into their own hands. Nor did he want Eckmann outside the compound until he determined what was wrong with him, if anything.

Gilman questioned him about the killing. He didn't remember it. He could only whimper repeatedly that Schliebert had been making love to his wife.

Major Borden arrived and, at Gilman's request, injected Eckmann with a sedative. While waiting for him to fall asleep, Gilman explained the events to Borden and asked for his offhand opinion.

Borden lit a cigarette, drew on it deeply, and said, "Pent-up frustration, war experiences he couldn't subconsciously justify—God knows. Could be anything. Just went crackers, huh? Well, I know he was preoccupied about his wife back home, always mailing letters and bugging us for the replies. I examined him a couple of times. The German medics claimed he was suffering depression, but I wouldn't say he ever exhibited any violent tendencies. The wife was all he talked about. You know— glowing. The most fantastic creature on the face of the earth—that sort of thing. Sensitive fellow, not really suited for prison life."

"Who is?" said Gilman.

"Some take to it better than others." Borden chuckled. "Don't happen to care for it myself." He coughed, and it turned into a deep smoker's hack. Recovering, he added, "Eckmann has some idealistic attitudes about fidelity, but I wouldn't call that abnormal."

"It is if it leads to murder," Gilman said. "What about claiming that Schliebert was banging his wife?"

"Paranoid delusion. Don't know what would bring that on, but then I'm not a psychiatrist. Maybe we ought to send for one." He hesitated. "I'll tell you, though—if I had sensed any homicidal tendencies—in him or anyone else—I would have drawn it to someone's attention."

"Okay," said Gilman. "Let's see how he is in the morning."

Hopkins was waiting outside with Steuben, who demanded to see Eckmann. Gilman refused. "He's been sedated. You can't help him anyway, Major. Everyone else in that room saw him crack Schliebert's head open. Either it's murder, or he's nuts."

"How will you handle this?"

"We'll conduct an investigation—psychiatric and otherwise—hold a hearing. If Eckmann is found guilty, he'll be punished. If insane, he'll undergo treatment."

Hopkins rolled his eyes, dissatisfied. Steuben stared at the solitary hut, and at the sentry posted just inside the door. "What's going on here?" he said.

A silence passed among them. Gilman and Hopkins both knew what Steuben meant. A series of bizarre events, particularly last night's "attack" on Vinge in the shower hut, and now tonight—a murder. Steuben found himself thinking of that and of all the other oddities he could trace back to . . . the arrival of Kirst.

Friction between Kirst and Gebhard. Gebhard's assertion that Kirst was a spy. Kirst running from the shower hut the other day, exposing himself to the camp. Kirst being removed for questioning. Kirst reciting details of submarine life by rote. Kirst's "blackout" at dinner. Kirst in Hut 7. Kirst in the same room with Eckmann. Eckmann murdering Schliebert . . .

Steuben quivered as a nervous chill shot up his back. Kirst. Could Gebhard be right? But how could Kirst have induced Eckmann to . . . ?

Gilman too had flashes of Kirst in his mind. Kirst's elusive image on Loats' photographic plates. Kalmus' story about Strann on the train. Kirst last night, accused by Vinge—and tonight in the corridor of Hut 7, the only one who hadn't looked frightened to death.

"What the hell are we standing here for?" growled Hopkins. "We ought to be questioning those bastards, one by one."

"Not tonight," Gilman said. "Major Steuben, I would suggest that you post a sentry in that room in Hut Seven."

"I was just thinking that myself."

"Do it."

Steuben turned and hiked back to the huts. Gilman imagined that he might do more than that—roust Eckmann's roommates and put them through a kangaroo court. That might not be bad, if it got closer to the truth.

"The whole thing stinks," Hopkins said as he hiked out of the compound beside Gilman. "They always stick together, never snitch on each other. So why were they so quick to point the finger at Eckmann?"

"They're edgy. Don't forget last night. We closed the shower hut. That didn't make them too happy."

"That wouldn't stop them. Monkey business is their only business, Major. I'm telling you, they're up to something. Maybe Eckmann didn't do it, or maybe he wasn't alone. Maybe they all did it and it's leading up to some kind of escape attempt, or a riot or—"

"What the hell are you talking about?" Gilman snapped. "They killed one of their own men and made it look like Eckmann went insane? Does that make sense? I should put *you* in a rubber room."

Hopkins' reply caught in his throat.

"Why don't you quit imagining conspiracies, Hopkins, and do something useful. Make out reports to the International Red Cross, the Judge Advocate General's Office, the Criminal Investigation Division—whoever is appropriate. Check the regulations under what to do in the event of a prison homicide. And make sure every move is right, so nothing backfires. What's important now is to make the prisoners believe we are *doing* something about this, that it's under control. Agreed?"

Hopkins forced himself to nod. "Agreed, sir."

"Then get on it."

Gilman quickened his step as he passed through the gate, anxious to get away from Hopkins. He glanced up at the sky and, even in the blackness, he saw thick clouds stirring above.

Hopkins watched Gilman slam back indoors.

Sonofa-fucking-bitch. You want to go by the book? Okay. But when it comes to a test of wills, asshole, I wrote the book.

Von Lechterhoeven sat on a rickety chair in the doorway of Room 2, Hut 7. The lights were out but, in the gloom, he kept a wary eye on the bunks. Steuben had posted him to a four-hour shift that would run until 0500. Bauhopf had left the room, taking von Lechterhoeven's bunk down the hall. He had begged out, claiming he couldn't sleep in a room where a man had

184

died. The others weren't too happy about it, either. They were lying awake, staring at the ceiling, glancing now and then at each other.

Gebhard stared at Kirst, hating him now more than ever. Kirst was asleep, oblivious, as if he didn't know or care what went on around him. Gebhard believed Kirst was responsible. Somehow he had engineered Eckmann's eruption. He was a spy, and a clever one. Always watching everybody. Well, he hadn't been careful enough. During the mad ruckus when the others were pulling Eckmann off Schliebert, Gebhard had turned to watch Kirst and had found him lying barely awake on his bunk, detached, aloof, indifferent.

How could anyone remain indifferent while a murder was being committed?

Easy, if he had caused it.

Gebhard did not know how, and he felt powerless in the face of his enemy's ability to manipulate in secret. He was conscious of the way others were regarding Kirst now—increased suspicion, wariness. Tomorrow there would be talk, and Gebhard wouldn't hesitate to throw in his two pfennigs'.

Mueller curled up in his bunk and thought about the killing. He was convinced that this camp would be a happy farm before New Year's, and that he was right in wanting to escape. He thought of the mine shaft, and the long dark tunnel he would have to travel to reach freedom. He didn't like tunnels. He had been lost in one once when he was a boy. Trapped without food or water for more than five hours, and ever since he had trouble dealing with long dark hallways, bunkers, crawl spaces.

But he would go through fire to escape this camp. He

would go into the bowels of Blackbone Mountain and find the other side, find the river, find freedom. . . .

If Kirst and Eckmann didn't fuck it up for him.

Bruckner had a small room of his own across from Steuben's. He lay in the dark on his bunk, Churchill curled up at his feet, convinced something was very wrong at Blackbone. It wasn't just Eckmann and Kirst and all the little things, it was all of that adding up to something big. And deep in his heart, he knew what it was. The Americans were behind it all.

Churchill woke with a start and looked around.

Do dogs dream? Bruckner wondered. Churchill edged up the bunk and found a warm spot between Bruckner's body and the wall. Ordinarily, Bruckner would boot him off but tonight they both wanted the company.

Night drew a shroud of thunderheads over Blackbone Mountain. The djinn pulsed inside Kirst with renewed energy and power, raw power, and hungered for more.

Part Three ═══════

As Loring stepped off the train, the stark winter chill bit through her clothing. The morning sky was dark and threatening, yet there was no smell of rain in the air. A sign identified WHITE SULPHUR SPRINGS, POP. 984, as the seat of Meagher County. The town looked as if it hadn't yet emerged from the nineteenth century. The old buildings were dwarfed by spectacular mountain scenery. Loring guessed the visibility at fifteen miles.

She saw a jeep parked beside the platform with an MP behind the wheel finishing a smoke and watching her, trying to appear only casually interested. The porter appeared on the steps behind her and handed down her luggage. Loring tipped him. He nodded politely and drew back aboard the train, which almost immediately sounded its horn and started up again. Loring looked around—she was the only passenger getting off.

She pushed her bags together and glanced at the jeep again. The MP was staring at her curiously. She crooked a finger at him. He jumped out of the jeep and hurried over, his expression shifting between a helpful smile and confusion.

"Are you here to pick up someone from the State Department?" Loring asked him.

"Uh . . . yes, ma'am. Fellow named Holloway."

She showed him her papers. "Surprise, surprise," she said.

The ride back to the camp was fifty miles over partly paved backroad that Army engineers had graded when the camp was installed. No one had worked on it since, so it was sunken, potholed, and overgrown with weeds. The jeep bounced so badly Loring thought her teeth would fall out. The MP, Faris, drove like he'd been born in these hills. He pointed out the sights—a creek here, a patch of woods there, a slope with near-dead bushes which he claimed bore incredible flowers in the spring.

"We sure had some excitement last night," said Faris. "One of our POWs went off his cork and killed somebody."

Loring forgot her rattling teeth for a moment as fear cut through her and made her think fleetingly of jumping out of the jeep and running back to the station.

"What do you mean, killed somebody?" she said. "Killed a guard?"

"No, ma'am. Another prisoner."

Loring caught herself leaping to conclusions, sure that one of the two had to be Kirst, hoping it was the dead one.

"First murder we've had since the camp opened," Faris was saying. "I sure don't know what it is. Maybe the Germans are getting wire-happy. Nobody likes it much in the winter. The nights are a pisser." He made a face.

They hit a bump and the jeep almost flipped. Faris made some quick maneuvers, spinning the wheel and thrashing the gears in sequence, and they were all right again. But Loring wished she had forgone breakfast.

190

They came around the loop and over the hills. The prison camp sprawled before them in a long valley beneath Blackbone Mountain. Loring studied the huts clustered inside the fence, the Germans on the slope doing calisthenics in their underwear.

Faris grinned. "Sorry, ma'am. Things are kind of free and easy here. Haven't got no women, and the krauts ain't got no shame."

Faris drove up to headquarters, shut off the engine, then jumped out and ran around to help Loring down. A squad of MPs double-timed past, led by a squad leader singing in a deep southern drawl:

> *"Sergeant Baker's outta luck—honey, honey;*
> *Sergeant Baker's outta luck—babe, babe.*
> *Sergeant Baker's outta luck;*
> *He found a girl he couldn't fuck!*
> *Honey, oh, baby mine."*

On the last phrase, the squad leader's eyes discovered Loring. His mouth fell open as he steamed past. "Awright!" he yelled. "Eyes front! Column right, march!" He took them around a hut and, when they were gone, Loring heard ringing laughter. She smiled at Faris.

"Surprise, surprise," she said again and followed him into headquarters.

Faris restrained a grin as Gilman stared at Loring. "This is Miss Loring Holloway of the State Department, sir. Picked her up at White Sulphur Springs as ordered, sir. Hope the Major is happy, sir."

"Dismissed, Faris."

"Yes, sir!" Faris saluted and left.

Gilman shut the door. "Sit down, Miss Holloway."

191

"Thank you." She dropped into a chair in front of his desk. Gilman sat across from her.

"Nobody said to expect a woman."

"Sorry, Major. Do I apologize for not telling you—or for being one?"

"Neither. Pleasure to have you. May I see your papers?"

"Certainly." Loring passed him a manila envelope.

Gilman shook the papers out on his desk, pulled off the clip, and scanned everything quickly. "Seems to be in order," he said, "although your position with State isn't exactly spelled out. Care to elaborate?"

"Is that really necessary? I'm here on a security matter." On the train she had decided that would be the best catchall cover: no one in the military ever questioned security. She couldn't just plunge right in and try to convince this major with the penetrating stare that she was hunting a demon. If he believed her—and looking at him she thought that highly unlikely—he would be alarmed. And being a soldier committed to the chain of command, he would alarm everyone else, setting up a climate of fear that would hamper her efforts and, worst of all, give the djinn a panic to feed on. She had already decided to keep as much of this to herself as possible, to work alone until she could hit on a plan for destroying the creature.

But Gilman was not so easily taken in. The sacred word "security" failed to set off the expected Pavlovian reaction. He leaned on his elbows and fixed Loring with that strong even stare.

"Let me tell you about security at Blackbone," he said. "We're holding just shy of two hundred thirty German officers, all of them potential security risks. We're off the beaten path for good reason—to keep these people isolated. We're so far out in the sticks that even nosy con-

192

gressmen tend to stay away. So, if somebody wanders in wanting a little chat with our prisoners, our curiosity gets aroused. Now . . . these papers indicate I should extend you my unquestioning cooperation, but they are signed by some State Department official who happens to be unknown to me, not by my commanding officer. Are you getting my drift?"

Loring nodded. "Ground rules—I come clean with you and maybe I get to do what I have to do."

"That's it in a nutshell." Gilman extended a pack of cigarettes. Loring refused. He smiled. "You're going to have a strange effect on this camp, Miss Holloway. These men—on both sides of the wire—haven't seen a female in a long time."

"I got that impression."

"They may not handle it very well."

"And how about you, Major? Can you handle it?"

"Why are you here?"

"I have to interrogate Leutnant Rolf Kirst."

"About what?"

"Why don't you sit in on the interview?"

Gilman watched her a moment then shrugged. "Well, there's no rush. Kirst isn't going anywhere and I've had quarters prepared for you. Like to freshen up?"

They stared at each other. Loring worried that Gilman wanted the time to check her credentials; she worried even more that they wouldn't stand up under scrutiny.

"The driver told me what happened here last night," she said, changing the subject. "You must be terribly busy. I really think delay would waste time for both of us, don't you?"

"I've got everything under control."

Loring wanted to slap him. He was so right: he had her boxed in. But there was one more question she felt compelled to ask. "Was Kirst involved in the incident last night?"

She hoped that would shake him. But he looked at her steadily a moment then said, "Did you expect him to be?"

Loring stood up. Gilman rose with her. "What are you?" he asked. "A diplomat? Foreign national? Red Cross?"

She shook her head. "After I've spoken with Kirst, I'll explain everything to you." That seemed a fair enough bargain to her. She could tell it didn't satisfy him, but at least she was admitting there was more to be revealed.

Finally, Gilman smiled graciously and said, "Come on, I'll show you to your quarters."

She followed him out of the building and down to a stairway entrance at the back. There were more MPs outside now and Loring felt at least a dozen pairs of eyes dart over various parts of her body. She quickened her step and trod on Gilman's heels in her haste to stay with him.

Upstairs, he let her into a small room with a cot, a desk with no drawers, a lamp, and a metal clothes rack. "If we'd had some advance warning, we'd have built you a bathroom, Miss Holloway," Gilman said. "As it is, you have an interesting choice. The latrine is outside; I'm sure the men would appreciate the company. But I recommend my bathroom down the hall, marked Commandant's Closet. It has a lovely shower."

"Thank you, Major. I shall always remember your generosity."

"I'll have the bellboy bring up your luggage. Please return to my office when you're ready." He went out and shut the door.

Loring had a fleeting worry that Gilman might inspect

the contents of her luggage. One look at the reading matter she was toting and he would definitely send her packing. She sat on the cot, feeling more alone than on the train. Now she was here, and ultimately she would have to put her trust in Gilman, but he seemed as narrow-minded and unbending as an anteater.

"I think she ought to keep out of sight, sir. Not only will she provoke our men, but she's bound to get the Germans excited." Hopkins had caught Gilman coming down the steps and was following him back to his office.

"I appreciate your concern, Hopkins, but if our men get out of line, they'll answer for it."

"What about the Germans?"

"I don't imagine they'll lose their minds over the presence of a woman, do you? What exactly do you envision —having to beat them back from the fence with whips?"

"I'm just thinking of morale, sir—"

Gilman turned on him. "Did you follow through last night?"

"Yes, sir. I contacted CID. They'll send someone out within a week—"

"A week!"

"They suggest in the meantime we hold Eckmann under observation."

"Shit . . . I don't plan to wait a week to get to the bottom of this." Gilman frowned and looked up at the second floor of headquarters. He fought an uncomfortable feeling that Loring Holloway might actually have something to do with this.

"What about Schliebert's body, sir?" Hopkins asked. "Where is it?"

"Wrapped in sheets over in the supply shed."

"That's cold enough. It'll keep."

195

"Not for a week, sir."

"Have Loats photograph the body, then move it to the dispensary. Borden can perform an autopsy. And get someone to build a pine box."

"Yes, sir." Hopkins nodded upstairs. "Have you found out yet what the lady wants with Kirst?"

"She wants to question him."

"Are you going to let her?"

"Haven't decided yet."

Gilman went inside. Hopkins stood on the steps, sucking in cold air, frowning suspiciously. State would never send a woman to do a job like this. They would send a smooth, faceless cop type, somebody like himself, somebody who knew how to get answers. Somebody forbidding. Miss Holloway looked anything but forbidding.

"He was crazy, that Eckmann. And it got worse the last few weeks. I watched him." Hoffman held forth in the POW mess hall, spearing sausages from a platter and wolfing them down. With his mouth full, he continued, "He would sit on the toilet and read those letters with his hand buried in his pants."

"Exercising his muscle," Dortmunder added.

Not everyone laughed. Schliebert had friends, even if Eckmann had few. They threw Hoffman some filthy looks.

"Ach, Schliebert," Hoffman said, his voice dripping with pity, "the only one innocent in all of this."

"Wonder why he picked Schliebert," Dortmunder mused.

Voices erupted. Arguments about Eckmann, about Schliebert, threats against Hoffman and Dortmunder.

Steuben shot to his feet. *"Achtung!"* he yelled.

Chairs skidded back. Feet scuffled. The men rose, instantly responding to his command. The room fell silent. They stood like statues. Steuben glared at those who had been squabbling.

"We are all here together," he said. "All Germans. Not separated into Luftwaffe, Army, Navy, SS, crazy and sane, masturbators and ascetics! We are men, and we all have weaknesses! Eckmann was hounded by certain men in this room because, in order to fight his loneliness, he retreated into fantasies about his wife! And *we* made him the butt of jokes!" His gaze flicked from table to table. "I am sorry for Schliebert, but I am also sorry for Eckmann. And the men who made those jokes I personally find *dishonorable.*"

There was silence and a few downcast looks. Hoffman stared ahead stiffly, burning with resentment, knowing he was being singled out, his mind searching for a scapegoat outside himself and deciding that this camp was to blame, this prison, this suffocating, demoralizing existence that he hated with all his being. Out—he wanted out! He glanced at Dortmunder, whose eyes were fixed on the sausage platter.

"I should like to see an end to it," Steuben said wearily. "An end to whatever is going on here." His gaze roamed among the men, and they all knew what he meant. All felt the same tense helplessness in the wake of uncontrollable events. "I don't know who or what is responsible," Steuben continued, "but I cannot allow our lives to become chaotic. We must have order and obedience and discipline. Our common welfare must come first. Though we have no weapons with which to enforce our rules, be assured *they will be enforced.* It is my primary goal that we all *survive* and go home in dignity. And those who wish to make it hard for others will be dealt with."

Steuben then asked for a moment of silence in memory of Schliebert. Afterward he said simply, "Sit."

They sat back down and the meal resumed, but conversation dried up.

At another table, Gebhard decided it was time to make his feelings known and to see who shared them. His voice was even and restrained, and intended for his table only, but it carried. "Kirst slept through it last night," he said, then looked around. "Did you know that?"

Eyes flicked at Kirst, who kept eating.

"Isn't that right, Bauhopf?"

Bauhopf nodded.

"Kirst didn't wake until the lights were on and we had Eckmann down on the floor," Gebhard went on. "I find that amazing. I mean, there was such a commotion—Eckmann yelling and banging Schliebert's head on the floor—we all heard it. It woke up everyone in the room. Others in the hut heard it too. And some of the men in Huts Five and Six—"

"I slept through it," Kirst insisted.

"Yes," agreed Gebhard, his eyes flashing. "But how is that possible?"

For a moment that Gebhard deeply relished, every unanswered question in every troubled mind in the room was focused on Kirst, as if he held the secret answer. Kirst never even looked up. He went right on picking at his food, eating mostly bread, fruit, and vegetables, ignoring the heavily spiced sausages. He never answered Gebhard. Interest faded, but now there were whispered conversations at every table, and that was enough to satisfy Gebhard. He wanted them thinking and talking about Kirst. If they thought and talked enough, they might do something, and the hell with Steuben.

Gebhard fixed Kirst with a smug, dark gaze. He knew

Kirst could feel the eyes on him, but Kirst still wouldn't look at him. Someone passed the salt and, when it got to Kirst, he refused to touch it. In fact, he sat back as far as he could and waited for the next man along to grab it.

Gebhard didn't understand that at all. He saw Steuben glaring at him. Gebhard snorted to himself and ignored the silent reproach. The salt came around to him and he held on to it a long moment, studying it, thinking. Then he looked at Kirst, who was helping himself to more applesauce. On impulse, Gebhard leaned across the table and shook salt into Kirst's food. A couple of the men nearby chuckled. Kirst froze in his seat. Gebhard put the salt shaker down and looked up, grinning.

The grin vanished from his lips as he felt the full shock of a malevolent stare from those eyes. In a brief instant, the memory of which was immediately blotted from his mind, Gebhard saw his own death, saw his own body lying naked and cold on a hard floor—

He recoiled in the chair. His hands shot out and gripped the edge of the table, causing the man next to him to spill his water and jump up.

The door banged open. Sergeant Vinge and two other MPs entered the mess hall. Vinge didn't wait for silence. He shouted immediately, "Prisoner Leutnant Rolf Kirst report here at once!"

The room fell silent. Steuben frowned at the man next to Gebhard, who was quietly swearing and mopping water off his trousers. Then Steuben translated the order.

Kirst stood up uncertainly. The MPs led him out and the door banged shut after them.

Gebhard stared at the empty chair, conscious that something had happened before Kirst had left but he couldn't recall what. He looked at his hands and discovered they were shaking. He felt curiously drained. A nag-

199

ging warning worked in the back of his mind. Kirst, they had taken Kirst out. Why? Because Kirst was indeed a spy and was being removed to make his report.

He looked at Steuben, who glared at him and threw down his fork.

The sentry removed the padlock and chains. Kirst stood before the opening gate, the imp filling him with strange sensations of freedom, release, and soaring anticipation. The sergeant prodded him up the hill. Kirst's awareness faded as the gate closed behind him, and the djinn took complete control.

Laughter roared in his head but Kirst was unaware. Blackness rebounded against the walls of his skull and tore through the intricate fabric of his brain. Joy leaped into his eyes and fastened them on the prey. Men. Men outside the prison, outside the cursed five walls. Here there were hosts for the djinn, from which the nightform could seek out fresh power, power from fear, energy from a new host, which it would soon need since this one would shortly be depleted. Already there was not enough will left in the body to generate fear. This host had become little more than a shell, a walking dead man, a desiccated spirit providing only one necessity, a hiding place for the nightform. But as a source of energy, it was drained. It could no longer fight. And if it couldn't fight, it couldn't fear. And from fear came the power.

But here on the outside there were men who had yet to feel the power of the djinn. If it could find the right host, someone with enough hidden fear to be mined . . . A new host! The djinn writhed in paroxysms of delight. Of course, it wasn't finished with the men inside the five walls, but to find a host who could move in and out freely would give it two feeding grounds, and being on the outside meant the possibility of growing even stronger and being able to leave and travel into the world again. Men! It sensed that men had multiplied in the eons in which it had been imprisoned. The djinn had listened to conversations going on around Kirst and had heard stories of large cities, huge cities, teeming with thousands and thousands of fear-racked souls. Tales of war and terror and natural catastrophes—the foundations on which the djinn could feed and build its power.

The djinn drew up inside Kirst's head, into a tight black ball soaking in his mind, calculating its rate of growth over the last few days, realizing with surprise and delight how much it had progressed from the puny, weak little thing in the bottle. All those men inside the five walls, with fear now the one emotion that held them together, not realizing that fear was the food itself—ripe, ready to be harvested like so much wheat. Never had the djinn known such an easy time of it—and the irony that men, soldiers, warriors would band together in their fear, thinking that gave them strength and determination to fight whatever was frightening them. Hah. The djinn burbled darkly over the folly of man's greatest instinct, his proclivity for lashing out at what frightens him. And when he can't see what it is, or he thinks it's something it's not, he lashes out even harder, he fights harder, and his fear grows, giving the djinn that much more to consume.

The djinn studied their faces as it passed—MPs moving out for guard duty—unwitting future prey.

Loring waited in Gilman's office, studying the camp map tacked to the wall, the only thing of interest in the room, unless she felt like making a detailed examination of Franklin Delano Roosevelt's portrait. Gilman had changed his mind. When she'd returned after freshening up, he had announced that she could interview Kirst, explaining that he would sit in on the session because there were things he wanted to know as well. But he had warned her that she would not be able to make this an extended stay: he wanted her to leave as soon as she was through. Loring hadn't argued. What she had in mind wouldn't take a lot of time anyway, but it would be bizarre. If Gilman objected, she would have to bull her way through.

Where is he? she wondered. This is taking forever. She sat down and stared at the map again. It displayed the entire camp, pinpointing every hut, every tree and rock, all the sentry boxes. . . . She studied the rectangular squares with the numbers on them . . . Huts Four, Six, Eight, Ten, all in a row . . . the *Krankenhaus*. . . . What's that? . . . Oh. Hospital . . .

She thought of the murder. On the way in she had spotted a report on the adjutant's desk and the names in caps, ECKMANN and SCHLIEBERT. Not Kirst. Kirst was not involved. At least that's how it looked. But not to Loring. She was sure the djinn had had a hand in it. Again she stared at the map. Her eyes traced the fence line from the northernmost sentry box on around the camp, stopping at each of the angular corners that bent the fence into a nearly perfect pentagon. . . .

She stared at the fence line again and realized what she was looking at. Five lines of equal length, with equal angles at the corners, forming a five-walled enclosure, almost a small city—like Ur-Tawaq.

He's here.

She quivered with certainty.

He's here because this five-walled prison is here. Because it's fate. Because, as the Arabs say, "It is written." Of course it is. It's meant to happen.

She should have known from the very beginning it was meant to happen. That she was meant to come here to battle this thing. To pay for disturbing its twenty-five-hundred-year rest, for drowning a dozen Iraqi workers in the Mesopotamian desert.

Preordained from the moment the first shovel bit into desert waste. It all led to this. She could drop it now. She should drop it now. She wanted to drop it now—

The door opened and Gilman entered. He sat down behind his desk, reached for pad and pencil, and said, "Mind if I take notes?"

"Fine."

The MPs brought in Kirst. He was younger than Loring had expected, a boy no more than twenty-three. She was not much older, but she had imagined him stronger, tougher, a seasoned submariner. Instead, he had a slack build, a strange pallor, haunted, sunken, sleepless eyes. He sat stiffly while the sergeant asked Gilman, "Want him cuffed, sir?"

"No. But wait outside."

The sergeant and the MPs stepped out and shut the door.

"Miss Loring Holloway, Leutnant Rolf Kirst," Gilman said.

Loring nodded politely. Kirst fixed dead eyes on her. She stared at his pasty skin and dry, chapped lips and was suddenly afraid.

He's the djinn. The djinn is him. They're somehow intertwined.

204

Again her eyes flicked to the map, and she realized the deeper significance of that five-sided fence.

This office is outside. We're outside. Kirst . . . the djinn is outside.

She panicked and thought fleetingly of demanding the interview be conducted inside the camp. Then she glanced at the list of questions on the chair next to her.

What good are questions going to be? If he is the djinn, he'll lie. I can't interview him. I have to expose him.

The door opened again and Major Borden entered. Gilman made more introductions. Borden asked if she'd like coffee. Loring said yes. He asked Kirst, too, but Kirst only gave him a blank look. Borden poured him some anyway. It sat on the desk in front of him. Kirst fixed his eyes on the curl of steam.

"All right, Miss Holloway," said Gilman. "Major Borden will interpret."

Loring glanced at the small suitcase she had brought down with her. Inside it were her books, the silver decanter that Yazir had given her, and some other things she thought would be useful in testing the djinn. But first she had to set the stage.

"Let me explain what I know about your prisoner," she said, waiting for Borden to translate. "Kirst was gunnery officer aboard the German submarine U-221, which sank the Liberty Ship *Delaware Trader* nearly two weeks ago. The submarine was almost immediately sunk by an American aircraft. Kirst was the only survivor. When he was rescued three days later by the USS *Sharpe,* he was found inside a floating crate, the only thing that remained of the *Delaware Trader*'s cargo. Whatever had been inside the crate was gone, presumably thrown out by Kirst. But we don't know for sure because, when he was interrogated aboard the *Sharpe,* he wouldn't talk. Now . . .

205

that particular crate is very important to us. It contained a consignment for the Metropolitan Museum in New York. We would like to know what happened to the contents."

Borden finished translating for Kirst. There was only silence. Kirst seemed to make an effort to lift his head and fix his gaze on Loring. She waited. They all waited. But not a word came out of him.

"What *was* in the crate?" Gilman asked.

"Artifacts," Loring replied, still watching Kirst.

"What sort of artifacts? Would they be of any interest to a German? Particularly one who is trying to save himself from drowning?"

"That's what I'd like to find out."

"You don't know precisely what was in the crate?"

"Yes. I do know."

"Well?"

Kirst's gaze had shifted. His eyes had dropped to Loring's chest. She frowned. Her hand moved protectively to where he was looking, and she felt the reassuring warm flatness of Yazir's pendant beneath her sweater and against her skin.

He's looking at it. He knows it's there.

"Miss Holloway," Gilman said patiently, "it might help if you jog his memory."

"Yes . . ."

She took her hand away and let his eyes rest on her bosom.

Let him wonder why I have it. Let him wonder about me.

"The, uh, the crate contained a selection of ancient artifacts from . . . from an archaeological dig in Iraq. . . . Among them, there was one item of vital importance . . . a flask."

Gilman frowned and glanced at Borden, who shrugged.

"Kirst," Borden said, following with a rapid patter in German. He stopped. Kirst was motionless, still staring at Loring. "I don't know, Major," Borden said. "Either he's not quite with us, or he just won't talk."

Gilman got up, came around the table, and squatted next to Loring, his back to Kirst. He spoke to her quietly.

"You want to tell me what's going on?"

"I don't know."

"If you have to get a straight answer out of him, you may be out of luck. He's a little strange. Been that way since he arrived."

"Yes. I'm sure."

"You're sure?"

"If we could just press on, some things might become clear."

"To whom?"

Loring looked at Gilman. He was staring at her now— almost as intently as Kirst. "Major, he's not your run-of-the-mill prisoner."

"You're telling *me.*"

"Something happened while he was floating around in that crate."

"What happened?"

"I don't know."

Gilman nodded, then touched her hand. "You're as mysterious as he is." Gilman rose and returned to his seat. Then he said quietly, "Borden, translate."

Gilman suddenly kicked Kirst's chair. Kirst and the chair slid back a foot. Kirst looked up in shock. Gilman stuck a finger in his face. "I'm tired of jacking around with you, Kirst. Now, this lady has come all the way from Washington, and she's not asking you about Hitler's underwear or Doenitz's battle plans, so there is no over-riding reason for you not to answer. She just wants to know what you did with a load of ancient pottery or whatever when you climbed into that crate. I think that out of pure decency you could bring yourself to answer. It doesn't sound to me as if the fate of the world hangs in the balance! So how about it?"

Kirst said nothing. He stared at Gilman.

"Don't give me that stupid look. You've been playing games ever since you got here, and I've had enough. I've got one man dead and another round the bend, and there's distinct suspicion in this camp that *you* are some-how involved. Now, it might be real smart of you at this time to open your mouth and let us hear a few words. Otherwise—"

"Major." Borden gave him a warning look, and Gilman realized he'd stopped translating. Gilman leaned back slowly and contemplated Kirst's empty face.

"Miss Holloway," Gilman said finally, "I don't think you're going to get anything."

Loring thought for a moment. "Let me try another way." She reached for the suitcase, stood up, and placed it on Gilman's desk. She opened a corner and reached inside, felt what she was looking for, and gripped it tightly. Kirst was watching her.

Now. If you can hear me, now let's see what you are.

She pulled it out and set it upright on the edge of the desk, directly in front of Kirst. He stared at the silver flask for an instant, then his eyelids dropped down, his lips spread, and out of him came a low chuckle.

Loring froze.

I can't be wrong. I can't be! It's silver, you sonofabitch. Just like the flask in the crate! You know what it means! It means I know what you are! Stop laughing!

208

The chuckling stopped.

"What the hell is this . . . ?" Gilman started to say.

Kirst sprang to his feet, eyes still closed. He snatched the flask off the desk and threw it with all his might at the window. It crashed through the glass and disappeared outside. They heard it bouncing off rocks then it rolled down the hill until it hit the compound fence and stopped.

Loring was motionless, frightened, one hand at her throat. Kirst sat down and opened his eyes. The blank look was back. Gilman got up and looked out the broken window. He turned back to Loring. "Well, Miss Holloway, I don't think he wants to answer your questions."

Loring caught her breath and said, "I think he did."

Gilman sighed. "Major Borden, get him out of here, and have someone retrieve that *thing* out there."

"Where are you taking him?" Loring's voice was shrill.

"Back to the camp. Any objections?"

"No. No, that's best."

"Good. I'm glad I consulted you."

Borden opened the door, motioned to the MPs and Sergeant Vinge. They escorted Kirst to the door. He stopped to look back and fix Loring with another empty stare. Again his eyes went to her bosom and she heard the chuckle as he went out.

Borden picked up Kirst's untouched coffee and took it with him to the door. "We might have ourselves a pair of Section Eights, Major. Eckmann *and* Kirst."

"We'll discuss it later," Gilman said.

Borden went out and shut the door. Before Loring could stop him, Gilman flopped open her suitcase and looked inside. He noted, among the queer old books, a carton of salt, an iron magnet, a battery flashlight, a steel

209

rod, a worn pocket edition of the Koran, a hunk of tar, a bag of herbs . . .

"This doesn't look like regulation Girl Scout equipment, Miss Holloway. What are you equipped for?"

She closed the suitcase. "I'd like to hear your interpretation of what just happened," she countered.

"He doesn't like you," Gilman said simply.

"When I showed him that flask, he exploded."

"Explain the significance."

Loring hesitated. "Look, Major, among the things in the crate was a flask, very much like that one, made of pure silver, but a great deal older."

"How old?"

"Twenty-five hundred years."

"I see. And of course this rather old bottle has some remarkable connection to the current hostilities between our countries. Correct?"

Loring searched for a reply. She wasn't quick enough.

"Just which hole in the State Department have you emerged from, Miss Holloway?"

"I don't think losing your temper will help—"

"I haven't lost my temper. I've lost my window. I'd like to know why. Obviously, you and Herr Kirst know a great deal more than I do, and yet you're asking *me* to cooperate. So what else do I have to put up with? What's he going to break next, and why?"

"Major, I'm trying to demonstrate something here—"

"What?"

"I don't think you're ready to listen."

Gilman laughed. "It must be a whopper." He picked up Loring's papers. "I don't think you're with State at all. I think you've pulled some hefty strings, but you're not what you claim to be. Right?"

"I'm an archaeologist, Major. I work for the Metropolitan Museum in New York."

"Now we're getting somewhere. What's it all about?"

"That crate was consigned to me. Its contents have disappeared. I'm trying to find out what happened to them."

"Lady, there's a war on."

"That shipment contained something . . . very dangerous."

"Explain dangerous."

Loring frowned. "I can't."

"You won't."

"No, I can't. I need time to find out some things, to study Kirst . . ."

Gilman turned to the window and peered through the jagged glass. His eyes scanned the fence line below and he located the silver flask resting against the wire, gleaming in the meager sunlight. "What did you expect would happen when you showed him that thing, Miss Holloway?"

"I don't know, really. I expected *some* reaction, but—"

"But you were looking for something a little stranger?"

"Yes."

"What do you think he did with the flask—the one in the crate?"

"That's what I have to know."

"But you don't want to tell me any theories because you're afraid of looking foolish. You'd rather handle this your own way, and you hope I'll cooperate."

"Yes."

"This doesn't have anything to do with the war, does it?"

"No."

"Uh-huh." Gilman snapped the suitcase latches shut, stood it upright on his desk, and pushed it toward Loring. "Okay, let's do it by the book. The purpose of your mission is to find out where your artifact is. You thought Kirst had it, so you followed him here. You've found out he doesn't have it. I can personally assure you he arrived in this camp empty-handed. No flask. It's not here. All done. Got it? Go home."

Loring stared at him, then at the suitcase. She didn't budge.

"Kirst is traumatized," Gilman went on. "Lost all his shipmates, his rescue was a miracle. He can't talk, he won't talk, he chooses not to—it doesn't matter. He's a prisoner of war. He doesn't have to cooperate. He can lie in order to confuse and confound the enemy, which is us."

"So can the thing that I'm after," Loring interrupted, "which is what's making this so difficult."

Gilman stared at her. *Thing. What did she mean by that?* He shook his head. "I suggest you pack up your bogus credentials and hightail it out of here, before I change my mind and hold *you* for investigation."

Loring grabbed everything, bristling. "Major Gilman, I am not obliged to reveal at what level these papers were generated. What you have to decide is not whether you're going to permit me to stay, but whether you want to risk official displeasure by booting me out!"

Gilman stared at her, then laughed.

Official displeasure. France. Window Hill. General Malkin bloated with rage. Gilman's fist—

His laughter diminished. He saw panic in her eyes. He thought about that for a moment, then he turned to the broken window again and looked down at the camp. He thought about Eckmann and Schliebert, the mirror in the shower hut, the other little things, and Kirst . . .

212

You want to get to the bottom of this, don't you? Don't you?

"Okay," he said. "You can stick around overnight. One day."

The djinn knew exactly what was happening, precisely how it would go. Because of the fear. Fear dictated the woman's actions. Fear motivated her. The djinn had sensed the fear, smelled it and tasted it in that moment when it had made Kirst pick up the silver flask and throw it through the window. It had been exactly the right thing to do to increase the fear. Fear had exploded from the woman, and the djinn had devoured it.

And there was fear in Major Gilman. Deep inside his soul, where all men hide their worst fears, it lurked and waited, and only the djinn knew how to coax it out.

Window Hill. France. Second battalion.

Through the entire meeting, not a word of Major Gilman's deepest fear had been spoken, but by the time Kirst had left the room, the djinn had known it all.

It didn't matter that at this moment Kirst stood before the gate, a near-somnambulist waiting for the fool to key off the lock and loosen the chains. It didn't matter that the djinn would be going back inside. Because now it had the measure of its enemies. It had two potential new hosts. And it knew they would bring Kirst out again. The game was starting. The woman would use anything she could to lure out the djinn. . . .

A few days ago, it might have worked. But the djinn was stronger now. And there was no trick in the world she could think of that could defeat him.

He made Kirst walk through the open gate. Then he made Kirst tramp down the hill toward the little knots of curious Germans.

Gebhard's skin prickled. He felt as if he were being enveloped by a cloud of seething hatred. Then Kirst went by, and the feeling passed.

When Kirst was out of earshot, some of the Germans turned to others and began to whisper. Traitors, spies, suspicions. By now, there was hardly a man left in the compound who trusted Kirst.

Bruckner stood apart, Churchill's leash looped three times around his wrist. Churchill was taking a pee. A little river of it ran down a furrow in the earth directly in Kirst's path. Bruckner watched Kirst stop and eye the steaming piss curiously.

Bruckner felt a tug on the leash and looked down. Churchill was edging backward, whining and eyeing Kirst mistrustfully. Bruckner snorted to himself. Poor bastard. Even the dog hates him. Bruckner glanced at his brother officers smugly. He watched them with their hands shoved in their pockets, kicking up little clods of dirt, talking about Kirst. *Spy. Traitor. They don't know the half of it.* Bruckner smirked. *Wait till they find out just what's really going on.* Images of his secret knowledge danced before his eyes and, when they faded, he saw Kirst's gaze fixed on him.

He knows. He knows, too.

Chapter 18

An orderly knocked on Loring's door and informed her that the commandant would escort her to evening mess at 1800 hours. Loring thanked him, promised to be ready, and shut the door. A minute later she had selected an outfit for dinner. She laid it out on the bed, then snatched up her toilet bag and went down the hall to the "Commandant's Closet."

She entered and locked it. Discovering there was an inner door that opened into Gilman's quarters, she was about to lock that, too, but curiosity got the better of her. She eased the door open and peered into Gilman's room. There was no one inside. She opened the bathroom door wider and stepped in, looking around.

The room was almost the same as hers—twice the size yet still tiny—like a sparse hotel suite in a New York fleabag. And it was neat; nothing was out of place. The desk was surprisingly bare, only a pair of pencils and a blotter. She resisted a temptation to open the drawers. She opened his dresser caddy instead—a handsome leather box with little compartments and slots. She picked up Gilman's high school ring.

What are you looking for? A wedding band? He'd be wearing that, wouldn't he?

She pictured his hands. No wedding band. No, he

215

wasn't married, not even engaged. He was *between*. She knew the type: hurt by someone in his past, no longer sure he would ever marry, no longer sure what he felt about women in general. Loring smiled and wondered if she was guessing even close.

She picked up a tie clasp: silver inlaid with mother-of-pearl, an odd thing for a man to choose for himself. She held it up to the light. There was an inscription on the back: Tiffany.

Loring shook her head. Soldiers didn't shop at Tiffany. Neither did mothers. Girlfriends did. Rich girlfriends.

She tossed it back and shut the box, then she hurried back into the bathroom and locked the connecting door. In a moment she had the shower running and her clothes off. She stepped under the needle spray and reached for the soap.

He does have a girl. Rich, probably beautiful. They're engaged, planning to marry. After the war a big church wedding in Manhattan. She will become Mrs. David Gilman. He will become wealthy and lose his soul. . . .

But why was there no picture?

Loring stopped soaping, threw the white cake back on the ledge, and stepped under the spray again.

No picture at all. No smiling rich face perched over his cot inside a silver frame. Maybe the rich lady wasn't his girlfriend anymore. Maybe it was over. Just like her "romance" with Warren Clark was over. She laughed and rinsed out her hair.

When Gilman picked her up, Loring had changed into a dress, combed out her hair, and doused herself with perfume. She looked radiant and smelled wonderful. She could see that Gilman was impressed.

Gilman told her she looked great, but they walked the

216

rest of the way to the officers' mess in silence. They made a place for her at headquarters table. Hopkins was out on duty; she found herself sitting with Gilman, Cosco, Blish, and Borden. There were five more at two other tables and throughout dinner they all had a hard time keeping their eyes off her. Her dress was burgundy taffeta, off the shoulder, fringed with a pink border at the bodice, cinched at the waist with a bow. She displayed creamy white shoulders and rested her arms demurely on the table. In short order, she was accepted into their company—one of the boys.

Gilman announced she was an archaeologist. Immediately, Borden opened up. "At last we can have some intelligent conversation around here." For the rest of the evening, he monopolized her, and she found out that he was an amateur archaeologist himself, that they knew some of the same people, that he even knew of Mahmud Yazir. After a while Loring realized she was very skillfully being pumped. Borden got her talking about Iraq and, since she saw no reason why Gilman shouldn't have the information, she explained about her dig at Ur-Tawaq, about Moulin and Bayar and the things they had found. She said nothing about Korbazrah or the flask or what had brought her to Blackbone.

"That was a rather cheap way to get information," Loring said, pulling the coat tighter about her shoulders.

"Pardon?" Gilman walked beside her in the dark, up the slope from the barracks to headquarters. The air had a biting chill. Spotlights swept the compound below them and illuminated the hillside.

"You know what I mean, Major. Your medical officer did all the talking, but he was asking *your* questions."

"Was he?"

"Don't play innocent. He knows Yazir, indeed. I doubt he ever heard the name before."

"You think Borden's a fake? Not an amateur at all?"

"He probably boned up on it this afternoon."

"I see. In our camp library, I suppose. We do have liberal borrowing privileges, but our stock is rather limited."

"Then you coached him."

"In a field about which I know nothing."

She whirled angrily. "I don't care if you're both experts. You've got something going on in this camp. You should be looking into that—not harassing me! I'm here to help!"

"Nobody's harassing you. And I don't need your help. The weather is going to change tomorrow. There could be snow, probably a storm. If that happens, they tell me the roads become impassable. Then we just have to sit until it stops. Nothing gets in; no one gets out. Now, I have no intention of keeping an unwanted guest. So first thing tomorrow, I'm going to have my adjutant contact the State Department and work up the ladder until he finds someone who knows you. Borden can call Columbia University and track down this Mock-mood Yazeer. And I will personally call the Metropolitan in New York. If you're not on the level, it's bye-bye so long. Whatever you won't tell me is either top secret or ridiculously silly, so you better come clean by tomorrow morning."

"You said twenty-four hours."

"I changed my mind."

Gilman left her at the stairway to her quarters and called back, "Nice gown, though! Makes you look like Rita Hayworth!"

Some of her anger melted. She watched him go across to the MP barracks.

Alone, she looked down at the compound, wondering about Kirst. The djinn was a night creature. Last night someone was murdered. How much more would have to happen before Gilman was ready to listen?

Gebhard lay on his bunk in the dark with the blankets hugged around his neck because he could no longer stand his own stench. Images stirred in his mind: the tight steamy quarters of his old U-boat, the sweat streaming off his body when the diesels were running, sticky shirts, greasy stubble . . . then he saw the locked shower hut, the pipes and spouts spurting water, the spray washing the sweat and grime off his skin. . . .

He sat up. Everyone else was asleep. Gebhard looked over at Kirst. He was on his side facing the wall, motionless. Gebhard swung his legs over and stood up in his long underwear. He grabbed a towel from the shelf by the door and slipped into the corridor.

Behind him Kirst stirred.

Gebhard stepped outside, threw the towel around his shoulders, then jumped off the stoop and started running. Dodging the searchlights and keeping to the shadows, he made it to the shower hut and flattened himself against a corner. He shook from the cold. He waited for the beam to sweep past his corner, then he slipped around the side to the furnace.

He fumbled with the valves. Luckily, when they closed the showers, they hadn't shut the pilot off. The furnace roared to life. Gebhard looked around, worried that the noise might attract a sentry. There were none in sight.

He waited for the light to pass again, then scuttled around the hut to the window. He reached under the hut to the little ledge in the foundation where he had hidden the spoon that morning. He found it, grasped it tightly with the bowl end in his palm, then he began prying the window out of the jamb.

In a moment, it eased out. The light came back. Gebhard dove under the foundation and lay still till it passed. About to get up again, he heard something and stopped. He turned and peered under the foundation. At first he saw nothing, then he thought he saw a black shape dart by on the other side. It disappeared. Gebhard waited, convinced it was one of the sentries, and he'd been spotted. But nothing happened. He heard the muffled roar of the furnace, but no one came to look. It was cold on the ground. He wanted that shower, so he rolled out, stood up, and opened the window. He grabbed the ledge and hauled himself up, then squeezed through and dropped inside.

He pulled the window closed, then stood up in the dark. It was quiet in the shower hut. He could hear the furnace but that was all. Water dripped somewhere. Gebhard smiled and hung his towel on a hook.

Eckmann slept fitfully. The sedatives weren't working, and no one had thought to increase the dosage. Borden had been back a couple of times today, but Eckmann had appeared docile, still in shock. Now he tossed about on the cot and his eyes popped open. He stared at the door, a dim outline in the gloom. A single bare bulb illuminated the corridor outside but was too far away to cast much light into his tiny cell. Eckmann thought he saw a shadow move at the base of the door—the guard going past?—but he heard no footsteps. Then the shadow vanished.

He closed his eyes and tried to go back to sleep. He started thinking of Frieda. Beautiful, sexy, buxom Frieda, with her long blond braids and eager smile. . . . Beautiful unfaithful Frieda! He pounded the pillow. But she wouldn't go away. She loomed against his closed eyelids, pursed her lips and leaned forward to kiss him, but it wasn't him she kissed. It was Schliebert. Frieda's beautiful breasts pillowed on Schliebert's chest, and Schliebert touched her hungrily—

Eckmann woke with a sob. Frieda was gone. He stared at the barred window and sniffled. He caught the scent of her perfume, long-forgotten but pungent now, as if she were in the room with him. He looked around.

Something rustled at the foot of the bed. Eckmann sat still, listening.

A rat?

Of course there would be rats in solitary, put there by the Americans—by Hopkins.

Eckmann's nose wrinkled. The smell was getting stronger—sweet and musky—filling the cell. He gagged on it, then he looked up and saw a figure standing in the darkness at the end of his cot. A female figure wearing a sheer negligee that stirred over her curves. Delicate hands were flattened against her hips. Eckmann watched, fascinated, as she shifted her weight to one leg. Her belly moved back, she thrust out her hips and rocked back and forth.

Eckmann closed his eyes to make her go away but, when he opened them again, she was still there.

Her face moved out of shadow: shiny, white, with a slash of red across each lip, teeth showing, eyes bright and smoky with lust. Her hair was long and blond and braided.

Frieda.

Eckmann blinked and rubbed his eyes. The apparition wouldn't go away. Frieda's hips kept moving. She licked her lips, ran the tip of her tongue under her teeth and

grinned. Her fingers clawed the negligee upward, exposing knee then thigh. Her movements became an insistent
undulation.

Eckmann wanted her. "Frieda," he said.

She leaned over. Her breasts swayed beneath the negligee.

"Frieda, please . . ." Eckmann's voice broke. The
tears came. "Why were you unfaithful?"

Frieda's knee came down on the end of the cot. Eckmann squirreled backward. Frieda yanked the negligee
up. Eckmann stared at her smooth white flesh. He
wanted it.

"I trusted you! Your letters! Frieda, how could you?"

She threw herself on the cot. Her eyes gleamed wick-
edly. She crawled toward him. He shrank against the cell
wall, curling his legs up. He wanted her, but he was
scared.

"Frieda, no . . ."

She sat on her legs and skinned off the negligee. She
was naked underneath. She drew the material across his
body. Eckmann quivered at the wispy touch. He watched
her eyes as she lifted her breasts, one plump globe in each
hand, selling lust not love. Eckmann didn't want lust. He
wanted his innocent darling Frieda, not this grotesque
amoral animal. . . .

She descended on him, pulling at him, urgently tug-
ging at his clothing, nipping his flesh. She pressed his
hand to her bosom and rubbed his palm over her nipples.
They were hard. Eckmann moaned. Heat flooded into his
crotch. He felt a potency growing that he had never before experienced with his darling Frieda. . . .

She soothed him, the back of one hand against his
cheek, stroking gently, the other tearing at his trousers.
Her eyes were distended with erotic need, her nipples

swollen and forcing themselves between his lips. Eckmann groaned and all fear left him. He sank into the sensual bath of her embrace, murmuring her name, letting her tear off his clothes. Then he was helping, flinging them aside. Her hand closed on the stiff, engorged center of him. Then she turned completely around and straddled him. Her mouth sucked him in deeply and hotly. Eckmann trembled with excitement and reached for her hips, pulling her down. His mouth closed on the hot wet center of her. Her movements quickened. She devoured him wolfishly. Everything she did demonstrated a wealth of whorish knowledge—

Schliebert, Schliebert. Frieda with Schliebert, riding him.

Eckmann panicked, remembering last night, remembering his unfaithful Frieda with that bastard Schliebert, and seeing in addition his beautiful darling Frieda with all the men she must have been with since their wedding, since he'd left. He fought those thoughts. He knew where they were leading, back to the truth that he had buried so deeply, the shame that he was so afraid of facing, that he had disguised so well in his thousand and one letters proclaiming love and devotion. He tried to get up. She kept him pinned down. His fear grew.

He wriggled and struggled to escape her. He whimpered and begged. She held him and worked him, and the pressure rose to an unbearable peak. He felt himself reaching beyond his endurance, rushing toward a plateau he had never scaled before. His body whipped beneath hers in a frenzy of excitement. He quivered on the cot like jelly.

She rose in front of him, gave him a wicked smile, then displayed what he had feared all along—his organ lying limp in her hand—the badge of his impotence—the trophy of his unconsummated wedding night—the shame of his failure with Frieda—

As he screamed out her name in a terrified protest, she ripped the sheet out from under their bodies and held it out to him, a silent offering. He stared at it.

The guard at the end of the hall started out of his midnight doze. He listened but heard nothing more. He didn't bother to check.

Gebhard let water run into his mouth and spill out. He ducked his head under the spray and shook his hair. Steam was building up in the tightly closed hut. Gebhard didn't care. And if they caught him, so what? He felt wonderful—clean, revitalized, defiant. He spread his legs and took a piss. The yellow river washed down the sloping floor to the drain.

Moving down the line of pipes, Gebhard reached up and turned on the other spouts. Within seconds every shower head was going full blast. The room was alive with spraying water, and steaming up fast. Mist swirled around him. He laughed and danced in it, grabbed imaginary beers off imaginary tables, downing them in wild flourishes.

A tendril of black smoke seeped under the padlocked door and wafted upward. It curled and tested the lowering cloud of moisture. Then the rest of the nightform came in and mingled with the vapor, saturating it with darkness.

Gebhard raised his imaginary stein to the heavens. His voice rang out, "Every god in his house, and every man in his shower! Give us this moment, and give us this power!" He held the back of his head and drank, then dropped the stein, stretched out his arms and prepared to let out a triumphant yell.

It never escaped his lips.

The sound was deafening, like a three-hundred-pound depth charge exploding in a tomb. The hut shook, and Gebhard was thrown to the floor. In shock, he looked around and saw the arch of an engine room overhead. He was naked on the deck. Rivets were popping around him. Walls of water slammed across the compartment, drenching the engines. The deck flooded quickly. Gebhard lay in a rising ocean, stunned and frightened. He heard voices yelling commands in German. A shadowy figure splashed by and nearly trampled him. Gebhard rolled. His bare ass hit the diesel casing and he screamed from the burn. He jumped up and looked around wildly, his mind screaming that this was impossible, but his eyes were telling him it was real.

A second blast slammed the boat sideways and threw Gebhard into a tangle of other frightened men. More rivets gave way. The compartment was filling up. Down at the end he saw a hatch close and the latch drop. A wheel spun, trapping him.

His worst dream was coming true. For an entire year of devoted, sweat-streaked service, he had avoided this, but now at last it had come—his moment, his final reckoning with God—

Pipes burst, drenching a man behind him with oil. The engine sparked and the man erupted in flame.

Gebhard charged away from him, toward the hatch. He hit his head on something and was spun around. The hull faded from sight. He reeled along the concrete floor, from shower to shower, under the sprays and out again, then his hand found the diesel casing. He shook his head to clear it. A stream of water hit his face. He tried to move out from under it, but his legs wouldn't work. His head throbbed, and the water stung his eyes. He closed them and heard voices reverberating dankly off the hull. Ripping sounds. Metal shrieking, giving, breaking up. His head lolled under the spray. His mouth and nose filled up, and he gagged and choked. He managed to stumble away and open his eyes, but he couldn't see: there was a misty darkness all around him.

The lights had gone. The sub's power was out. He could no longer hear the men or the diesels, only a throbbing rush from someplace, the hiss of water, the racketing splash as it pummeled the deck.

Heart pounding, Gebhard reached out and felt nothing. He stumbled faster, his bare feet splashing. What's making it so dark? He hit the wall full force and cracked his head.

He stood against it, dazed and dizzy, trying to stay upright. His hand moved along the wall and felt his hook and the towel. He snatched the towel down but couldn't hold on to it.

It fell into the stream at his feet and was carried along toward the drain.

Salty warm wetness flowed down Gebhard's cheek and into his lips. He tasted blood and the knowledge made him weaker. He staggered after the towel, a white beacon in the dark, covering the drain. A pool of water was forming and backing up toward him. The room began to spin. Gebhard's knees buckled. He collapsed into the water pooling around the plugged drain. He tried to move and couldn't. All strength had gone out of him. The water slopped over his cheek, washed off some of the blood. It bubbled into his mouth.

Gebhard screamed at himself to move, but his body wouldn't cooperate.

The blackness descended over him, embracing his body, devouring the fear and panic that drove his heart to its wildest contractions. His body was seized with violent pain. His jaws snapped open involuntarily. He couldn't get his breath. Water flowed through his lips and filled his lungs. The djinn fed and fed and fed . . .

Until there was nothing more.

Seconds later, the nightform left the hut and flowed quickly across the chilled ground toward the back end of camp, toward the base of Blackbone Mountain and the mine shaft. Black tendrils whipped against the night air, lashed out in triumph, as the djinn felt power course through its essence. Power from fear. Even greater power from death. Power enough now to move mountains.

In Hut 7, Mueller sat up and tried to figure out what had disturbed his sleep. Drawn to the window, he rubbed mist off the pane and peered out. Light swept the back end of the camp.

There was something out there. Below the fence, around the caved-in part of the old mine shaft, blackness moved against the light. Then the light was gone.

Mueller hesitated a moment, wondering if it was an animal. He turned and pulled on his boots then threw on his coat. That wouldn't be warm enough: Mueller was sensitive to the cold. He wrapped himself up in his blanket and went out.

Keeping to the shadows and out of the roving searchlights, Mueller passed the shower hut, ignoring the rush of the furnace and the faint sound of running water. He was intent on getting to the back fence. He went around the last hut and peered up the slope. Something was different about that tiny patch of terrain. He had stared at it so often, had seen it so frequently in his dreams, that he more than anyone else in the camp would know if something had changed. Something had.

With mounting excitement, Mueller sprinted across the remaining ground. He reached the base of the slope and looked up. He couldn't believe what he saw. Where before there had been a solid wall of rubble over the mine shaft entrance, now there was a gaping hole.

Mueller scrambled up the slope. He flopped on the ground just beneath the hole as the spotlight swept toward him. He threw the blanket over his body and waited. The light passed.

Mueller poked his head out and stared at the hole. It was better than he could have hoped for—large enough to crawl through! Gripping the edges of it, he pulled himself higher. He stuck his head and shoulders inside and whistled softly.

There was an echo. The shaft was open.

Cursing himself for not bringing a light, he withdrew and looked around. It wouldn't do to be caught here now —not with the find of the century. Nor could he leave it as he'd found it. In the morning the MPs might spot it and dynamite it closed again. What to do? The blanket. The spotlight had moved right over Mueller's blanket, which was olive drab, and almost matched the ground here. The sentry operating the light hadn't noticed it.

Mueller stuffed the blanket into the hole then climbed above it and, cupping his hands, pulled dirt down over it. When it was completely concealed, Mueller ran down the slope, turned, and looked back up.

From this close, which was as close as the MPs ever got in daylight, the hole was invisible. So was the blanket. Mueller hurried back to Hut 7.

Tomorrow. Tomorrow night!

As soon as he was gone, the nightform wafted out of the hole, seeped around the blanket, and crept down the slope.

Chapter 19 ==========================

Hopkins charged down the slope, buttoning his shirt, a coat slung over one arm, murder in his eye. He flew through the open gate, signaling two MPs to follow. Vinge was waiting at the shower hut. Hopkins paused to listen to the running water. A look of intense pleasure crossed his face. Someone had defied orders and was having himself a little midnight wash. Hopkins pulled the key and slipped it into the padlock. He ripped the lock off and kicked open the door.

A cloud of escaping steam swirled past him. The MPs held their tommy guns at waist level. When the mist cleared, Hopkins saw the showers going full blast, a deepening pool of water where the floor sloped to the drain— and in the pool a body.

"Alert the camp. Sirens, lights, the works!" Hopkins snapped. As Vinge took off, Hopkins walked forward, slopping into the pool, turning off the showers one by one. Finally, he stood over the body in calf-deep water, looking down at Gebhard's staring eyes beneath the surface. There was a gash on his forehead, but most of the blood had been washed away.

The air-raid horn erupted outside, mixed with MP whistles. Sweeping lights filtered through the back windows. Hopkins saw that one was slightly ajar and smirked. So that's how the stupid sonofabitch got in. But who killed him?

In Hut 7 men collided in the corridor in a mad scramble to get outside. Mueller collared Bauhopf and wordlessly dragged him into Room 2 and pointed out Kirst, who was sitting up in his bunk, slouched against the wall, his chin on his chest, eyes narrowed, brows lowered. Through bared teeth, his voice came in a ghostly rasp—

"Gebhard . . . Eckmann . . . deeeeaaaaaddddd . . ."

Bauhopf's eyes widened. Mueller ran to get someone else. Bauhopf realized he was alone with Kirst and backed swiftly to the door.

The outer door opened. Cold air blasted in. With it came an MP shouting, *"Raus! Raus!* Everybody out!"

Bauhopf turned in time to see Mueller and two other men being shoved past by the MP. Mueller pointed into the room.

"You, too!" the MP shouted at Bauhopf. "And your sister there."

Bauhopf jumped at a touch on his sleeve. He whirled. It was Kirst, stumbling past him, dazed, confused. He went out after the others. Bauhopf followed, no longer sure of what he had seen or heard, but determined to confer with Mueller about Kirst.

Loring Holloway stopped at the bottom of the stairs in the shelter of the entryway and stood with a blanket over her shoulders, watching the commotion below. There was Gilman running through the gate. MPs double-timed down from the barracks and into the compound. She saw the Germans forming up, the MPs surrounding them with weapons. A cold spot blossomed deep in her stomach. She knew instantly that the djinn had been at work.

230

Gilman stared down at Gebhard's naked body lying in a pool of reddened water. Hopkins showed him the contusion on Gebhard's head, the soggy towel plugging the drain and the open window. "Someone forced him in through the window, made him strip, bashed him on the head, then helped him drown. Made it look like an accident."

"But not to you," said Gilman.

"They've got a lot of tricks, Major, but I've seen 'em all."

"Evidently."

"If you want, sir, I'll prepare a report for your signature."

"No. I may file a different report."

Hopkins frowned thoughtfully. "Suicide, sir?"

Someone stumbled through the door—the guard from solitary. "Sir—" he said, choking on the word—

"Sir, it's Eckmann!"

Gilman swung the cell door open and stared at what the guard had discovered only a few minutes earlier. One end of a sheet from Eckmann's cot was tied securely around the eight-foot-high window bars. The other end was around Eckmann's neck. Eckmann's body lay flat against the cell wall, hanging from the window like a grotesque human tapestry. His face was blue, his tongue swollen and nearly bitten through. His eyes bulged and displayed his final fear and madness.

Hopkins stepped in and stood behind Gilman. The guard refused to enter, remaining in the corridor, shivering—and not from the cold.

"What happened?" Gilman turned and asked him.

"I don't know, sir. I heard a sound a while back, sort

of a yell, but—but the prisoner had yelled out a few times during the day. I didn't think it was unusual. He never wanted anything. So I didn't check this time. Sir, if I'd thought something was wrong, I'd have come back here. That's the truth."

"I'm sure it is. Go on."

"When the siren went off, I got worried it might set him going again, so I came back and—" He motioned toward the cell. "I found—that."

"You want to know what I think, Major?" Hopkins said.

"Not particularly."

"I think the fucking krauts are bumping each other off."

"Hopkins, you've got a particularly nasty habit of jumping to conclusions."

Hopkins slammed a fist against the cell door. "Well, what the hell do you think is going on, sir?"

"I don't know!"

"Great! I suppose you think Gebhard's an accident, and Schliebert slipped and strangled himself, and nobody else had anything to do with it! That's three bodies, Major! I don't know about your head count, but to me that's a lot! Or don't you care? When people are under your command—*don't you care?*"

Gilman whipped around, his fist balled for a punch.

Hopkins held his ground, wanting it, needing an excuse.

"Outside," Gilman said quietly.

In front of the formation, Gilman reported to Steuben that Eckmann had evidently hanged himself, but that Gebhard's death would require a full investigation. Bruckner interrupted in a torrent of angry German. Steuben snapped at him to shut up.

232

"It's all right," said Gilman. "What did he say?"

Steuben translated wearily. "He is saying that since Eckmann was in the custody of your guards, they could have 'arranged' his suicide." Bruckner jabbered more German. "And they could have taken Gebhard to the shower hut and killed him."

Bruckner eyed Hopkins, as if to suggest who was responsible. Churchill obligingly helped by erupting into a barking frenzy aimed at Hopkins.

"Shut that fucking dog up!" Hopkins yelled. He made a move to grab it. The dog leaped backward and bared his teeth. Hopkins grabbed his sidearm. There was an answering surge from the Germans. Almost as one, they stepped forward.

"Hopkins, knock it off!" Gilman bellowed.

Hopkins glared at the Germans, then released his grip on the weapon. He turned away from the dog. After a moment, Churchill stopped barking. Bruckner soothed him. Gilman caught the Germans whispering to each other and casting unpleasant looks at the surrounding MPs.

"Major Steuben," said Gilman, "no purpose is served by standing here throwing accusations. Dismiss your men back to their huts. Tomorrow morning, we will conduct an investigation."

Steuben dismissed the prisoners. Gilman watched them fall out into little muttering groups and slowly move back to the huts.

"Hopkins, get them back inside."

Hopkins came instantly alive, shouting orders at the MPs, who moved in and prodded the Germans along, busting up the groups. Gilman watched Mueller and Bauhopf approach Steuben and tell him something. They were pointing at Kirst. Steuben's face fixed in a stunned frown. He glanced once at Gilman then scolded Mueller and Bauhopf ferociously, dismissing them and stalking back to his hut. Mueller and Bauhopf stared after him then were shoved toward Hut 7 by an MP.

Gilman watched Kirst shamble up to Hut 7 and feel for the doorjamb to pull himself up. He moved as if completely preoccupied. Gilman didn't know why, but he felt something curl in his innards.

What's going on? What did they tell Steuben?

Hopkins confronted him. "Let me in there, sir. I can sweat the truth out of them."

"You've got a sweaty solution for everything, Hopkins. Get those bodies picked up and over to Major Borden right away. I want cause-of-death first thing in the morning."

Hopkins watched Gilman turn and trudge back up the hill. Hatred bloomed in his frustrated brain. It was time to put the screws to Major Gilman. Take off the gloves. Make use of all that shit Chilton had dug up. He wouldn't wait any longer. Now, while everyone's confused, and their confidence in Gilman hangs by a thread, now is the time to give him a little push. He glanced around. The MPs were mopping up, slamming doors, shouting "Lights out," and moving out in little groups. Hopkins went up to one of them and bummed a smoke. Then he started talking.

Gilman ran into Loring at the gate. She was wrapped in a blanket and wearing a woolen nightdress beneath it. She'd gotten the news from the gate guard, a PFC named Cokenaur.

"I think we'd better talk," she said urgently.

"Given the circumstances, Miss Holloway, you'd better leave in the morning. We'll be crawling with CID in

234

the next few days. I can't deal with them and with you at the same time."

"Major," she said tightly, "three deaths in two days. Don't you find that odd?"

Gilman grabbed her arm and hustled her away from the curious MPs. "Stay out of it," he said, "unless you want to tell me who's responsible."

"Kirst."

He stopped and stared at her. She watched fear and confusion cut through his eyes, then they clouded over with anger as he rejected her flatly. His mouth opened. He was going to tell her off again. She turned her back on him and ran up the hill, ran all the way upstairs and slammed inside.

Gilman stared after her again. The fear came back.

"Someone from another hut had to know Gebhard was going out," said Bruckner. "They had to know what time."

"Or they sat up all night waiting," Dortmunder suggested.

"They could have been waiting *in* the shower hut."

Churchill was curled up at the foot of Steuben's cot. Steuben's room was crowded with officers and cigarette smoke and full of the tension of frayed nerves. They were trying to figure who'd gotten Gebhard. Eckmann they didn't even want to think about. If he'd committed suicide, it was only fitting justice after what he'd done to Schliebert. But if, as Bruckner suggested, the Americans had rigged it to look like suicide, that was another matter. That they would discuss among themselves tomorrow.

"No one saw Gebhard go out of Hut Seven," Bruckner said. "They were all asleep, but it's well known Gebhard liked his showers, that he was upset over the shower hut being closed down. Yesterday he talked openly about breaking in. Whoever killed him must have overheard that."

"Gebhard had no enemies," said Steuben.

"Yes, he did," Dortmunder piped up. "Kirst."

That set everyone to muttering. Steuben reconsidered what Mueller and Bauhopf had told him. He had ordered them not to repeat it, but what good would that do? By morning, the story would be all over camp—Kirst speaking the names of the dead before anyone knew they were dead.

Steuben tried to short-circuit the budding rumor. "Kirst is a heavy sleeper. He sleeps through everything. He slept through Eckmann's attack on Schliebert."

"That could just be an act," said Bruckner.

More muttering. Steuben had to concede it was possible. If no one had heard Gebhard leaving Hut 7, they could just as easily have missed Kirst.

Bruckner's voice rose above the chatter. "I think what's most odd about Hut Seven is that all three dead men—Schliebert, Eckmann, now Gebhard—were from the same room in that hut. And so is Kirst."

More muttering. Louder.

"What do you propose to do?" Steuben snapped.

"What does it take, Walter?" said Bruckner. "More deaths?"

"You want to kill him? Is that what you want? What if you're wrong?"

They were quiet a moment. "Let's clear out Room Two and lock Kirst in alone," said Bruckner.

There were murmurs of agreement.

"Before we go dancing off on the wrong foot," said Steuben, "let us examine facts. Kirst did not kill

Schliebert. Eckmann did. There were witnesses. Kirst did not kill Eckmann. He couldn't get into solitary—not with a guard on duty. Eckmann either hanged himself or was murdered by the Americans. The only death where Kirst had either a physical possibility or a motive is Gebhard's. But out on the field"—he shot a finger at Bruckner—"*you* suggested Hopkins was to blame!"

"Kirst is a spy," Bruckner replied. "He's working for the Americans. Gebhard was onto him. Hopkins *ordered* Kirst to kill Gebhard."

More muttering, louder than before, outright hostility. Steuben knew he had lost: it was what they *wanted* to believe. It gave them something to fight over, a rallying point. Kirst a spy, in league with their jailers, a traitor. Steuben sighed, and though he tried to shout them down, he knew he wouldn't be able to control this.

The meeting split up a few minutes later, the men under strict orders from Steuben not to take matters into their own hands, to wait for the results of an investigation tomorrow.

Dortmunder slipped out and scurried across to Hut 7. Mueller let him in. "What did they decide?" asked Mueller.

"What do you think?" Dortmunder replied bitterly.

"Well . . . too late anyway." Mueller nodded down the corridor. Dortmunder hurried down to Room 2 and peered in. All the bunks were empty except one. Kirst was lying sprawled in a heap. There was blood on his face. His breathing rasped. He quivered now and then.

"Couldn't stop them," said Mueller. "Just about everyone had a hand in it."

Dortmunder whistled. "Steuben won't be happy."

"Who cares? Besides, what can he do?"

"Shouldn't we get him to the medic?"

"He's not that badly off. Look, if Bruckner's right, and Kirst is a spy, they'll remove him tomorrow." Mueller leaned into the room and spoke quietly. "Good-bye, Kirst. May you rot in hell."

Churchill raised his leg against the side of the hut and decorated a foundation block. Finished, he romped happily around Bruckner and sniffed at the ground. Bruckner snapped his fingers. Churchill jumped up the steps and ran inside ahead of him. Bruckner glanced around, always afraid of discovery when he took his dog out for a nighttime piss. He paused on the top step and looked over at Hut 7. It was dark and silent. A chill brushed the nape of his neck. Something was very wrong in Hut 7 and Kirst was at the center of it. Bruckner's accountant's mind kept seeing details that wouldn't add up. He turned, went in, and shut the door.

A cloud of blackness rolled out of the crawl space above Hut 7, descended like liquid shadow to the ground, and flowed across the compound in darkness.

The djinn chortled to itself over its success. Fear was on the rise. The djinn was playing it carefully, manipulating the Germans, terrifying them one minute, letting them think they had power the next. Right now the men in Hut 7 believed they had matters in hand. Kirst lay in a battered stupor, his insides rearranged by their angry fists. That had been worth a lot to the djinn. Power from their anger. Power from Kirst's feeble terror. But the deaths of Eckmann and Gebhard had been the most nourishing so far. The explosion of spiritual terror at the moment of death was the vital nutrient that the djinn needed for growth. Tonight it was bigger, more powerful. After tonight, it would be able to do bigger things, cause more death, gain more power, and grow grow grow. . . .

Overhead, the stars were crowded out by thick black clouds rolling in from the west. Deep winter had arrived at last.

Gilman couldn't sleep. Plagued by confusion, he sat at the desk in his quarters and smoked.

What the hell does she know about what's happening here?

One cigarette burned almost to the end. He lit another. He kept seeing Gebhard and Eckmann—one drowned, the other hanged. When the reports went in tomorrow, there would be a volcanic eruption in Washington. Investigators would be dispatched immediately, but they would have to come by train. There was no airfield within a reasonable distance. That might give him some time.

For what?

Gilman's hand shook. It was France all over again. Men entrusted to his care. Men dying because David Gilman wasn't decisive enough. At Window Hill, he had protested the general's order enough to get himself relieved, but he hadn't carried the fight any farther than that.

Hell. How could you have known there would be a slaughter?

"Caution does not win wars," General Malkin had said. "Aggressive action and bold, decisive moves win the battles and save lives." It was Malkin's bold, decisive move that had killed Gilman's men.

But you didn't do enough. You could have gone around Malkin. Directly to General Patch at Seventh Army HQ. If your battalion had come back victorious, you would have looked foolish. Isn't that why you held off? You didn't want to appear a coward. So you kept quiet, and the men got wiped out.

Gilman looked out the window. Things were getting out of hand here at Blackbone. If the story of Window Hill got around, would anyone look to him for leadership?

Gilman punched out his cigarette, pulled on his boots and a coat, and slammed out of the room. The barracks were dark when he came out on the hill. Spotlights swept the camp slowly. Gilman passed several MPs on duty. Their conversation stopped as he passed. He felt their eyes on him, heard their thoughts, and in that moment he knew.

The story was out.

He just knew it. He had nothing to base it on other than one tiny little incident, but he had a commanding officer's sensitivity—he knew when trust was no longer there.

He moved on slowly, feeling their eyes still on him. He passed the day room. There was an NCO inside. Gilman could see him through the window, sitting under a conical light with his feet up and his cap on the table, reading a magazine.

He passed the gate. The sentry on duty came to attention and saluted. Gilman returned the salute and went on by. From there on, he was alone, walking the perimeter, heading down the long slope to where the valley flattened. White flakes appeared ahead of him, a few scattered bits of snow. He stopped and looked up and, in light reflected off the ground from the spotlights, he saw the dark overhanging clouds and the first snowfall drifting down.

Just in time for the holidays.

Gilman smiled. A white Christmas at Blackbone. Back

up the hill, he could see snow falling on the barracks. Inside the compound, the fall was illuminated by the sweeping spots.

The guard in the nearest tower was watching Gilman, his tommy gun leaning against the railing as he worked his light. Gilman gazed through the fence into the prison grounds. On the slope between the fence and the huts, he saw dark splotches scattered over the earth.

What the hell are those? Shadows?

Gilman pressed against the fence to see without the links obstructing his vision. Light swept by. They weren't shadows. They were recognizable human forms. Bodies. Dead, torn apart, pieces of them scattered everywhere. . . .

Gilman stood rooted against the fence. The scene was impossibly quiet. He blinked, scrunched his eyes shut and kept them closed as long as his curiosity could stand it. When he opened them again, the bodies were still there. Faces were twisted in horror. Eyes gazed sightlessly back at him, pleading against the final indignity of violent death.

Gilman began to shake. His fingers clutched the chain link fence and began to rattle it. He couldn't help himself. He knew who they were. American soldiers killed in battle, murdered by a general's stupidity and a commanding officer's failure of nerve. They were his men, Second Battalion, lying in an open-air grave on Window Hill—

Gilman sprang back from the fence, stumbled, and ran up the long slope, legs pumping, arms clawing at the air. . . . He tore past the day room. The MPs he had encountered on the way down stared at the mad major dashing uphill. Reaching headquarters, Gilman flung an arm out to grab the corner of the building and stop himself. He ducked into the shadows at the bottom of the

241

stairs and stood flattened against the wall. His heart slammed against his ribs. He waited for it to slow down then worked up his courage and looked out at the compound again.

They were gone. There was no trace of what he had seen. There was only the snowfall beginning to lay a soft white carpet on the ground. Gilman stared at it, his mind gripped by an even greater terror. It hadn't been real. It was a waking nightmare.

I'm cracking up.

The nightform seeped back into Hut 7 and returned to Kirst undetected. The djinn settled into place and tested the host body. Still alive. No real damage, just pain and bruises. He kept the mind tapped out, comatose. Kirst had no need for consciousness now. The djinn could bring it back easily in the morning. Only one thing was bothersome: the head had taken such a beating that the eyes were out of focus. The djinn ignored Kirst's other aches and pains but went to work on the eyes. Moments later, the djinn was able to see through them again.

Satisfied, he curled up in Kirst's dormant brain and considered the night's accomplishment. At last he had gained the key to capturing a new and more effective host. Tomorrow, Kirst's beating would be discovered, he would be separated from the others, removed from the compound, taken outside the five walls. Then the djinn would have Gilman at his mercy.

Chapter 20

The snowfall continued the next morning as the Germans turned out for roll call, and Kirst was discovered missing. Gilman immediately dispatched MPs to search the camp, while he and Steuben went together to Hut 7. They found Kirst exactly where his hut-mates had left him the night before, sprawled on his bunk, alone. Steuben was furious, Gilman methodical. He summoned Major Borden as well as one of the German medics, Leutnant Cuno. While they examined Kirst, Gilman ordered Steuben to isolate all the men from Hut 7 for questioning. Steuben hesitated.

"Do you know something about this?" Gilman said.

Steuben nodded.

"Do you want to explain? Or should I go out and knock heads together?"

Steuben sighed. "They think—and I can't say that I don't agree with them—that Kirst is somehow responsible for everything that's happened. For Eckmann, Schliebert, Gebhard, and the general disruption in morale."

Gilman glanced at the cuts and bruises on Kirst's face, the dazed, unseeing eyes, at Borden trying to coax him back to consciousness with ampules of smelling salts.

"They think he's responsible, but they don't know. So they beat the crap out of him to be sure. Is that it?"

Steuben nodded. He said nothing about the other suspicions—that Kirst was a spy planted by Hopkins, that his men believed the two were in league and were jointly to blame for the deaths. He wanted to see what Gilman would do first. If he would take his spy out.

"I think, for his safety, we ought to get him the hell out of here," Gilman said. "Don't you?"

"That might be advisable, Major."

Steuben felt a stab of disappointment. He too glanced at Kirst. The men may have been right. They may have acted stupidly, but they may very well have been right.

Borden stood up. "I don't know what the hell's wrong with him, sir. He's got a few contusions and some split skin, and his belly's kind of lumpy, but he's not coming around. Seems to be in a coma. But his vital signs are all normal. It's like he took whatever they handed him then slept it off."

"Can he be moved?" Gilman asked.

"I think so." Borden conferred briefly with Cuno. Then Cuno hurried off for a stretcher. Gilman ordered two MPs to help him.

"You're taking him out then?" asked Steuben.

"Yes. And I want everybody who belongs in Hut Seven to get his ass back inside. They're confined to quarters until further notice. If I catch even one of them outside, I'll throw the whole mob into solitary. In the meantime, I leave it to you, Major Steuben, to isolate the perpetrators."

Steuben frowned.

Gilman thought he had everything under control, but he hadn't counted on Loring Holloway. She was waiting

244

at the gate and, when she saw him approaching with Borden and the MPs carrying a man on a stretcher, she tore past the sentry and ran down to see who it was. Discovering it was Kirst, she stumbled back to catch up with Gilman.

"Where are you taking him?"

"Out."

"Why?"

"His friends don't like him. They rearranged his face. Next time they might kill him."

"Why did they do it?"

"They're beginning to think like you—that he's behind everything."

She glanced back. Germans were everywhere on the hill, deriving great satisfaction from the procession.

"The only way I can improve the situation is by getting him out," Gilman continued. "If they want to believe he's responsible for three deaths, then at least it looks like I'm doing something."

"Don't take him out," she said urgently. "If you do, I swear you have no idea how bad it's going to get."

Gilman stopped. *"Lady, what are you talking about?"*

Loring searched desperately for a way to convince him. Her eyes fell on the fence. She wanted to tell him about Ur-Tawaq and how the five-walled city had imprisoned the djinn 2,500 years ago, but she quickly realized that telling him would accomplish nothing: she had to show him.

"Major Gilman, you've got to trust me," she said. "Those men are right—Kirst *is* responsible. Only it's not Kirst."

Gilman stared at her then smiled. "Lady, I really do think the time has arrived for you—"

"Oh, stop playing that game! You know you haven't

245

got the answers! You just want them to *think* you're doing something!"

Gilman bristled.

She pointed to Kirst. "Let me work on him. You've got no plan other than conducting interrogations. *Please let me work on him!*"

The MPs were stopped behind them, exchanging puzzled looks. Borden frowned skeptically. "What do you mean, work on him?" Gilman said.

"Let me *show* you what's wrong with him."

"Why not just tell me?"

She moved to the stretcher and looked down at Kirst's staring eyes. "I can't—because you won't believe it. But I'm positive I can show you. He's inside there, but I can bring him out. I can force him to show himself. Then you'll see what you're dealing with."

Gilman met Borden's suspicious gaze, then he looked down the hill at the Germans. They were waiting for the parade to resume, for Kirst to be taken the hell out of their midst.

"I'm sorry, Miss Holloway," said Gilman. "Whatever you want to do, it'll have to be outside."

"No!" She stabbed a finger at Kirst's chest. "That's what he wants!" She swept a hand around. "In here, he's contained! He can wreak havoc, but he can't get out and make it worse! Take him somewhere isolated and let me work on him, but it's got to be inside this fence!"

Gilman was wondering if she was crazier than Kirst when he caught sight of Steuben and Bruckner hurrying toward them. Before they caught up, Gilman moved to the stretcher and studied Kirst then made his decision. He told the MPs, "Take him down to the *Krankenhaus*. Clear everybody else out. Miss Holloway, get whatever

246

you need and meet us in ten minutes. Borden, I want you along."

"Yes, sir."

Loring turned and ran back through the gate, as Gilman explained to Steuben what they were going to do. When Gilman invited him along, Steuben accepted grimly.

The MPs marched Kirst back down the slope, passing nearly two hundred dismayed German prisoners. As Steuben started to follow, Bruckner grabbed his sleeve and warned him, "Be careful. They're up to something."

Steuben shook him off and tramped angrily after Gilman.

Confined to Hut 7 by Gilman's order, Mueller lay on his bunk and stared out the window. A door creaked; he heard footsteps clumping down the hall. As Dortmunder and Hoffman entered, Mueller motioned them to the window and pointed to the back fence. Now the dirt-covered blanket concealing the open mine shaft was further cam- ouflaged with fresh snow, but when Mueller described the hole, they got excited. They saw what they had been waiting for: freedom.

"Until last night," admitted Mueller, "I wanted to get out of here just for the sake of being free. Now—" He didn't have to voice the rest: they all felt the same fear— that more was going to happen, and the longer they stayed the greater the chance they would become victims.

"We are the only ones who have the means of escape," said Hoffman, stroking his chin. "If we share it, we risk discovery."

"We have to keep it quiet," Dortmunder agreed. "Too bad about Eckmann, though. It would have been fun having him and his letters along."

"Maybe you'd rather take Kirst in his place," Mueller said.

Nobody laughed.

Mueller turned over and stared at the ceiling. "We'll move tonight."

Loring spread everything out on a tray beside the cot on which they had placed Kirst. In a row she arranged the silver flask, the carton of salt, the magnet, the steel rod, the flashlight, the bag of herbs, the lump of tar, and the copy of the Koran.

While Steuben and Borden studied the display, Cuno finished patching up Kirst. The German infirmary was otherwise deserted. They were alone in the long ward with its row of neatly made-up cots. Toward the rear were a storage closet, an isolation cubicle, and living quarters for Cuno and the other medic, Heilbruner.

Gilman stood at the window watching the snowfall. If the storm hit tonight, the CID investigators wouldn't get through, and Gilman knew his own options were limited. He couldn't stomp around the camp playing Sherlock Holmes—he wasn't trained for it. Damn the Army anyway—why hadn't they built an airstrip? He frowned. Loring's hand was at her chest, fingering something beneath her sweater. Gilman studied her figure: with that tight woolen pullover and those stylish baggy trousers, she looked even more attractive than in that Rita Hayworth get-up—at least to Gilman, who noted that no one else was interested.

Cuno finished and backed away. Loring pulled up a chair next to Kirst. Borden sat on the next cot over. Steuben moved to the foot of the bed. Gilman stayed at the window. Kirst lay very still, his eyes milky and staring, lips parted, his breathing shallow.

Loring reached for the Koran, opened it to marked pages, and started to read—flatly, as if it were an ordinary ritual. "In the name of Allah," she began, and continued, intoning passage after passage, invoking the power of Allah to rid them of this troublesome spirit. . . .

Gilman was speculating on why she was subjecting them to this mumbojumbo when she stopped abruptly and studied Kirst. They waited in silence, but nothing happened. Quietly she put the book aside and reached for the flashlight.

Steuben grunted something.

Loring flicked on the light and waved it to show that it was an ordinary instrument. Gilman immediately recalled Kirst's reaction to having his picture taken: flying across the room when the flash went off. He glanced over and could see that Borden remembered it too.

Loring held the flashlight over Kirst and directed the beam into his eyes.

His head jerked sideways and his lids snapped down.

She waited then put her thumb against his left eye, pried up the lid, and directed the beam into his pupil—

Kirst's arm shot up and hit her wrist, knocking the flashlight to the floor. Loring grimaced at the pain.

Kirst's arm fell to the bed. His head rolled up, revealing unseeing eyes open again. Everybody stared at him. Loring twisted her hand to counteract the pain. "It doesn't like light," she said.

"What do you mean, it?" said Gilman.

"A creature of darkness, Major Gilman. Haven't you noticed that all three deaths occurred at night?"

Gilman had visions of Kirst rising in the night like Bela Lugosi and gliding forth for a midnight drink.

Loring watched a slight flicker in Kirst's eyes. "I think

he's going to wake up soon," she said. "Perhaps someone should make coffee."

While Cuno got the water boiling, Loring reached for the lump of tar. Using the edge of the magnet, she pried off a bite-size chunk and held it over Kirst's parted lips. "Now keep your eyes on him," she said, and quickly jammed the lump between his teeth then held her hand over his mouth. Steuben moved to stop her, but he wasn't fast enough. Kirst's jaws flew open. His teeth clamped down on Loring's hand, and she screamed. Steuben froze, frightened by her scream and by a menacing growl from Kirst. Gilman reached over but Loring was quicker. She slammed her fist down on Kirst's chest. His grip relaxed and she yanked her hand free.

Gilman stared at the bloody teeth marks in her flesh then watched her rush to the sink and hold her hand under running water. As he turned back to the cot, he saw Kirst's head again loll sideways. Hot melting tar leaked from his lips and spread in a steaming pool under his head.

Gilman, Steuben, Borden, and Cuno—all were immobilized, staring at the black goo on the sheet. Borden finally reached over and cautiously dipped a finger into it, scooping up a glob and letting it run down the back of his nail. "Jesus Christ," he said, staring at Kirst's blistering lips.

They waited while Cuno used disinfectant on Loring's hand. When she returned to the chair, she was pale and shaky.

"Maybe we'd better call a halt before he bites your head off," Gilman suggested.

"No."

"It's your party, but I'm beginning to wonder what you're going to do with that rod."

"Very funny." She unbuttoned Kirst's shirt and exposed his torso. They were all surprised at how thin and gray he was; his ribs stood out. "There are certain substances that he—that *it*—reacts to violently. Kirst is permitted to eat only enough solid food to keep his body in minimal working order. Eventually, though, he'll die. Major Borden, would you lift him, please?"

Borden raised Kirst by the shoulders, allowing Loring to arrange the rod on the bed so it would lie parallel to Kirst's spinal cord, then she gestured for Borden to lower him on it. She picked up the magnet and gripped it so the polarized tips pointed downward and were just touching the surface of Kirst's flesh at his collarbone. His skin at that spot quickly blackened to the color of a bad bruise. As Loring drew the magnet down the length of his torso, following the approximate position of the rod beneath his back, the blackening followed.

Kirst began to writhe painfully. His mouth opened. He made a choking sound.

"All right, Miss Holloway, that'll do . . ." Gilman said.

Loring ignored him. She held the magnet directly over his belly and worked it up and down. The blackness rippled with the motion. Kirst's head rolled from side to side. His hands snatched at the bedclothes. His body stiffened.

They were all staring now.

"It was in the flask," Loring said, glancing at their astonished faces. "It was in the crate he climbed into after his submarine sank. He threw everything else out, but not the flask. He opened it, and the thing that was inside got out. And now it's in him."

"What *thing?*" Gilman said hoarsely.

"Can you see it?" she snapped, indicating the rippling blackness. *"Tell me you can't see it!"*

They exchanged looks.

"All right," said Gilman. "We see something."

Satisfied, Loring continued. "It's not a trick. I didn't make him swallow iron filings while your backs were turned."

"What *thing?*" Gilman demanded again.

"A demon."

There was silence. Not even a look was exchanged. They watched the moving magnet and Kirst alternately writhing and stiffening.

"It holds itself together by manipulating its molecules inside a magnetic field. Historically, this type of demon reacts adversely to iron, and it was easy to figure out why —iron disrupts its magnetic field. Right now it's helpless."

Gilman's anger grew. He was tired of this, tired of her tricks and pronouncements. For a moment he watched her continue to draw patterns on Kirst's stomach, then abruptly he snatched the magnet from her hand and returned it to the tray. "All right, Miss Holloway, do you work for State, the museum, or Blackstone the Magician? Which is it?"

Loring was quiet a moment.

"What else are you going to do? What about the salt?"

Loring reminded Cuno about the coffee. Gilman angrily hoisted Kirst up and yanked the rod out from beneath him.

"Look!" said Borden.

The black bruise was still there on Kirst's belly. As they watched, it continued moving, as if the magnet were still manipulating it. It burrowed up to Kirst's throat and pulsed there, changing color back and forth from black to gray, then it shot back down and described figure eights on Kirst's chest. Borden choked on a laugh.

"Oh, Christ," said Loring. "It's playing with me."

As if it heard her, the black spot stopped moving and gradually disappeared. Steuben reached for a chair and sat down. Loring leaned back, some of her anxiety going. It was there, no longer a figment of her imagination. It really existed. She had chased across half a continent to find it and now she knew—

There is a djinn. And it's inside Kirst.

They sat around a card table and had coffee, and Loring told them where it came from, how she had found it, how it draws energy from fear, how it gains power by killing its victims, how it thrives on an atmosphere of chaos.

The djinn moved inside the body. It used Kirst's eyes to watch the little group around the table. It had mixed feelings about the woman. On the one hand she was a nuisance, but she could be dealt with. She could sit there and talk to them until the seasons changed, but they would still not be convinced. The djinn could sense that they didn't believe her yet, and that was good, it gave him more time. *Confusion, indeed.* The djinn chuckled and rolled inside Kirst—*How could she know she was only adding to the confusion?* And when she finds out how little she has accomplished her fear will return. And that will bring us to the other hand: she too could make an excellent new host.

"If it's not stopped," she was saying, "it will kill everyone within reach."

"I'm sorry. I just don't understand this," Borden said. "You mean at night Kirst walks around like some zombie and does these things?"

"No. The djinn comes out of Kirst in some way, does

253

what it wants, and goes back in. All it requires in order to function is a host to live in during the day and the regular consumption of emotional energy." She glanced at Kirst. "It's in there right now. We've got to keep it in there."

"How?" Gilman said.

"I don't know."

Gilman's chair scraped loudly as he got up. He went all the way to the back of the infirmary, found a sink with a medicine cabinet mirror over it, ran some water, and washed his face. He couldn't decide whether or not he believed her. He didn't *want* to believe her, that was the whole thing. Would it make his job easier if he did? God, no. He reached for a paper towel. She was standing a few feet away.

"I'm a scientist," she said. "I've got nothing to gain by promoting a load of hogwash. What has to happen for you to believe me?"

He chucked the towel away. "It just seems so convenient. The thing never shows itself, yet people get killed. I'm not as scientific as you claim to be, but I want *proof.*"

She glanced around to be sure the others couldn't hear. "The biggest danger we're facing right now is that it wants to get outside this prison compound and into a more wide-ranging host. And if that happens, there's no way to stop it. It can go on and—"

Disgusted, Gilman walked away from her. She followed him back to the table and watched him sip coffee. She felt angry and hurt but tried to get past that.

"This thing has a history," she went on. "It's been written about. There are similarities between some of the deaths it caused in Ur-Tawaq and what's been going on here."

"What similarities?" Borden asked.

"Major Steuben, why did Eckmann kill Schliebert?"

254

Steuben hesitated. "He imagined Schliebert was making love to his wife."

"Which sounds crazy, doesn't it?"

Steuben was silent.

"But suppose Eckmann really did see Schliebert with his wife? Suppose he didn't imagine it but *believed* he was seeing it. It was as real to him as I am to you. Were Eckmann and Schliebert friends or enemies? Did they like each other or hate each other?"

Steuben thought carefully. "It was . . . Hoffman and Dortmunder, and a few others, that Eckmann didn't get along with. Schliebert was a friend."

"So why would Eckmann imagine the worst of a friend? There would have to be a history of frustration and mental pressure with Schliebert at the center of it. Even a psychotic behaves within a discernible pattern. But the djinn doesn't care about human motivations. It induces psychosis! It feeds on the fears of its victims, setting friend against friend—you see, there were *two* victims in that murder. Schliebert *and* Eckmann!"

They still weren't sure. Loring grabbed a notebook out of her suitcase and slapped it on the table. She flipped pages until she found the one she was looking for.

"Here. This is an account of two citizens of Ur-Tawaq. A blacksmith, believing that his wife had been unfaithful with a carpenter, killed the carpenter. But his wife was able to prove her innocence—she had never even met the carpenter. Just before he was to be tried for the crime, the blacksmith hanged himself in despair." She closed the notebook and looked at Gilman. "I think that's goddamned similar, don't you?"

No one answered.

Loring shot a finger in Kirst's direction. "It worked so well twenty-five hundred years ago that the djinn thought it would be swell to try it again! Don't you see what you're up against?"

Borden frowned skeptically. "How does it accomplish these things?"

"By conjuring delusions. There's a lot of fear and demoralization floating around this camp. It capitalizes on that, provokes more of it by applying a form of hypnosis to weakened, fearful minds. It can pick these men off one by one or in twos or—In the city of Ur-Tawaq, eventually there were mass delusions!"

Gilman's hand lashed out and swept his tin coffee cup off the table. It clattered off to a corner. Fixing Loring with an angry glare, he said, "You're not making things easier, Miss Holloway. You're telling Major Steuben that there's a monster after his men."

"It's after all of us, Major. It's only starting with the prisoners."

"Presuming you're right, how do you propose to stop it?"

She indicated the tray. "That's what I'm trying to find out. We're testing it."

Borden shrugged. "Why don't we just kill Kirst?"

Steuben jumped up. He assailed them with a string of German epithets. He shouted and thundered then stopped abruptly and crossed to the cot. He stared at Kirst.

"I guess that's one vote no," said Borden.

"We may have to at some point," said Loring, "if only to expose the djinn, force it out in the open, deprive it of its host. But it won't do any good—in fact, it would be more dangerous—unless we have a surefire method of killing it." She looked at the cot and raised her voice for Steuben's benefit. "Kirst is going to die anyway. He can't last long with the djinn draining him this way. He's not really in a coma, you see. There's just . . . nothing left of him. No will, no emotions, no thoughts of his own. And now that the djinn knows we're aware of its presence, it *has* to find a new host. And soon."

"How will it do that?" Gilman snapped.

"I don't know. The same way it got into Kirst, I suppose."

Steuben studied Kirst's staring eyes. Some of his superiors' orders had defied credibility, but this woman put them all to shame. She was remarkable—so convincing!

Bruckner is right—the Americans are up to something. They brought her here, just like they brought Kirst. They're all in it together. But why? What are they doing to us?

He moved to the tray and picked up the bag of herbs. "What is this for?" he said. At that moment, his gaze fell on the window and he saw something happening outside, between Huts 9 and 10, that made his blood freeze.

Ten minutes earlier, Hopkins had entered the camp alone, armed with a .45 automatic holstered at his waist.

He felt like the marshal walking into a town full of bank robbers, cattle rustlers, and mother rapers. That's all the Germans were to him anyway: the bad guys, the black hats in the Saturday matinee serials he had devoured back in the thirties. In high school, while the other guys had spent their weekend afternoons lining up dates, Hopkins had wallowed in fantasy at the movies. It had never mattered to him that he couldn't find a "nice girl" to go out with. He had known a few who weren't so nice, and they had suited him fine.

Hopkins had learned a lot from Tom Mix, Buck Jones, and Hoot Gibson. He had learned that if you really wanted to show them who was boss, you had to do it alone. You had to buckle on your six-gun and walk onto their turf. You had to go looking for it.

He knew the Germans were responsible, that the deaths of Gebhard, Eckmann, and Schliebert were all part of some vast, well-coordinated kraut plot, and that Bruckner and Steuben were the ringleaders. Gilman couldn't see it, because Gilman had no experience with Germans, except to lose his fucking command to them in France.

Spreading the story hadn't worked out as he'd hoped. The MPs were too uneasy over the recent mysterious deaths to concern themselves over something Gilman had done in Europe, so Hopkins had decided to dispose of the mystery first. One step at a time.

The Germans were using lengths of board to clear snow off their volleyball court. He felt their eyes on his back as he swaggered past.

That's the way it should be: they hate me and I hate them, and no bones about it.

He walked on, contemplating means and ends. Their scheme was obvious: murder a few of their own and blame it on the Americans. Hopkins would expose that. But Gilman would never mete out sufficient punishment and, among the MPs, that would be a strike against him. They would come to Hopkins and say, What's with this asshole, anyway? Then Hopkins would remind them of what they had ignored before. Gilman in France—Second Battalion—Window Hill—weak jerk-off coward Major former-Lieutenant Colonel David Gilman. Well, what do we do about him? they would ask. Give him the treatment, Hopkins would suggest. Put the screws to him, let things go wrong, make him crack, make him request a transfer. In the middle of winter, the brass wouldn't bother sending up a new C.O. They'd look around to see

258

who was already in place, holding all the crap together. They would discover Hopkins. The number two man would become number one. It was easy, the best plans always were.

Hopkins walked on, smugly satisfied.

Yes, sir. Can't miss. Like sliding into home.

Hopkins went between Huts 8 and 9. Damnit, where was Bruckner? Should be out somewhere walking that fucking dog. Step number one, shake Bruckner up. Invite him to the shower hut for a conference, pretending concern for what's been happening. Once alone with him, Hopkins would grab him by the throat, shove the automatic down his pants, and threaten to blow off his cock if he didn't squeal and say exactly who had cut Gebhard's water, and who had stretched Eckmann's neck. And if he didn't talk, maybe Hopkins would accidentally shoot his fucking dog.

A twig snapped. Hopkins glanced back. There were four Germans strolling up behind him, hands jammed in their pockets, blank-faced. Ignoring them, Hopkins rounded the corner of Hut 9.

Three more of them were blocking his way. Hopkins stopped. They closed in on him a bit, then they stopped too. Hopkins braced his hands on his hips and glowered at them—the marshal surrounded by black hats.

"Well, sprechen me zum English!" he barked. He figured they wanted something, some complaint or other. He could deal with it quickly and still find Bruckner.

But it was Bruckner who stepped into view next, around the corner of Hut 10 with the dog on a leash. In broken English, Bruckner said, "How did you kill zem, Hopkins?"

Hopkins glanced back. Surrounded, he decided to bluff it out. "With my prick, kraut."

They glared at him. An alarm went off in his head. Mentally, he spelled the word *backfire.* "You think I did it?" he said.

Bruckner nodded.

"That's funny. I think *you* did it."

Bruckner shook his head—universal gesture meaning a flat no. But to Hopkins it translated as, I'm calling you a liar. And that made him mad. He hitched up his pants; his right hand settled on the butt of his automatic.

Bruckner wasn't fazed. Carefully he enunciated, "And who vill you kill next?"

Hopkins started to worry. As they drew closer, he saw hatred in their eyes. They all had a few days' growth of stubble. It made them look like derelicts, like the angry and haunted jobless he recalled from the early years of the Depression. Robbed of their self-esteem, their only solace lay in occasionally beating the crap out of somebody better off than themselves.

Fury broke in Hopkins' brain. He yanked out the .45. He was grabbed from behind. He tried to get his index finger through the trigger guard, but they took the gun away from him and pinned his arms back. He started hollering. They threw him to the ground and shoved his face into the snow.

Standing over Kirst with the bag of herbs in his hand, Steuben saw through the window what was happening between Huts 9 and 10. With a guttural curse, he flung the bag down on Kirst's cot and bolted for the door.

An instant later, Gilman ran after him.

Chapter 21

The wind was up, whipping at Steuben's clothes as he bellowed in German at his men, flung them aside, and reached down to help Hopkins up. Hopkins scrambled away and backed against a wall. "You fucking krauts!" he screamed. "I'll rip your fucking balls off! You'll all end up like Eckmann . . . !"

The man holding Hopkins' gun leveled it at him. Steuben's fist came around so hard the man was knocked flat on his ass in the snow. Steuben scooped up the .45 and pointed it at his own men. They froze, their own anger checked by the fury in Steuben's eyes. Slowly they backed off.

"Give me that," Hopkins growled, his hand outstretched toward Steuben. "Hand it over right now, Major, or you'll be playing oom-pah with the Pearly Gates Band."

Steuben's gaze shifted to Hopkins. His finger closed on the trigger. Gilman stepped between them and said calmly, "I'll take that."

Steuben relaxed and handed it to him.

Brushing snow off his clothes and retrieving his cap, Hopkins joined Gilman and balefully eyed the Germans. "Jumped me, sir. I was just out here minding my own business—"

"Alone. And they took your weapon away."

"Well, yessir, but—"

Raising the automatic over his head, Gilman fired till it was empty, snapping off an entire clip as the Germans flinched around him. When the sound of echoing cracks had died, he glared at Hopkins. "Loaded, too, huh?"

Hopkins glanced at the Germans. They were grinning. "Sir, are you insinuating this was my fault?"

"Hopkins, the dumbest MP in our barracks wouldn't walk in here armed and alone with the prisoners out of their huts. You could have gotten yourself killed, which I can promise you would not make headlines in the *Army Times*. Or they could have used your gun to kill someone else, in which case you'd be court-martialed!"

"You'd give those krauts a medal if they killed me."

"I don't understand how you ever made captain."

"I don't understand how you only got busted to major!"

Gilman stiffened then abruptly grabbed Hopkins, propelled him around Hut 10, and slammed him against the wall. "You think you know something?"

"I know plenty."

"Do you know where your asshole is?"

"What are you gonna do, Major? Punch me like you did the general?"

Gilman hesitated, listening to Steuben, around the corner, angrily dismissing his men. Shoving the .45 back into Hopkins' holster, he released him and said, "Get out of here."

Hopkins saluted stiffly and stalked off.

Steuben fell in beside Gilman and they walked back to the *Krankenhaus*. Steuben was apologetic for the behavior of his men. Gilman brushed it off. "As far as I'm

262

concerned, Major, the incident was provoked. It's over. Nobody gets punished."

Steuben thanked him, then added, "I must tell you, Major Gilman, there is suspicion among the prisoners that your soldiers were responsible for the deaths of Eckmann and Gebhard, and that Hopkins himself was behind it."

"Do you believe that"—Gilman opened the door to the *Krankenhaus* and gestured inside—"now?"

Steuben shook his head. They went in.

There was an empty space where Kirst's cot had been. For a moment, Gilman and Steuben both stood staring at it, thinking the worst—that Loring Holloway's demon had somehow broken loose and demolished the bed, Loring, Cuno, and Borden in one stroke, and now it was loose somewhere in the camp.

Gilman edged farther into the ward, looked around, then in great relief heard voices coming from the back. They found everyone in the rearmost cubicle, gathered around Kirst's cot.

"For a light sonofabitch, it just about threw my spine out to carry him," complained Borden. "She made us drag him back here. She wants him isolated."

Gilman checked Kirst. He was still out. "What have you got in mind now, Miss Holloway? More tests?"

"No." She was opening the bag of herbs and carefully sprinkling them over the bedclothes and around the cot on the floor.

"What's that going to do?" Gilman asked.

"Hopefully, keep the djinn from getting out tonight," Loring said. "One or more of these herbs should have some effect and conceivably could keep the thing at bay."

"Like the tar?" Borden said with a grin.

263

"I take it you have an explanation for that, Major Borden?"

Borden's grin faded and he shook his head.

Loring sprinkled the last of the herbs at the rear threshold, just beyond the cubicle, then she turned to Gilman. "You've got three dead men, Major. If you don't want more, I suggest you stop laughing at me and post some guards in here tonight—men who can stay awake! I want Kirst watched! If you're not convinced I'm right, at least humor me."

Gilman frowned then finally nodded. Behind him, Steuben muttered, "Thank you, Major."

Steuben stood outside the *Krankenhaus* as the MP detail summoned by Gilman double-timed down the slope and ran up the steps inside. Curious prisoners were slouched outside the huts. Catching Steuben's eye, a few gestured with their hands, "What's up?" Steuben ignored them. Borden emerged from the rear door with Loring Holloway. Gilman held the door open so Steuben could see the arrangement inside.

Kirst was stretched out on the cot as they had left him. MPs were stationed one at the cubicle, one at the rear door, and the rest deeper inside the ward as relief. Satisfied, Steuben nodded to Gilman and backed off. Gilman shut the door and said, "Any problems tonight, Major, don't hesitate to scream bloody murder."

"At the top of my lungs, Herr Kommandant."

Gilman prodded Loring Holloway and, with Borden hefting her suitcase, he followed her out of the camp. Watching them go, Steuben saw the way she glanced at Gilman, and the way Gilman ignored her. Steuben smiled to himself and contemplated how he would handle her. Mentally, he had her pants off and her legs spread on the bed before the image of his wife intruded.

He walked back to his men. Bruckner met him with Churchill on a short leash, several loops of it wrapped around his wrist. After that brush with Hopkins, he was taking no chances: he expected reprisals, and he knew Churchill would be an easy, cheap target.

"What's going on with Kirst?" he asked Steuben.

Steuben thought carefully before replying. It wouldn't do to describe everything that had happened in the *Krankenhaus*. That would most certainly provoke panic among his men. "They have agreed to isolate him," Steuben said. "They will keep him under guard tonight."

"Why?"

"To prove to us that he's no spy. To put our minds at ease."

Bruckner laughed.

"Hans, listen to me. I want you to reassure the men that the Americans had nothing to do with the deaths of Eckmann and Gebhard. If there were a plot to exterminate us, Gilman would have to know. But he's as concerned about the deaths as we are. I think we have to trust him."

"I see. Trust him, even if we all die."

"Hans, we are prisoners. They have no reason to murder us. If they were our prisoners, we wouldn't do it to them."

"No?"

Bruckner pulled Churchill along, motioning Steuben to follow and gesturing at the other men to leave them alone. He led Steuben behind the shower hut and stopped. Churchill sniffed at the foundation then took a healthy piss.

"Do you really know what is going on in this war, Walter?"

"We are losing it."

"Have you ever seen a concentration camp?"

Steuben sighed impatiently. "No, Hans. No, I haven't."

"I have. I've been inside one. I've tried to forget it, tried to put it out of my mind but, whenever I hear our friends carry on about their lofty ideals and their grand moments in this war . . . all I can think is, You fools! You don't see. You haven't been there."

At Steuben's puzzled look, Bruckner managed a tense smile. "I know what you think of me. Hans Bruckner is afraid of his own shadow. Paranoid. He clings to that dog as if it's the only reality left in his world." He drew Churchill closer on the leash. The dog was licking up snow. "Well, if I appear suspicious of everything and everybody, there is a reason—rooted in what I saw in that concentration camp."

He looked Steuben in the eye. "If we could do it, Walter, so could the Americans."

"Do what?"

"Because I was an accountant in private life, they made me a paymaster. In that capacity, I was sent to Auschwitz to deliver an SS payroll. Do you know about Auschwitz?"

Steuben shrugged.

"An industrial commune in the south of Poland, near Krakow. Also the site of a huge concentration camp where they . . . process people."

"Process?"

"Where they kill them. The SS has a highly efficient system for disposing of Jews and Poles. Men, women, and children are collected and brought by rail to Ausch-

266

witz, housed in filthy barracks where they wait their turns to be executed. They are taken in lots to be gassed, then the bodies are burned . . ."

Steuben's ears were flushed with blood as he listened to Bruckner describe details of the showers that weren't showers, the ovens, the sifting of ashes for valuables, for gold teeth and jewelry hidden in bodily orifices—He couldn't believe what he was hearing.

Bruckner continued, the details pouring out of him in a flood of disgusted remembrance. "But the worst of it, Walter, is that this *processing* is done by German soldiers —*our men* who went off to fight a war in the name of the Fatherland! This is how we have ended up! This is our legacy! This is what we will be remembered for!"

"Hans—"

"When I was captured in France and shipped to the United States, all I could think of was that the higher powers in this war—Hitler, Churchill, and Roosevelt— had somehow agreed that the innocent of all countries should be done away with and that, in America, they would put me in a camp like Auschwitz, beat me and starve me, then shove me in a chamber and gas me, then burn the remains! Can you imagine the state I was in when I arrived here? Until I realized there were no ovens, that the shower hut was truly a place where water and not gas ran through the pipes. Now, after Gebhard and Eckmann and Schliebert, I can't help myself. I'm afraid. I don't care what they tell you, Walter. *I believe they are going to kill us.*"

Steuben was silent, feeling the chilling wind ruffle his hair. "Why don't you . . . tell the others?" he said.

Bruckner sagged against the wall. "We're prisoners. We have little enough to cling to. To expose the truth about our aims in this war . . ." He shrugged. "If I could make every man in this camp see what I have seen, it would undermine their will to live."

"Why should the SS do it?"

"Walter . . . do you find it so hard to believe? They've always been free to kill enemies of the state. They have merely extended that sanction to include Jews, gypsies, Poles, and others."

"Russians?"

"Of course. They processed nearly a hundred people while I watched. On a daily schedule, multiply that by five or ten, and that by as many concentration camps as there are in Europe—"

"They're doing it all over Europe?"

"Of course."

"But it can't just be the SS. The authority must come—"

"From the top, yes."

Steuben stared at Bruckner, who gazed sadly at the ground. Though Steuben did not share Bruckner's fear that the Americans were in collusion with Hitler and the British to massacre "undesirables," he could without much trouble imagine Hitler and his lunatics coming up with the idea by themselves. He thought of all the commanding officers he had known in the Army. Not one would ever behave in a manner unbefitting a soldier. Their duty was war, not genocide. Yet the SS and the Gestapo—they could be persuaded to do such things. Some would pay for the privilege. Kill Jews? Why not? Kill Poles and gypsies, certainly! How many? When? Where? Is this what Aryan supremacy was all about?

Bruckner clucked to Churchill and they walked away together. Steuben stayed where he was, slumped against the wall of the shower hut. This was the black finale to his career, to the Army, to Germany itself. From this,

Germany would never recover. And those idiots in charge probably thought no one would care if they murdered a hundred thousand Jews more or less. Maybe a million. But why stop at a million?

Steuben thought of his family in Germany, in the path of the Russian advance, and of the reprisals the Russians would take using the concentration camps as an excuse. His family. Steuben was now sure that he would never see them again.

Despite the winter chill, he was sweating. His shirt was sticking to his back. He wanted to strip his uniform off, tear it, and burn it! Wasn't there some way he could recover the dignity those lunatics in Berlin had stolen from him? Wasn't there some way he could get back into the war and die a soldier's death, an honorable death?

Steuben pushed away from the wall and walked back to his quarters.

Settled deep inside Kirst, the djinn rested, preparing itself for tonight. Its strength was nearing peak. Now its exploratory tendrils could invisibly range far beyond Kirst, almost to the five walls themselves. Now it could find fear anywhere in the camp, analyze it, and store it as reference for the nightform. So had it picked up the extraordinary emotional outpouring from Bruckner, and logged Steuben's tortured response. It reveled in Bruckner's paranoia. Through him it now had the means to create chaos. But tonight? First it would need more energy, more victims, build up just a bit more power before it could unleash the full terror.

Testing the air in the cubicle, the djinn swirled in amusement. Hyssop, mandragora, rue, belladonna, and even death camass the stupid woman had scattered about the room. A few days ago the djinn might have been

269

slowed by such folly, but no longer. Now it was too strong. Now nothing could stand in its way. Not all the power of Korbazrah or any other ancient mage. And never again, either!

The djinn rolled up into Kirst's eyes and studied the soldier standing guard at the door. Poor fellow, thought the djinn. It drew back and waited. Night was coming.

Part Four

Chapter 22

Snow flurries whipped between the huts for the rest of the day. There was no volleyball, no calisthenics, and only a few prisoners braved the storm to stretch their legs. With the weather getting worse, the Americans got lax about the enforced confinement at Hut 7.

Lurking around the back of Hut 10, Mueller eyed the thick blanket of snow building up over the mine shaft entrance. To mark the rapidly disappearing spot, he threw a small branch up the slope. It would be disastrous if he and his companions lost valuable time tonight just trying to find the damned hole under the snow.

A few minutes later he was in Bruckner's quarters. "We're going tonight," he said.

Bruckner listened to the storm outside and glanced significantly at Mueller.

"We'll be all right," Mueller said.

Bruckner nodded. "Good luck."

Mueller backed out and shut the door.

Bruckner let his breath out slowly. Churchill was asleep at the end of his cot, curled up in a ball, his tail twitching against his nose. Outside, winter screamed at the camp.

"Good luck," Bruckner repeated to no one in particular.

From a window in Hut 7, Bauhopf and von Lechterhoeven watched the rear of the *Krankenhaus* through the driving snow flurries.

"What if we killed him?" Bauhopf said.

"Difficult. Too many MPs in there."

"What if we get Heilbruner or Cuno to do it? Inject him with something?"

"How do we get to them?"

Bauhopf leaned against the wall thoughtfully. Then he took several deep breaths and abruptly slammed his hand through the window. Glass shattered. He gasped sharply. Wide-eyed, von Lechterhoeven stared as Bauhopf drew his hand back. There was blood welling from several cuts.

"I've had an accident," Bauhopf said through gritted teeth. "Better call the medic."

From the window in his quarters, Steuben watched absently as von Lechterhoeven, bundled in a heavy coat, thrashed through the deepening drifts and headed for the *Krankenhaus.* Steuben turned away, too preoccupied to wonder what he was up to.

He lit a cigarette and smoked lying on his cot, going over what he had witnessed today. Strictly on the human level, demons notwithstanding, Kirst was a menace, a threat to camp morale. That alone made him dangerous. If he was somehow possessed by a demon on top of it, then perhaps this chitchat about eventually having to kill him wasn't idle.

Steuben smoked the cigarette through, then stubbed it out and got up. Climbing onto his cot, he reached up to the ceiling and shoved a board out of the way. His fingers felt around in the crawl space until they closed on steel.

274

He brought down a knife fashioned out of prison cutlery and honed to a sharp edge, a little item he had confiscated from Dortmunder a few months back. It had seemed foolish to just turn it over to the Americans, so he had hidden it.

Now perhaps there was a use for it. If anything happened tonight . . . *Kirst, I have a present for you.*

In a foul mood, Hopkins finished reaming out Chilton for some minor infraction, the nature of which Hopkins forgot before the end of his tirade. But he didn't forget to postpone Chilton's leave. "The weather, Corporal. No one gets out in this shit."

"Yes, sir. Maybe after it lets up, sir."

"Yeah, maybe."

Chilton saluted and fled before Hopkins could dream up something worse.

Hopkins growled to himself. The story of how he had failed as a uniformed Gary Cooper up against a mob of unarmed Germans had circulated fast. The MPs had been joking about it at lunch, and Chilton had been laughing right along with them.

Sonofabitch, that's what you get for trusting the little bastard.

Hopkins kicked the side of his desk and spun around once in his swivel chair. *There's got to be some way to short-circuit this mess,* he thought. They had been making a big deal about Kirst all day, and they hadn't let him into the Krankenfuckinghaus to see what it was all about. Some folderol involving the skirt from State. As assistant commandant, he could insist that they keep him informed but, after today, he stood little chance of insisting on anything where Gilman was concerned.

Suddenly it struck him—Gilman must have something

on Kirst. That's why they were in the *Krankenhaus.* Gilman was giving the bastard the third degree, getting him to admit that he'd killed Eckmann and Gebhard. Hopkins swore to himself. *If Gilman manages to stick that feather in his cap, it's the end of my bid to replace him as commandant. Can't let that happen. But how to stop it?*

Get Kirst.

Cuno tied off the dressing around Bauhopf's hand and taped it. Glancing up, he saw that the room in Hut 7 had filled up, and there were more prisoners standing in the doorway. He looked at Bauhopf, puzzled.

"It's been decided," said Bauhopf. "We have to get rid of Kirst, and we want your help."

Cuno frowned. "Who decided?"

"Steuben."

"I don't believe you. He wouldn't give such an order."

"He wouldn't dare countermand it," an angry voice piped up.

"How much morphine have you got?" Bauhopf asked.

"None. It has to be issued by the Americans." Cuno quickly packed up his bag. The men watched him.

"If you won't help," said Bauhopf, "we'll do it without you."

"You can't get in."

"You'll take me. I'm wounded."

Cuno's jaw worked as he studied their faces, so full of determination. "You weren't there today. You didn't see . . ."

"Didn't see what?"

"Steuben knows—"

"The hell with him. We'll handle this—"

276

"What are you going to handle?" Cuno jumped up, eyes blazing. "Do you know what Kirst is?"

"A spy."

"A traitor!"

"A killer!"

"It's not Kirst doing the killing!" Cuno snapped.

Bauhopf touched his arm. Their eyes met. "Who then?"

Looking around, Cuno saw that he wasn't going to get out of this room unless he told the truth. So he did.

Loring Holloway sat by the window in her room, distracted by the storm boiling up outside. Somehow, out here in the wilds of Montana, a snowstorm seemed far more fearsome than in the canyons of Manhattan. She thought of her warm little apartment in Midtown, and the way the windows rattled all through winter. She thought of her cozy, dry office at the museum, and her parents' sumptuous country home. She thought of a crackling fire and Warren Clark and his pathetic attempts at courting. And then she thought of Gilman.

David Gilman. Pigheaded, authoritarian, narrow-minded but handsome. She sat back and entertained thoughts about him that she had never even considered about Warren. For instance, what was he like in bed?

She found herself wanting to know all about him, and that was a hell of a lot more than she had ever wanted from Warren. But why? What made him so interesting? Because he hated her? Because he thought she was a nuisance?

Because he doesn't yet think of me as a woman. To him, I'm just another guy around here, just another pain in the neck.

So, how would he behave if he suddenly discovered

that Loring Holloway was a woman? How, indeed? And how would it help her with Kirst? She sat up sharply then, frightened at herself. Was she so deeply into this that she might offer herself to Gilman in order to gain control over Kirst?

There was a knock at her door. She opened it to find an orderly standing stiffly outside. "Excuse me, ma'am," he said. "Commandant's having evening mess brought to his quarters and wonders if you'd care to join him."

A laugh escaped her, puzzling the orderly. "Tell him yes," she said, adding with a chuckle, "and ask him if it's formal."

They knew all about it now—Loring Holloway and her strange experiments, Kirst's even stranger responses, Loring's story about finding a demon in a bottle in Iraq, and Kirst somehow ingesting it, and that being the likely cause of all the trouble. They hadn't found it hard to believe, and that had surprised Cuno until he'd realized they were ready to believe anything that would give them a scapegoat—and Kirst had been elected long before tonight.

Leaving them arguing over what to do, Cuno had fled back to the *Krankenhaus,* ashamed for opening his mouth. Steuben would be furious. It would be all over camp by evening mess. Cuno tried to convince himself that he had spoken out because there was too great a danger in ignorance, but he knew perfectly well that knowledge was the greater danger.

He slammed through the back door of the *Krankenhaus* and stopped facing Kirst's cot. Startled, the MP on guard had his weapon up but relaxed when he recognized Cuno. Cuno stared at Kirst, still lying comatose on the cot, and thought maybe it wouldn't be so bad if they lynched him. A second later, he disappeared into his own quarters.

Drawn by the voices, Mueller came down the hall and caught the tail end of the argument in Bauhopf's room. He buttonholed von Lechterhoeven and quickly got an explanation. Leaving the men making big talk about storming the *Krankenhaus,* he returned to his room in a daze and stopped at the door to stare at Kirst's empty bunk.

The man has a demon inside him? What the hell kind of nonsense is that?

Just the kind a campful of trapped and demoralized prisoners would believe, he thought, listening to the spill-over hitting other rooms, voices rising, the outside door slamming as men took off to spread the tale. *Just the kind of nonsense the Americans might use to create a panic, maybe even a riot. But why?*

So they can slaughter us.

Bruckner is right. The Americans are behind the whole thing.

Mueller entered his room and went to the window. Outside, it was snowing harder. His mind raced. They wouldn't make everybody troop over for a regular mess call tonight—not during a storm. Instead, they would run food details from the kitchen to the huts. That meant there would be no roll call. So why wait? Better to get his little band in place and out of the line of fire before those idiots decided to invade the *Krankenhaus.*

Quickly he wrote a cryptic note, snagged one of the men in the corridor, and asked him to run it over to Hoffman. Then he ducked back into his room and ferreted out his warmest clothing.

By 1630 hours it was dark. The storm was at full intensity. The wind howled down the valley, banged off the steep slope of Blackbone Mountain, and fell back on the camp, pummeling the huts with sleet. A curtain of icy particles swept horizontally across the searchlight beams from the sentry towers, where the guards were wrapped in heavy coats, their hands encased in sheepskin gloves. Their weapons were too slick with ice to handle, but they took comfort in knowing no one would try to escape in this weather. And they found injustice in the thought that the Germans were snug and warm inside their huts.

From windows all over the compound, Germans watched the *Krankenhaus*. They stared with keen interest when NCOs from the MP mess kitchen came through the gate, struggling against the storm to deliver food to the guards watching Kirst. Bauhopf conferred with some of the POWs, and they were busy hatching a plot to overpower the kitchen NCOs and steal their uniforms when the detail emerged from the *Krankenhaus* and slogged back up the slope.

Bauhopf was growing more obsessed by the hour, conscious that night was coming and with it the time when whatever was plaguing them would go to work again. So far, no one had come up with a workable plan for getting to Kirst. And they probably wouldn't until after the next meal. Arguing had made everyone snappish and hungry. Bauhopf stayed by his shattered window, ignoring the cold wind breezing through, intent on watching the *Krankenhaus*, as if his riveted attention might produce inspiration.

Mueller buttoned up his coat, tightened the heavy shirt about his neck and ears then pulled the door open. Snow and wind flung him back. He forced himself out and shut

280

the door. He jumped off the top step and landed in a crunch of foot-deep snow. Plowing as fast as he could across to Hut 9, he went in the back way and ducked quickly into the bathroom. Hoffman and Dortmunder were waiting for him, bundled up and ready to go. Mueller nodded and they moved quickly to the exit.

"You're going out?" someone called after them.

"To the rec room!" Hoffman hollered back.

They were out the door a second later. Dortmunder slipped and fell in the snow. He got up cursing and followed the others in a crouched scramble toward the shower hut.

They flattened themselves at the corner and waited for the searchlights to pass then moved to the back windows. In all the excitement over finding Gebhard's body in the shower hut, no one had remembered to seal the window he had used to gain entry. Mueller had found it unlatched and had stashed provisions and gear inside.

Hoisting himself up, he scrabbled for footing against the slick wall. Hoffman helped him over the sill then he and Dortmunder followed. Once inside, they shut the window.

Mueller lit a match. His gear was stashed in the farthest toilet cubicle: food, handmade digging tools, blankets, and candles.

Dortmunder listened to the wind outside. "We may escape," he said, "but we could die of exposure in this storm."

"We'll be fine," said Mueller. "It'll be dry in the shaft. We'll shore up the hole, let the snow cover it, then move on up the tunnel. When the storm lifts, there will be more than twelve inches of snow out there. Nobody will ever think to look, and no one will ever know where we've gone."

"Except Bruckner," Hoffman said.

"He won't talk."

"Why not?"

"He's leading the next group."

The door to Gilman's quarters was standing open, but Loring knocked anyway. Gilman motioned her in. She stood aside as he helped the orderly convert his desk into a dining table, opening a beer-barrel-sized canister and hauling out the dinner in fitted trays. Gilman placed a candlestick at the center of the table and lit the candle, with a wink at Loring. She was wearing a wool sweater and dark slacks. She spun around and gestured for his approval.

"What do you think?"

"Very nice," said Gilman. "Beats that thing you were wearing last night."

"I thought you liked that."

"I did, but it's a little too glamorous for this place."

The table was finally set. Two steaming plates of roast beef, boiled potatoes, vegetables, bread, and peach cobbler for dessert. The orderly uncorked a bottle of wine, poured two glasses, then killed the overhead light before leaving. As the door closed, Gilman held a chair for Loring and she sat down. He sat across from her in the shimmering candlelit gloom. She smiled as the storm howled outside.

"It's like a private room at the Waldorf," she said.

"Actually, the chef is vacationing from the Plaza, but he has to go back tomorrow, so eat hearty because pretty quick it's back to K rations."

Loring picked up her wineglass. "To the chef."

"To the chef."

Gilman filled his face like he hadn't eaten for a month.

Now and then he grinned at Loring, who for the occasion mustered all her best finishing-school etiquette.

"I was thinking," said Gilman, "maybe later for fun we could go down to the camp and beat the crap out of Kirst. What do you say?"

"I think you still don't want to believe me."

"I'm only curious, Miss Holloway—"

"Loring." She smiled. "As long as we're having a romantic evening together, you might at least use my given—"

"We're not having a romantic evening. We're having dinner."

She gestured at the layout. "Do you dine like this with Major Borden?"

Gilman put his fork down. "Just tell me one thing. Why are you here?"

"Oh, come on, Major—"

"David."

She caught his determined gaze. "All right. David."

"Thank you. Now, I don't mean *why* are you here. I mean why are *you* here? Why *you* and not somebody else?"

She stared at him. "I thought we were sitting here pretending nothing else existed."

"Sorry. I don't believe in time out."

"Evidently not. So, let's put it on the proper footing. Finish this sentence—You're trying to find out what would make a woman like me . . ."

". . . come rooting around a detention camp, behaving as if she's on a dangerous mission."

Loring stared at him darkly. "Major, I've had about enough of your pigheaded attitude."

"And I've had enough of your magic tricks."

She stood up.

"Sit down."

Surprised, she sat.

He poured more wine. "Miss Holloway . . . Loring. We are going to sit here until you tell me what I want to know. We may sit here all night, in which case we are both going to get very tired. I at least have a cot to take a snooze on. I sure don't know what the hell you're going to do. But you're not leaving until you come clean with me."

"You want to know why *I* came."

"I think you're getting my drift."

Loring drank more wine and studied the glass, pursing her lips in a bitter grimace. "I'm here . . . because I killed some people in Iraq."

Gilman looked up slowly, sensing the first glimmer of recognition, of commonality between them. "Go on," he said.

Sergeant Vinge came out of the barracks bundled up against the storm. His eyes were slits underlined by a heavy muffler that protected his nose and mouth. He stood at the crest of the hill and looked down at the compound, irritated that he couldn't get inside tonight, sure that in the storm his black wildcat had come down to seek shelter beneath one of the huts. Ever since the other evening he had grown increasingly certain that his life simply could not go on unless he had that black pelt tacked to the wall over his bunk.

He tramped over to the armory and checked out his carbine. Then, fighting the wind and sleet, he made his way down to the fence and peered through the chain links.

"Hey, Vinge—what are you doing?"

It was Cokenaur, standing in the gate guard post,

freezing his buns off. Vinge trudged over to join him. Cokenaur made room for him in the tiny phone-booth-sized shelter and they stood facing each other. Vinge hugged his weapon and kept an eye on the compound. Cokenaur's carbine was slung over his shoulder.

"Bring any smokes?"

Vinge produced a crumpled pack of cigarettes. Cokenaur shivered as he lit one and offered it to Vinge, who shook his head. Cokenaur drew in the smoke and studied Vinge.

"Expecting something?" he said.

"Waitin' for the A train."

"Yeah, well, it ain't coming through tonight." Cokenaur sneezed. "Shit on this post. Hey, I can't see anything with you standing in the doorway. What are you looking for anyway?"

"Nothing." Vinge glanced at Cokenaur thoughtfully and debated telling him the truth. He decided not to—better to bag the little mother and surprise everybody. He cracked a smile. "Keep warm."

Vinge hiked back up the hill and entered the rec hut. Parking himself by the window, which gave him a view of the entire compound, he turned the table lantern down low and glanced once at the five guys playing poker in the opposite corner. They were oblivious to him. Vinge leaned closer to the window, looked out, and waited.

Mueller poked the shower-hut window open a few inches. Shielding his eyes against the blizzard, he tried to see past Hut 10 and up to the fence surrounding the mine shaft. From here it seemed covered in white. The branch he had thrown to mark the spot must have been buried in snow hours ago. He let the window drop back into place then turned and walked the length of the shower, glancing up at the cold, dead pipes.

Dortmunder studied the fine ash on the end of his cigarette. For the fourth time since they had climbed through the window, Hoffman went to the toilet.

Mueller returned to the window for another look. They could go now, but there were still lights on in some of the huts. Men were awake. Anyone who happened to be looking out the back side of Hut 10 might see three figures scurrying through the storm and disappearing into a hole in the ground.

If we find the hole again. . . .

And what about Kirst? So far, nobody had made a move against the *Krankenhaus*. Maybe the air had gone out of that idea. Or maybe they were all waiting, like he and Dortmunder and Hoffman were waiting.

We could wait ourselves to death.

Mueller turned his back to the wall and dropped to a squat on the floor. It was the first time he had sat down since they came in here. A moment later, he sprang up again.

He had the uneasy feeling that he wasn't safe, whether he stayed in the shower hut, returned to his quarters, or went up that mine shaft. Something was waiting for him. But whatever it was, it would be easier to face than more of this sitting around.

"Let's go," he said.

The window at the back of the shower hut banged open. Mueller's head and shoulders appeared. He hauled himself through and tumbled into the snow. Wind-blown icy particles bit into the exposed areas of his face. The gear came out next. Mueller gathered it all together and called softly. Dortmunder came through and, after him, Hoffman.

For an instant, a passing searchlight beam reflected off the snow. The men went rigid until darkness returned, then they snatched up their gear and charged off, floundering through the snow toward Hut 10.

Loring finished her third glass of wine and leaned back, warmed by the liquor, the storm forgotten, the djinn forgotten. All she could think of was David Gilman sitting across from her with his eyes boring into hers, intensely interested in what she was saying, his hand wrapped tightly about his own wineglass, the remains of dinner ignored between them.

"They all drowned? Every one of them?"

She nodded. "Never found a single body. Searched the entire riverbed. Vanished as if they'd never been alive."

"And you think it was your fault?"

Her voice slurred. She caught it and tried to force the words past her uncooperative tongue. "I'm the one who recited the spell. I'm the one who brought the water."

Gilman let go of his glass. His hands dropped beneath the table, and he clasped them together out of sight. Loring watched his frown deepen. "What's the matter?" she said. "You don't believe that, either?"

"Oh, I believe it. It's just . . ." He looked up, pained. "You're not alone."

"What do you mean?"

France. Second Battalion. Window Hill. General Malkin. Scorched grass and rivers of blood. Tramping among the dead.

He told her all of it, his whole remorseful tale, and at last she understood what drove David Gilman: the same thing that had brought her running to Blackbone—atonement.

They sat quietly, both a little drunk and both thoughtful until finally she said, "We have the same weakness. What if the djinn plays on that?"

Gilman looked at her briefly, then got up and moved to the window. He studied the storm-swept compound outside and realized that there was no general topping the chain of command. There was only destiny. Somehow, he had been brought here for a reason. So had she.

And so had the djinn.

He felt her body behind his, her hand on his shoulder. He turned quickly and kissed her, and her heated response surprised him. His hand brushed her breast, then both hands were moving rapidly, touching her all over. Her mouth covered his, and he tasted wine and flesh. His fingers curled in her hair and he held her against his mouth, in a sweeping motion picking her up and carrying her to his cot. Her mouth broke free and she gasped for air, then came back even harder.

They tumbled on the bed and tore at each other's clothing. In a moment, he was inside her and driving hard, deep, and she groaned, her head whipping to one side, her hand feeling for where they were connected. Her hips arched upward, engulfing him. He gasped. Wildly, she followed his movements and helped him. The cot creaked. Gilman threw his body upward and locked his arms in place. Looming over her, he drove himself deeper, anxiously reaching for his peak. Her hips moved faster, the muscles inside starting to contract and pull. She stiffened and let out a long groan. Gilman exploded inside her.

The nightform spilled out of Kirst's mouth while the guard's back was turned. Black smoke boiled over the side of the cot and gathered in the shadows beneath. The djinn thinned itself out to a light mist, then seeped

288

through the floorboards and re-formed beneath the *Kran-kenhaus.*

After a moment, it moved out into the storm. Its fragile form took a terrific buffeting from the wind but held together and let itself be swept along toward the back of the camp.

In the next flash of lightning Vinge spotted a shadow moving between the huts. Through the driving snow he couldn't be sure it was anything more than a trick of the light, but he was out of the rec hut like a shot, carbine held crosswise in front of him as he bounded through the snow and down to the gate.

Cokenaur saw him coming and held out the pack of cigarettes. "Knew you'd be back—"

"Open up!"

"What?"

Vinge missed his footing and skidded into the gate. The nearest sentry heard the rattle of fencing and swiveled his light to fix Vinge in its beam. Vinge sprang back and threw up his hands for a second, holding the carbine aloft so the sentry could see it.

"Open the gate!" he snapped again at Cokenaur, who stared at him in surprise.

"What's going on?"

"I saw something! Come on, open it!"

Cokenaur jammed the cigarettes back in his pocket and came out of the booth. His gloved hand fumbled for the key and he undid the padlock. "I'll get some men—" he said.

"No! Nobody else! I'll handle this. Just stay here and keep watch. Give me your flashlight."

Cokenaur handed him the heavy-duty light and an extra pair of snow goggles. Vinge fitted them on, slung the carbine over his shoulder, switched on the light, and went through the gate. The searchlight beam followed him until he signaled it away.

Then he was alone, lunging through the drifts.

Mueller was frantic. He couldn't find the entrance to the mine shaft. Every time the searchlight came around, he and the others had to burrow into the snow and lie still. Then they would get up and resume digging for the branch or the blanket.

Dortmunder found the branch, but there was nothing beneath it except a foot of snow and hard ground. "It must have moved," Hoffman shouted above the wind. "Probably slid away in the snow."

Mueller started digging in a line directly up the slope, pitching snow behind him like a mole. When his fingers closed on the edge of the blanket, he let out a sharp laugh. They worked quickly then, ahead of the next pass of the light, piling snow up around the hole, digging out the blanket, one by one crawling into the hole and dragging gear after them.

Once inside, Mueller and Hoffman repacked the hole with dirt and the blanket until there remained only enough room to slip an arm through and sweep snow down from above the hole. It didn't matter if any dirt was still visible, because in five minutes it would be covered with fresh snow. By morning no one would know there had ever been an opening.

Finished, Mueller drew in his arm and looked around. Hoffman had a candle lit. Dortmunder was lighting another. The chamber they had entered was littered with rubble. They had to crawl over twelve feet of it until they could stand, and then only in a crouch. The shaft was low and narrow. "Dug by elves," snorted Hoffman. The beams and braces were old and far from sturdy. There was only enough room to move through in single file. But at least they were in and dry, and they had provisions and tools and light. They looked at each other and grinned. Two minutes later, with the gear hoisted on their backs, stooped low, they started up the tunnel.

The nightform found the armhole left by Mueller. It spilled into the shaft and nosed up after the flickering lights.

Gripping his wrist and applying intermittent pressure to the artery just above the bandage, Bauhopf managed to reduce the pain in his hand. "Keep doing that," von Lechterhoeven said quietly, "and it will rot and fall off."

"Who died and made you medic?" Bauhopf growled. Slipping the back door of Hut 7 open an inch and disregarding the blast of cold air that ripped at his eyes, he gazed over at the silent *Krankenhaus*. Nothing had happened over there for quite a while. There was still a light on in the front of the ward, but in the back it was dark. Cuno and Heilbruner must have gone to bed. And Kirst —if he was anything but unconscious, there would be a light burning in the rearmost cubicle. There wasn't.

"Those MPs should be good and tired by now," Bauhopf said.

"I'm good and tired," von Lechterhoeven replied.

"Where are the others?"

"Gone to bed. I don't think anybody's up for a midnight raid. What if we . . . ?"

"Shh!" Bauhopf held up his bandaged hand. Von Lechterhoeven fell silent and watched him stick his head out the door. "Someone's out there."

"Who?"

"Can't tell."

There was a long pause with the only sound the wind whistling through the door, then Bauhopf abruptly shut it, leaving just a crack to look through. "It's an MP. That sergeant, I think." He turned. Von Lechterhoeven watched his eyes work thoughtfully. "He's alone. I think we can take him."

"What?"

"He's got a weapon—we need it!" Bauhopf opened the door.

Von Lechterhoeven shut it and grabbed him. "Wait a minute."

"Let go of me."

"Use your head! Think for a moment! They don't let anyone patrol the compound alone when there's a storm!"

"Their mistake—"

"So if he's not authorized, what's he doing here?"

Bauhopf stopped struggling and looked at von Lechterhoeven a moment, then he edged the door open again and peered out cautiously, shielding his eyes against the snow. The MP was gone, had disappeared around another hut most likely, and with him had gone Bauhopf's chance.

"He's up to no good," said von Lechterhoeven. "Maybe Hopkins sent him."

"All the more reason . . ."

". . . to be careful."

Vinge's goggles were icing up. He looked back up the slope from his position behind Hut 9 and could vaguely make out the gate and the guard post next to it. But he couldn't see Cokenaur and assumed he was back inside the booth, smoking another cigarette. The wind changed and blew snow up Vinge's nose. Cursing to himself and shivering against the biting chill, he turned his back to the wind and let it propel him ahead.

There was no sign of that shadow and, now that he was back here among the huts, he was even less sure that it had been his elusive wildcat. Maybe it was a German making a latrine run. Or it could have been one of the MPs from the *Krankenhaus*.

What would make that damn fool cat come down in this weather anyway? Why wasn't he up on the mountain in some nice warm cave, hibernating with the rabbits and squirrels?

Hearing an unfamiliar noise, Vinge stopped to listen. But all he heard was the wind howling between the huts and loose tar paper flapping on the roof of Hut 9. Wait— there was another sound. Wiping his goggles, he looked around and saw only snow covering the compound and the dark huts. The wind changed again and swept off to the east, up the side of Blackbone Mountain, rattling the chain links on the back fence. He struggled to separate sounds and finally he caught it—a hollow sort of rush. He tensed and looked up at the mountain.

It was Blackbone itself, howling back at the storm. Wind blasting through the mountain's secret orifices, rushing through the old abandoned shafts and emerging somewhere above so that the sound was directed back at the camp. Vinge shuddered. Even the goddamned mountain was creepy.

Sweeping the flashlight before him, Vinge tramped off, warily keeping an eye out, promising his frozen legs he would give this only another few minutes.

Hunched over, Mueller moved up the shaft. His candle cast an eerie glow on the dry dirt walls and rotted timbers around him. Carefully, he tested the ground before putting his foot down. Each step took several seconds, but it meant avoiding a fall through a rotted floor or a shift in the timbers that might bring the whole shaft crashing down on his head.

Hoffman and Dortmunder were right behind him, the gear on their backs making it difficult for them to move. Dortmunder had resorted to a crab walk. Hoffman, who was taller, had shifted the weight higher on his shoulders, almost up on his neck. He moved apelike, walking with his knuckles dragging.

Mueller carried very little gear. If a beam fell or the floor gave, somebody needed both hands free to rescue the others. As his cautious forward movement became more automatic, Mueller listened to the wind howling somewhere above him through an open shaft, turning the entire mountain into an echo chamber.

They had traveled about fifty yards up a twenty-degree incline. Suddenly there was a sharp left turn and the shaft switched back steeply, up into the heart of the mountain. Mueller stopped, worried. If that was a permanent bend in the shaft and it didn't switch back the other way somewhere up ahead, then he was wrong and they wouldn't exit on the northeast slope of Blackbone Mountain. This detour would bring them out on the northwest side, visible from the camp.

Mueller extended his candle around the bend, casting light on the nearby rock walls. Ten feet beyond that, all was blackness. Dortmunder and Hoffman caught up and asked what was wrong. "Nothing," Mueller said, frowning to himself. They had to give it a try. There was no other choice. He took a step forward, again testing the ground. It was solid. But glancing at his candle flame, he saw something peculiar. The flame was angled toward him, bent by an almost imperceptible force. Putting his

295

face close to the flame, he felt a gentle breeze cool against his cheek. It grew gradually.

Dortmunder and Hoffman felt it too. "God," Dortmunder said gratefully.

Hoffman laughed. "It's the old man of the mountain breaking wind!"

"We must be near an exit," Mueller said, relieved. He stepped forward. The breeze was still angling his candle flame, making the light flicker on the walls. Hoffman and Dortmunder followed, anticipating freedom only moments away. Then Mueller noticed that, though the breeze was still gentle, it was getting colder. Surely that meant they were almost out. His excitement grew, although practical reality nagged him that it would be dangerous to emerge within view of the camp.

The incline got even steeper, thirty degrees now. Tougher for Dortmunder and Hoffman. Mueller's candle flame was bent almost horizontally. The breeze was like ice on his cheeks.

He stopped.

Something was happening to the light. Before, the candle flame had illuminated almost ten feet ahead, but now blackness crept down the incline, swallowing the light. The breeze stung his face. The candle flame whipped.

Dortmunder grunted as his light went out.

All three stopped and watched, fascinated, as blackness engulfed everything in their path—walls, ceiling, and floor. The wind rose abruptly, tore at their clothing, and put out the two remaining candles. Mueller held his ground, straining to see in the dark, but the wind pushed him back. Or was it the wind? It felt like a huge hand against his chest. He stumbled and heard another sound, a distant howling. It built from somewhere up ahead and grew in volume. They backed away.

Mueller fumbled in his trouser pocket for matches and lit one. Something black brushed his hand and put the light out. Behind him, he heard Dortmunder struggling with matches that wouldn't catch. Mueller flung himself against the shaft wall, cupped his hands, and struck another match. It flared briefly and, in that instant of illumination, he saw what the blackness was.

A thick, oily, smoky substance that curled over his hands and snuffed out the light.

Mueller dropped his matches. Hoffman swore. All three were hurled back by a fierce gust of frigid wind. Then Mueller heard footsteps retreating—Hoffman charging down the incline. Dortmunder fell to his knees, murmuring a prayer. The howl grew louder, deeper, throatier. Then sound erupted around them. They were assaulted by deep, cavernous rumblings, cackling, echoing quakes, and the edgy strain of cracking wood.

At that moment, Mueller knew they had not entered a mine shaft at all. They were in the mouth of hell, about to be devoured by blackness.

Dortmunder frantically shrugged off his gear and flung it to the ground then ran down the shaft toward the bend. In the darkness he couldn't see and smashed into a brace, which exploded into dust. The crossbeam dropped and shattered his shoulder. He screamed and dodged a hail of falling rock.

Following the sound, Mueller ran to it, ran through the cave-in, holding his gear over his head, ignoring Dortmunder on the ground screaming about his shoulder, gagging on a mouthful of pebbles. Mueller found the bend and whipped around it, losing his footing on a river of gravel, hitting the ground and sliding down the incline. A scream tore from his throat as sound rose behind him —the roar of an avalanche, a breaking, spilling, crashing 'sound as of a mountain giving way. He hit the side of the shaft and grabbed a brace beam to stop his slide. The beam came away in his hands and he slid on, at any second expecting to be crushed by collapsing rock. He struck the side again and jammed the brace beam into a protruding boulder. He stopped sliding, scrambled to his feet, and ran. As behind him the sound swelled to a demonic shriek, Mueller's fear took a quantum leap to terror.

He threw out his hands in the dark, beating against the walls to keep himself centered in the tunnel. "Hoffman!" he called, his voice drowned out by a roar that shook the entire shaft. He heard worm-eaten braces give way behind him and a distant scream cut off by a crash. Dortmunder.

Hearing sharp grunts ahead, Mueller charged on, feeling the uneven crunch of the spill underfoot—the dirt and rock pile left when the American engineers had blown up the entrance. Then he cracked his head on the low ceiling. Ignoring the pain, he dropped on his belly and crawled up the spill to where he knew the hole must be. He thought of the storm out there, the welcome difficulty of plowing through deep drifts to return to his bed. The grunts came from Hoffman, trying to claw through the dirt.

"It's me," Mueller called. "Where are you?"

"In front—"

Aiming at the voice, Mueller sprang forward and landed on Hoffman, who yelled. His voice was picked up on the wind coming from back in the shaft and was bounced around the walls beside them. It came back intensified. And with it came the demon's roar, rushing toward them on a black cloud that now they could even taste—like sulfur on the tongue. It burned their throats and clogged their lungs. They began to cough. Then it reached into their minds and laid bare the raw nerves of terror.

Oh God, Mueller thought. *Not in here! Please not in here!*

Gasping for air, feeling his heart pounding in his chest, he grabbed Hoffman's trousers and yanked him out of the way, kicked him down the spill. Then he pulled himself forward and clawed at the dirt, with the blackness stinging his eyes and filling his brain with an icy coldness. The mountain creaked around him. His fingers found the loose dirt and the edge of the blanket. He tore at it, shoved it aside.

Just as Mueller's hand punched through and he felt the relief of cold snow on his fingers—snow he recalled from his boyhood—innocent, heartwarming, holiday snow—there was a sharp crack above him, and then the ceiling dropped. Something incredibly hard and sharp bit down on his neck.

In the last second of life, Mueller thought the beast from hell had taken off his head. But then he felt the cold weight of rock against his ear and knew it was nothing quite so terrible.

Only death.

Over the wail of the storm, Vinge heard a crash up on the slope behind Hut 10. Stopping with his legs sunk calf-deep in snow, he played his beam around the corner of the hut and up the slope to the fence, but the driving snow reflected the light back at him. Hoisting one leg up at a time, Vinge plowed through the drifts, crossing the broad empty space toward the base of Blackbone Mountain. Reaching the bottom of the slope, he played the light in a side-to-side arc, working slowly upward. He held the beam on something dark that looked like cloth. Two colors. Blue and gray. The Germans wore gray.

Leaving the carbine slung on his shoulder and holding the flashlight in his left hand, he started up the slope, figuring that if it was a German, and he was unconscious or dead, he would be easy to deal with. If he was faking, Vinge could hit him with the light to get him under control.

Struggling for footholds in the snow, Vinge worked up the slope toward the blue and gray cloth. Stopping to aim his light at it, he realized it was nothing more than a blue blanket. But the gray thing—that looked like a coat sleeve.

Something growled at him.

Vinge froze. Only his eyes moved, darting around and —It growled again. Then it snarled.

That's no goddamned fucking wildcat.

He flicked the light around quickly. The growl came from above and to the left. There, in the bushes up against the fence, he saw two jewel-like eyes glinting back at him. And beneath the eyes were snarling lips and slavering teeth. It crept forward a couple of feet, shoving the bush aside, scattering snow, and coming into the beam of Vinge's light. It was a wolf, the biggest one Vinge had ever seen or had ever even dreamed about. It was immense and black, and its hide was slick with melted snow as steam rose off its back. The jaws opened wider, exposing sharp yellow fangs. The wolf cocked its head to one side and roared at him.

Wolves don't roar, Vinge thought, as his knees buckled and he slid backward. *Wolves howl. What the hell . . . ?* Bracing his legs, he quickly unslung the carbine, snapped off the safety, and took aim. When he fired, the weapon bucked, and he knew a bullet had gone right for the animal's heart—

Then why was it in the air, leaping at him? No. Not leaping. Flying! He fired again. The wolf roared in midair and slammed into the snow. For a second, Vinge felt a thrill of triumph. He had killed it. He lowered the weapon and took a step forward and, as he did, the wolf sprang to its feet.

Vinge turned and bounded down the slope into the drifts. In eight inches of snow it was hard going, but he refused to stop. Glancing back, he saw what he already knew: the wolf was coming after him. He stopped to fire again, missed, then yelled, "Goddamn it, help me!" He stumbled and nearly lost the carbine, recovered and kept moving, urged on by the sound of the wolf behind him, growling wetly, slobbering with hunger.

Glancing back again, he stumbled sideways and crashed into the side of Hut 7. He stopped and realized he was foolish for running. Scrambling to the door, he turned the knob. The door was stuck. He shouldered it but it wouldn't open. Something was braced against it on the other side. Using the butt of his carbine, he bashed it and kicked it at the same time. It swung open. Vinge was startled to see Bauhopf sprawled in the corridor, staring at him in surprise.

The roar sounded above him. Backing up a few steps to glance at the roof, Vinge saw the wolf crouched to spring. As he raised his carbine, Bauhopf, convinced he was the intended target, slammed the door. Vinge fired. His shot tore away a chunk of tar paper directly in front of the wolf. It didn't budge. It only roared at him again.

Whimpering with fear and cursing his aim, Vinge turned and plowed away from the huts. To reach the gate he had to negotiate the snow-covered slope, all of it uphill. Looking back, he saw the wolf leap off the roof of Hut 7 and come bounding after him.

He fired into the air to attract attention, hoping the nearest sentry would swing his light and see the wolf and cut him down with submachine-gun fire.

At the gate, Cokenaur heard the shots. He bolted from the booth and over to the gate, clicked off the safety of his carbine, and raised it to his shoulder, aiming the barrel through the fence. He heard somebody yelling and saw a shape bounding toward him through the storm.

Vinge is after someone, he thought. *Flushed out a German trying to pull some stunt.* Cokenaur watched the approaching shape. It was big and black, and it loped through the drifts, ignoring the storm.

That's no German.

He saw the teeth, the steaming hide, heard the rising frenzied roar. Twenty yards away and closing, it looked big enough to crash through the gate. Mixed in with the roar, he thought he heard Vinge's voice yelling for help. *What's the asshole in the tower doing with the light?*

There was no time to think anymore. The wolf was ten yards away and as big as a tank. The eyes blazed at him. Cokenaur fired.

*

The last shot woke Gilman up. For a moment, he didn't know where he was as he stared at Loring Holloway's body curled against his under the covers. She was awake, too, her eyes working with fear. "Was that shooting?" she asked.

"I'll find out," said Gilman, jumping up and quickly dressing.

Loring threw off the covers and, naked, reached for her clothes. "We'd better hope that's not Kirst," she said.

Gilman paused. "Why?"

"Because if he gets killed, the djinn will get out, and then we won't know where it is."

"Oh, Christ."

Gilman bounded for the door.

Chapter 24

As the siren sounded, Bauhopf came out of Hut 7 and stood looking up the slope toward the gate. Spotlights from two towers beamed through the storm and picked out something dark lying in the snow. Soldiers rushed down from the barracks, their movements hampered by swirling snow. Everywhere around him, Bauhopf saw lights snapping on inside the huts, doors opening, men edging out into the freezing night, frightened, curious. Von Lechterhoeven appeared at his shoulder. "What's happened?"

"I don't know," said Bauhopf. "It sounded like shooting."

As the gate was opened, Hopkins came thrashing through it, leading the soldiers down toward the spotlit shape. After them came Gilman.

Bauhopf glanced at the *Krankenhaus.* The rear door was open. Cuno was huddled in the entrance with the MP on duty, both looking up the slope. Sensing his chance, Bauhopf plowed across. "Cuno!" he called. "Someone's been shot! They need you!"

Cuno glanced at the MP, who eyed him blankly. Cuno shook his head and refused to budge. Germans came out of the huts and grouped near the *Krankenhaus* to stare at the scene uphill. Bauhopf melted in with them and waited, eyeing Cuno. Von Lechterhoeven joined him and said through his teeth, "What are you doing?"

"Keep your mouth shut."

Steuben emerged from his quarters, stamping hurriedly into his boots and buttoning his coat, shielding his eyes from the storm and sizing up the growing crowd of prisoners. "Stay in the huts!" he called out. They ignored him. He caught sight of Bruckner standing in the doorway he had just come out of, worriedly looking up the hill with Churchill at his side. Steuben was conscious of eyes glancing at him—of anger and resentment.

Staring up the hill at the black shape surrounded by MPs, he thought, *They'd better have an explanation.*

Loosely holding his carbine, Cokenaur stood by the gate in shock as MPs formed an armed ring around the thing in the snow. Hopkins moved to one side and, with his hands on his hips, glared at the Germans below. Gilman circled the body, taking in details. Blood-stained snow, sprawling limbs, bared teeth, cheeks drawn back in an impossibly contorted grimace, the tongue lolling out one side of the mouth. He examined the entry wound that had left a meaty hole between the eyes.

Vinge was stone-dead.

Gilman got up and went to Cokenaur. "What happened?"

"I—I shot him, sir."

"You shot him?"

"Yes, sir."

Hopkins turned, his mouth opening to vent surprise. Gilman silenced him with a look. To Cokenaur he said, "Why?"

"I thought he was a—a wolf, sir."

"A wolf?"

"He came at me, sir. In—in—in the snow and the wind and everything, he looked like a wolf, sir. He was big and black and he had teeth like—" He made a face to demonstrate. The way his lips drew back and his teeth parted, he looked almost like the death mask on Vinge. Wolf-like.

"It moved like a wolf, sir. I mean, I couldn't see all that well, but goddamnit, sir, I can tell a wolf from a man and that was a goddamned wolf!"

"Take it easy, Cokenaur."

"I swear I didn't know it was Vinge, sir!" Cokenaur's eyes were wild. He was crushing a pack of cigarettes in his free hand. "It was a wolf! *I shot a wolf!*" Every MP within range heard him.

Gilman gently relieved him of the carbine and nodded to Hopkins, who came over with a scowl on his face. "Have someone get him up to Borden and sedate him."

"Yes, sir."

Gilman looked over at Vinge's body and felt himself begin to shake with helpless rage. Now he understood Hopkins a little better. That feeling of powerlessness in the face of the unknown. The djinn. Somehow, Loring Holloway's demon was responsible for this. Cokenaur was no fool. Even in a storm, how could he mistake a khaki-wrapped human being for a *wolf*? No. Cokenaur had been made to *believe* that what he saw was a wolf. *Just like the djinn made me believe I was seeing Window Hill the other night.*

The wind bit into the back of his neck but it was no colder than the chill of fear gripping his body. She was right—deep in his logic-obsessed brain, he knew she was right.

Kirst.

Gilman whipped around and detailed two MPs to double-time down to the German infirmary to check on

306

Kirst. Then he gazed downhill at the Germans. Walking away from Vinge's body so he could be seen better, Gilman shouted through the storm, "Major Steuben!"

Blackness swirled into the crawl space beneath the *Krankenhaus* and became a thick, shadowy cloud pulsing on the cold ground. Out of the wind and snow, the nightform was able to relax and let the waves of new energy suffuse its being. With its increased power, dispatching the men in the tunnel had been easy. Most of the djinn's ancient talents were fully effective now: shapeshifting, sound mimicry, molecular interference, commanding the elements . . .

But now fear would take over, and fear would bring more victims. Before this night was through, it would devour them all.

As Steuben started up the slope, Bruckner forced Churchill back inside the hut with his boot then came out, hurrying after Steuben. "Walter," he called.

Steuben waited for him to catch up, then they continued together, heading toward the Americans. "God only knows who's been killed now." He glanced back at the milling men. "Or how many more will die refusing to go back to their beds. We're in for it now, Hans. Any idea who it is up there?"

"It could be Mueller."

"What?"

"Mueller was going out tonight, Walter."

"What do you mean, out?"

"The mine shaft. He found a hole. He was going out tonight with Dortmunder and Hoffman."

Steuben was silent a moment. "Are any of them still here?"

"I don't know."

"You'd better find out—quickly!" Steuben swore. "Why wasn't I informed?"

"Your opposition was a matter of record. The men were determined."

A moment later they were both staring down at Vinge's body, Bruckner confused and Steuben relieved. Relieved that it was not Mueller or Dortmunder or Hoffman, that this time it was an American and not a German. Relieved because this death punctured forever Bruckner's conspiracy-to-kill-Germans theory and paved the way for the prisoners to be told the truth about Kirst.

Steuben glanced at Gilman. "What happened?"

Gilman had to shout over the roar of the storm. "He was mistaken for a wolf and shot by one of our own sentries."

Steuben's lips parted in surprise. He looked down and studied how the body lay, the distance to the gate, visibility. "Is that possible?" he asked. Gilman didn't answer.

Bruckner tugged at Steuben's sleeve, wanting to know what had been said. Steuben translated for him, and he too looked puzzled. To Gilman, Steuben said, "You think the woman is right about Kirst?"

"Maybe," said Gilman.

The MPs returned from the *Krankenhaus* and reported to Gilman that Kirst was still out like a light. "Hasn't been awake the whole time, sir. Hasn't even been to the can."

Steuben wasn't paying attention. His mind was running back over the things Loring Holloway had said earlier today, about people trapped in a city twenty-five hundred years ago, plagued by a demon who murdered them in dozens of different ways—"by strangulation, by fire, chased by imaginary beasts, beneath collapsing buildings—"

Mueller. Mueller in the mine shaft. Sergeant Vinge there on the ground, shot because he was mistaken for a wolf. Gebhard, the submariner, drowned in the shower hut. Eckmann murders Schliebert because he thinks Schliebert is making love to his wife. Paranoia and fear. What was Vinge running from? Kirst? No, Kirst was asleep in the *Krankenhaus*. But the djinn had gotten out. And now it was after—

"Mueller," Steuben said.

Bruckner's eyes widened.

"What's that?" Gilman said.

"Mueller. He's trying to escape."

Bruckner lunged toward him, horrified.

"He's in the mine shaft with Dortmunder and Hoffman!"

Gilman whirled. "Hopkins!"

Scattering the Germans in their path, Gilman and Hopkins led a squad of armed MPs past Hut 10. Steuben and Bruckner hurried along behind them, Bruckner's face working with anger, Steuben frightened and concerned. They climbed the slope and found what Vinge had seen: a gray sleeve and part of a blue blanket protruding from a small hole. Gilman cleared snow from around the sleeve, revealing a bloody, frozen hand.

"Oh, shit. Another one," said Hopkins.

Ignoring him, Gilman ordered the MPs to use the butts of their weapons to dig the body out. They worked as fast as they could, hampered by snow and dirt crumbling around the body as they struggled to free it. Finally, they had the head and shoulders clear. Two MPs grabbed the arms and jerked. Mueller emerged like a newborn child, his head dangling oddly as they lowered him to the snow. Examining him, Gilman immediately found the gash at the base of his neck where his spinal cord had been severed.

Bruckner stared at Mueller and shook; tears froze on his cheeks.

"There were two more!" Steuben called out against the wind. "Dortmunder and Hoffman!"

While a couple of MPs carried Mueller's body down the slope, two more went to the *Krankenhaus* for a stretcher. The others jammed their weapons into the ground to widen the hole. When there was enough room to crawl through, Gilman took a flashlight and wriggled in.

Inside, the ground was dry and cold. He shoved piles of dirt and rock aside and played the light around until he spotted Hoffman's shoes sticking out of the cave-in. The rest of the body was buried. Gilman withdrew.

"One of them's dead for sure," he told Steuben. "The other one—probably."

Steuben let snow collect on his face without brushing it off. He felt an overwhelming surge of sadness. It was all slipping out of his control. Morale was gone, courage was gone, men were dying. Soon they would all be dead. These deaths were only portents. The worst was yet to come. He was on the verge of the final battle, and he knew there would be no survivors. Why should a demon give quarter to anyone? When he met Gilman's gaze, they were both thinking the same thing. Steuben voiced it. "Kirst," he said.

"Kirst," Gilman agreed flatly.

Bauhopf watched the two MPs barge in the back door of the *Krankenhaus* and shout something to the MPs inside. Then they charged through to the main ward, leaving the door wide open. Most of the other prisoners who had come out of their huts were preoccupied watching the MPs up on the back slope. Bauhopf stood halfway between the *Krankenhaus* and the nearest hut and stared at that open door. He glanced up the hill to the gate and saw more MPs rolling the American sergeant's body onto a stretcher. He saw the American woman at the gate, watching them and peering through the storm to the shifting lights at the back of the camp.

He waded through the snow and approached the open door. Peering inside, he could see that the rearmost cubicles were dark. Down the corridor in the main ward, the two MPs were selecting a stretcher. Kirst. Where was Kirst? With the light on in the front and the MPs making all that noise, he would have to be awake now. Unless he was in the back.

It's worth a try.

He waded a few steps closer and was at the door looking in. It was dark in the rear cubicle. He could see the edge of a cot but couldn't tell if there was anyone on it. There was an empty chair by the wall and, standing against it, a carbine with fixed bayonet.

Bauhopf stared at the bayonet, a plan instantly forming in his mind. Beads of sweat froze on his upper lip. Keeping his eye on the men in the ward, he ascended the steps cautiously, trying to appear merely curious.

The two MPs in front had their stretcher and were headed out the front door. Nobody was looking in Bauhopf's direction. He threw a glance to his right. Only von Lechterhoeven, standing ten yards away in the snow, was watching him, aghast. On his left, up the slope, the MPs were carting the sergeant's body past the woman, who tried to get through the gate. A guard held her back.

Bauhopf entered the *Krankenhaus,* stepped quickly into the shadows, and peered into the darkness. Kirst was asleep on the cot. The MPs in the main ward had let the stretcher-bearers out and had shut the door after them. Now they were strolling back this way and talking among themselves. Bauhopf slipped past the cot and flattened himself against the wall. He grabbed the carbine and hurriedly worked the bayonet free, glancing once at Kirst's sleeping face and feverishly promising to put him to sleep forever—

Boots banged on the steps. Von Lechterhoeven filled the doorway and hissed a warning: "Hopkins!"

Bauhopf ignored him and finished detaching the bayonet.

"Hey!"

Von Lechterhoeven looked up. MPs were rushing at him from the main ward. He leaped back and jumped off the steps, pausing to glance back, seeing Bauhopf huddled against the wall with the bayonet—

He collided with Hopkins, who shoved him aside, looked once at his terrified face, then bounded toward the open door. Von Lechterhoeven glanced around and saw Gilman leading the rest of the MPs back with Steuben.

In the cubicle, Bauhopf waited, counting heartbeats. Two MPs flew past him. The first one shot out the door and crashed into Hopkins. The second one whipped around to check Kirst—and caught the carbine butt on his chin. As he went down hard, Bauhopf dropped the carbine and, clutching the knife, moved to the bed.

Disentangling himself from the MP, Hopkins cursed him and flung him into the snow, then bounded up the steps and flicked on the light. Bauhopf was bent over Kirst with a knife in his hand. "What the fuck are you doing?!" Hopkins yelled.

Bauhopf stopped with the knife poised. Hopkins clawed for his .45 then stared at Kirst. The look of shock on his face drew Bauhopf's attention. He too looked down and froze at what he saw.

Kirst lay on the cot, most of his body covered by a blanket. His mouth was open, his eyes closed. Unseen before Hopkins had switched on the light, a thick cloud of black smoke was rolling up the bed, coming in like the tide, crossing Kirst's chest and approaching his mouth—

Bauhopf yelled. The knife shook in his hand. Kirst's eyes flashed open. For the first time in twenty-four hours, Kirst was *aware*. He glimpsed Bauhopf's horror-stricken face and the knife in his hand then he saw the blackness rear up above his chest and descend on his mouth. His scream was cut off as the nightform disappeared down his throat.

Bauhopf gave a loud grunt then swung the knife down in a wide arc and sliced open Kirst's throat. Instinctively, Hopkins jerked out his .45. As blood spurted from Kirst's wound, Hopkins' gun spat flame. The bullet hit Bauhopf in the right temple. He was slammed back against the wall, then he sank to the floor, still clutching the knife.

Kirst sat bolt upright, his wild eyes connecting with Hopkins, who sprang back in shock and watched him vault off the cot, hands flying to his throat, trying to stop the jetting blood. Kirst swooped around the cubicle like a trapped bird, plunging, gagging, fluttering, retching. An MP coming in from the ward ran right into his fist and dropped like a stone. Cuno came in after him. Kirst slammed him to the floor.

As Kirst's body was gripped by a series of violent, spasmodic convulsions, Hopkins shakily leveled his .45 but couldn't bring himself to shoot: he was so fascinated by the sight of this dead man insanely thrashing about in front of him.

Kirst crashed against the medicine cabinet and froze as he saw his reflection in the mirror.

Hopkins saw it too. So did Cuno, getting up from the floor. It wasn't Kirst's face. It was a twisted parody of human features. It had a wolfish snout with large, curved canine incisors, thick lips fixed in a permanent snarl, deeply hooded and burning eyes, quivering, pointed ears —the entire head was encased in a leathery reptilian skin covered with mottled eruptions. A glistening forked tongue flecked with blood darted from between the lips. It was the face of the djinn.

Cuno turned and vomited on the floor. Hopkins raised the .45, but Kirst lashed out and struck the weapon from his hand. Hopkins shrank into a corner and cowered, and Kirst bolted to the door, shouldering the jamb hard enough to splinter the wood. Then he sprang off into the storm with an inhuman howl, one hand clutching his split-open throat.

Hopkins stumbled down the steps and fell into the snow. Gilman arrived with Steuben and the rest of the MPs and, dumbfounded, they watched Kirst's fleeing figure with its head rocking back as if on a hinge.

Hopkins was first to gather his wits. He jumped up and snatched a tommy gun from the nearest MP. He fired a warning burst over Kirst's head.

Gilman reached out to stop him, but Hopkins lunged forward and bounded through the snow after Kirst. "Don't shoot!" Gilman yelled, charging after him with Steuben following.

At the gate, Loring and the MPs on guard heard the warning burst and turned to see Kirst running toward them, holding his throat and screaming and roaring like a pack of wild animals.

Loring shouted at the men behind her, "Shut the gate! Don't let him out!"

They did it quickly, leaving Loring inside with two MPs readying weapons. Kirst was hit with a spotlight from the nearest tower.

Hopkins floundered up the slope, yelling at Kirst to halt. Kirst bounded past the MPs and bolted for the fence. He sprang four feet off the ground and grabbed the barbed wire with both hands. His head flopped back. Loring saw the gaping throat wound and the dead eyes. Instinctively she backed away. The MPs stared in disbelief.

Ignoring the sharp barbs, the djinn forced Kirst to climb the fence. The flesh was torn from his hands. His legs kicked wildly, trying to dig into the links for footholds. He was hit with a second spot. Everybody was shouting now.

Hopkins reached the base of the fence and positioned himself directly beneath Kirst.

Realizing what he was going to do, Loring yelled, "No!" and charged toward him.

As Kirst reached the top, Hopkins raised his tommy gun and fired one long burst. Bullets tore into Kirst's back. Blood spurted. His body stiffened at the top of the fence. Loring stopped and stared up at him, horrified.

Gilman, Steuben, and the others arrived in time to see the spotlights converge on Kirst's body, limp and hanging from the topmost strands of barbed wire, gently twisting in the wind. Kirst's head hung by gristle and bone, lying all the way back between his shoulder blades.

From the gaping slit in his throat, illuminated by the spotlights, a thick cloud of black smoke poured out of the body. It flowed against the fence and recoiled with an echoing howl of rage. Then it appeared to be caught on the wind and whipped away into the camp. It disappeared into the storm.

Gilman, Loring, and Steuben looked at each other.

Chapter 25

As the fence swayed from the impact of Hopkins' gunfire, feathery clots of snow broke off the top and blew about their faces. Around them a trackless ocean of white continued to draw down a curtain of swirling flakes from the sky.

Gilman watched the trail of blackness vanish among the huts. The Germans gathering at the bottom of the slope were unaware of it as it rushed over their heads.

"Is it gone?" Gilman asked Loring.

"I doubt it." She looked up at Kirst's body. "Killing him drove it out, but it couldn't get past the fence because of the way the camp is shaped—with its five sides. It's trapped in here, and the only way it will ever get out is inside a new host."

The MPs exchanged nervous glances. They didn't like what they had seen. They didn't like the idea that Kirst had run around for several minutes with his head nearly severed from his body. They didn't like the gory, gaping smile where his neck had been, or his cold dead eyes.

Hopkins stood very still, clutching the tommy gun tightly to his body, trying to make sense of what he had seen. Cuno appeared behind him, his eyes darting toward Kirst as he described to Steuben what had happened in

Kirst's cubicle and what he and Hopkins had seen in the mirror.

As Steuben translated, Hopkins kicked snow with his boot, muttering to himself.

Gilman turned to Hopkins and, indicating Cuno, said, "Is he telling the truth? Did you kill one of the Germans?"

Hopkins stopped kicking snow. "Bauhopf. He took a knife to Kirst, sir—slashed his throat. So I shot him. But then—" Glancing up at Kirst, he struggled with the memory. "Kirst got up, sir, and he was holding his throat and kind of crashing about, and then he stopped in front of the mirror, and instead of his face we saw this . . . this *thing* . . ." His eyes traveled back up to Kirst and stayed rooted to the body while Cuno gave a clinical description of the face of the djinn. Steuben provided an artless translation. The MPs listened, liking all of this even less than what they had witnessed.

Gilman turned and slogged through the snow, down the fence line, away from the MPs. Steuben, Bruckner, Cuno, Loring, and Hopkins joined him, huddled against the storm.

"Look, it's vital now that we all know what we're up against, because its purpose—according to Miss Holloway—is helped by keeping us in the dark. So the lid is off. Major Steuben, you will please inform your men—and Hopkins, you'll pass the word to the MPs."

"What word?"

Gilman drew a breath. "What's been going on around here—the killing—is due to something that was living *inside* Kirst."

Hopkins stared at him.

"It's sort of a parasite," said Loring, aiming for a cred-

318

ible description. "In point of fact, a demon. It's called a djinn."

"Hopkins, that's d-j-i-n-n," Gilman added. "It's not in any field manual, so there's no regulation procedure for dealing with it, other than initiative. That black cloud we all just saw leaving Kirst's body? That was it."

Hopkins' expression became a halfhearted smirk.

"You'll have to force yourself to believe it," said Gilman, "so you can convince the others."

"Me?"

"It killed Gebhard in the shower hut. It forced Eckmann to kill Schliebert. It even made Eckmann hang himself."

"Why?"

"It feeds off the death of its victims," said Loring, "whether it does the killing itself or just *causes* them to die."

"So far tonight, it's killed Sergeant Vinge and the three men in that mine shaft. And even though you pulled the trigger, the djinn was responsible for Bauhopf." Gilman glanced back at the body on the fence. "As well as Kirst."

"What are you giving me?"

"Hopkins, you saw its face in the mirror. You and Cuno."

"I saw some trick!"

"The mirror . . ." Loring was momentarily lost in thought, then she brightened. "That's why they saw it! That's what the silver is for—it'll show us where the djinn *is!*" She tugged on the chain at her neck and pulled out the silver talisman Yazir had given her. "No matter what shape or substance it takes on or where it hides, we can find it by catching its reflection in silver. We need mirrors!"

"Which we may be a little short of," Gilman said.

"Look, the more it kills, the stronger it gets. It's going to keep killing. But from now on, it's vulnerable. It has no place to hide. We've got to do something while it's deprived of a host—and before it finds a new one! At least when it was inside Kirst, we knew where it was! Now it could take any one of us—anybody inside this compound! And if it does, we won't know who!"

She fell silent. Snow blew around them. They glanced at the MPs waiting beneath Kirst's body, at the Germans still emerging from the huts, disregarding the storm and forming a growing mob.

"How is it going to get a new host?" Gilman asked.

Loring was thoughtful a moment. "It has to be ingested. The sorcerer in Ur-Tawaq *fed* it to his assistant. Kirst apparently drank it. It will disguise itself as something edible. It could become food, drink, cigarette smoke . . ." She looked at Gilman. They both stared at the mob of Germans down the hill.

"Well, that does it," said Gilman. "We've got to get everybody out of here—right now."

"Wait a minute!" Hopkins snapped. "Those men are prisoners. They're not getting out of here!"

"Hopkins—"

Hopkins brandished his tommy gun. "Uh-uh, Major. You can believe all that hocus-pocus if you want to, but not me. What do you think you're dealing with here? They're Germans! They're going to escape any way they can! This may be the best act I've ever seen, but it stops right here!" He slammed the bolt action back and steadied the weapon.

Steuben stepped forward. "Major Gilman, I give you my word my men won't attempt to escape—"

"What about the three in the mine shaft?" interrupted

320

Hopkins. "What were they doing—digging a new latrine?"

"They were fools. They wouldn't have gotten far in this storm. Captain Hopkins, we all have a common enemy now. Vinge was *your* man. This demon is no longer killing only Germans."

Hopkins smirked again then glowered at Gilman. "What about Window Hill, Major? The last time you trusted a German?"

Gilman's eyes went cold. "Hopkins, who I trust and why is none of your business, unless it happens to be you—which it's not."

With the storm growing around him, Gilman leaned into the wind and motioned the MPs over. They slogged up close, eyeing Hopkins and his readied tommy gun.

"Shit," Hopkins said, lowering his weapon. Handing it to the nearest MP, he turned and stalked off through the gate.

A few minutes later, MPs were removing Bauhopf's body from the *Krankenhaus* and taking it across to the rec hut past a line of grim-looking Germans. As Steuben called a meeting of hut captains outside the *Krankenhaus,* Cuno regretfully admitted his part in the night's tragedy. "I was trying to prevent this," he told Steuben. "Bauhopf and some others were determined to kill Kirst. I had to tell them what we had seen this afternoon—"

"So it's all over camp by now," said Steuben. Cuno nodded. Steuben turned to confer with the hut captains. "Kirst is dead," he began. "So is Bauhopf. So are Mueller, Dortmunder and Hoffman, and the MP, Sergeant Vinge. But the Americans are not to blame—nor are any of us. There is a story going around that something was living inside Kirst. That story is true. There is a monster loose in this camp."

The hut captains regarded Steuben blankly. Bruckner grunted.

"It doesn't matter to me what you choose to believe," Steuben added. "I only care that from this point you follow orders and regard this as a military operation. That means no committees, no discussion, no voting— only orders." He paused, glancing at each of them, his gaze settling on Bruckner. "Major Gilman wants all of us out," he said.

"Out?" said one of the men. "What do you mean, out?"

"Out of this camp. Outside the fence." They looked at him in surprise. "This is not an invitation to escape. It's a necessary move to save lives. Hut captains, round up your men, return to your huts, pick up only warm clothing and blankets. Leave behind all edible food and drink, and all cigarettes. You are to give the men strict orders not to eat, drink, or smoke anything that is presently inside this camp. Tell them the food is poisoned. Tell them anything you like, but every bit of it stays here. As soon as you're ready, assemble outside the huts and wait for the MPs to escort you out. Any questions?"

Beneath Hut 7 the nightform gathered into an undulating pool of blackness. The djinn listened to feet pounding against the floorboards overhead and the muffled chatter of frightened men, the snap of orders, pushing, sliding, things dropping, flurries of movement. Panic. Panic and chaos.

Relishing those emotions, the nightform drifted under the steps that led up into Hut 7. From within its blackness, two yellow jewel eyes took form and peered across the compound. Everywhere, men could be seen coming out of the huts, carrying armloads of clothing and blankets and forming lines in the storm. Eyes furtively glanced about, each man unsure of the one standing next to him. Talk diminished as fear and suspicion took over. Beneath the steps, the djinn trilled happily to itself. Smoky black tendrils whipped out excitedly, as if even from this distance the djinn could grasp victims and pull them in.

Time. Time enough. Wait. They're not going anywhere. They think they are, but they're not.

The nightform withdrew up the corner of Hut 7 and settled across the roof as, within it, the djinn gathered all its force for a major assault.

Bruckner emerged from his quarters with a terrified look. "What's the matter?" said Steuben.

"I can't find Churchill."

"Enough with that damned dog—"

Bruckner shot him a look of fury then moved down the corridor, banging on door after door, calling his dog. Steuben watched him throw open the outer door and holler into the storm, "Churchill!"

Steuben turned and shoved the homemade knife into his belt then buttoned his coat over it. He no longer needed it for Kirst, but perhaps against this djinn . . .

Huddled against the storm, Loring stood with Gilman as two MPs came by, headed for the gate with Vinge's body on a stretcher between them. Other MPs worked Kirst's body free of the barbed wire and brought it down, but Gilman ordered his remains sent to the German rec room. Loring said nothing as he leaned over to explain, "I'd just prefer leaving him inside the camp." When she didn't respond, he added, "You're not really suggesting I send my men through this compound holding up mirrors. Can't you come up with something a little better?"

"Nothing else seems to have much effect."

"What about salt? You never got around to that earlier."

"I just wish we could test it. I mean, what if we're face to face with the djinn, and we throw salt at him, and nothing happens?"

"Is there any reason to think it might be effective?"

"The dig at Ur-Tawaq was heavily salted. In those times, they salted tombs to keep evil spirits in check. The Romans used to salt the graves of their enemies killed in battle so they wouldn't rise up again—"

"Look, I don't need a history lesson. I need ways of killing this thing."

Loring stared at him. He apologized then looked at her —with her hair storm-blown, her hands clutching the coat tightly about her body, her nose blue. She was shivering.

"Let's get you out of here."

"I'm all right. I'll take care of myself."

Gilman thought back, recalling what they had been doing a short time ago. It already seemed distant, part of the unrecoverable past. He wanted to ask why she had made love to him, but he already knew. Desperation. Fear. Need. No love at all.

He looked up as two squads of MPs double-timed through the gate, led by Lieutenant Blish but slowed by the storm as they headed down the hill to take charge of moving the Germans out. Behind the MPs came Hopkins. He stopped at the gate and shouted down to Gilman:

"General headquarters on the radio, sir! They want a word with you!"

The radio shack was a separate cabin behind the MP mess hall. Loring opened her coat and warmed herself at the potbellied stove. Hopkins took the extra chair. Gilman replaced the radio operator at his seat and grabbed the microphone.

"This is Major Gilman. Over."

A voice crackled from the speaker. "This is General Hawthorn. What's all this crap about moving the prisoners, Major? Your assistant commandant wisely thought to check that order through channels. Are you aware that it's against regulations? Would you care to discuss it? Over."

The last thing Gilman wanted was to get boxed into an explanation that would sound utterly ridiculous to an outsider. He opted for vagueness. "Sir, we have a condition here," he said. "Some unexplained casualties. So far, eight Germans and one MP have been murdered. For the security of all concerned, I intend to move the prisoners out of the compound and quarter them in one building where they can be carefully watched. We've got a hell of a storm going, sir, and that's making it difficult to conduct an investigation. Over."

Hopkins smirked, confident that the ploy wouldn't work. They waited through the hash coming from the speaker as Hawthorn evidently conferred with other officers. Loring glanced out the grimy, iced-up window, but she couldn't see the compound. Even the fence was obliterated by the storm. She felt as if she should be down there right now, because something was happening.

The general came back on the line. "That's a negative, Major. Your orders are to keep the Germans inside the compound and confined to their huts. Do not move them. Repeat, do not move them. Do you read me? Over."

Loring closed her eyes. This was getting out of hand.

Gilman thought carefully before answering. *France. Window Hill. Second Battalion.* "I read you, sir. Over."

"I will send a detachment as soon as the weather lifts, Major. Do you read me on that as well? Over."

France. Window Hill. "Yes, sir. I read you, sir. Over."

"Good, Major. I'm glad we understand each other. I will enter this conversation into my records. I advise you to do the same. Over and out."

Gilman turned the microphone back to the radio man and stood up. Hopkins was gloating.

France. Window Hill. Never again.

"Hopkins, haul your ass over to the office and write down that conversation. Add that you failed to obey my order and on your own initiative took the matter up with General Hawthorn. Say that upon signing off I decided to disobey the general's orders"—Hopkins blanched—"and proceed on my own authority. Have your stooge, Corporal Chilton, type it up for my signature. I'll be outside, supervising the move—"

"Sir, if you refuse to obey the general's orders, I'll have to assume command—"

"You'll assume shit!" Gilman leaped over to Hopkins. *"I am not going to lose any more men!* Now"—Gilman rebuttoned his coat—"get some guards into our mess hall. We'll put the Germans in there. Are you with me, Captain?"

Hopkins rose and nodded bitterly. "Yes, sir."

Gilman left with Loring. Outside, the storm had calmed; the wind had slowed. "It must be reassuring fighting your own officers," Loring said.

"That's why we have captains and majors. The major doesn't have to be right—he outranks the captain."

"And the general?"

326

"Fuck the general."

Gilman slowed at the crest of the hill, expecting to see German POWs filing out the gate past armed MPs. But the gate stood open and there was no one guarding it.

"Goddamnit." His anger rose and he lengthened his stride, intent on chewing somebody out. Loring grabbed his arm and pointed into the camp. He paused and followed her arm and saw . . . nothing. Nothing but the fence and the sentry towers running to the left and the right. Nothing but searchlights stabbing an impenetrable darkness. Nothing beyond the fence but blackness. No huts, no Germans, no MPs, no snow-covered slope. A black shroud hung over the compound, concealing everything. Even light couldn't break through. Swirling snow was swallowed up in blackness.

Gilman hardly heard Loring's muttered gasp because of the sounds rising from within the camp. Howls of terror, screams of shock and fright, shooting—

Yanking himself free of her clutching hand, Gilman floundered toward the gate.

"Major!" she called.

On his right, the sentry in the nearest tower descended quickly and hurried to join him, rifle ready.

"Major—don't go in there!"

He went in.

Chapter 26 ════════════════════════════════

With the storm thinning out overhead, Blish had moments earlier been checking the ranks of prisoners wrapped in coats and blankets and waiting in front of their huts. Then he authorized the first hut to move out.

Armed MPs fell into step around the prisoners, but they never got beyond the circle of buildings. They stopped and looked up curiously as a thin veil of black rose up into the sky from the roof of Hut 7 and expanded to create a canopy over the entire compound, blotting out the searchlights and plunging the camp into pitch-black darkness so thick that men two feet away couldn't be seen.

As the MPs tried to prod the Germans into formation, they began shuffling and muttering in the blackness. One shove too many and suddenly there was shouting and cursing.

Panic erupted. The Germans broke ranks, shoved past the MPs, and ran. Within seconds, Steuben stood alone on the steps of his hut and stared into blackness, listening to the sounds of his men running and shouting.

The first blast of tommy-gun fire made him flinch. Then he felt something cold and wispy touch the nape of his neck. He turned abruptly. It brushed his face. He tried to grab it and caught something. He brought his hand close to his eyes and in the gloom saw black mist curl from his fingers then shoot upward to be lost in the cloud overhead.

A light stabbed Steuben's eyes. A frightened MP roared something at him. When the light wavered, Steuben glimpsed the MP aiming his carbine one-handed. Steuben dove through the hut door as a burst of gunfire chewed up the threshold behind him. He kicked the door closed and flattened himself on the floor. More bullets ripped through the door and plowed overhead only inches from his body. Then he heard boots crunching away fast in the snow. More fire elsewhere. He looked down the empty corridor.

What's happening?

Lieutenant Blish stood in utter blackness at the corner of a hut—he didn't even know which one—.45 in hand, fear making a lump pulse in his throat as he waited for the next German to charge by. So far, he had fired at two of them, two rifle-bearing soldiers wearing long greatcoats and coal-scuttle helmets. Somehow, these helpless, unarmed prisoners had acquired a stash of war gear and weapons and, under cover of this freak darkness, had become a fully equipped little army. At least that's what he *saw*, but common sense told him it was impossible.

Again, icy coldness brushed at his ears and he swatted it. Blackness stirred past his eyes. He had never seen fog like this—thicker than the proverbial London pea soup and so unrelievedly black.

A man lumbered around the corner of the hut and collided with Blish. Shoving him away, Blish had a fleeting glimpse of his helmet and rifle and, hearing his guttural war cry, fired point-blank into his face. The soldier crumpled in the snow.

Got one at last.

Dropping down before the blackness could move back in and obscure the body, Blish prodded the soldier over with the muzzle of his .45 and stared into the gory, pulpy face, unrecognizable in death.

Blish froze. This soldier had no weapon or helmet, because it was no soldier. It was an unarmed prisoner.

Blish felt a surge of horror. Blackness closed over his face. Icy fingers of gloom seeped into his mind and siphoned off his fear. Aware of what was happening, Blish's terror mounted. He screamed and leaped to his feet. He fell back against the wall of the hut and clawed at the blackness, the .45 still in his hand, his finger still hooked around the trigger. He got off a shot, but the force extracting his emotions gripped him even tighter and, where it drained him, he felt freezing cold injected in its place.

Squirming in terror, Blish fired the .45 again and again. The last time he squeezed the trigger, the muzzle was against his eye.

Glacial cold pierced Gilman's brain as he trudged down the snow-crusted slope, blind in the overwhelming darkness. The sentry who had come in with him crunched off to the right. In a few seconds, his footsteps were lost in the rising pandemonium from below.

Something flitted into Gilman's face. He brushed it away. *Snow,* he thought. *Just snow.*

But if there was any snow falling through this murk, it was invisible to him. He stopped, realizing he was no longer walking on snow. He was standing on something that had the consistency of mud. Squatting down, he peered at the ground and was able to discern only a shapeless dark mass. He ran a hand over it. It felt wet and slimy. In the midst of it, his fingers encountered something hard and sharp—like a meaty stick.

Disgust surged in Gilman's stomach. It was a human rib, and the pulpy stuff around it was the remains of a body. The gloom thinned a bit, and he found himself on a dark familiar hillside, squatting inside the rib cage of a dead GI whose entire torso had been blown apart. Around him on the hill were more bodies, scattered like split broilers waiting to be cooked.

Gripped by an uncontrollable sickness, Gilman vomited over the body beneath him. The bile came in nauseating waves, convulsing his neck and shoulders. Gasping, he crouched to recover, heart pounding with horror as he smelled burnt flesh and cordite on the air. His worst nightmare had come to life.

Window Hill. Second Battalion.

Gilman released a shout of denial then staggered away from the bodies and back into darkness, sensing something pulling at the back of his head, a numbing chill trying to suck the fear from his mind.

He collided with someone, hit the snow, and rolled. When he looked up, Loring was beside him, lifting him up. He grabbed her hand. "I saw them," he croaked. "My men—"

She grinned. Her mouth opened and he saw the blackness through it. Her hand became black wisps in his fingers, and then she wasn't Loring anymore. She was a black tornado, spinning out of what he had thought was Loring's flesh, rising over his head.

Gilman scrambled backward, letting out a long, drawn-out scream of pain.

Huddled against the back of the shower hut, Bruckner listened, terrified, to the screams and shooting around

331

him. He could see nothing anyway, so he closed his eyes. But being alone with his inner darkness only made it worse. Unable to stop himself, he was shaken by sobs.

Somewhere a dog barked.

Bruckner's eyes snapped open. He sniffled and peered through the darkness. Was that Churchill loping by, disappearing beneath Hut 9?

Chancing a dash in the open, Bruckner hustled across the open space, hoarsely calling his dog. Reaching the side of Hut 9, he peered under the foundation, but the snowdrifts were piled so high he realized the dog would have had to dig through them to get beneath the hut. It wasn't Churchill, he decided. It was part of the nightmare. With his rejection of the image, blackness again closed in. Bruckner straightened slowly, conscious of voices nearby. . . .

Peering through the gloom, he was gradually able to make out the shadowy figures of men standing in a long line outside the shower hut. His heart filled with relief. The madness was over. Order was restored.

Pushing himself away from Hut 9, he waded through the snow toward the line. As he got closer, he realized they were his men, Germans, his friends, and they were lined up—some twenty of them—waiting to get into the shower hut. And every one of them was stark naked.

He stopped to study their hangdog faces and huddled bodies and hands covering their genitals. They seemed embarrassed and terrified. Other shapes moved into view. MPs carrying tommy guns, prodding them one by one into the shower hut. Behind Bruckner, an MP brandished his weapon and nodded at him to join the line.

Bruckner stumbled forward, a hideous certainty trying to break through the fog in his brain. Despite the inner warning, Bruckner joined the line and almost in a zombie trance stripped off his uniform. He became one of them, edging closer to the open door, naked and freezing. A chill breeze struck like the snap of a whip on his body, and he saw stinging welts spring up on his flesh. He remembered that nightmare from his boyhood. He had grown up and learned to laugh at it, but this was no nightmare. . . . This was real. . . . Real? Dread screamed in his mind. Looking up, he saw Mueller in the line, Hoffman and Dortmunder, Eckmann and Schliebert, the dead. . . .

Gebhard stepped through the door into darkness, beckoning him to follow.

Bruckner watched the MPs shove Schliebert through next. A dog barked nearby. Bruckner turned and, though he knew Churchill was only a few feet away, the dog was invisible, lost in the darkness beyond the shrinking line of men, barking furiously as if to warn him where his own inner alarm had failed.

Then he was on the steps and about to enter. Churchill's bark was cut off, replaced by a vicious snarl, sounds of a terrible fight, Churchill's frightened whine—

"No!" he shouted. He flung his arms out to keep himself from entering. The dog sounds vanished, replaced by a deep, throaty, mocking laugh. A frigid unseen hand shoved Bruckner through the door. It slammed shut after him.

He was in the shower hut with twenty other naked men, all of them talking in low whispers that slid like ice cubes into his blood. Bruckner looked up at the shower heads. No water yet. The others looked up with him. There was a clanking sound as a cover was removed from a vent directly above him.

For a second he glimpsed Hopkins' grinning face, then

a canister of crystals was emptied on his head. Water sprang from the showers. The crystals erupted into gas.

Around him the naked men coughed and choked. Bruckner stumbled backward, at last aware of what was happening. He flung himself at the door and hammered on it. It wouldn't open. He whirled as the hut filled with gas and he saw he was alone—there were no other men.

He ran to the back of the hut and slammed a fist through the window and reached up to climb out through the jagged glass. But blackness flooded in and obscured the opening.

Stumbling back, Bruckner whirled and saw two MPs open the door to the toilet stall, but there was no toilet. Inside, there was a roaring oven.

They reached for him. Bruckner choked on his scream and clutched his heart. He jerked several times then went rigid. When he hit the floor he was dead.

Retreating to his quarters, Steuben had stood pressed into a corner in darkness, listening to the occasional screams and bursts of gunfire outside. Struggling to make sense of what was happening, he concentrated on the sounds and detected something very odd. Two succeeding bursts of gunfire were followed by the same scream.

He realized he was hearing imitations. There were delusions going on outside, but whose?

Clutching Dortmunder's homemade knife, Steuben edged into the empty corridor, which was as pitch-black as the outdoors. Detecting no human presence, Steuben opened the bullet-riddled door and looked out. He was surprised to see the gloom had diminished. Flicking his thumb across the edge of the blade to be certain of its sharpness, he stepped out and looked up.

The blackness hung a few feet above him, blotting out the roof of his hut. Knowing it was waiting for him made him feel better. Seeing the enemy made escape at least possible.

A woman shouted.

He thought for a moment it was Loring Holloway and automatically looked for her. He saw nothing. Then the same woman screamed and cried for help.

Plunging into the snow, he followed the sound to the rear of Hut 7. As he approached the door, the cries grew louder. Then the door burst open in front of him and men tumbled out, dragging women behind them. Thinking they were MPs, he backed up, brandishing the knife. But they paid him no attention. Then he saw their uniforms. Russians. One of them leered at him, while another swung a woman around and threw her into the snow, then pounced on her and tore at her clothing. She screamed and, seeing Steuben, stretched an arm out to him and called—

"Walter!"

Steuben was momentarily transfixed as it sank in—a Russian was raping his wife. Then a young girl was dragged from Hut 7 and stripped bare before his eyes. "Papa!" she cried. Russian hands clawed her breasts. Her eyes were saucers as she screamed for help. Hands ran up her thighs and forced their way into her—

Steuben let out a bull-like roar and rushed into their midst, slashing with his knife. His shoulder hit solid flesh and then he was rolling in the snow with someone, thrusting his blade repeatedly into the man's neck. The blade pierced flesh, so he knew this was real, but then images exploded in his mind—Eckmann and Schliebert and Eckmann's imaginary wife—and he told himself there were no Russians in this camp and—

Schrecklichkeit!

Systematic terror. And now he was a victim.

He rolled free of the body and sprang up to see who it was. It lay in a heap in the snow, alone, a German—one of his own men. Steuben sucked in air and shut his eyes. The others were gone—the Russians, the women, his wife and daughter. Gone because they had never been there. Only in his tortured, fear-ridden mind.

He snarled at the blackness overhead, and at its tendrils licking his face. He stabbed at it, and it quickly wisped off. Hearing men running through the snow, Steuben bounded off, leaving the body behind.

Around the front of Hut 6, he found a knot of POWs huddled in fear. He waved the bloodied knife. "We're getting out of here," he said. Without question, they fell in behind him and he led them up the slope.

Overhead, the black fog was thinning out, admitting more dim light.

If we find the gate, we're out, Steuben told himself. *And if they want to keep us in here, they'll have to shoot us.*

Loring paced anxiously at the gate, staring at the blackness and wanting to charge in after Gilman but aware that if anything happened to him she was the only one left with a hope of defeating the djinn. From either side, the tower sentries continued to crank their sirens. MPs were gathered behind her on the hill, and she had pleaded with Hopkins not to send them through the gate. Hopkins waited at the crest, watching for Gilman to reappear.

While the wind banged the gate against the fence, Loring began to think she could see shapes moving around inside and the outline of huts below. She assumed the darkness was lifting. Clutching the silver talisman to her chest, she darted through the gate.

Inside, she ran without thinking until her legs sank into a snowdrift. Climbing out, she glanced back and saw the gate nearly obscured by blackness, Hopkins and his MPs invisible beyond it.

While she was looking toward the gate, a curtain of black abruptly descended around her. Sprawling backward, she held up the talisman and waited, motionless.

You're not going to get me.

The blackness settled.

Then, from the direction of the gate, she heard water trickling. With her legs sinking deeper into the snow, she listened to the sound growing louder. It became a bubbling rumble from the ground almost directly in front of her—a sound that she recognized—

Iraq. The water spell.

She held up the talisman as if to drive it back, but the rumble shuddered up from beneath her. Snow split open and a torrent of water gushed from the ground and cascaded over her head. With it came bodies—men in ragged clothing with bloated, staring eyes—

Spewed forth like broken dolls, their limp forms wrapped around her legs as she stood against the flood and screamed, her eyes automatically closing to shut out the horror.

Something cold and wispy touched her cheeks. She dared to look and saw the blackness reaching for her. Ignoring the bodies piling up around her and the water hissing over snow, she ripped the talisman from her neck and, using it as a knife, sliced at the blackness as she would a curtain of cobwebs.

Something splattered into her eye, and there was a terrible roar. She stumbled back, wiping black blood from her face.

The blackness retreated upward and folded back into the cloud above. The water vanished. And with it the bodies.

Loring looked at the talisman. Even in the gloom she could see that it was covered with a dark, sticky wetness. She felt a thrill of satisfaction. She had wounded the djinn! She set her teeth in determination.

If it can be wounded, it can be killed!

A jumble of sounds behind her. She looked back. Steuben was leading a crowd of POWs up the slope toward her. Gilman joined them. Their eyes fixed on the gate, they plowed through the snow, ignoring the blackness diving down to tease their faces.

Less than ten yards away, they stopped, bumping into each other. MPs came up alongside, some without weapons, all with horror etched on their faces as they stared at Loring. She backed away and held the talisman tighter until she realized they were not looking at her, but past her.

She turned.

Positioned in the opening at the gate, just inside the camp, was Hopkins. With him were two MPs manning a .50-caliber machine gun. Behind Loring, the Germans saw with sinking realization what they had suspected all along.

Hopkins said nothing as he faced them sternly. Loring knew he would not let anyone pass.

Gilman appeared alongside her. He seemed different. Changed. Hollow-eyed and haunted. Without taking his eyes from Hopkins, he placed a hand on Loring's shoulder and gently but firmly pushed her away. She watched him lurch forward.

Hopkins eyed him coldly then rapped the gunner on the head. The gunner pulled the action back and tightened his hold on the trigger grips.

"Get away from that weapon," Gilman commanded.

Beneath Hopkins' brow, two burning coals flicked over the Germans. Gilman took another step toward the machine gun, unwilling to believe Hopkins would really fire. There was a click. The gunner's finger tightened. Hopkins grinned at Gilman.

The machine gun spat flame in the night.

Part Five

The racket was deafening. Germans dove into the snow and covered their heads. Two of the MPs returned fire. Their bullets punched up snow sprays around the gunners. The machine gun swept back and forth in front of Gilman, who wondered why his body wasn't already punctured in a hundred different places. Tommy guns clattered behind him. An MP appeared at his shoulder, angrily emptying his clip at the gunners to no effect. When his bullets were gone, he dropped his weapon and a frightened sob escaped him. The machine gun kept spitting fire but hitting nothing. Loring crouched in the snow and stared. Even the Germans began to look up. A mocking laugh overwhelmed the gunfire—it came from Hopkins.

"What the hell is going on?"

Men came through the gate—MPs, led by Hopkins. Another Hopkins. He stopped just behind the other and stared incredulously at his double.

Loring scrambled to Gilman. "It's the djinn!" she shouted. The machine gunner locked his weapon on Gilman, blasting at his midriff. Gilman stepped forward.

"What is this?" the second Hopkins bellowed.

Gilman moved right up against the muzzle of the gun.

343

It fired harmlessly at his legs. He felt nothing. He looked into the eyes of the thing that was posing as Hopkins—

Abruptly, the entire illusion—Hopkins, the machine gun, and both gunners—turned to oily black smoke and billowed up around Gilman, skimmed over the Germans and back up into the cloud overhead, which quickly began to collect in on itself and rush back into the camp.

Hopkins—the real Hopkins—was immobilized at the gate, staring at the ground, looking for shells, for some proof that he had seen something real.

Gilman angrily erupted at the spot where the illusion had been, kicking up great feathery drifts of snow and swearing at the unseen enemy.

Loring grabbed his arm. "Now, while we have some control back—get everyone out of here!" He stared at her. "It pulled this stunt just now to keep everyone inside. It's not enough for it to kill. I'm telling you, it needs a new host. Without a host, it's trapped in here alone."

Gilman looked for Steuben. "Major!" he called. "Collect your men and get them out of here. And from now on, ignore what happens on this side of the fence!"

Steuben hesitated, slipping the knife back into his belt, not wholly willing to trust his eyes and ears anymore, but recognizing his duty as a commanding officer. He turned and barked orders to the men with him. They lost no time hustling through the gate.

Grim-faced, Hopkins came down and deployed his guards to help Steuben round up the rest of the Germans. At this point, even Hopkins saw the sense of Gilman's order.

They came hurrying through the snow, shielding their faces against the storm, intent on one thing—getting past the gate. Steuben moved along with them, repeating

Gilman's warning to ignore anything that got in their way.

Loring stayed close to Gilman, watching the POWs run a gauntlet of armed guards through the gate and up the hill into the mess hall. She looked down into the camp. The blackness had completely vanished under cover of the storm. The djinn could be anywhere now. She wondered why it didn't continue its attack. Maybe it needed time to recover from the massive effort of the last fifteen minutes. Or maybe it had already found a new host, and it was leaving the camp right before her eyes, inside one of the Germans. She watched them carefully.

Hopkins stood at the gate, shaken and fighting hard not to show it. Snow swirled into his face and he batted the flakes away with a gloved hand. Suddenly it was no longer important to bully the prisoners or worry about what they were plotting. There was a *real* enemy to fight. Hopkins decided he would kill it himself and leave Gilman flatfooted.

The last of the Germans came through without incident, accompanied by the remaining MPs. Steuben stopped to comment to Gilman, "There are quite a few dead men down there, Major—some of yours, some of mine."

Gilman nodded. As the last man went out, he turned to Loring. "Couldn't we just clear out and let the djinn have the camp? If it can't find a new host or any more victims, my guess is it'll die, or at least become manageable."

Loring indicated the men going up the hill. "It may already be out," she said. "In a new host. We've got to go down there and be sure."

"It's going to be desperate, isn't it?"

"Yes."

"And careless?"

"We're not dealing with something that operates by the rules of human behavior, Major. We can't outwit it. We have to find it and kill it. If we wait for reinforcements—for the general's detachment—we'll have to go through all of this again, trying to convince other people. They may not be as open-minded as you," she added wryly.

"Thanks."

"And worse—fresh troops determined to show you what a bunch of cowards you are will be easy pickings for the djinn and simply add more possibilities, more ways for it to escape and get out into the world. And if it gets loose—if it leaves these mountains—"

"It'll what?"

"It will grow and consume and kill and grow larger and more powerful and, eventually, there won't be any way to stop it." She shielded her eyes from the snow. "We've got to do it now, right here."

Hopkins stood apart, staring into the camp, almost positive he could see a shadow moving against one of the huts. He drew his .45. "There's still someone down there," he called to Gilman, then took off at a run, broadjumping the drifts.

"Hopkins!" Gilman shouted.

In a moment, Hopkins was a shadow himself, swallowed up in the storm. Gilman swore and looked back. There were MPs gathered at the fence, watching, waiting for his next move.

"I guess it's me and Hopkins," Gilman said.

"I'm going with you."

"No!"

Loring flared. "I *brought* the damned thing here!"

346

Steuben joined them. "If there really is a straggler down there, Major, it's one of my men. I'm going, too."

Gilman thought of calling the MPs down to remove both Loring and Steuben, but they were already trudging down the slope toward the huts, and he knew they were not after any straggler. They were after the djinn.

He turned to the MP nearest the gate. "Close it," he said. "And no matter what you see, don't open it again. Not to let anyone in or out."

The MP swung the gate shut and snapped the padlock.

Hopkins rounded the *Krankenhaus* and peered through the open door. It was dark inside. He called softly. No one answered. Leveling the .45, he went up the steps and called again. Silence. He backed out and shut the door.

Where the hell is that straggler?

He crunched through the snow, the .45 extended in front of him as he swept the huts with a steady gaze, alert for shadows. Moving searchlights helped a little, but he saw nothing. The huts were deserted. Somewhere, an open door banged against a wall repeatedly.

Between Huts 4 and 5, Hopkins stopped and tried a shameless ploy. "I see you," he called. "Come on out."

No one came.

Something moved beneath Hut 6. Hopkins bounded to the wall and tripped over a body in the snow. He picked himself up and looked at the crumpled form half buried in a drift. He brushed snow from where the head would be and stared at Blish's cold dead face with half his head blown away.

Hopkins scrambled away from it, stared at it a moment, then grimly turned back to Hut 6, moved to the wall, and crouched. Peering beneath the hut, he saw the glint of a pair of eyes. He stuck the .45 under the foundation, his finger tightened on the trigger. "All right, asshole—out! Now!"

The eyes vanished. A shadow moved. Hopkins fired. The blast was a deadened *prang* beneath the hut.

The thing scurried out of sight. An animal, Hopkins realized. Maybe Bruckner's dog.

Shit, I hope I hit it.

Hopkins hauled himself up and looked around again.

A man ducked into the rec room.

Hopkins stood still, trying to decide if it was a man or just a trick of the eye. "Hey," he called. "You in the rec room!"

Kraut. Probably heard the shot and figures we're shooting prisoners.

Hopkins plunged toward the rec room. He heard Gilman calling his name and stopped. Three figures were coming down from the gate. At this distance, obscured by the storm, he couldn't see them clearly. Just as well: that meant they couldn't see him. He ignored Gilman's call.

The rec-room door was open. Hopkins slipped in, flattened himself out of the dim light at the doorway, and waited for his eyes to adjust to the gloom. He swung his .45 around slowly.

"Okay," he said. "I know you're in here. Come on out."

Nothing moved.

He groped for the light switch, found it, and flicked it on. Nothing happened. He moved back to the doorway, where he would be silhouetted, and the German could see him holster his weapon. He slid it down snugly into the leather and removed his hand from it.

"See? I'm not going to hurt you. Come on."

Nothing moved, yet Hopkins sensed a presence. Something in this room didn't belong. He sniffed the air. It was cold and smelled of stale cigarette smoke and sweat. And blood. Hopkins' eyes darted about. Blood. A metallic sweetness that had burned itself into his sense memory over the last few days.

Moving forward, he stumbled against something. It scraped loudly across the floor. A card table. Both his hands shot out—one to his .45, the other to the table for balance. His hand touched something soft. Rough wool. A blanket. There was something beneath it. He jerked his hand away, backed up, and looked at the table. Dimly he could make out a long object concealed beneath the blanket.

His other hand tightened on the .45. His heart beat faster and his mind raced. He was sure the straggler was hidden beneath the blanket with a gun or a knife—

Then he realized what it was.

Kirst's body, put there by the MPs and draped with a blanket. That's why he smelled blood. And on the next table under another blanket was Bauhopf.

Hopkins choked on a laugh. There was no one in this hut. No one living, anyway. The figure he had seen dart through the door?—only in his mind. There was no one. Only Kirst.

"And you ain't going nowhere," he said to the corpse.

He laughed again and turned to leave.

The blanket moved.

Hopkins froze.

Maybe it wasn't Kirst. Maybe it *was* a goddamned straggler.

Shit.

He turned back.

"Maybe we ought to split up," Gilman suggested. They were walking along the outer line of huts, he and Loring and Steuben, calling Hopkins and getting no answer.

"No!" Loring shouted over the storm. "You saw what the djinn was able to do at the gate. It had enough power to make us believe that whole tableau. If we separate, it could disguise itself as any one of us to get near the others. We have to stay together and find something to use against it. Protection. Then we'll think of a way to let Hopkins know where we are."

Gilman nodded. "All right—protection. Name something."

"The one thing we haven't tried—salt."

Gilman grunted. "The one thing we haven't tried, eh? Very reassuring. Well, anybody got a shaker?"

Steuben pointed between the huts. "There's a supply of salt in the mess hall. Bags of it."

"Let's go," said Loring.

"Okay. . . . Everything is going to be just fine. . . . You've got nothing to be scared of. . . . Daddy Hopkins is here to haul your precious German ass up to our own good old American mess hall, where you'll get some really fine chow. . . . You hear me, kraut? I'm talking to you."

Hopkins cautiously reached for a corner of the blanket. His other hand rested on the .45.

"I'm standing right beside you, and there's no one else with me, and my gun is holstered, and you don't have one fucking thing to be afraid of, okay, Mac? Okay, here we go. I've got the blanket now. You just stay calm and—"

He whipped off the blanket. A gust of wind from the

open door blew it into his face. He clawed it off and flung it aside and looked down.

On the table was a body. Not a straggler, not Kirst, not Bauhopf. Hopkins was certain that he could see the two silver bars of a captain. U.S. Army. An American. Moving closer, Hopkins thought he recognized the face. The hairline, rumpled and greasy with matted blood, looked familiar. He came around the table for a better view and discovered dark, mottled stains along the shirtfront— dead, staring eyes and a ripped-out throat with torn arteries protruding—

This is Kirst, isn't it? No, it's not.

Hopkins trembled as he stared at the face, knowing who it was but wanting not to know it because it was someone he knew, someone he saw every day. It was Hopkins' own dead face lying there on the card table— with no throat and the body stretched limp from the slaughter and blood all over—

A maddened howl echoed through the rec room. Hopkins' hand shook on the butt of his .45 when he realized it was his own terrified scream reverberating in his ears—

The door slammed shut.

Alone in the dark with the thing on the table, Hopkins blinked to dilate his pupils. He leaned closer to the table to prove to himself he had made a mistake, hoping that even in this pitch-black darkness he would see what was really there. Kirst—it had to be Kirst. But then the body was in motion, and there was only time enough for him to glimpse arms rising from either side of the table before huge clawed hands seized him around the throat.

Hopkins flailed at the hands. Their grip tightened. He backed and stumbled and tried to get away, but the claws held him and, as fear dilated his pupils and let him see in the gloom, he discovered that these were disembodied hands, vanishing at the elbows, not connected to the body on the table at all. They forced him down.

His knees buckled and he was slammed into the floor, one leg bent almost double beneath him, but that pain lasted only an instant and was wiped away by a numbness spreading downward from his neck.

The djinn materialized out of the dark above, and now he saw what the arms were connected to. It towered over him, leering, its jaws opening wide, and its forked tongue flicking at him.

Then the claws punctured his neck and ripped out his throat.

The djinn's immense hand rose, offering Hopkins' gory flesh to an unseen god. Then Hopkins' head dropped to his chest, and gratefully he saw at last that there was no body on the table after all. There never had been. It had all been in his mind. Only the djinn was real.

And in his glazing eyes, even the djinn became darkness.

Chapter 28

Rummaging in the pantry, Steuben found several large bags of salt, which Gilman helped him drag out to the mess hall. Each grabbing a bag, they began salting the hut. Loring poured a line of it across the doorway. Steuben scattered it on the floorboards. Gilman covered the windowsills. Loring brushed some under the back door then returned to watch Steuben stoke a fire in the potbellied stove.

When it was going strong and they could feel the warmth, they sat down in front of it and tried to relax, figuring that the smoke from the roof stack would eventually draw Hopkins. No one spoke. They all knew they had set themselves up as bait. The djinn would come for them sooner or later.

After a while, Gilman opened the door. The storm had died down. Snow was still falling, but it was no longer whipped about on raging winds. Gilman watched a breeze stir the grains of salt at his feet. The white line remained in place.

Looking up, he spotted a figure stumbling out from between the huts, coming toward him. As it got closer, he recognized Hopkins. Gilman signaled him. "Over here!"

Loring and Steuben joined him at the door. Loring studied the approaching figure intently.

Within a yard of the door, he stopped. Salt stirred on the threshold. Gilman urged him on impatiently. Hopkins stayed where he was, his gazing moving slowly from one to the other of them. All at once, his eyes rolled back into his head, he swayed, and toppled into the snow.

Gilman made a move to help him. Loring grabbed his arm. "Wait a minute," she said.

"He's hurt."

"Let's just wait."

Hopkins didn't move. Gilman shrugged off Loring's restraining hand and descended the steps. He stopped, beginning to think about why she wanted him to wait. He stared at Hopkins' body sprawled in the snow and wondered what was wrong with him. Why had he collapsed? Had there been a fight? Had the straggler attacked him? Hopkins' .45 was still in its holster. Something about this struck Gilman as not being right.

Loring's hand was on his arm again, pulling him back. He went back up the steps and watched her hold up the silver talisman and angle it to catch Hopkins' vague reflection. She looked into it and gasped.

Gilman and Steuben looked. In place of Hopkins' body lying in the snow was the reflection of something half-man, half-beast, crouched and watching them with the hungry look of a starved dinosaur.

Loring dropped the talisman. It dangled on the end of the chain as she stooped and grabbed a handful of salt from the doorstep. She flung it at Hopkins.

There was an unearthly howl of pain and rage as Hopkins' body erupted out of the snow, twisted into impossible shapes then collected into what resembled the blistering stump of a tree made of smoldering flesh. In its place then rose a thick column of oily black smoke that coiled backward then hurled itself at the mess hall.

The smoke clove into two bands of cloudy blackness that encircled the space beneath the eaves. It seized the mess hall and began to shake it.

Gilman, Loring, and Steuben sprang back into the room. The salt jumped and flew about the doorway. The floor banged and cracked beneath their feet. The walls heaved. Clouds of black boiled against the windows and exploded the glass inward. Shards tore past them and ripped their clothing. Salt blew from the exposed windowsills and whipped about their bodies in a white swirl.

Gilman shoved Loring to the floor and held her down as the boards bumped and heaved beneath them. Steuben dove under a table.

Blackness seeped upward between the cracks, forcing the floorboards apart in an attempt to get through. Salt dropped through the openings and the howl rose again. The floor stopped moving, but the entire building began to shake. Then, beneath the potbellied stove, the floorboards finally buckled. They snapped and, on a roiling black cloud, the stove was hoisted into the air and tipped over. Hot coals spilled from the open grate. The dry floor ignited.

Behind them, boards splintered and one whole wall opened up. An impossible wind blew in, fanning the fire and carrying sparks to the opposite wall.

Gilman got up, pulling Loring with him, trying to reach the door, but the wind gathered force and propelled them across the room toward the fire. Sparks and salt blew around their heads. The floor around the stove was already an inferno, and the east wall was burning.

Steuben scrambled from beneath his table and tried to run for the kitchen. Boards splintered under his feet. He tripped and nearly fell through the floor. Blackness rose through the opening and gripped him. He screamed.

Grabbing one of the half-empty salt bags, Gilman threw it to Steuben, who turned it bottom up and emptied it over the lower half of his body. The blackness howled again, immediately released him, and shrank out of sight beneath the hut.

Steuben struggled to climb out of the hole as Gilman moved to help him. The wind blasted Loring backward. With a shriek, she crashed into the tables and was shoved back with them.

The nightform came billowing in on the wind, through the gaping hole in the west wall. It formed a black tornado in the center of the room and spun around at incredible speed. As Loring fought to disentangle herself from a crush of tables and chairs, Gilman struggled to free Steuben from the hole in the floor.

With a lurching shudder inside the tornado, the nightform abruptly became the djinn.

It stood stooped beneath the ceiling, its reptilian hide covered with dark, greasy fur. From the waist down, its body was goatlike, with yellowed cloven hooves. Long, powerful arms with clawed hands lashed out at Loring and Gilman, separating them. It took another swipe, and one of its talons hooked into the chain at Loring's throat. She screamed as it was yanked away. The chain and Yazir's silver talisman were flung into the flames.

Inches from the spreading fire, Steuben crouched and stared at the djinn's burning eyes, its flicking tongue, its blood-flecked teeth.

Shoving a hand inside his coat, Steuben groped for the knife. He pulled it out and signaled Gilman to get Loring out the door.

Loring stared into the flames, searching for the talisman, but she couldn't find it. As Gilman lunged toward her, the djinn swung at him and tore a strip off his coat.

Steuben jumped between them and plunged his knife into the djinn's thigh. The knife sliced deeply into thick flesh but drew no blood. Steuben wasted no time and yanked the knife out for another stroke, but the djinn caught him with a backhanded stroke that knocked him to the floor.

As fire roared along the north wall, descending from the burning roof, Gilman caught Loring about the waist and headed for the door with her. Seeing Steuben jump back up and crouch to attack the djinn with his knife again, she cried, "No! You can't fight it this way!"

Gilman shoved her out the door. As she sprawled in the snow outside, he whirled to see the djinn backing Steuben into the fire. Something cracked above Gilman. He dove backward as a section of burning ceiling crashed down where he had been standing.

Looking up from the doorway, he saw that he was cut off from Steuben and the djinn. Through the flames, he could see Steuben thrusting and slashing with the knife. The djinn danced with him, intermittently snarling and roaring, imitating fearsome animal cries to frighten him.

Gilman tried to edge around the fire. He saw Steuben thrust again, then the great claws slammed downward and ripped away half of Steuben's coat. Steuben bellowed in pain. Across his exposed side, Gilman glimpsed blood welling up from three gaping streaks. The flesh hung in strips.

Smoke from the fire was filling the mess hall, and it stung Gilman's eyes. Coughing, he was driven back to the door and strained to see through the flames. Steuben vainly and furiously continued to slash at the djinn, which took his cuts with mocking laughter.

Then it abruptly evaporated into black smoke. In a soundless rush, it wrapped itself around Steuben and tried to crush him. He slashed at it frantically. Fire rose up from the floorboards around him.

"Steuben, get out of here!" Gilman called.

Flames shot up in front of Gilman, obscuring his view. The heat was intense. Smoke billowed into his face. He was forced out into the snow. Loring jumped up to help him.

Choking, Steuben continued to slash the air with his knife. Through eyes nearly blinded by smoke, he finally realized the blackness was gone from around his body, but now he was surrounded by flames. Panicking, he lunged through them toward the open wall.

The djinn rose up in front of him and forced him to stop with his body standing in fire. His trousers ignited. One of the djinn's immense arms snaked around his shoulder. The djinn clutched him to its body and pressed its face close to his. Its jaws opened and the forked tongue darted out, leaving an acid burn on Steuben's forehead.

Steuben stabbed upward with the knife, intending to disembowel the beast. But its free hand snapped his wrist. He screamed and dropped the knife. Both of the djinn's hands went to his throat. Claws dug deeply into the back of his head. Roaring, the djinn lifted him off the floor by the neck and shook him violently.

One thought blossomed in Steuben's tortured mind as the djinn ripped him in half—while he had lost the certainty of ever going home again, he had never lost hope. And now, he was truly on his way.

Loring pulled Gilman away from the mess hall only seconds before the entire west wall exploded outward. Splinters and fragments of board were scattered in the snow, and among them was Steuben's mangled body.

Gilman instinctively moved toward him, but Loring yanked him back. "He's dead—there's nothing you can do for him." She had seen the djinn standing in the flames, turning to whirling blackness and beginning to spiral out through the burning roof.

They ran for the nearest hut and crashed against the door. It was wedged shut. They banged on it and kicked it, but it wouldn't open. Stumbling off the steps, they looked back. The mess hall was engulfed in a pillar of fire, lighting up the camp, spraying smoldering ash into the snowfall, dirtying the white blanket around them. Gilman wondered if the MPs were still watching from the fence on the hill and if they would obey his last order and stay out.

He could no longer see the djinn. The black whirlwind had disappeared, changing into something else. Loring tugged on Gilman's arm and together they floundered through the snow to the next hut—the *Krankenhaus.*

The door was open.

They stumbled in and slammed it shut. Gilman searched for a lock then remembered there were no locks in the prison huts. He leaped across the room and, grabbing a chair, braced it against the door.

"You think that will keep it out?" Loring asked quietly.

Gilman glanced at her. She was shaking. He sagged against the wall to catch his breath. "It finished Steuben," he said. "Why didn't it finish us?"

"I think—" Loring choked back a nervous sob. "I think it only wanted to separate us from the salt."

"The salt, hah! What good did that do?"

"Didn't you see what happened when Steuben poured salt all over it?"

"It got out of the way, but *it didn't die.*"

359

"Because it was in that cloud form. That's like an in-between state for it. But when it takes on substance, I'm willing to bet—"

"Don't bother betting."

"Look, Gilman," she said with a hard edge to her voice, "Major Steuben got in the way, so it killed him. But it wants us alive. One of us has to become the host."

Gilman knew she was right. Maybe he had outsmarted himself by insisting they face it alone. "If we don't kill it," he said, "we might not walk out of here alive. If the djinn doesn't get us, those men waiting on the hill won't open the gate. And if they see us still walking around tomorrow and no sign of the monster, they may assume that *we're it*. Then—bang, bang."

Loring reflected on that while Gilman moved to a window on the east side and stared out at the burning mess hall. Steuben's body was disappearing under a layer of ash and snow. The fire was dying down slowly.

"Do you think we can hold it off till dawn?" he said. "And if we do, will it die?"

"I don't know, but if it's as desperate for a host as I believe, and it doesn't get one, something will change."

"Christ, we're operating on two volts of guesswork."

Her eyes flared. "I'm sorry. The only thing I'm sure of is that it will come after us—soon. So we'd better be prepared."

"You and me and the Boy Scouts."

They searched the entire hut to be sure the djinn wasn't already inside with them. They peered under the cots, between the sheets, unfolded the blankets, studied jars of medication, shook out towels. Gilman had no idea what they might find, what form the djinn would be inclined to turn itself into, or how they would recognize it.

They turned the back rooms inside out but found nothing, nor was there anything in the rear cubicle where Kirst had spent his last hours. They searched the medicine cabinet and found only a sealed bottle of iodine and a sponge.

There was still a closet left to search just ahead of the back rooms, but Loring was tired. They had been up all night, and she was beginning to fade. There wasn't much time left until dawn, and she reasoned that if the djinn were going to make a move, it wouldn't bother hiding in some stupid closet.

In a cupboard Gilman found a windfall: a large brown bottle filled with salt tablets. Loring found saline solution bottles and Gilman hit on the perfect weapon.

"Molotov salt cocktails." He unstoppered the solution bottles, dropped a couple of salt tablets in each, then stirred them, increasing the ratio of salt to water. He hefted one like a grenade. "Should be enough to make that overgrown pain in the ass piss in his pants."

Loring was too tired to tell him how clever he was. Gilman lined the bottles up on a rolling cart and left them unstoppered. Stuffing more salt tablets into their pockets, they tried to think of what else to do.

Gilman rolled the cart to the window and looked out again. The wind had died down completely, leaving a light snowfall descending in the night. Gilman leaned against the wall and thought of his childhood winters, of snow blanketing his parents' home in Pennsylvania. He closed his eyes and saw the woods, thick stands of pine, branches heavy with snow, pools of slush, the sun warming the chill ground. . . .

The djinn's face loomed before him with jaws distended and fangs dripping gore. . . . His eyes snapped open and he jumped upright. He blinked and realized he had gone to sleep standing up.

Loring lay on the nearest cot, one hand massaging her forehead as she struggled to stay awake. She was worried now. Yazir's talisman was gone, and with it any semblance of safety and security she had felt since arriving here. She had grown dependent on it, but what good had it been? Would anything work against the beast? Then she recalled how violently the djinn had reacted when she slashed it with the talisman, how it had drawn black blood, and how Steuben with his peculiar knife had stabbed at it, pierced its flesh but had been unable to harm it. Why? What was the difference between her attack and his?

Then she realized what it was. "Silver," she said aloud.

The knife was made of steel, the talisman of silver. The talisman had drawn the djinn's blood. The knife had not.

"Silver," she repeated, looking at Gilman. "Something made of silver might hurt it. If we can get close enough."

Gilman reflected for a moment then walked to the back cubicle. A moment later, Loring heard a loud crash. She forced herself to get up, though she was so tired she just wanted to stay on the bed no matter what.

Gilman returned carrying the jagged remains of the medicine cabinet mirror. He tossed the pieces on a cot. "Mirrors are glass backed with silver, right? Choose your weapon."

Loring nodded. "Brilliant." She dropped onto the bed again.

"Don't go to sleep. It's not that long till dawn."

Loring braced herself on one extended arm. Gilman admired the swell of her breast beneath the open coat. She was gazing out the window.

"Sky's getting lighter," she said.

Dawn was coming. The djinn had to move soon or lose its chance.

They waited.

Gilman sat on the cot next to Loring. Her face was close to his, her eyelids drooping. She leaned against him. His arm went around her shoulders. He moved a length of hair out of her eyes and bent to kiss her cheek. She didn't respond. He kissed her lips then covered her mouth with his. Her eyes were almost dead with tiredness, but her arms went around him and pulled him down.

Something scratched at the door.

Chapter 29

Flooding out of the burning mess hall as Gilman and Loring ran off, the nightform shot away into the camp, the djinn anticipating where they would go and determined to complete the trap it had laid. In the center of its consciousness, the djinn was furious with them for interfering in its hellish war. Anger turned to rage as the djinn realized that, if it failed to find a new host before first light, it would lose all it had gained and be completely at their mercy.

Fear drove it now, welling up from an awareness of its vulnerability, its need to keep feeding on the fear of others to gain energy, its compelling drive to create chaos and havoc and death so its power would grow. If not allowed to range outward and escape the compound, its power would eventually turn inward and feed on the djinn's own fears. The one emotion upon which the djinn depended so heavily for its own sustenance could slowly destroy it from within, creating an inner panic greater than that of any of its victims. And now, concern over this possibility threatened to cloud the djinn's judgment with irrational, desperate need.

It rushed forward across the compound, skimming over the icy white earth, hell-bent on preserving what it had carefully created—the image of vast, overwhelming, all-consuming power that no human could hope to defeat. Yet at the forefront of its mind lurked the knowledge that its enemies already held the key to its corporeal destruction. The djinn had used up too much power dealing with these frightened animals and, since it no longer possessed the element of secrecy, finding a new host became imperative.

With its appetite for energy growing in direct proportion to the amount expended to kill, it now felt a hunger unlike any experienced by mortals, and that hunger was rapidly, insidiously driving the djinn mad.

A muffled whine accompanied the scratching. Loring stayed absolutely still on the cot while Gilman slowly rose and both listened.

Scratch. Scratch.

Gilman moved cautiously to the door. Loring rolled off the bed, adjusted her clothing, and followed.

Scratch.

More whining. Gilman put his ear to the door and listened.

Scratch. Scratch. Scratch.

A pitiful, lonely whine.

Gilman grunted, recognizing the sound, growing certain of what it was, or what it should be. Loring was at his shoulder, intent on the sound.

"Bruckner's dog," he whispered.

"Don't be so sure."

Gilman went to the rolling cart with the row of salt cocktails. He picked one up and, returning, moved the chair and reached for the door handle.

Scratch. Scratch.

Gilman opened the door.

Churchill darted inside, scooted directly to the nearest

cot, and dove under it. Gilman stared after him, ready to throw the salt cocktail. A chill spread from the open door.

"Sure looks like a dog," Gilman said.

Loring shut the door quietly and moved the chair back into place. Churchill poked his head out from under the cot and watched them, his eyes flicking from one to the other.

"Come on out, fella," said Gilman. "Come on." He handed the salt cocktail to Loring then crossed to the cot. Loring followed, her arm back, ready to throw the bottle.

Bending over, Gilman gently snapped his fingers at the dog. He whistled through his teeth and flashed a friendly, encouraging smile. The dog just stared at him.

"What do you think?" Gilman said.

"I don't know." Loring turned on all the feminine charm she could muster and coaxed the dog. "Come on, sweetheart. Nobody's going to hurt you. Are you cold? Want to get warm? Can't be too warm under that cot. Why don't you climb up here and we'll rub you down with a blanket? What do you say?"

Churchill's front paws edged out, then he stopped and eyed them uncertainly, making up his mind if they were worthy of his trust.

"Nice doggy," Loring said. "Come on."

They both stood over the cot, coaxing the dog. He emerged inch by inch, making a game of it. He came out a bit, they offered approval, he came out a little more. At last he wriggled free, stood on all fours, and panted up at them.

Loring let him lick her hand then rub against her leg. Gilman got a shard of mirror from the other cot. "Maybe we shouldn't take the chance," he said.

She glanced at the shard of silver-backed glass in his

hand then shook her head and gave him a firm "No." Gilman tossed the shard back on the cot. Churchill sniffed Loring's legs then rose abruptly on his hindquarters and planted his front paws against her knee. Loring leaned over and let him lick her chin. "Why do they call him Churchill?" she asked.

"I think it's supposed to be a joke."

"Oh."

Gilman crouched and extended a hand. Churchill obediently came to him and licked at his fingers. "Probably hungry or thirsty," he said.

"Don't give him anything," Loring said. "He's as much a potential host as we are."

Glancing up, Gilman saw Loring pour some of the salt solution into her palm then extend her hand toward the dog. While Gilman tickled Churchill's ears to distract him, Loring quickly rubbed the salt solution into the dog's fur. She yanked her hand back and waited.

Churchill swung his head to gaze curiously at the wet spot. Disappointed in Loring, he slunk back under the cot.

Loring was relieved. "It's not the djinn. It really is a dog." She managed a tired laugh then apologized to Churchill. "I'm sorry, old boy. That was a nasty trick. I should have asked first, right?"

Churchill watched her carefully.

Loring put out her hand to be licked, but it was the one with the salt on it. The dog jumped up, shot past her, and retreated down the length of the ward, disappearing into the back cubicles.

"Win a few, lose a few," said Gilman, getting up and moving to the cot. "Where were we?"

"Oh, Christ. I'm sorry, but I'm one of those girls who just can't do it with a monster on the loose."

Gilman snorted a laugh. They looked out the window. The snowfall had slowed to a trickle. The sky was starting to lighten. Dawn was only a few minutes off.

"As soon as the sun comes up, we should be relatively safe, at least for the day," said Loring. "The djinn will be dormant, hidden somewhere. Whatever it turns itself into, it will have to stay in that form. We'll have to figure out what and where. But at least we can hunt it down without worrying about being torn to pieces."

Churchill was whining.

They hurried across the ward to investigate and found him hunched in front of the closet door, his hindquarters raised and front paws extended. He glanced up at them and whimpered.

Gilman stared at the closet door. Loring ran back to the cart for a couple of salt cocktails. Handing one to Gilman, she hefted the other herself. Gilman studied the door.

Wouldn't it be smarter to just clear out and run?

He reached for the handle. It turned easily.

Churchill ran and hid under the sink. His whining grew increasingly worried.

With a glance at Loring—she was ready with her bottle of salt solution—Gilman turned the handle until it stopped and he could feel the door loosen in his hand.

The djinn is in the closet. It's been there all the time. It's waiting for me to open the door.

Gilman fought panic.

"Now," Loring said, braced with her salt cocktail.

Gilman yanked open the door.

For an instant, nothing happened. Then something stirred in the darkness within. It leaned out and the light fell on it—a brutally mutilated human corpse, its clothing torn to shreds, its arms dangling from their shoulder sockets, held in place only by the remaining stretched and exposed tendons. The throat was gone and the head hung back on the shoulder blades, chin pointed to the ceiling. It wavered a moment then crashed to the floor.

Gilman stared at the face. Hopkins.

Loring's salt bottle slipped from her fingers and shattered on the floor. The liquid splashed away, most of it running under the corpse. Gilman whirled and saw Loring stagger a few steps, white as a sheet. Her eyes rolled back, her knees buckled, and she dropped to the floor.

Gilman backed away, for a moment too stunned to do anything. Then he remembered that wasn't just water running across the floor. It was a triple-strength saline solution, and it was pooling under Hopkins' corpse.

But there was no sizzle or spark, no reaction at all. This time it *was* Hopkins, the real Hopkins, dead Hopkins. It wasn't the djinn.

Gilman's gaze darted to the closet.

It wasn't the djinn, but the djinn had put it there. It knew they were in here. It was in here with them.

Gilman put down his salt cocktail and kneeled beside Loring. Trying to revive her, he kept glancing over his shoulder to be sure Hopkins didn't get up and walk. He slapped Loring's cheek, pinched her arm, talked to her urgently. She stayed out. Maybe sleep had finally caught up with her, and she was too exhausted to wake up.

Gathering her body in his arms, Gilman carried her to a cot and stretched her out. He glanced at Hopkins' corpse—it still hadn't moved. Relieved and trying to laugh off his fear, he looked outside.

Dawn was breaking. Light was spreading over the crest of Blackbone Mountain.

Maybe it would be all right, Gilman thought. Maybe in a few minutes, he wouldn't have to worry. Maybe the djinn had given up. Maybe he could let Loring sleep. Or carry her to the gate and get her out. Then he could sleep too. No. No sleep. Not until the djinn was found. He glanced at the dog.

Churchill was still huddled under the sink, staring at Hopkins' body. The sink. Gilman grunted.

That's how you wake them up from the faints. Water.

He crossed the room. Looking for a glass, he found one in the cabinet next to the sink. He filled it with tap water and hurried back to Loring. Slipping one arm beneath her shoulders, he raised her up. The motion helped. She stirred and started to come around woozily. He held the glass to her lips and tried to get her to drink.

She blinked and forced her eyes open. It seemed to Gilman that she wasn't seeing anything; she could still be asleep. He tilted the glass slightly. Her lips remained closed. Water moistened them. Her eyes fluttered and finally she looked around.

"Come on, Loring," he said. "It's just water."

She looked at Gilman, at the room, at the body on the floor, then her gaze settled on the glass, and her eyes widened sharply.

Her hand crashed into his, knocking the glass away. It smashed on the floor. The water splashed away in a widening circle.

Gilman grunted in surprise, but before he could say anything, the spilled water rushed together and out of it grew a column of oily blackness, whirling toward the ceiling like a dervish, spreading and turning into the djinn.

Its immense head lunged at them and fouled the air with its breath as it let out an enraged roar.

Loring spun off the bed to the floor. Gilman dove over the cot and rolled, then pulled his legs up under him, sprang to his feet, and darted toward the salt cocktail he had left beside Hopkins' corpse. Snatching up the bottle, he turned to see the djinn in the air, leaping across the room at him. Its cloven hooves crashed heavily on the floor. Its arms shot out, the claws jumping in the djinn's frenzy to get at him.

Gilman threw the bottle. It smashed against the wall behind the djinn, splashing some of the salt solution on the demon's back. Wherever the liquid touched his hide, fire erupted.

The djinn sprang upright. Both its arms shot high into the air. Its roar of rage turned to an agonized shriek of terror, the sound of a thousand demons writhing in mortal pain. Flames sizzled on its back, emitting a greasy gray smoke. Bits of ash were whipped about as the djinn threw its giant arms behind its back to claw at the pain.

Dodging past it, Gilman reached Loring and looked up in time to see the djinn spinning itself into a black tornado that quickly became a cloud of black smoke and rushed toward them.

Gilman threw Loring to the floor. The cloud blew over the cot and exploded out the window, shattering glass.

Leaping up, Gilman stared through the empty frame. The blackness whipped off in the growing dawn, around a corner and out of sight, trailed by an agonized howl that rolled up the side of Blackbone Mountain and came down as a resounding echo. Then it diminished to silence.

He turned to help Loring up. She pointed out the window and said, "Look."

The sun appeared over the top of Blackbone.

"It's gone," Gilman said. "Dead. Finished. Right?"

She shook her head sadly. "We didn't see it die. We saw it leave."

"Screaming in pain!"

"That could be another trick."

"For God's sake, how many does it have?"

"Before we let anybody back into this camp, we have to be sure!"

Gilman looked past her and saw Window Hill in his mind. He shook his head. "But it's daylight now. If it's supposed to be helpless, what can it do?"

Loring stepped away and stood over the shattered glass cup on the floor. Churchill wandered over and sniffed the pieces.

"It has to remain in some dormant form until dark," she said. "The only thing that makes sense is to turn itself into something that can be eaten. Like it did with the water. It doesn't matter if that trick didn't work the first time. It just has to keep trying."

"Won't do any good. There's nobody in here to do any eating except us. And frankly, I'm not hungry."

"That's not the point. If it's in food, we can find it. Even though the mess hall was burned flat and all those supplies are gone, there is still food left in this camp. When the prisoners were evacuated, they left behind everything edible, remember? That's where the djinn is going to be, waiting for someone to come back and have a snack."

Gilman opened the door and they stepped out. The snow had finally stopped. The black clouds were moving on to the east, leaving clear sky and sunlight. The ground was wearing a thick white carpet. Gilman looked over at the remains of the mess hall. Though reduced to a blackened ruin, it too was covered with a layer of snow.

Churchill bounded between their legs and ran off, romping and barking happily.

There was a shout from the gate. Looking up the slope,

Gilman and Loring saw POWs and MPs gathered on the other side of the fence, dozens of them looking in, waiting.

Borden met them at the gate. Gilman studied the men crowded against the fence, all of them—Americans and Germans alike—afraid, uncertain, wanting to know.

"Hopkins is dead," Gilman explained. "So is Steuben. The thing we're after is still on the loose, though it might not be dangerous at this moment."

Borden nodded but looked at him suspiciously. Gilman realized he and Loring were getting funny looks from all the men, and that some of the MPs had their weapons casually pointed in his direction.

"Look," said Gilman. "What I said before still stands. No one goes in or out until we all know for sure that this thing is dead. But if anybody gets itchy right now, you'll never know."

A few held their looks then lowered their weapons.

"Got a call from headquarters during the night," said Borden. "General Hawthorn was concerned you might not follow his orders and keep the prisoners in the compound. We had to tell him the truth."

"And?"

"He was mad as hell. Said that storm or no storm he was sending a detachment by truck convoy. At last report, they should be here in thirty minutes."

Loring felt hope sink in her stomach. She looked at Gilman and saw his despair and knew what he was feeling. Window Hill. Once again, he would be in hot water over a disobeyed order. But this time, more was at stake. When the detachment arrived, they would find a lot of corpses and a screwy, unbelievable explanation. This time they would throw the book at Gilman.

"The orders remain the same," said Gilman. "Every-one stays put. No one comes through that gate."

"Major, General Hawthorn isn't going to wait for your permission to enter," said Borden. "If we don't open the gate, he'll drive through it."

"Stall him. I'll handle the rest."

Gilman turned his back on the mob at the fence and strode quickly through the snow, back down to the camp. Loring hurried after him.

Snow crunched under their feet. The sun was up, but it would be a while before the white blanket began to melt and turn to slush.

"Red Cross parcels," Gilman said.

"Pardon?" Loring gave him a puzzled look.

"The International Red Cross supplies parcels to war prisoners. Everybody gets the same thing, usually books, baseballs, underwear—useful stuff like that."

"And food?"

Gilman nodded. "Not just a few candy bars and cookies, either. There might be a whole shipload of plum puddings scattered among the huts."

"We'll find them. We'll gather them all up and bury them in salt."

"Salt went up in the fire."

"There must be more salt in your own supplies."

"Do you want that general to walk in here and find the two of us burying food in salt?"

"Will you stop worrying what he's going to think?"

Gilman paused outside the *Krankenhaus.* He looked at the sky, the mountain, the snow. "Time," he said. "There isn't enough time."

"There is, too! Now let's split up and get busy!"

Loring stalked into Hut 4. Gilman stared after her.

Why should she be right about what form the djinn would take? Why should it conceal itself in food? Wouldn't it realize they might guess? Wouldn't it try to outsmart them? Sure it would.

Gilman set off around the huts, determined to find it. Dislodging thick drifts of snow piled up against the foundations, he poked and prodded under the huts.

It could turn itself into anything. A rock, a stick of wood, a window pane, mattress ticking . . .

Gilman stomped into Hut 5 and stood in the corridor, listening. There wasn't a sound. He entered the first room and stared at upturned mattresses draped with belongings: books, pictures, and clothing. He opened the single storage cabinet. Inside he found two tin cups, a chocolate bar, a small sheaf of prison stationery, pencils, a box of tea bags, and two cans of condensed milk. He debated whether to bother with it and finally decided to leave it. If in the next fifteen minutes he couldn't find the djinn, he could always make an end run from hut to hut, grabbing up food stocks and throwing them on whatever pile Loring started outside. Then they could burn the whole lot and salt it later.

Not that he believed it was necessary.

Gilman went on to the next room.

Loring dumped an armful of food into the snow outside Hut 4. She had found ten chocolate bars, several boxes of tea, four cans of condensed milk, and a stale sponge cake. She looked around for Gilman and, not seeing him, went into Hut 7.

She rummaged through the first two rooms, finding more tea and chocolate. She was loading it into a pillow case when she heard the scratching sound.

The outside door. Someone trying to get in.

376

She heard it open and creak on its hinges, then it banged shut. Something padded down the corridor. Loring turned, the pillow case clutched in both hands. She shrank back, her heartbeat quickening, her breath coming in short bursts.

There was a low whine from the corridor.

Loring expelled her breath in relief. She had forgotten about Churchill. Lowering the sack, she went to the door.

He was standing in mid-corridor, looking right at her. Loring smiled and wiggled her fingers. "Come here, boy. Here, Churchill."

He watched her uncertainly then slowly made his way toward her. His tail was down, his eyes on her all the time, alert and suspicious.

Loring's hand remained outstretched, but as the dog got closer, her fingers instinctively curled inward, and she withdrew her hand as it occurred to her that something didn't seem right about Churchill. He looked subdued, different. . . .

Loring backed into the doorway. Churchill stopped and met her gaze. They stood watching each other for nearly a full minute, as Loring wondered if she had been all wrong about the djinn, if maybe it wasn't dormant during the day at all but had somehow changed into the dog and now it was going to . . .

Churchill was intent on the sack. His ears pricked up. He edged his nose forward and sniffed. Ignoring Loring, he padded closer and sniffed the bottom of the sack. His nose left a trail of dampness. Loring held the sack out so he could get to it easier.

Churchill sat down on his hindquarters and looked up at Loring expectantly. At last, she decided to accept him for what he appeared to be—a lonely, hungry dog.

But he wasn't about to get anything from that sack.

She crouched and extended a hand, and Churchill sniffed it. In a moment, they were friends again, with the dog panting, thumping his tail on the floor and licking her fingers.

He followed her from room to room and patiently watched her gather up the rest of the food. He waited and hoped and kept his eyes on the sack, but he never got anything.

Gilman sat on the stoop outside Hut 9 with the sun warming his face, trying to think. In his state of mind, that was nearly impossible. He was immobilized with worry. All he really wanted to do was lie back and let the sun burn away the night and its memories. He pulled off his coat and threw it into the snow.

Out the corner of his eye, he saw Loring emerge from Hut 7 with a sack slung over her shoulder—Santa Claus weighted down with Christmas goodies.

Damn. Christmas is coming. Where will I spend it this year—in Leavenworth? Or consigned to some icy outpost in the Aleutians? While the djinn moves into Meagher County, Montana, and makes mincemeat of the local residents.

Resting his head on his arms, Gilman again tried to think: *Where would that sonofabitch hide?*

Dormancy. He kept thinking of dormancy. *Why should Loring be right about that?* He watched her tie up the ends of the sack, which he now recognized as a pillow case, then dump the load into the pile outside Hut 4.

Then he saw Churchill watching the pile. Loring shook a warning finger at the dog, shooing him away. Churchill trotted off but, when Loring moved away, he turned and eyed the pile again.

Gilman had just stuck two fingers in his mouth to whistle the dog down when he heard the first distant roar of a vehicle. He listened. Loring was about to enter Hut 6. She stopped too.

Gilman rose and went to the bottom of the slope. The men were still lined up along the fence, but their heads turned as they too became aware that something was approaching.

The roar grew louder. Something rounded the distant bend and came into view. Gilman swallowed. A snowplow.

He glanced back. Loring stood outside Hut 6, watching the snowplow come down toward the camp.

The relief detachment would be right behind it, probably in trucks. Gilman felt all hope sink in his chest. There were only a few minutes left and he had done nothing. He hadn't a clue where to find the djinn. And all Loring had managed to accomplish was to pile up some food in the snow. Churchill was scratching at the pillow case full of food, trying to open it. Gilman gave the dog one short, sharp whistle.

Churchill scurried back to Loring. Gilman returned to the stoop he had left, shoving his hands in his pockets and encountering the salt tablets he had stuffed in there last night.

Loring walked around a puddle in the snow and joined Gilman on the stoop. They sat quietly and watched the trucks come down the valley road and grind over the hump above headquarters, then brake as they came down to the gate.

Gilman couldn't watch anymore. Churchill sat down in the snow in front of Loring and raised a paw to be held. Gilman wondered if Bruckner was still among the living, up there at the fence maybe, watching them take care of his pet. Starving him to death, but otherwise taking care of him.

Gilman absently scratched Churchill's ears.

"I'm sorry." Loring's voice was soft next to him.

"For what?"

"Getting you involved."

"You did what you had to do. We both did."

She bit her lip. "What's left?"

Gilman shrugged. From his pocket, he pulled out the remaining salt tablets. He juggled them and looked up at the trucks. "Maybe I can keep *them* away with these."

One by one the trucks drew up to the fence. The rear gates dropped and armed soldiers poured out, and they didn't care who they were prodding into formation—Germans or MPs.

General Hawthorn climbed out of one of the trucks and clumped over to the gate, a large man with heavy jowls and thick glasses and a stern expression. Borden and Cosco were waiting for him. Gilman watched them salute then listen to the general, who did a lot of talking very quickly, very hotly. Borden tried to guide him away from the gate, talking to him, reasoning with him.

"Shit. He's stalling the bastard."

"That's what you told him to do," Loring said.

"But can't he see that it's useless? That we're not doing anything?"

"He's following orders. What did you expect?"

"Does it matter?" said Gilman. "Any second that one-star pain in the ass is going to turn and see me sitting on the steps of Hut 9 chatting with a woman. Then he'll order the gate blown open and storm down the slope with his entire army, then—" Gilman got up and took a deep breath. "No sense letting Borden take all the heat," he said. Loring rose with him. She reached for his arm and pulled him around, then she was kissing him deeply, her eyes closed, her breath warm against his cheek. He held her and wondered if the general had turned around yet.

Churchill barked.

Loring pulled away. Gilman drew back and looked at her hair, disheveled but still pretty in the sunlight. He wanted more time to spend looking at her, time to think of her as a woman and not just someone with whom he had survived an ordeal. Despite the passion of last night —which he had known at the time was little more than desperate lust—he really hadn't begun to know Loring Holloway until this morning. He could see in her eyes that she felt the same way.

Churchill barked again—twice.

Gilman glanced over and saw the dog standing before the puddle in the snow, looking at him and panting happily. His tail wagged. He bobbed his head several times at the water.

"We've been so hard on him about food," Loring said. "I think he's actually *asking* if he can have a drink."

Gilman grinned.

There was a yell up the hill. The general was storming toward the gate, motioning a soldier with a tommy gun to come with him. Borden hurried after him and tried to stop him at the gate. The general thrust a finger in Borden's face and Borden backed off, looking down into the camp, right at Gilman and Loring. The general nodded to the soldier, who braced himself and sent a burst of gunfire into the lock.

Churchill leaped back in surprise and crouched in the snow, whimpering.

"It's okay, boy," said Gilman. "Just some asshole from headquarters."

Glancing at Gilman, Churchill hesitantly returned to

his puddle, circled it, territorially staked it out, growling at the armed soldiers tromping through the snow and kicking up drifts. General Hawthorn was in the lead.

Conscious of the salt tablets crumbling in his palm, Gilman was about to pitch them into the snow when it occurred to him that something was not right. Something was very much out of place.

"Major Gilman, I want to see you right now!" Hawthorn called from halfway up the slope.

Ignoring him, Gilman stepped back from Loring, his eyes shooting to the nearest hut, to the eaves, to the snow on the rooftops, snow and ice on all the huts, snow and ice everywhere he looked. But nowhere, nowhere in the entire camp for as far as he could see was there anything like the puddle of water Churchill had found.

Everything else was still frozen solid and would remain that way until after noon, when the sun climbed higher and it got hot enough to melt the snow and ice and—

Churchill was down on his front paws, about to drink.

"Get out of there!" yelled Gilman. "Yah—yah!" He ran across the snow, waving his arms at the dog, hoping the troops coming down the slope wouldn't think he'd gone nuts and open fire. "Yah—yah!"

Churchill scurried away from the puddle and circled back to Loring.

Gilman floundered in the snow with the crumbling salt in one hand, his other hand plunging into his pockets for more. He took all he had in both hands and flung it into the puddle, then he threw himself backward, tripped, and fell in the snow and crawled madly—

The water sizzled. In full view of the soldiers coming down the hill, and the general waving his drawn .45, the puddle of water erupted out of the snow, sending up a column of oily flame thirty feet high. The force of the blast knocked Loring off her feet. Churchill shot past her and dove under Hut 7.

Within the column, out of a central core of blackness, the djinn appeared, writhing in agony, flailing its arms and legs as its body was carried off the ground by the building inferno. It screamed rage in a hundred voices that echoed off the steep slope of Blackbone Mountain and froze General Hawthorn and his soldiers in their tracks, awed by what they saw and heard.

The flame slowly dissipated, turning the djinn's twisting, burning body into an oily black smudge that greased the air and shortly turned to smoke that trailed up into the sky. It leveled off and became a fine gray ash that rained down on the snow.

The soldiers on the hill held their ground but went no further. The general was still backing up when the ash rain stopped.

Gilman helped Loring to her feet then coaxed Churchill out from under Hut 7. The dog emerged cautiously, frowning at the ash around his paws. As Gilman and Loring headed up the slope, he trotted along with them.

"Still want to send me away?" Loring said.

"What? Oh, I don't know. I thought you might want to stick around and watch General Hawthorn tear a strip off me."

"Just let him try."

He glanced at her. She smiled. "Maybe we ought to get to know each other, Miss Holloway."

"Not a bad idea, Major."

"What if I invite you up to see my etchings?"

"Any time. And I've got a few things I'd like to show *you*."

Gilman chuckled and watched the general cautiously

wade through the snow to meet them. He was holstering his .45.

Window Hill. Survivor syndrome. They died and I didn't. What if I had died with them? Then who would have been in charge here at Blackbone? And what would he have done?

Gilman smiled. General Hawthorn's scowl was clouded with uncertainty as they exchanged salutes. Before words could be exchanged, Gilman grabbed the dog and held up his front paws.

"This is Mr. Churchill, General. He would like a cigar."